# BODHI RISING

Andrew Sweet

Copyright © 2021 Andrew Sweet

All rights reserved.

ISBN: 9798734125670

Forever grateful to my beautiful wife, Hollee, my partner in crime and my final editor!

Special thanks to Leila Garrett, beta-reader for both this and Models and Citizens.

# 1

## The Dying Boy

### *Tuesday, June 2, 2201*

Bodhi survived on the knowledge that if he died right now, his mother would be equal parts guilt-ridden and angry. He had been stupid not to bring enough extra food. The disease that ravaged his body stalked him through the halls of a thick-walled mansion just outside of Winnipeg, Canada. He scowled realizing that he could no longer recall how to navigate the monstrosity of a home.

His supporting hand slipped against the white marble walls, struggling to keep his body upright, and his thin shoulders slackened as he neared a potential exit. He slowed to listen for voices, hoping that it led to freedom, confused and directionless in his weakened state. Bodhi lifted his head and strained to distinguish among the sounds emanating through the pale ivory door. He distinguished the high, rich tone of his mother's voice and Aiden's deeper masculine vocalizations as they drifted in from the garden outside. The sound of a United States newscast lay beneath. He pushed against the cold metal, swinging the door outward and revealing four overgrown stairs descending toward a garden as anemic of vegetation as his body was of iron. Any discussions ceased when he crossed over the threshold. Bodhi stiffened his back and let out his breath slowly.

They had been talking about him again.

That probably meant another course of treatments that wouldn't work.

Bodhi's mother swept dark black hair away from her hazel eyes and smiled up at him from where she'd been pulling weeds.

"Hey, Bodhi, how are you?"

A different question hid beneath that veneer of simple greeting. She wanted a rundown of his physiological condition to determine how anxious she should be for the day. His head began to swim as the temporary effects of his back-up chocolate bar faded faster. If he didn't get more food soon or a session with the damned erythropoietin pump to boost his failing kidneys, he would collapse.

He refused to give her the ammunition to lock herself into a downward emotional spiral.

Bodhi pushed his lips up at the corners to reassure, but his knees failed him. He re-positioned his feet to stabilize himself. Bodhi's shoes found no purchase and he tumbled forward headlong toward the dry, rocky dirt. His mother screamed. Aiden rose to lunge for him, but the man was too far away and too slow. The last thing Bodhi saw was the ground advancing toward his head.

Awake.

A fire burned between his eyes.

The world brightened before him with natural sunlight and warmth as the flash-blindness waned.

He closed his eyes against the repetitive thud of pain in his forehead, diminishing as the grogginess dripped from his mind. Re-opening them, he looked to his left, where his haptic gear lay, an invitation to escape from reality. The nearby erythropoietin pump caught his attention next. This resembled a swag light hanging overhead, issuing forth vibrations that, on some level, told his body to produce more blood cells. His cheeks flushed and he grit his teeth. Weeks of effort to gain more autonomy over his life evaporated due to an inept sense of direction. Collapsing before his overprotective mother would siphon away what was left of his freedom.

He rolled over toward his haptic rig.

"Don't even think about it, Bodhi," came his mother's voice from the opposite direction. Startled at not having seen her, he turned back over and tried to gauge how angry she was. Her eyebrows furrowed over her eyes, set against her sandstone-brown skin. Her fixed jaw usually meant that nothing he told her would matter. He gulped and tried anyway.

"Mom, I just got lost. That's all."

Embarrassment flashed through him, and his cheeks grew hot. Anger flared in his mind at what he knew was coming. He'd made yet another mistake.

"You got - lost?"

"I went exploring and took a wrong turn. That's all that happened."

She sighed, and her jaw loosened slightly.

"Would it hurt you to be more careful?"

He had been, but he couldn't tell her about the two back-up chocolate bars that had lasted less than thirty minutes between them. Nor could he share that even when they did work to give him energy, the mental clarity was hit or miss. In Aiden's half-underground mansion, the walls all looked the same when his mind went fuzzy. To tell her that would mean that his condition had deteriorated, and he wouldn't do that to her.

But now she would find out anyway.

Later, alone and feeling a little stronger under the pump, Bodhi mentally prepared for what he knew would come next. The best and worst thing about living with Aiden was that Aiden could afford to have a doctor on site at all times. Every time Bodhi's illness flared, his doctor appeared on the scene almost immediately. The routine check-ups and interviews that happened weekly remained tedious, but worse were the visits when Bodhi hurt himself.

The doctor didn't even knock, but barged into Bodhi's room with his mother in tow. Despite the doctor's ongoing feud with his mother over formalities, Bodhi liked the man. His crooked teeth beneath a coal-black bowl cut of hair could be off-putting when he wasn't expected though.

"Mrs. Periam," the doctor addressed his mother, and Bodhi felt her reaction before it erupted from her mouth.

"Rawls," she corrected. He always made the same mistake, as though he insisted that the Aiden and his mother be married. The doctor ignored her and engaged in an examination which involved a lot of wand-waving around Bodhi's body and questions about his exhaustion.

"Your son can't keep his blood count up."

"We knew that already." She scowled at him now.

"It's gotten worse, Mrs. Periam."

"Rawls, doctor. It's Ms. Rawls." Again he gave her no response.

"Can I speak to you in private?"

Bodhi started up from his bed to leave the room and make his way to the virtual reality jump point down the hall. He was still sore from the previous day's fall, but he could use some escape time. Before he reached the door, his mother grabbed him by the arm and pulled him back.

"No. You stay. You're fifteen - you need to know what's happening with your body. Go on, doctor."

The doctor shifted his weight and stammered as he began.

"Very well. Even the erythropoietin pump isn't keeping up. Its effects seem to be wearing off. His body -"

The man stopped for a moment then turned to Bodhi directly.

"Your body is shutting down. The increasing shakes and seizures are signs of advanced degenerative muscle and nerve disease. The lack of oxygen is starving it. Your life expectancy is lower than it says in your chart because of all the recent changes."

Bodhi's heart skipped, and he leaned forward.

"To what?" Bodhi whispered.

The doctor pulled his lips into a tight line.

"One year, maybe less."

Bodhi's mother's hand shot up to cover a gasp. She drew her head backward and stared at Bodhi with glassy eyes.

His expected life span had just been sliced in half.

"Mom, it's okay," he tried to reassure her, the words falling empty from his mouth as he processed. She only shook her head at his attempts.

"Don't do that," she said. "Nothing about this is okay. It's shit."

For Bodhi, the moment was fuzzy and distant. The idea that he could be dead before his sixteenth birthday seemed ludicrous. Many assumptions about how his future would unfold crashed down around him. Part of him had expected to meet someone and fall in love. A family he would never have disappeared before his eyes. Somewhere in the back of his mind, a voice told him to be upset and to rage. But it was small and hidden and easy to ignore as all feeling drained out of him.

Bodhi stared up at the ceiling and imagined that he was free of his body, flying around over the trees. He longed for that type of freedom, with the sky stretching before him and the warmth of the sun on his back. Then he tried another coping technique from his endless supply. He imagined running through the forest, in a body that never tired. He dove into a lake in his mind, feeling the cool rush of water as he slid through it. The dirt beneath his healthy feet gripped as he walked, clawing him to the earth. Thick, muscular legs carried his broad shoulders. He jumped and soared up into the sky, landing a few meters away, and it took no more energy than to blink.

But when his eyes drifted back down and landed on his mother, her tears were still there, and his life was still over.

# 2

## The Coma Girl

"Mom, I'm ready."

Christine stamped a ballet-slipper clad foot against multicolored tiles at the bottom of the stairs as she awaited her mother's grand entrance. After an hour, she expected her mother's emergence - even her mother couldn't drag it out much more than that. The hem of a forest-green dress with gold trim poked out through the door to the master bedroom at the top of the stairs. In a way that only her mother could, the woman exuded elegance in colors normally reserved for wrapping gifts.

"I'm ready too, honey. Where's your father?"

"Getting the volantrae." Their vehicle was the newest model, and levitated using distributed ion drives, freeing it from the traditional automobile shape to the less obvious visage of a floating box.

Her father's taste needed refining, and Christine had told him as much many times.

"Shall we?"

Her mother extended a gloved hand and rested it atop the

banister where it glided down as she made her descent. Her smile, wide and generous, floated down effortlessly, despite the fact that she fumbled to keep her footing on the last step. When she transitioned to the tiles, she wrapped her arms around Christine, who inhaled the day's airy cotton perfume. Her mother's arms squeezed her tightly against the woman's body.

"I'm so excited," Christine told her as she pulled away. Her mother looked down with that same persistent smile, and her mouth barely moved when she responded.

"Me too. You look so beautiful, Christy."

That name caught Christine off-guard and she furrowed her eyebrows and looked up into her mother's eyes - eyes which didn't see her, focusing instead on the door over her shoulder.

"Mom, don't call me Christy anymore. It's Christine."

"You'll always be Christy to me."

When Christine heard the door open behind her, she twisted her head back to look over her shoulder with such haste that her chestnut hair whipped around into her eyes. There, in a top hat with a cane, stood her lanky father, the picture of sophistication. Tonight they would see a live performance in the Canopy in the Byrd Theatre. She'd never been to Strata 20 before, even though her father worked higher and often spent happy hour schmoozing in the restaurants that littered the entertainment district. The image of her school friends' jealous faces already bounced through Christine's head. She couldn't wait to tell them.

"Are you ready to go yet?"

"Of course, dear," her father told her, extending his elbow for her to loop her arm through. On his other arm, her mother gripped tightly and they stepped through the doorway. Before them the lime-green volantrae, now reminding her of a giant breadbox, hovered just at the end of the walkway, side-hatch wide open and retractable steps extended for them to board.

A beep echoed through the sky from a source she couldn't identify. Then another sounded, and another as they continued to keep time. Her father didn't seem to hear, nor her mother. A moment later, she felt herself whisked far up into the sky. She became an onlooker to her memory. Implications of the scene crashed through her consciousness. Christine wanted to scream at the family not to go but all she could do was watch and remember. The smell of her mother's perfume, her father's terrible jokes. The volantrae trying for the exit ramp and missing.

Self-flying mode didn't work.

It had died the week before—a series of stupid accidents.

The volantrae careened from the sky. From Strata 7, and she counted four other strata before the first collision with another vehicle. She remembered that at first, it was fun - like a roller-coaster ride, as the volantrae tried to latch onto each strata signal and level off. The self-correction proved its inadequacy repeatedly, staying level just long enough to play pong with other cars before falling again.

When the blood started flying, it wasn't fun anymore.

Stop! She called out to herself, trying to hide the memories away. She pushed them down, and her ghost flew up farther into the clouds, into space, beyond, and then into blackness.

How long had she been reliving this moment? Years? Hours? And why this moment, out of an entire lifetime to choose from? All of these thoughts occurred within the space of a heartbeat, and then she was pulled toward her body, screaming inside yet making no noise to disrupt the scene. Then, there was only one of her.

"Mom, I'm ready."

# 3

## The Order

### *Sunday, June 7, 2201*

"Captain Bentley?"

Ordell looked up from his pinamu tablet, a device the size of a sheet of paper but two millimeters thick that allowed him access to the Labyrinth virtual network through a graphical touch interface, and met Monica Caldwell's deep green eyes across the kitchen table. He ran his fingers through his thick black hair and instinctively scratched at the beard that now hid the scars along the left side of his face as he chuckled.

"Captain Bentley, huh? What?"

She reached out and grabbed his hand.

"What do you mean, what?"

"I heard what you said. Just thinking this through. Emergent Biotechnology is now partnered with Beckett-Madeline Enterprises, right?"

"Yes," she told him, stroking the back of his knuckles with her fingertips. He pulled his hand back, but not far enough to escape her light caresses.

"And you think that Alexander Toussaint is wrapped up in that?"

"You know who owns Beckett-Madeline?"

He nodded. Gallatin Hamilton owned Beckett-Madeline, benefiting from majority ownership, which also gave him control over Prescient.

She shook her head, thick reddish-brown locks swaying on either side of her face.

"I don't think it. I know it. Rochester's been watching them since January."

"Why does it matter if they've teamed up? One enemy to fight instead of two - easier if you think about it."

"It means something is happening we need to know about. Isn't Dr. Toussaint an 'old friend' or something?"

Ordell stretched his memory backward over the years. Once, almost two decades before, he'd seen the man briefly when Emergent Biotechnology tried to settle a court case with him. Rather, with his dead girlfriend's daughter, Harper, by proxy. And he met the man at the funeral of Harper's friend Railynn Marche.

"Not really, Monica. I've *met* him twice. Hardly friends."

"Calm down, I'm just letting you know."

She smiled, and he raised an eyebrow toward her, aware at his quickening pulse and the heat behind his eyes. He forced his clenched jaw muscles to relax.

"What are you smiling about?"

"Just remembering how long it took you to call me Monica," she laughed and kissed his hand, then stood from the table. "But why do you only do it when you're agitated?"

He shrugged his shoulders.

"I guess you're Caldwell to me. It's hard to switch off the habit."

Every day, all day, they worked together in a military

compound. Like him, she was a Captain, so he called her Captain Caldwell, or just Caldwell. He carried the habit back home.

"There are a lot of us Caldwells. I wouldn't want you to get us confused," she smirked. Then she pivoted away from the table and walked toward the replicator.

"Check the fridge," he told her absently, considering the implications of their conversation and trying to remember what else he knew about Alexander Toussaint.

"I guess it makes sense," he said. "If Prescient and Emergent are working together, then that's over seventy-percent of the market share. Toussaint Labs focuses on models, speeding development, I think. The cloning industry hasn't had a boon like this since before my first birth."

He cringed as he said it. The very idea that people like Alexander Toussaint existed - people who tinkered with human biology with clinical detachment - now turned his stomach. Without such individuals, he wouldn't be alive, though. He was a model, or a genetically-altered clone created for a brief life of difficult labor. Caldwell was also; the same was true about almost everyone else in the Siblings of the Natural Order - the resistance movement that they both worked for.

"Thanks. Yes, they do. But we found out something else, too," Caldwell said as she opened the refrigerator door. "His latest project is something he calls the animus module. This device maps out brain network functionality."

She retrieved a covered plate from the refrigerator and turned to face him. Then she reached into her slacks and pulled out a data-coin and threw it across the table. A schematic that looked like a dandelion flower pulled up on the tabletop display. He tapped it once, and the image popped up into three dimensions.

"What am I looking at?"

"That's the module after it's been learning brain patterns for a while. We pulled this out of the head of a discarded model we found at the new reclamation facility in Minneapolis."

The mention of reclamation bristled Ordell's neck. Caldwell had rescued his longtime friend Lancaster from being killed in one of those obscenely boring-looking factories. The crippled man, his legs stolen by an Overseer's laser whip, now led the Siblings of the Natural Order, but he had once been seconds away from death.

The life-cycle of a model began with the first birth. This resembled human childbirth in that a screaming infant was unleashed upon the world. Robots reared and trained the child from their emergence from the egg-like birthing pods through their twelfth year. When they reached that age, the children were re-submerged into stasis pods and stayed until their second birth, which depended entirely upon consumer demand for their pre-ordained trade. Ordell's own second birth had been delayed for over a decade during the climate change event that wreaked havoc on the continental United States during that time.

A useful model could expect to work for thirty to forty years, and then "retire," which meant a celebration, pomp and circumstance, followed by transportation to a reclamation facility, in which the model may or may not be given sedatives before being submerged in a sealed vat of chemicals designed to reduce the model into constituent proteins - re-use for the next generation. For less useful models, or deformed models, the trip to reclamation occurred as soon as the "defect" was detected, even if that "defect" was inflicted by an owner, like the man who had laser-whipped Lancaster's legs until they couldn't heal correctly.

From a polli perspective, these factories increased efficiency and facilitated the re-purposing of resources. For models, they were death camps.

Not all parts of the model recycled cleanly. Heads were likely to remain mostly intact except for the soft parts like eyes and tongues. The skull and other bones often survived and were discarded with the trash, which the Siblings of the Natural Order, SNO, routinely searched in order to provide proper burials for whoever they could find and piece together. It was one of the most solemn jobs one could have within the order. Ordell assumed that this was where the remains of which Caldwell had spoken were discovered.

"What was that doing in someone's head?"

"As near as we can tell? Failing to override his neural pathways."

"Over-ride? You mean to take over?"

"Exactly."

"Why?"

"I asked Rochester the same thing." Caldwell paused, and he looked from the device's image up to her face. She pinched her lips together before speaking. "She said that they're trying to transplant consciousness. She thinks that polli want to live forever, and use us to do it."

His jaw dropped. The thought wedged itself in his brain. Living forever, and with every life, a death. He ran his hand through his hair, pondering the implications. A few minutes later, a flabbergasted Ordell and unusually silent Caldwell shared a volantrae ride toward SNO regional headquarters just north of League City.

They approached the tall fence around the industrial complex where Jarro used to sit, a dive bar that Harper's family used to own which she abandoned to Ordell when she left. The origins of the new industrial complex traced back to a failed uprising, which produced a requirement for more security and the necessity to move money faster. Turning Jarro and a few surrounding acres into an industrial park solved both problems. Sixty of the seventy-five billion dollars had gone into this project - half to build the industrial park and the other half to pay lawyers, builders, in that order. The gate before them swung inward, and Ordell pulled his Galaxy volantrae, which looked disappointingly like a very practical shoe-box, onto the grounds.

The building they sought stood where the old Jarro bar had before. A level parking lot had replaced the sloped and destroyed driveway, and a short wall surrounded the lot at the marsh edge.

"Let's go," Caldwell told him as the vehicle pulled to a stop and she stepped out into the heat. Ordell followed, putting on the grim face of a military man as they approached the building and passed through the door to where biometric security sentries waited to scan them.

He tried to imagine Jarro in the tall, cream-colored walls and the shimmery tiled floors. The bar would have stood just about where the hall ended at an elevator bank. Caldwell stepped in briskly and spun, causing her hair to swing over her shoulders and her perfume to waft over him. Lilacs - always some flower, though he didn't remember her wearing a lot of it before dating her. The doors slowly slid shut behind him.

"Fifth floor," she said. Ordell smiled at how she blurred the sounds at the end of the word 'fifth,' as though the 'f' and the 'th' were a special new letter.

"Do you remember when we decided to build this complex?"

"Are you getting sentimental, Ordell?"

He smiled. "Always. But it was after Mara, just after I picked up Captain. That night we had dinner, and I asked you back to my place."

"Which was very inappropriate."

"You said no."

The elevator passed the second floor and beeped a subdued groan of a sound.

"I had to. We'd just made you Captain the week before. What would that have looked like?"

"Yeah, but you were pining after me the whole time."

"Pining? Right. But the complex, that was Lancaster's idea wasn't it?"

"I think it was all three. Instead of dinner, we met Lancaster at your place. When he saw the documents and data-coins scattered around, he said his place looked the same."

"And what if someone broke in…"

The elevator came to a stop.

"Just thinking about that. We've come a long way since, you know? Sometimes I forget it wasn't always like this."

"I know what you mean."

The doors opened to an aisle that ran between two groups of desks. A transparent glass partition ran along the back wall, and a group of Lieutenants examined the data on it. Ordell could easily make out a map of the United States translucently displayed on one of the six panels combined to form the far wall. They proceeded down the center, and people on either side looked up at them as they entered and grinned or waved. Chatter was ubiquitous around them. Building out the complex was easily one of the most important things they had done to help the organization grow.

"Reports," said Caldwell, as someone handed her a coffee. The act made Ordell smile, and he wondered how long the Sergeant had watched for them to get the replicator timed perfectly to produce coffees that were the right temperature when they arrived. He felt a coffee shoved into his hand as well. A Lieutenant stopped dead in front of Caldwell and turned to face them.

"Ma'am," he said, as Ordell struggled to maintain his bearing.

"Well?"

"Captain Rochester is in your office waiting to debrief you on the situation in Seattle. Construction has begun on four of the destroyed reclamation facilities. This time, they're being built like prisons instead of factories. Walls, automated sentries, and drones. We're not optimistic that we can destroy them again."

"If we don't, thousands of discarded models die every month."

"I know, and I reminded the general," the man said softly. "He's asked to speak with you when you're through with the debrief."

Caldwell met Ordell's eyes as he stifled a smirk. The man swiveled his head. "Both of you."

"Very good. At ease."

The Lieutenant left and made his way back across the room to join the others in tactical planning. Ordell watched a red light illuminate near a cluster of three on the map of the United States. The latest reclamation facility. Then he followed Caldwell's rapid pace to the right side of the room and through the doors to her office.

"You should come too," she told him. "This will be about what we talked about this morning."

"Rochester, what's the news?" Caldwell wasted no time as they crossed the threshold into her office.

"I wanted to tell you personally," the tall woman said, looking down at Caldwell, but just on par with Ordell's height. "We've been monitoring disposals at the Seattle site. The number of transplant failures has been decreasing over the years, and even more quickly over the months."

"Are they giving up the program?"

"We don't think so. Less failures means more successes. We can't be sure how successful, but good enough not to kill the models anymore. Last month there were no bodies discarded."

Caldwell's eyebrows furrowed, and she grabbed her left arm, rubbing her hand up and down across her elbow. Ordell caught a flash of her bar-code tattoo on her left wrist - the inescapable mark of the model.

"There's more. Gallatin's granddaughter has been in a coma since before the program began. There's a rumor that they feel confident enough about the program to try it on her."

"Wait. They're that far along that he's willing to risk his granddaughter's life?"

"Apparently."

"Any idea when?"

"Next week."

Ordell gasped involuntarily as his mind swam through the implications. He could see one person, hopping from body to body, each hop a murder. Then he saw millions and millions of people, all doing the same thing. What he saw in his mind wasn't yet a reality, and if they acted quickly, perhaps they could prevent models from being killed. But immortality was a temptation that could very easily seal the fate of models for good. From the look on Caldwell's face, she'd come to a similar conclusion.

"Attack?"

"The facility is in the Seattle Canopy."

He blew out through his teeth. Akson society had installed the Canopy when they reigned decades before. The minority government had been paranoid about being displaced, which happened within five years anyway. During that time, they built Canopies in several large cities and fortified them. And strengthened the towns as well: the entire reason they hadn't attempted an attack yet.

"I don't think we can. Not yet."

Caldwell walked in slow steps away from Ordell and toward the window. Sometimes, she did that when she thought, although the only thing out there was a dying forest being slowly devoured by a marsh. He looked through, trying to see what she saw, and only saw the clinging tree moss and hidden quicksand. Alligators lurked back there too, waiting to eat anyone who wandered through - something he knew from personal experience. He shuddered and turned away to look at Rochester.

"What does intelligence think we should do?" He asked. Sometimes they had great ideas.

"Start moving troops in. We can start buying up houses in the lower Strata - that should be simple enough."

He nodded, and Caldwell turned to rejoin the conversation.

"We have to attack," she said, with her voice lacking emotion.

"People will die. Lots of people will die."

"More than in the uprising?"

Rochester looked to her right for a moment and turned back. "Maybe. An all-out assault would fail miserably. If we don't mind-blowing our cover, we can have our investigators open the doors to let us in."

"That would be a one-time thing," Ordell said. "If it doesn't work, then we lose visibility into anything they're doing for at least as long as it takes to plant more bodies in there."

"Six months. Flying blind for six months," said Caldwell, shaking her head. "I don't like it."

"The program still isn't ready for the public," Rochester said, making eye contact with both in turn.

"We wait then," Ordell suggested. "Wait and watch the situation. Even if she's a success, it will take months, even years, to ensure no side effects. Would you buy into an immortality program if it meant that life was a chronic disease?"

"Propaganda?"

"That might be the right move. Maybe double-down on some of those rumors about clones not being quite human," Rochester suggested.

"We can't do it. Models, others like you and like me - we internalize that. We need to go the other way. Clones are human. That's the message."

"We've been pushing that for years. It hasn't worked yet. And with immortality on the line, how many people will rationalize it away?" Ordell commented, playing the role of a skeptical realist.

"We never had an intelligence branch before."

"Intelligence can handle it," Rochester stated flatly. "We can get going now, and if we get Canada and Brazil to join, a combined campaign - it may be more effective than just us."

"It's something," Caldwell said. "That and we watch - see what happens. Ordell?"

"Yeah. I know."

The stakes were rising. Ordell would have to reach out to Alexander Toussaint somehow. He didn't have the man's Seattle contact information, but there was one person he knew who did have it, though it might take a while for him to work up the courage to reconnect after such a long silence.

"Did you say when they are going to try with Hamilton's daughter?" He asked.

"Not sure," Rochester replied. "Soon."

# 4

## Awakening

### *Saturday, June 13, 2201*

Something bright chased a cooling sensation along her arm just under the skin.

Wait, no.

She was confused.

Bright was to do with sight, not touch. But still, the description seemed to fit. Euphoric weightlessness swept over her chest and expanded through her body.

Was it just another endless dream?

No, it felt different.

She focused on the cold. The brightness expanded all around her. Then it condensed, collapsing from a feeling into a concentrated laser piercing her eyelids. She tried to blink, but nothing happened. Her neck refused to respond to her repeated commands to turn her head. Christine's pupils slowly adjusted to make out an older man's face, smiling down at her through a hazy glow.

"Christine, how do you feel?"

She thought about the question as she searched her memory for his name. Her mind flitted briefly across the mental scene of the volantrae plunging downward through strata after strata. The man hadn't been in the vehicle with her then. She tried to stretch her mind farther but failed to find him. Then she found someone who kind of looked like him but seemed much, much younger. This new memory was of her grandfather. They even had the same green eyes. She strained at his face until she could make out a younger man behind the wrinkles.

"Grandfather?"

The man's smile widened, pushing the corners of his mouth further apart and forming more folds around the edges.

"Baby girl," he said, with tears in his eyes forming as she watched him reach toward her. He stopped just before wrapping her up in a bear hug.

"Not yet," he told her, "not yet. It will take a few hours for you to adjust."

He smiled as he folded his arms back across his chest. Splotches blotched his weathered forearms that jutted free of rolled-up sleeves of a plaid blouse. Christine noticed that he was clean, very clean, as though he had never been dirty in his life. His fingernails trimmed immaculately, his eyes set in his wrinkled face were clear and focused and piercing. His teeth were whiter than any teeth should be. She raised a hand toward his face, curious about the texture, but the arm moved too quickly prompting him to jerk backwards. She stopped to examine the back of her hand. Tiny blonde hairs poked out all over it, and long, slender fingers extended from the end.

It wasn't her arm. Her grandfather must have seen the confusion as a frown spread across his face.

"Christine, there's something you need to know."

A voice interrupted from behind him somewhere beyond her range of vision.

"Gallatin, it's not time yet. She won't understand. Give her a few hours to get adjusted. The animus module is still integrating."

"She needs to know."

"I know, but not yet. Just tell her you love her and let me get back to work, please. We need to put her back under for a bit."

The idea of submerging back into the endless dreams frightened her. Christine struggled to move in protest, but the rest of her body wouldn't respond to her commands.

"N-no," she interrupted, "not back under."

Her Grandfather's eyes furrowed as he watched her struggle.

"Does she have to?"

"She needs to lay still. It would be easier if she were asleep."

"But not necessary, right?"

"No, but..."

"Okay, princess, you don't have to," Grandfather told her, smiling with his wrinkly face. She wondered what happened to him to make him so old. In the background, she heard someone clearing their throat aggressively, but Grandfather ignored it.

"Why are you so old?" she asked candidly, which made him laugh and seemed to force the tears in the old man's eyes out and down his cheeks. He bent forward and wrapped his arms around her, holding her so tightly that she gasped for breath. Christine felt pressure on her chest and then a rasping sound as the air went in and out against his crushing embrace. Another sound came of a clearing throat, and Grandfather pulled himself up to his feet, somehow looking even older than he had looked when the hug began.

"I'll be back, little one," he told her and then stroked a hand across her face before turning and leaving the room.

"How are you, Christine?" A male voice called to her, unfamiliar and clinical.

"I'm okay," she said.

"Good," said the voice. "What do you remember?"

"You mean about the car crash?"

"Anything that you remember. The car crash is a good start if you want to talk about it."

"I don't. I remember Grandfather, though."

"I saw. What else do you remember? Do you remember your full name?"

"Christine Chase Hamilton."

That was an easy question, she thought, and she hoped they would all be so easy.

"Age?"

"Fourteen."

"And… what year is it?"

"2177," she replied confidently. She heard the man's throat clear.

"Good."

"No, it wasn't good," Christine corrected. "What year is it?"

"In time, Christine. We don't want to shock you too much."

"Now, or I won't answer anymore of your stupid questions."

A second passed, and then another. A host of seconds followed, each creeping by in silent succession as she awaited the man's response.

"Okay, but make sure to keep breathing. Your animus module is still integrating, and the shock could make you forget."

"Forget to breathe?"

"Kind of. It's a little more complicated than that, but you should be fine as long as you keep focusing on breathing. Are you ready?"

She tried to nod her head, but it was still beyond her control. She could now move her left arm, so she flashed a thumbs up, which elicited an unexpected laugh.

"Okay, then. Today is June 13th, 2201."

Christine's breathing stopped. She willed herself to inhale twice before her body responded. Her autonomic processes kicked in, and she recovered, gasping for oxygen.

"Twenty-four years?!"

The man said nothing at first.

"Has it been that long?" The man offered the question, but she thought he probably didn't expect an answer. "Your grandfather is a determined man."

Christine had been in a coma longer than she'd been alive.

"Do you want to talk about the accident now?" the man asked, as though the shock may have somehow changed her mind.

Christine got flashes of the rain, and the skyway, and the screaming - her screaming. With just enough focus, she pushed the memory away. Christine knew already what she would find within.

"No. Why is my arm hair blonde?" Christine asked to change the subject.

"What?"

Christine held up her left arm again and examined the blonde hairs poking softly up out of her skin in little goosebumps.

"Oh, that."

But the man didn't continue. Instead, he mumbled something Christine couldn't make out, though a device somewhere picked up the man's vocalizations with a confirming beep. Clinical bedside manner hadn't improved in twenty-four years. Christine turned her head toward the sound of the mumblings. The man seemed taller than the image Christine's mind created. At a guess, he was near 5'7, four inches taller than Christine. The man wore a lab coat that hung open with green and blue scrubs peeking out. He focused on that far-away place doctors look when they're recording medical notes using sub-vocals. His nametag read Dr. Alexander Toussaint.

"Dr. Toussaint," Christine said, pulling the name from the man's nametag. "Why is my arm hair blonde instead of black?"

"Torrent, please."

Torrent swiveled his azure eyes at her and focused crisply behind thick glasses. Christine thought for a second that she saw a look of sadness before he propped the stooped eyebrows back into just the right amount of concern.

"You have a new body, Christine," Torrent told her, as his face set.

"A new body? Did I get a brain transplant?"

"Kind of. That's pretty close. There's been a bit of an experimental breakthrough out of Toussaint Labs. We moved your consciousness into this body."

Christine lacked the right words to respond to something like that. As she tried out different phrases in her mind, he continued.

"We couldn't get approval to try the experiment with a fourteen-year-old body - even a model, so this one is eighteen years old. We didn't have a lot to choose from either. Still, I think that you'll find that it's a good body in excellent physical shape."

Christine didn't want a good body in excellent physical shape; she wanted her body. Her lungs expanded in her chest, and oxygen flooded her nerves. Her belly announced its presence with a thick grumble, and feeling spread through her legs and feet. She glanced down with her eyes and noticed a rise in her chest. At fourteen, she'd already mostly grown into her body but had never had boobs. That part was a pleasant surprise, and it occurred to her that it would be something her schoolmates would be shocked to see.

What schoolmates?

All of them would be nearing forty now. Nobody in her life would recognize her. No friends. No acquaintances. Not even the stupid little girls she used to bully would be the least bit interested in her anymore. Christine gulped at the notion and turned away from Torrent to hide the tears she felt forming.

"It is a shock, Christine," Torrent continued, "but don't worry. We'll figure it out."

"We?"

"My room is a few floors up. I'll be in here so often you'll get sick of me."

"I already am sick of you."

She kicked angrily with her leg and was surprised when her leg jumped up and nearly hit him in the face.

"I'm sorry. I didn't think that leg would move."

"That's okay. The module is going to take a long time to get used to."

She reminded herself that Torrent saved her life. Her emotions fluctuated between annoyance and outright rage, but she could maintain bearing. Her private school had taught her how to hide her feelings.

"Are there any others...you know… like me?"

"You are the first and only full success so far," he said, "but your Grandfather has an animus module too, and he's started shopping for a new body as well. You won't be alone for long."

"My parents?"

"Your...parents ... were in the car with you, Christine. Neither of them made it."

"And my stepfather?"

"Grandfather wouldn't let him in to see you. He gave up

after three years, and we haven't heard from him since."

Good for Grandfather, she thought. She hadn't told him about Davey's advances, but Grandfather must have picked up on how uncomfortable she was around the man. She shuddered to think what Davey might have tried with her, completely unable to fight him off. That man would have probably considered the coma an opportunity. Her body shook, but like her tears, she soon put that to a stop.

"Do you want us to try to find him?" Torrent asked, misinterpreting her reaction.

"Please don't, no. I never liked him anyway."

Torrent smiled at her, something that seemed just slightly warmer than the clinical detachment he had worn to this point. The sympathetic look made Christine believe that he understood after all, perhaps without her having to explain. She smiled back at him.

"Christine, would you like to see your face?"

She nodded at Torrent, relieved when her neck responded. She could feel her toes now, and the brisk, sanitary air that flowed over them. Torrent pivoted and grabbed something small from a nearby tray. As he picked it up, Christine noticed beyond what looked like a mound of pink on the counter that she realized then was a white gauze that had soaked through with blood. Then Torrent turned back around, and Christine gasped at what she saw in the mirror.

Large blue eyes stared back at her from the reflective surface of the tiny surface. Thick lips pursed beneath a slightly excessive nose. Still, traces of baby fat lingered around her jawline, so she could tell the body was maybe not as young as she had been, but only a few years older. Brownish-blonde hair lay to one side of her oval face, and dark brown eyebrows contrasted with it and made her face take on a mysterious look. She saw the eyebrows furrow up around her giant blue eyes, and it took her a moment to understand that she was doing it.

"I'm pretty," she said.

"We did try."

Bodies didn't materialize from the air, but she was somehow in a new one. She tilted her head up to see the rest. Still, she couldn't see anything beneath the crumpled hospital gown.

"Who was it?" she asked quietly.

"Who was who?"

"Whose body was this?"

"Oh, it was nobody," Torrent said, "just a model, that's all."

Even before her twenty-four-year coma, models had exploded in use after the Equilibrium climate disaster, partially due to the subsequent declining birth rate. The federal government even provided free child care to anyone who would go through the trouble to have a baby. The program, though successful in some degrees, failed to address the problem of an aging population. Every time they'd had an essay assignment at her school, at least half of the submitted papers were about Equilibrium and a third about the population crisis and models.

The big news from her childhood had been when an all-model construction crew rebuilt hurricane-ravaged Pike's Place Market. Seattle had been praised as a leading city of technology yet again because they had been the first to use only models for that purpose after climate change slowed. It was safer to keep humans out of harm's way.

She was ten when all of that happened. By her fourteenth birthday, what pundits on holovision called the Cloning Revolution dominated the news. Models would soon be everywhere, they predicted.

"Good," she remarked.

"Don't worry. We took every precaution. Your Grandfather commissioned this body as soon as he knew we could pull you out. He thought - well, he thought you would like to look more like your mother. There's some of her in there."

Her grandfather was mistaken. Christine's mother shined with beauty, completely unlike Christine, and the way she navigated life exploited that beauty daily. The asinine idea frustrated her, but it wasn't like she was going to hop into another body. A wave of exhaustion washed through her. She acknowledged to herself that she'd been too hard on Torrent and would have to do better. For now, she needed rest.

"Torrent, I'm tired."

"I know. That's why I said we should put you under again. Physical therapy is going to be real work."

"Physical therapy?"

"Yes. That's not the body you're used to, Christine. The broad strokes will work, larger muscle movements. But it would be best if you learned how to use the smaller muscle groups again while you're still with me. Fine motor skills may be complicated for you." He paused, then continued. "It'll be harder for you than others. After that coma, your mind will have to re-learn a lot."

Christine allowed the hand holding the mirror to fall to her side, too exhausted to hold it up any longer. Torrent retrieved the mirror and placed it back on the little metal table.

"You need rest."

"No."

Christine couldn't shake the thought that if she closed her eyes, even for a second, she wouldn't open them for another twenty-four years. In response to Torrent's request that she rest, Christine screwed together her courage then twisted her tired body around to the sitting position on the hospital bed. Tubes that she hadn't realized connected to her pulled taught and threatened to come out.

"Hold on, Christine, you'll hurt yourself. Let me."

Torrent pulled each of three tubes from her body. One was

a drip of some fluid, which was probably the source of her original cooling sensation in her arm. That one had been easy. Another similar one was attached to her other arm. A moment later, she closed her eyes and felt flush as the catheter slid from her groin. She didn't feel any physical sensation when the tube came out since she was still numb in some areas, but the idea embarrassed her. She opened her eyes again in time to see Torrent carrying something into the bathroom, and then return.

"If you want to get up, I won't stop you. But please wait here, and I'll bring you some clothes, and we'll get you cleaned up, okay? Then we'll go present you to Grandfather clean and ready," Torrent told her, and then left her alone on the bed.

Christine had many questions, but she agreed to this. She inhaled again, exhilarated at the air moving through her lungs. Oxygen spread through her body. She didn't remember breathing feeling so wonderful. She stretched her arms up into the air and marveled at the tiny blonde hairs.

Legs still tingly, Christine slid herself toward the floor. Her toes touched first, and she nearly recoiled from the freezing stone tiles. Her right foot flattened out against the surface, and Christine attempted to push away from the bed, shifting her weight to her right leg. As she did, the leg immediately bucked beneath her and then kicked out and dropped her to the floor on her bottom in a harsh thunk. Christine winced as she tried to bring herself to her feet. Just behind her, she heard the sound of Torrent's running feet.

He must have heard the fall.

Embarrassed more than anything, Christine struggled to pull herself up off the ground, but her legs wouldn't listen. She commanded them to straighten, and they folded. She tried to use her arms to help. Though she had more control, the weak fingers on her hands were nowhere near strong enough to allow her to pull herself up completely. She leveraged herself into a position so that she could stay clear of the ground. Christine felt hands beneath her arms, lifting her onto the bed, and turned to see Torrent and her grandfather, both helping her.

"Why can't I move?"

"You have to get used to this. Your mind still thinks this is your atrophied, old body. You've been in a coma, remember? You have to work up to it," Torrent told her sternly, almost rebuking her for her audacity to try to stand.

"How long will that take?"

"As long as it takes, Peach," Grandfather told her, eyes fixed on her in a stern gaze.

Christine settled back into her bed, frustrated and bewildered. She pulled the blanket up to her chest and closed her eyes.

"I guess I will rest now, then."

Christine's grandfather and Torrent left her alone to recover in the vacant and sanitized space. One tiny window allowed her a view of the world beyond, and through it the world seemed unchanged. She could believe that twenty years hadn't passed except that the styles of the volantrae that zipped by had deviated even more from the traditional automobile. A pretzel-shaped vehicle floated by and she couldn't help wondering where the people actually sat inside of it.

Then her eyes clouded over and she looked away. Her heart collapsed and she felt a lone tear trickle down her cheek. Suddenly Christine felt cold and the room grew more empty. Each beep from the equipment that she could find no reason for bounced around the empty walls. She was a stranger to this world, made different by years of absence. Her friends would be in their thirties now, with families. Some would even have daughters her age.

She closed her eyes, this time longing for the repetitive coma-induced dream where at the very least, she would be able to see her parents again. Mental creations or not, they knew who she was, which was more than she could say of herself.

# 5

## The Mother

### *Sunday, June 14, 2201*

Harper's communicator buzzed in her hands, and she stared at it as though it were an extra body part sprouting from her fingertips. The impatient way that the device screamed at her betrayed that Torrent called, eager for his regular conversation with Bodhi - conversation she would have preferred to skip. The need for Bodhi to recover outweighed Torrent's need to make paternal overtures, but Torrent wouldn't feel that way. He would think that the right thing was to act the father and try to talk to him. She sighed, resigned to the fact that it wasn't her decision, and pressed a button on the tiny cylindrical device and deposited it on her nightstand. An image slammed against the far wall proving her clairvoyance.

"Hi Harper, how are you?"

"I'll get him - hold on."

"Wait, I want to introduce you to someone first."

He swiveled the communicator, pulling someone else into view. A petite, blonde girl stood between Harper and his shadow. For the briefest of seconds her muscles tensed in her face before she forced them to relax. When she examined the girl, she saw a bubbly eighteen-year-old smiling back. Inappropriate, but he could do what he wanted. Harper had made that decision ages ago. The girl sat in a hovering chair and as she pivoted her head back to Torrent and then around again toward Harper, she could see premature bags in the shadows beneath her eyes.

"Ms. Rawls, hello."

"Who is this?" Harper addressed the question to Torrent who now hid almost completely out of sight. The girl answered instead.

"Christine Hamilton," the girl said, in a tone that matched her smile more than her eyes.

"Tell her how old you are," Torrent said.

"Fourteen."

"No, your real age."

"Oh. Thirty-nine?"

He swiveled the camera back until he once again took up the entire image.

"Remember that treatment I told you about? We figured it out! Look at this."

Torrent reached toward the communicator, and another image took the place of his projection. Harper saw a mousy girl with dark brown curls. Harper's mouth dropped as she processed what he'd said.

"You did it?"

"We did. Christine was in a coma until a day ago. You remember Gallatin? This is his granddaughter. And because of the treatment, Christine is up and moving around. The Hamilton line continues."

He panned the camera back over to Christine again, who

stared forward into it in silence. She seemed to be thinking about something and the smile had left her face.

"Christine," Harper said. "How do you feel?"

"Aside from being a bit tired, fine. I can't describe what it feels like to be back in the real world. You wouldn't believe me if I told you what a coma is like."

"I would. But you don't feel any side-effects? I mean, the chair. Is that permanent?"

"No. It was just that I'd been in a coma too long. I have to re-learn how to walk. Balance is tricky."

Harper nodded in acknowledgment.

"That's not all," Torrent interrupted and reached for the communicator again. This time an image flashed of a boy, around the same age as Christine, with a fit body and a wide smile. The way he stood with his arms in the classic Superman pose, Harper saw the tattoo on the inside of his left wrist.

"This one's for Bodhi," Torrent told her. "Isn't he great? Thanks, Christine. Nurse, can you take her?"

After Christine was gone, Torrent addressed Harper again.

"I've already prepped everything. All you have to do is bring Bodhi to Seattle. The H Hotel is where we do the procedure. It's a one-stop-shop."

"Can you let me talk to him about it?" Harper asked. She could only imagine the way that Torrent, in his excited state, would railroad her son into the decision. His projected image clenched its teeth slightly.

"I guess, but tell him soon. Gallatin's doing me a favor here."

"I will. Hold on, let me get Bodhi. Not a word."

Torrent nodded.

Later that evening, Harper took her dinner in the kitchen while Bodhi reclused into the virtual reality of the Labyrinth.

That would occupy hours of his life unless she stepped in to intervene, which she had no intention of doing until it was time for his treatment. The time alone gave her freedom to think through what she'd just learned. At the counter in the kitchen, Aiden nursed a mug of yaupon hot brew.

"Late for coffee, isn't it?"

"I guess so. It's been a busy day." He shifted to look at her and she noticed wayward strands in his normally precise hair.

"Well, I'm glad you're here."

"You seem upset. Is something bothering you?"

He sat on the stool beside her. She moved away from him and turned until they sat face to face. A gentle sigh escaped her lips when she exhaled and then sucked in another breath. She told him everything that Torrent had told her, and waited for his response.

"That's a lot to take in," he said. She watched his eyes. He searched her face looking for clues how to respond, but she gave nothing away, valuing additional insights over feel-good remarks.

"It's a tough position to be in," he told her. "I'm not sure what I would do. On the one hand he gets a chance at a longer life. What is the cost of the life of someone you don't know?"

"That was no answer at all."

"What did you expect? "

"Something more than what you gave me." Harper narrowed her eyes and grit her teeth together.

"I can't tell you what to do. I don't think you can decide this anyway. It's Bodhi's choice, isn't it?"

"What choice?" Harper cringed as Kiera entered the conversation and the room. The blonde-haired woman, taller than Harper by an inch, had become her surrogate sister over the contentious years. Aiden, in a completely isolated and scandalous incident, had rescued Kiera from a brothel in the states, brought her back to his complex and she'd never left. Even today, every time Kiera entered the room Harper's eyes drew to the tattoo on the inside of her left wrist.

Aiden shifted over a seat to allow Kira space, but she didn't take the offering. Harper studied the far wall and avoided eye contact, unwilling to tell Kiera about the operation.

"There's a way to save Bodhi, but it's not easy," Aiden said.

"It never is," Kiera replied. "What way is that?"

"It's worse than you think." He shifted his eyes from Kiera to Harper and Kiera's followed. Harper took a deep breath. Then she went on to explain to Kiera what she just told Aiden. She watched Kiera's jaw lock in place, and her eyebrows lower in anger.

"You can't be serious," Kiera whispered harshly.

"What do you mean?"

"How can you possibly think it's okay to trade someone else's life for his?"

Harper's eyes narrowed, and her breath shortened. She returned Kiera's glare with one of her own.

"That's easy to say when you're not the one dying."

Harper's body tensed as she prepared for whatever altercation came next. She'd never seen Kiera so angry. As she looked at Kiera, she imagined her younger, trapped and held back my straps with a bit drilling into her scalp.

Harper fled to the privacy of her room as judgmental eyes followed after her.

## *Monday, June 15, 2201*

She spent most of the day in bed not getting up. Harper had to tell Bodhi something, but the selfish part of her desperately wanted to lie. If she gave him the truth, she risked losing her son. Forcing herself from the bed, Harper made her way towards Bodhi's room. She knocked twice but didn't wait for him to answer, instead pushing through and seating herself on the edge of his bed. Harper took a deep breath.

"Bodhi, I wanted to talk to you about something."

"What?"

"There's an experimental treatment in Seattle we can try. Aiden and I learned about it yesterday." It wasn't fair of her to bring Aiden into it, but she didn't want to take the journey alone. Bodhi looked away from her, and she heard him exhale as he squeezed his hand into a fist. She was about to put him through the medical circus again, and he knew it. But the door was closing on keeping him alive. She swallowed as he turned back around, expecting a fight.

"I can't do anything with this fucking disease. I only went for a walk through the house, and that nearly killed me. I need more than just a few hours to live each day."

"Okay, good. Torrent presented a possibility we should consider," she said.

"What is it?"

"He created something he calls the animus module. It - well, it maps your brain."

"My brain? How does that help for my anemia?"

"I'm getting there," she said, flipping her hair out of her face and re-establishing eye contact. "How do I explain?"

She paused.

"There's only so much they can do for your body, Bodhi. You've been too sick for too long."

"What do you mean, Mom. You're not making sense."

"I'm saying that maybe," she sighed. "Maybe it's time to leave this body behind."

He cocked his head and stared at her with his eyebrows raised. Then Bodhi examined his arms and legs as though he'd never seen them before.

"Behind?"

"Yes. The animus module maps your mind, and your consciousness - that thing that is you - moves over to the device. Eventually, the device holds everything that makes you, you."

"What is the treatment, Mom?"

Harper opened her mouth to speak and then closed it again. Big, trusting brown eyes looked back at her. She could lie. In that single moment, she could lie, and if the consciousness transfer worked, he would have the rest of his life to hate her. She blinked away the tears that collected in the corners of her eyes. Then she told him everything.

For a moment, he sat there staring dumbly at her. Then he arched his left eyebrow.

"Where does a new body come from?"

Her caring and sensitive son. Of course, he would ask the one question that she didn't want to answer. But she had already invested in the truth, so she continued with it.

"A clone, Bodhi - one especially picked out for you."

"Like Aunt Kiera? What if someone did this to her?"

"Nobody is doing this to her, Bodhi. She's free."

"She still has the tattoo."

"By choice. In Canadian law, she's a full-fledged citizen."

"But it could have been her."

It could have been. Bodhi was right, and nothing she said could change that. Harper could feel that the opportunity slipped away. Her child slipped away with it.

"Please, Bodhi."

"I won't do it, Mom. I'm not going to take someone else's life so that I can live."

"Bodhi," she gasped.

"Mom, what are you asking me to do? How…"

"Please, Bodhi. Do it for me. I can't lose you. You're my

son."

That was when she finally broke, and the tears erupted down her face.

"You have to, Bodhi. A son shouldn't die before his mother."

"Mom…"

"Just - please. Just do it, okay? That's all you have to say. Just say - say you'll do it."

He looked at her with a mixture of confusion and pity in his eyes. At that moment, Harper didn't care which of them did the job. She saw that his resolve wavered. It only took her complete humiliation.

"Okay, Mom," he whispered, and turned away from her again. She squeezed him so hard that he tapped her shoulder to be released.

"Thank you."

He still wouldn't make eye contact. He might hate her, but she would have the rest of his life to convince him not to. Harper wiped at her tears and stood up to leave.

"I love you, Bodhi."

He responded with silence as the door latched behind her.

The next day, she awakened to see Kiera looming over her bed, glaring down at her with squinted eyes and a deep scowl. Harper rubbed the sleep away, and when she verified that Kiera was still there, she sat up at once.

"What are you doing in my room?"

Kiera flashed her tattoo at Harper.

"What am I doing? What are you doing? Do you want to kill me?"

"He's my son. That's all there is to it."

"Ordell would say that you have betrayed us."

Harper glared at Kiera. Knowing her life's story didn't give Kiera a right to make judgments about her friends.

"I know what Ordell would say. I'm not part of the Siblings of the Natural Order. I don't care what Ordell would say. Bodhi's my son, and I'm going to save him if I can."

"By killing someone else?"

"If that's what it takes. I'll kill twenty people if that's what it takes. And I don't need your permission."

Kiera ground her teeth without breaking eye contact.

"I have no alternatives, Kiera."

"You always have a choice. Your problem is your precious son. Does he know?"

Harper didn't answer. She would leave her son out of the fight if possible.

"It doesn't matter."

"Kiera…."

"Don't. Don't talk to me."

Kiera left Harper sitting alone at the foot of her bed.

# 6

## Roommates

### *Wednesday, April 26, 2186*

Stunned, Harper stared after Kiera as she left, feeling the loneliness close in like an old friend, triggering the rise of a long-hidden memory. This one was of Bodhi, and her transition from fleeing fugitive into the protection of Aiden's home.

When she'd brought Bodhi home from the hospital, he was so tiny and fragile, she'd feared breaking him in two accidentally, as though even shifting the weight of his tiny body between her arms might be enough to crack him open. That was something she'd had to get over quickly, as his anemia required strength that she didn't know she had.

He sat in Harper's lap, swaddled in a thin blanket, as the volantrae banked gently to the right on strata 11.She poked at his nose with her finger, and his face shriveled up like he was going to sneeze. Harper stifled a giggle. She watched the clouds go with only occasional interruption. Her shoulders strained together as if tugged by some invisible thread, her head throbbed and other body parts ached under the strain of delivery.

A little boy. Her reflection smiled as she wrapped her arms around him, and leaned closer for a better look at the clouds. The air in the volantrae was cool, and Aiden busied himself giving the driver corrections and then correcting those corrections, which the driver took with admirable aplomb, in her estimation. Leaving the lonely skyway caught her off guard, as suddenly the clouds below that she'd been admiring lifted towards them. For a second, she mistakenly thought her sickness had returned, before she realized that the feeling she had was from rapid descent.

"There, over there."

Aiden motioned furiously to the driver, who remained stalwart in his control of the vehicle.

"It's off the ramp, sir. I can't do it."

"There's literally nobody around, Gregory. Surely you can just go there. The ramp is nearly a mile away still."

"We'll be there quickly sir. Can I encourage you to calm down and let me drive?"

Harper watched the situation with amusement before deciding to come to the driver's rescue. She had no reason to expect it, but she gently touched Aiden's arm, and collapsed back into the seat beside her, still disheveled and flustered.

"It's right there. We could just drop down to it. I do it all the time when I drive."

Harper had only been in a volantrae once before, and had little idea what the rules were, but she was reasonably sure that straying from the lane would cost someone a license.

"You don't make a living driving this thing."

At the same time, she looked toward where he pointed,

and her mouth dropped. A massive dome structure extended into the sky almost as high as Strata 5. In the center at the top was something that resembled the automatic door at her old home, only it was much, much larger and lay horizontally on the surface.

"But he's got to go all the way to the end, come around, and then *back* up over the dome to gain entrance."

"Are you in a rush?"

Aiden tilted his head and stared ahead, eyebrows furrowed together.

"I guess not," he said. "I've already canceled meetings this week."

After he said that he grinned. "Okay I'll relax."

The ride to the end of the off-ramp, which wasn't really a ramp as much as a series of floating lights, only took another three minutes. And then the driver swiveled the car around and drove along another skylane only visible through the augmented reality windshield. The volantrae flitted up and over the dome to descend through the opening at the top.

The dome was extravagant, but not unusual. Smaller houses near the skyways had grown the equivalent of three-dimensional privacy fences, half-spheres or connected quarter-arcs toward the traffic. To have a fully enclosed dome meant full privacy, and nobody in her previous life even came close to that kind of money, save for Gallatin Hamilton who permanently lived in a hotel.

The interior of the dome was a perfect projection of the sky outside. The clouds through which they descended appeared again over their heads as the volantrae lowered gradually toward the earth. Even a crow which she'd passed on the way in fluttered across the sky in search of its mate. With the exception of a seam that connected the two halves, the image looked flawless.

The volantrae landed just in front of an old wooden door

built into the side of a hill. Trees cluttered the landscape, thick and green and lush.

"This is climate controlled," she remarked in awe.

"A few generations beyond the Mars dome fields. I'm really just trying it out. For a friend."

"What kind of friend lets you try out his environmental dome?"

"The kind who likes to stay secret," he replied. His eyes darted from hers to the driver, who had exited the front to open their doors. The volantrae lifted off shortly after, and when the doorway had closed, Harper didn't have any idea where it had been.

"Aiden, why do you need a driver? You just argued with him the whole time. Couldn't you have gotten a self-driving volantrae and saved the trouble, not to mention however much money you just gave him?

He smiled at her.

"It's a little selfish. I'm busy all the time, making deals here, and negotiating there. Some weeks, every single person I talk to is someone who wants to cut some sort of a deal. The driver - even the arguing - connects me to a real person. I never fly without a driver for that reason. They make me sane."

She staggered a little then, finding her legs, but Aiden caught her arms and helped her through the doorway.

On the other side of the unassuming wooden door lurked halls of pure marble. Aiden half-pulled and half-carried her down the hallway past three doorways. One opened up to a kitchen with slightly more color - reds and browns. The next lacked a door but clearly was a living area with easily the largest holovision she'd ever seen. The third must have been the guest room, although looking further down the hall, there were plenty of other doors - secrets to be discovered, she thought.

"You're in here," he told her. "The maid will be along soon and you can ask her for whatever you think you need."

He stepped backwards through the door, but paused there, staring at her as she took in the room. A queen-sized bed was centered on the far wall, covered in thick comforters. To the left was a bassinet, empty except for a thin pad. One side of it collapsed down to allow her easy access to the child. The sight of all of the preparation that Aiden had done lifted her heart, until she saw a bank of machines behind it. She saw the rounded chamber that she would have to abandon her child to as part of his treatments. Harper mentally went through the steps again. Place the child inside, then close the opening. This was the part that scared her. She only thought of how abandoned he would feel for that minute alone. Against a far wall sat a magnetic-glide rocking chair with a rocking ottoman.

"That machine in the back is for transfusions. The doctor will come on-site to do them. I thought it was probably better to have it here in case - you know - we had to do it ourselves if there's an emergency or something."

She lifted her tired eyes up to his face.

"How much was all of this?"

"It wasn't that bad. Don't worry - I wouldn't have done it if I couldn't afford to. Is it okay if I go check up on some things? Even though I'm not *booked* I still like to keep an eye on my investments."

She smiled at him.

"Only if you tell me where the bathroom is first."

"First door on the left past this one. Did you want a tour? I should have offered."

Harper eyed the bed. Plush down sheets draped languorously over the side, dripping down toward the floor. She looked back at Aiden, then down to the sleeping child.

"No, definitely not. I am exhausted and I feel like I could

sleep for years."

"Okay then, I'll leave you. Please just yell if you need me. I'm not really all that far. It looks a lot bigger than it is."

After he left, she placed Bodhi's sleeping body gently into the bassinet. Then she lay her head down on the pillow of the queen bed and closed her eyes. She postponed sleep for a few minutes as she tucked the blanket in around her body and chin and ducked her face into the soft mass. She smiled and sank down into the cushions. Then Bodhi cried out.

She jumped from her bed and ran to the bassinet, to find him turning bright red as he screamed with his entire body. He'd just gotten a treatment before they left the hospital, so she knew he wasn't due for another one until an hour from now. She scooped him into her arms and carried him against her chest, where he began to force himself downward on her. Taking the hint, Harper carried the infant to the rocker. She grabbed the throw pillow and took its place, using the pillow to prop his head up. Then she unbuttoned her dress and exposed her breast to him. He latched on quickly and settled, working with his tiny mouth to pull in every nutrient she could provide. Harper closed her eyes and rocked slowly until he'd finished and fell back to sleep. She carried him over and placed him back in the bassinet before she buttoned her maternity dress back up and made her way back into her bed to close her eyes once again. Next time she would have to put him in the pump, and that seemed impossible.

Two hours later, Harper awoke to more screaming. It was time for the chamber. She scooped up the crying infant and placed him inside. The machine came to life as soon as she closed the door. As she listened to its sounds, she heard Bodhi's cries over them all. Her heart sank as he screamed out in fear again and again. She grit her teeth and waited.

Her communicator buzzed from somewhere in the room.

Her purse was still on the floor next to the rocking chair. Harper recovered it and fished her communicator out. She glanced at the machine. It would take at least another five minutes to complete, so she answered the call.

"Hey Harper," came a voice she recognized.

"Torrent - how did you get this number?"

"When you disappeared, I started looking. I figured you were in Canada, and Winnipeg was the closest city. Then it was easy. You weren't very discrete traveling with Aiden Periam. How did you manage that?"

"He found me. What do you want?"

"I feel shitty about how we ended things. I just wanted to see if you're okay? And the baby?"

She sucked in her breath and didn't respond.

"The baby, Harper. Is - is it mine?"

She smiled at the idea that he could have thought it was anyone else's. Still, she didn't answer - curious what else he might say unprompted.

"I guess it must be. Did you know? I mean is this why you left?"

"I suspected. But he has nothing to do with me leaving. You do. Ordell does. Railynn…"

"Her kids are fine. I sent them into the Orphanage program in Washington state. We've already lined up a good school for them to go to when they get old enough. Harper?"

"What?"

"Is it a boy or a girl?"

"A little boy. He was born six pounds eight ounces."

"Did you name him?"

"I did."

"Well?"

"Bodhi Alexander Rawls."

She waited as he processed the information.

"Can I meet him?"

A beep sounded in the background.

"Torrent, I have to go. Bodhi needs to be let out of his erythropoietin chamber."

"Wait - does he have a blood disease?"

"I can't right now."

With the machine off, Bodhi's screaming became louder and more desperate.

"Bye, Torrent."

She hung up before he could say anything else, and then rushed to let Bodhi out. His frantic little body punched at the air and his eyes squeezed so tightly that little tears were forced out and down the sides of his face. He kicked the air with his tiny feet in frustration.

"Mommy's here," she told him as she picked him up. Nursing calmed him down, and within another twenty minutes, the child was asleep again. Harper yawned and made her way back to bed. One session down, and a lifetime to go.

## *Thursday, April 27, 2185*

After a night of rotating shifts, Harper found herself longing for the post-maternity ward, where the nurses brought Bodhi in for nursing and then whisked him away again so she didn't have to listen to the his ragged breathing, preventing her even from the short stretches of sleep she might have had in between feedings. When morning came, she somehow was even more exhausted. At nine o'clock in the morning, Harper fed the baby, then put him down and made her way through the hallways to the kitchen. The marble felt cold against her bare feet.

There, she searched the cabinets for coffee, and finding none, decided to try her luck with the replicator. Having her mother's lack of any cooking skill, she produced a cup of brown paste. As the device shook and emanated the strong burning odor, the maid came in and placed a hot cup of coffee on the counter beside her.

"Thanks, maid."

It beeped and then left the room. She sat at the kitchenette counter and sipped on her coffee. It trickled through her body and she felt energy being restored. Her mind refused to catch up though, so that she stared dumbly through at the wall in the windowless kitchen.

"You're awake," Aiden said, shaking her from her stupor.

"I don't know that I'd call it that."

"Well your eyes are open," he said, smiling. "It seems like taking care of that little guy is a lot of work. Can I give you a hand?"

She thought hard about that question. So far this man had done so much for her that nobody else in her life had ever done.

"I don't want to take advantage."

"Harper, you can't tell by now? I'm in this with you. We're a team. You and me."

The words made her feel lighter and a little focus returned. She was a new mother, and as a mother, she had to take care of her baby. If someone wanted to help, and she believed Aiden did, she should accept it.

"Okay, but you're going to regret this. And however you feel about me now, it's going to get weird."

"I can do weird. What do you need?"

"The pump," she told him. Her eyes watered and her face tightened. "I can't listen to him scream while he's in there. Can you do that for me?"

He nodded as the maid handed him a cup of coffee as well.

"Anything else? We could get a nanny in here too if you want - give you some time."

She shook her head.

"That would only get in the way right now with nursing. If you can handle putting him in the pump, that would mean so much to my sanity."

"Okay, done." He smiled at her and reached over toward her hand. She reached out to grab his, and looked at him in his eyes, seeing nothing there but kindness.

"Thank you."

"You keep saying that. You really don't understand, do you? You amaze me. I've never met anyone like you. The desert? Really?"

"I didn't start off on foot. My car broke down."

"But how many people would even try that trip?"

She could think of one more person. Ordell would have, if he had had to. But thanks to her, he didn't have to try it, though he probably would have fared better. Being pregnant in the sun was a bad combination.

"I guess you're right," she said. "I am kind of amazing."

He leaned forward across the table and kissed her cheek, then let her hand go.

"I told you so," he whispered as he leaned back to his stool. He picked up his coffee and brought it to his lips. She realized then that what he meant was that, for some reason she would never understand, he liked her. She lifted her own coffee to her lips to hide her smile as she watched him over the rim.

# 7

## Calling All Allies

### Sunday, June 15, 2201

Ordell pushed the thick blanket off of his shoulders and stared up into the darkness. He rolled over onto his right side, tucking it between him and Caldwell, and getting a face-full of her thick red hair as strands explored his mouth. Still unable to sleep, Ordell rolled away from her onto his left arm in another motion. The sound of her deep breaths tinted at the edge with the rattle of a snore grated as she sank farther into her peaceful world of dreams while he danced around its periphery. He kicked his legs out from beneath the covering and shifted to sit on the bed's edge.

Emergent Biotechnology's attempts at transferring consciousness haunted his nights. The Siblings of the Natural Order kept close monitoring on the union between Emergent Biotechnology and Beckett-Madeline Enterprises. As they went, so went the modeling industry. And the fact that both had partnered to investigate the possibility of consciousness transfer was an inauspicious sign.

Thoughts tumbled through his mind every time he closed his eyes. As he rubbed them with the thumb and index finger of his left hand, he saw visions again. An endless line of models, one after the other, Bentleys - he could tell by their size and the similarity of their features - moved ceaselessly forward. At the end of the queue was a doorway emanating a blinding light through which they stepped, coming out the other side as varied as polli in their appearances. Rewritten, with their previous destinies erased, these abominations disappeared out into the world.

But that's not how it would happen. Polli don't want to look like other polli. Non-clones enjoyed more variety than that offered. Bentleys all had the trademarked broad, flat noses and the coarse hair, no matter what color that hair happened to be. His body was the same shape and size as any other Bentley. They didn't share his brown eyes or his complexion, and sometimes the ears varied, body fat percentage. Even with the differences, it was easy to tell who was a Bentley or a Briggs. But polli would want their uniqueness. An entirely new industry would spring out of this program. Middle-income people would get reclaimed models, and rich people would get designer ones with mods like Caldwell with her color-changing eyes and slim nose.

He took a deep breath.

The SNO wanted to stop it. It was a new program, and like any other, the companies would need to make sure things were safe. Rochester kept assuring him of the fact. The thought that they had at least a couple of years made him feel better sometimes, but tonight it didn't help him sleep. Ordell pulled himself to his feet and stepped away from the side of the bed. He crossed the floor as quietly as he could, conscious of the fact that his size made every board he touched creak beneath his feet.

"Are you okay?" He heard Caldwell's voice behind him in a half-whisper, but he could tell by the drawing out of the vowels that she wasn't fully awake.

"I'm fine. Go back to sleep."

She muttered something he couldn't decipher as he continued through the door to the master bedroom and into the hallway. As he walked the long hallway toward the living room, where he planned to use a couch cushion as a meditation support pillow, he ran a hand absently along the wall, feeling soft paint. Occasionally, his fingers slipped over an imperfection where an image used to hang.

In the living room, he pulled the cushion down from the plush couch. As he settled himself onto it, he heard a sound near the mantle and he pulled his head around. In the dim light of kitchen appliances, he only saw the mantle's outline. He squinted into the darkness as another shape materialized before him. Ordell continued to sink onto the cushion as he waited for the figure to form.

"Aayushi."

He would recognize her outline anywhere.

"What have you gotten yourself into now, Ordell?"

"I didn't know you were still here."

He smiled at her as her form became more evident, and her brown skin emanated light. He could see her broad smile and contented eyes that she'd never had in life. Ordell's mind settled as his body did into the cushion's surface.

"It's been some time. I'm so happy to see you with someone. For a long time, I thought you were lost to the world."

"I did too."

"Why aren't you sleeping, odd one?"

He considered that she probably knew the answer, but she still wanted him to say it out loud, so he did.

"The Immortality Program."

Her smile twisted downward.

"That is troubling."

"Can you tell me? Will any of what I've been seeing happen?"

She smiled in response.

"As always, you overestimate me, Ordell. I can't see that far, but I can feel something. You will have to choose between tomorrow and forever."

He'd forgotten how frustrating it was to talk to her like this. She was incapable of expressing anything in concrete terms.

"Can you tell me anything else? Anything helpful?"

Her glow began to fade. Her teal sari darkened into a light gray and then to black.

"Yes. Be happy when you can. Don't take now for granted."

As she disappeared, he made out another shape behind where she stood. Caldwell leaned against the wall with one hand on her hip.

"Are you okay? I saw you were gone. Who were you talking to?"

"Nobody. Just thinking out loud."

He motioned to the cushion on which he sat, inviting her to join him. She staggered sleepily over.

"Can't sleep?"

"Not for some time."

She seated herself beside him on the pillow and pushed her head into his shoulder so that he wrapped his arm around her body.

"We'll figure this out."

He wasn't sure, but he said nothing and instead took in the smell of her warm hair and smiled. In the next few days, he had to reach out to Harper Rawls - however much he hated the idea. But for the moment, he didn't have to do anything and took respite in the warmth of her body.

\* \* \*

## *Monday, June 16, 2201*

Ordell stared at the communicator on his rubicund desktop, willing himself to pick it up. He'd been there for fifteen minutes since he'd left Caldwell in her office. He intended to make the call to Harper, but this call would be different from the informal, friendly conversations they used to have. This one was an effort to get information from a friendship that had gone cold, about another friendship that had gone colder still. He sighed and picked up the communicator.

"Call Harper Rawls," he said, hoping that the year-old a.p. address was still unchanged, while at the same time, crossing his fingers that it no longer worked and he could say he tried his best. Her fuzzy image projected against the far wall. Lacking words, he smiled, admitting to himself that his worry was pointless, as the feelings of familiarity came rushing back at the sight of her. She smiled broadly back at him.

"Ordell, it's so good to hear from you."

"Likewise. How are you?"

The picture became more apparent as her features darkened in. The lines at her eyes seemed more numerous, and the cracks at the side of her smile as well. Ordell saw then that she'd finally become her mother Aayushi, in that her smile, however authentic it might be, stopped just below her eyes. In those glistening eyes, he saw sadness linger, and he knew the cause.

"I'm fine. How are you? Are you still in …"

She stopped, apparently remembering that it's probably not a good idea to speak directly of SNO over a commlink - advice he'd given her years ago. Since then, he'd learned that commlinks were now encrypted end-to-end by default.

"SNO? Yes, I'm a captain now."

"What's that?"

"Just a rank, like the military. Lieutenant, captain, then general."

"Congratulations?"

"More work, of course. How's Bodhi?"

He asked the question because he had to out of obligation, but he knew the response already, confirmed as her shoulders fell and she let out a thin breath.

"I wish I could say he's thriving, but…"

She didn't have to say anything else, and he felt guilty for even asking the question. Now might be the time to change the subject.

"Can you give me Alexander Toussaint's communicator number?"

"Torrent? What for?"

Her arms closed in tightly around her chest, and she squeezed her shawl more closely around her body. Her head turned to the side, and she no longer looked at her communicator but examined something at the edge of the room. It was a simple question, and a direct one, and one that she failed to answer.

"Just wanted to catch up," he lied. "Do you have is commlink number?" Her head snapped back to examine him. He doubted she believed his motive. He and Torrent hadn't parted on good terms and had never been close enough to warrant "catching up." The lie was a thin one. Intelligence would probably be able to get the number if she didn't. Calling her gave him the ability to say that he'd gotten it from Harper, a better story than none at all.

"What do you want his number for?"

He turned his attention back to Harper. This time her eyes were fixed on him, and she'd pulled up her eyebrows into a concentration stare that bordered on anger. He needed a better story, and quickly.

He paused then took a deep breath. "I need to know more about the process, the modeling process. What his lab used to work on, remember? Maybe need isn't the right word. Want to know?"

Her eyes softened, and her smile returned.

"I can give you his number, Ordell. I'm sorry. I've read about the SNO bombings across the United States over the last few years. I was afraid -"

"Those were reclamation facilities. Torrent's not in danger from us."

True enough - for now. But Harper didn't need to know that Torrent may be soon, and Ordell would try to keep Torrent from harm if he could. Friend or old acquaintance, he couldn't be the cause of the death of someone who had once cared so much for Harper.

"I have to look for it. It wouldn't be on this communicator; this is new-ish."

The way she said it - offering more detail than she usually would - made him suspicious. She wasn't telling him everything. He guessed that she would take the time to reach out to Torrent and give him a warning, and the possibility of that happening caused his stomach to churn. Once, there would have been no secrets between he and Harper, and yet here they both were, deceiving each other with every other word.

"If he gets in touch with you, can you give him my contact information then? It would mean a lot."

"Okay, Ordell," she said, suddenly seeming so exhausted that she might fall over.

"I guess… goodbye, Harper."

"Goodbye. We should talk more."

The way she said it conveyed the idea that they really should talk less. And she closed the commlink before he had a chance to respond. The door to his office burst open, and he glanced up to see Rochester barreling through the entry way.

"Come with me," she said. Although they were both Captains, he out-billeted her, so it was unusual that she ever gave him commands to do anything. He rose anyway and stepped around his desk to follow her, no questions asked.

Rochester and Ordell entered Caldwell's office, and she, as usual, gazed out over the ruins of what used to be farmland. She turned as they entered.

"Sit down, Ordell."

He and Caldwell held similar billets, but again, unused to being commanded, he obeyed without thinking, finding a seat just to the right of her desk. Rochester plopped herself down on top of Caldwell's desk and crossed her legs at the thighs, dark slacks covering down to her ankles.

"I just got off of the comm with Kiera."

"Kiera?"

"Another Caldwell. I knew her at Didactics before she was shipped north up to Washington State for a brothel there. It's a long story, and not important right now."

He pondered at the fact that he was only just now hearing about someone so obviously close to her. There were still some secrets she kept. He decided he was in a mistrustful mood after Harper.

"Go on."

"As luck would have it, Aiden Periam is one of her former clients. He's the one who helped her escape, and now she lives with him in his compound near Winnepeg."

"Isn't that where…"

"Where Harper lives? Yes, it is. Like I said - lucky. She just argued with your girl Harper two days ago. This is going to be hard for you, Ordell, but you need to know."

Caldwell met his eyes directly. Her fierce irises were green this time, the same as the first time he'd seen her. Her red hair flared out behind her, sticking out from the otherwise professional bun. He gulped as an idea formed about where the conversation was going.

"Her son is dying. He has a year left. She's convinced him to be a trial participant in the Immortality Program. They'll be in Seattle a few days from now."

He gulped and squinted his eyes, concentrating on controlling his anger, cognizant now of the real reason for Harper's evasiveness. The same program they were trying to stop, and she had already enrolled. He'd always thought of Harper as an ally but now began to wonder if she was the enemy.

"What?"

The words came out before he could stop them. He'd heard, but that was the only word he could think to say.

"It's true," Rochester confirmed. "We correlated that story with inbound flights. They're taking a private jet through SeaTac."

The anger refused to stay. Ordell slammed his fist into the desktop, leaving a round indention haloed by tiny fractures in its faux wooden surface. Caldwell jumped when he did this, but Rochester seemed unfazed. He met Caldwell's eyes and grimaced at her.

"I'm sorry. I didn't mean to do that."

"Sometimes I forget how dangerous you can be."

"Not dangerous to you."

She only smiled and turned to Rochester.

"We need to decide what to do," Rochester interrupted. Caldwell nodded.

"Call the council," Caldwell said. Ordell watched Rochester see if she would jump to the command, only to realize the order wasn't for her as the wall behind Caldwell changed from transparent to solid-colored. Five of the seven members of the high council came onto the screen, one at a time. The last two, Ordell and Caldwell, were already present.

"Did you get the brief I sent?" She asked. All who were present nodded.

"What should we do?"

"Kill them," the representative from the western region called first. "This is already a problem for us. Models are being collected and experimented on to get this program going. We need to stop it now."

"I agree," said the man's face who occupied the center-top panel. "It's too dangerous. We need to stop it now. Blow up the experiment site and be done with the whole thing."

"Let me talk to them," Ordell offered. "Try to talk them out of it. Give me a chance to do that."

"Your sentiment will get people killed, Ordell. I respect you, but these friends of yours are opening the door to further entrenching the system we're trying to overcome."

The man leaned into the word friends and drew the end out to sound like hiss.

"We have time, though," said a woman who represented Hawaii and Alaska. "And we shouldn't look at the short game. Right now, we kill them. How many copies of the data do they have? This will pop up somewhere else with more security. On the other hand, if we let them sink billions into it, and then pull the rug out - that's a mess that even Emergent Biotechnology can't ignore."

"Who says this is the only location?" Another voice chimed in, one that Ordell didn't recognize. He glanced to the bottom right and saw the speaker as a white-haired woman in a suit. Everyone looked back toward Rochester then. She was the leader of intelligence. Her words would likely make the decision.

"I don't know," she admitted. "Security is better than we'd like. A lot of the intelligence we have came from being in the right place at the right time more than any comprehensive intelligence strategy."

"We need to find out more," Caldwell suggested. "Maybe we can do two things at once. We send in Ordell to have those conversations. He might be the right person to get us to some better understanding too."

"I can do that," volunteered Ordell, happy to be delaying the violence.

"All in favor?"

Other than the west coast representative, the others all voted for the motion. They made their greetings and disconnected the call.

"Excuse me," Rochester said and left the room. She would have to get Ordell to Seattle now, and being a model, state-to-state travel wasn't straightforward.

"Caldwell," he said, when the two of them were alone. "Monica."

She crossed to him and wrapped her arms around him, and he did the same.

"I'm sorry, Ordell. I didn't want to tell you this. You're on the council, so you had to know."

"It was the right thing," he told her as he pulled back so he could see her eyes. A lonely tear trickled down the side of her face. He cupped her face in his hands and wiped the tear away with his thumb. Then he kissed her.

"It's the right thing," he assured her. He gulped back the lump forming in his throat. "She was my friend. She risked her life for mine. Why do this now?"

"She has a son now, Ordell. No matter what you are to her, you will never be that."

# 8

## Flying to Seattle

### *Wednesday, June 17, 2201*

The puddle-jumper that Aiden rounded Bodhi and his mother into barely occupied the same size as their living room carpet. The entire plane could have fit into the VR room, yet another distraction Bodhi wouldn't have while dealing with the crippling issue of his mortality. He sighed and watched the compound become smaller and smaller while they lifted up into the sky. The turbulence jolted the vehicle upwards as it gained altitude, slamming the top of Bodhi's head into the ceiling. He grumbled and rubbed the aching spot as the plane flopped through the air like a fish on a dock. Bodhi smiled at the grim thought that if the plane went down then, the impossible decision would no longer loom over him. He stole a glance toward his mother, whose eyes had locked onto him since before they left the house. Nothing had changed.

The only good thing that Bodhi could observe about the

flight was that no waiting lines and no customs meant the cramped ride only sucked away two hours of his life. He let out a sigh of relief when touchdown finally occurred at SeaTac airport, where Aiden made a quick consult via communicator while the pilot taxied the plane into a small terminal. The thought of moving from the plane into a volantrae and the hoisting back up in the air made Bodhi nauseated.

"Aiden," he said, but only got a pointer finger in response. He lifted his hand to his mouth as a precaution until the feeling subsided. His mother reached out and put a hand on his shoulder, sending shocks through his body, and he shrugged the hand off. He would live, for her, but he didn't have to be happy about it - or her right now.

"Bodhi, it'll be okay," she told him.

"You don't know that. We could kill someone and it could all not work." The words flew out of his mouth and by her physical recoil connected right between her ribs. She retracted her still extended arm.

"Okay."

Bodhi's stomach heaved and he ducked is head down between his legs, but it was a false alarm. The force of the sensation brought tears to his eyes, and he looked up at his mother through bleary eyes.

"I can't do a volantrae, Mom."

"We don't have to. There's a no-flying zone around the airport. It'll be a car."

An actual car was something Bodhi had never seen in his life. After his nausea passed and the trio made their way down the exit stairs, Bodhi's heart jumped when a long black limousine met them on the ground. Even if the ride downtown added another thirty minutes before they pulled into the H Hotel, Bodhi felt energized by the sensation of the wheels beneath them. Within the hotel, there was even more to examine as Bodhi soaked in the scenery. Mostly, when they traveled, getting a hospital room to himself excited and amazed. When the manager escorted the three of them to the elevator, Bodhi crossed over highly-polished marble floors and through gold-plated elevator doorways. They squeezed in together as the hotel manager who escorted them apologized for a finger smudge on the frame surrounding the antique push-buttons before pressing the one for the top floor.

A loveseat and two chairs, expensive looking with actual leather, adorned the living area. He staggered forward, staring ahead into space. To his left, a dining table and full bar sat tucked against the wall. To his right, and past a holovid base the size of a small car, a door entered his sight. He assumed this to be a bedroom.

Aiden caught up to him as he ogled the holovid.

"Hey, come this way," Aiden motioned, and they turned right past the holovid and through a door that Bodhi hadn't noticed before. Aiden smiled as he held the door aloft.

"I had this place prepped."

As Bodhi entered the room, his eyes complained about the change in light. The darkness swallowed him before pieces of metal began to materialize and take shapes. He recognized it as a virtual reality den, in which three benches covered with black leather sat side-by-side. On the wall near the foot of each were unopened haptic gear – the new kind lined with programmable nanites instead of the classic combination of accelerometers and servos. Nanites created continuous haptic feedback over the entire body and were more sensitive to human reactions than pressure pads or servo-based resistance. He couldn't help grinning when Aiden showed them off, despite everything else he felt.

"One for each of us?"

"Brand new, state of the art," Aiden said, with a twinkle in his eye. The man seemed as excited about the gear as Bodhi.

"Are these the Kelso Model 3 suits?"

He knew they were but sought validation anyway.

"Exactly! I own stock in the company and could get them before release. What do you think?"

"And that one," he pointed to the blue with black trim, "belongs to me?"

"If you want it. The suits form to your body, so any of the three will fit."

"Amazing," was all Bodhi said in response as he reached out his hand to touch the cool fabric. He couldn't see nanites, though he knew they were there. When he felt the suit, it resisted just slightly to his touch. Bodhi recalled the specs. The nanites were nearly 2 micrometers each. They created resistance by interlocking their proportionally long 0.1 micrometer arms in different formations called a resistance mesh. More or less resistance depended on the numbers of nanites that were involved in forming the mesh.

The wide smile that the new gear brought out of him died as quickly as it was born. The treatment loomed too large in his mind. He kept what he could of the grin intact so Aiden would know that he appreciated the gesture, but as soon as Aiden left the room, Bodhi plopped on a bench and folded his head into his hands. Five long minutes passed until he decided that if he lingered longer, someone might come to check on him, so returned to the main living area.

Bodhi's mother drifted ghostlike from room to room of the expansive penthouse before landing in the kitchen. He watched her from afar as she pulled garden vegetables from her bag and immediately located a simmering pot in the cabinet beneath the replicator. She moved with lethargic motions, stumbling here and there. Bodhi joined her when the food was complete and the three of them set out the places. He glanced at his mother as she dug into a bowl of brown that had probably originated as a nameless tuber. All of her foods were superfoods that were also high in iron, and mostly they tasted like precisely that. He hid a grimace as he scooped some up and shoveled it into his mouth. It tasted like a grainy turnip - not the worst of her attempts. Still, he had to choke it down and chase it quickly with water. All he had to do was make it through dinner without anyone mentioning the procedure. One day at a time. Turning the conversation before it began, Bodhi took the opportunity to find new answers for old questions.

"Mom," he started, "what happened in the states?"

Aiden's eyes went wide, but Bodhi ignored them and focused his gaze on his mother, who had stopped chewing through something green. She swallowed before she answered.

"You mean, why did I leave?"

He nodded. He'd always been curious, but his mother clammed up usually. She owed him now, though, and he thought he had a good shot at actually getting the story this time.

"You told me about leaving and about Ordell being a model. But you left out a lot of the details. I'm old enough now, right?"

"There's not much to it," she said and turned back to her food.

"I still want to know."

"Where did this come from, Bodhi?"

She stopped chewing and stared at him, red eyes puffy and bags hanging beneath them.

"Emergent Biotechnology. Alexander Toussaint. These old connections. It doesn't make sense. Why would you want anything to do with Emergent Biotechnology, after what they did to you?"

"I'll tell you. Just not now, okay."

"It's never now," he said, even after he saw her eyes misting up again.

"It was a long time ago," she told him. "Some things are better left in the past. If I hold grudges…"

He felt as though he was losing the fight. Unwilling to let it go, he gave it one last try.

"I'm fifteen, and I have a year to live. It has to be now."

"Later," she assured him.

Bodhi refused to be set aside so easily. There was one sure way to get her attention.

"I'm not hungry."

"Bodhi, eat something," his mother pleaded. "You can't not eat."

"It's important to me to know, Mom."

"Okay. I will tell you. Just please, eat your food. There isn't much to tell. The first thing you have to realize is that I left for love."

Aiden looked at her with an arched eyebrow, and she smiled back at him.

"No, I didn't know about you yet."

She smiled at him, but Bodhi could tell it was forced. Part of him now regretted asking the question as she began.

"I told you about Ordell Bentley, but what I didn't tell you was that he was my mother's boyfriend."

Bodhi's mouth dropped open.

"After my parents died, I was alone. No family, no friends. I had pretty severe anxiety, and I wasn't the calm, relaxed person I am now."

Both Aiden and Bodhi chuckled at this, and she seemed to relax a little more, too, as she took a sip of something brownish orange.

"I'd almost decided to end my life when he came barging in from the Texas swamp. I don't know. If I hadn't had to take care of him, I wonder if I'd even be alive."

She paused and made eye contact with both of them.

"But he didn't come for me. He came for my mother, and some Human Pride Movement terrorists had attacked him in Tribeca."

"You were involved with the Human Pride Movement?"

They were the most well known international anti-clone activists. More active in the United States, but even Canada had to deal with extremists like them.

"More than I'd like to admit right now. But Ordell showed up, and then he never left."

"Wasn't that illegal?"

She nodded curtly.

"Harboring or grand theft, depending on which state you're in. Eventually, we settled with Emergent Biotechnology. But there's the problem of grand-theft. According to Texas law, I stole Ordell, and therefore was a criminal and needed to be locked up as much as he needed to be returned."

"That case wouldn't have worked," Aiden said. "He's twice as big as you. He could have left any time he'd wanted to."

"Still, after the legal battle with Emergent Biotechnology, how could I put the people I loved through another round? What would the fallout be from Human Pride Movement if we continued to be as high-profile? Besides - I struggled then figuring out who I was. I felt like I couldn't be me anymore - not there."

"So you left?" Bodhi asked.

Again, she nodded. Her eyes focused on something far away as she pulled back the memory.

"Torrent - I mean, Dr. Alexander Toussaint, stayed. He patented a new cloning process, and Emergent Biotechnology was first in line to license it. Despite everything I told him, he used the new, cheaper models for his experiments. Maybe that was my fault too. There may be some spite in it - I don't know."

She let out a deep sigh before she continued.

"He's perfected it now - the process, I mean. He's got it down to a pill that you swallow - Railynn's idea. But that's another sad story."

"So I could just take a pill?"

"I don't know. That's why we're here for the consultation. We have to find out."

Aiden grabbed her fingers and squeezed as she posted a smile on her face. Bodhi recognized that smile as one he had seen throughout his childhood, whenever he had a bad spell. As close as they were, or in the lighting somehow, he noticed now that the smile seemed shallow and pretend.

"Mom, you're a hero," he told her honestly. By this time, her eyes were heavy with tears, and she had a far-off look like she could visualize every scene. She wiped her eyes on the back of her hand.

"No," she said, "not a hero. I was young, just a little older than you. I made a lot of mistakes."

"What? I don't see them. You did great."

"Well, I was pregnant with you. It had become too much and I couldn't handle the emotions, so I carried you through a fucking desert."

"So? You made it."

"But at what cost?" She asked the question, and her eyes floated up to Bodhi at the same time.

"What do you mean?"

Unnoticed by Bodhi, Aiden had worked his way closer to her, and now he lay his arm across her back.

"I mean you. The desert, the heat - and a baby on the way. It was insane, and you paid the price," she said.

Bodhi blinked. It hadn't occurred to her before that his mother's reluctance to discuss her past might be his condition.

"Mom, I don't think you can blame yourself for my disease."

"Of course I can."

After dinner, they settled into the expensive-looking couch to watch murder mysteries on the holovid. The silence that they'd begun dinner with returned, and Bodhi thought through his feelings for the millionth time. He longed to forgive his mother, but ever since what she'd asked, her flaws seemed to jump out at him.

*I can do this.*

His resolve weakened. No matter which way he twisted the idea, he still had the problem that he would be taking a life when it was over. After the operation, if it was what his mother and Aiden claimed, Bodhi would awaken in a new body that used to have an occupant. He would take over the body like a parasite.

*I can do this.*

The idea sickened him as he thought it. Nothing about the decision felt right, but neither was the fact that he, Bodhi Rawls, would die. Fairness had nothing to do with the situation. There was only one way forward, and Bodhi would have to do it. Or, he would have to resign himself to non-existence. That prospect made him even more nauseous.

A lump formed in his throat as he considered the competing alternatives. In one scenario, the guilt of a murder would follow him for his entire life, a burden which he already felt. In another, there was no guilt because there was no him. His mind oscillated between these two extremes.

A hand fell across his, interlacing his fingers with warmth. He turned to see his mother smiling at him with sad eyes and this time he smiled back, and at that moment, understood why her smiles sometimes seemed to fall short.

\* \* \*

The next morning, Bodhi awoke with actual energy. However, he suspected it was the kind that came of having impossible choices. At first, realizing that the sun hadn't even broken the horizon through his bedroom window, he closed his eyes to return to sleep. Sleep was impossible, though, so Bodhi decided to make good use of the energy he had and made his way toward the VR den.

Bodhi pulled the suit over his legs and winced as the material tightened first and then expanded to form-fitting. The suit finished adjusting, and he lowered over his head next. It vacuum-sealed to the suit, and he was surprised as a cool, wet sensation touched his lips and receded. Part of him wondered if this suit enabled taste as some of the new ones professed. Still, he would have to see the difference.

Bodhi fell toward the tiny dot, and this time instead of only inertia, he felt the wind push against him. Then the inertia built, slowing his acceleration until he hit terminal velocity. In his old suit, only the inertia translated by micro-movements in the suit's arms. He hadn't even realized that Labyrinth encapsulated the information to do that. He slowed himself by stretching his arms and, instead of stopping just before the collision, was able to steer his landing. When he landed, he couldn't help laughing at the sensation of being a super-hero, at least until an elephant knocked him to the side. The pressure on his side grew intense as he went flying through the air. Bodhi made a note to adjust the sensitivity when he returned as he righted himself.

The world around him lit up with colors he didn't recognize. The optical unit of his new suit interpreted the information to give full retina colors. Buildings that had looked blocky and washed out before suddenly became full of detail. He could see the stress cracks in the bricks of the community library.

Bodhi surmised that the latter was probably because, in downtown Seattle, they were very close to an ansible trunk, which could deliver high-detail information very quickly. However, the equipment still had to interpret all of that information in real-time, so he was duly impressed that the suit could keep up. With a shove off of his feet, he propelled himself into the air and punched his arm out to communicate flying to the equipment. He soared between buildings as he headed for his favorite game: Event Horizon. The video game allowed individuals to create planets and establish rules for the evolution of creatures in them.

Even the new haptic suit couldn't improve the immersive experience on-world in the game, though. The game involved too many interdependent equations for allowing the transmission of very much information. The trees were blocky, and the animals grainy. But it wasn't the graphics that brought Bodhi back to Event Horizon, but the gameplay. He had an entire world that he had created, complete with moons in a dual-star solar system.

He descended through his atmosphere and landed on the dark volcanic stone islands that he'd created. Walking across the surface, he felt the sharp rocks beneath his feet and marveled at them. A new sensation, the smell of molten iron, accosted his nostrils. That was one trick behind which he didn't fully understand the technology.

Bodhi sat down on one of the rocks and stared out across the ocean. There, he saw monstrous waves crashing into one another, a system he'd designed so that he could surf whenever he wanted. He didn't feel like surfing. As he lay back over the rocks, he felt finally able to relax. The sun warmed his skin, and the crash of waves in the background lulled him into a sense of peace. Nothing existed but him and the ocean.

The peace wouldn't last. In all its glory, the seascape

couldn't remove the truth from Bodhi's mind. Death stalked him like a tiger, relentlessly gaining ground while he fought in vain to stay ahead of it.

# 9

## Physical Rehabilitation

### *Friday, June 20, 2201*

"It's impossible!" Christine exclaimed, swinging her arm out in a wide circle as she struggled to walk. Anger flooded her mind as she tried to stand only to fall. With tears in her eyes, Christine directed her hostility toward her rehabilitation coach, rising again. The woman's frustrating, monotone voice reasserted that Christine should try harder.

As if she wasn't fucking trying at all.

"It's lack of toes, not lack of trying," she explained again. The woman ignored her.

"Listen to me," Christine said, not budging from her spot on the floor.

"Try harder, ladybug," her coach told her gently.

"I'm trying as hard as I can. You aren't listening."

"I know what I'm doing, Christine. Trust me. You need to try it again."

The woman had a plain face, even with layers of make-up

covering her cheeks. No amount of make-up could hide the crooked slant in her nose.

"There's something wrong with the module. It won't work, and I look like an idiot limping around like this," Christine told her in frustration, but she didn't respond.

Mirrors all around her told her the same thing. She couldn't walk, and how sad was it that such a pretty girl couldn't walk. Christine slammed her fist upward into the supporting bar and felt a crunch as a stab of excruciating pain shoot up her arm. She screamed in rage at her weakness. The coach stepped cautiously away as Christine tried to rise but slipped.

"No, no, no!" she screamed, seated on the floor. Her eyes wandered, and for just a moment, she caught the face of a sadly beautiful woman in tears from the mirrored walls. The image taunted her, telling her that not only would she never walk again, but she also wasn't even real.

"Christine! Are you okay?" the coach asked. It was too late for that, though. By then, Christine had curled into a quivering and sobbing mound.

"Stop whimpering. Get up!" a masculine voice interrupted. Christine went silent as she looked around for the source, and then her eyes fell on her grandfather.

"Your mother was the same way," he told her, dropping the volume of his voice. Embarrassed, she pulled herself up to her feet.

"She was?"

"You don't remember?"

He waved away Christine's coach, who feigned sadness at being dismissed, yet left the room at almost a run. He approached the bar that Christine used to support herself and placed his hand casually atop hers. She pulled herself up with her arms and looked at him directly in the eyes.

"Your mother always had to be the center of attention," he

continued, "like you. Even if there was nothing wrong, she would rather fight for an hour than not be noticed."

"It's impossible, Grandfather."

"It's not," he told her. "I've seen it twenty times already. Do you think you're the first? We tested this entire process thoroughly. All you have to do is keep walking, and the module will figure it out."

He wasn't going to change his mind. Christine had forgotten much of her previous life, but she remembered that about him. He was ruthless when he wanted to be, no matter what his current demeanor seemed to indicate.

She straightened her back, stood up on long legs that jutted out from orange gym shorts, and ended in quaint bare feet, small for her height. She picked up her leg and then tried to place her foot down. When she shifted weight over to it, she nearly toppled again. To her surprise, her big toe flexed and kept her balance.

Christine smiled as she looked up into his face to see her smile reflected there as well.

"Then she would do that. When you thought she was going to give up, she would always surprise you."

"I remember."

"Yes, you should. Your mother was always in need of attention, just like you. The two of you together..."

He trailed off. She moved closer to him in a wobbly, staggering gait, never letting go of his hand. Then she threw her arms around him and pulled him into a tight hug. Her toes still fought her, but she nearly had them under control. Just then, over his shoulder, she saw Torrent enter the room.

"Are you ready for some lessons on the animus module implant?" He asked. Grandfather released her from her hug and pulled away enough for her to turn to see Torrent standing there.

"I think we're ready," her grandfather said to her in his

gravelly voice.

"Good. So, let's begin."

After a quick shower, she made her way to Torrent's suite, flanked on either side by Torrent and her grandfather. Once seated, Torrent reached into his pocket and pulled out a tiny metal object that was the size of the tip of her pinky finger.

"This is an animus module," he began and extended her hand toward Christine, who gingerly accepted the metallic sphere. It was tiny and cold. She rolled it between her fingers, examining it. There were no markings on it that she could make out. Torrent continued.

"While you were in your coma, we installed something like this behind your left ear. You can also swallow it like a pill, but your coma made that risky."

Instinctively Christine reached up behind her left ear and ran her fingers over the skin there. As her fingers brushed against the bottom of her earlobe, she felt a raised line of scar tissue.

"Yes, we installed it the same way on this body. While in your old body, the animus module gradually took over your higher-order brain functions by building a network of nanites to emulate brain communications. Then, we extracted it from your body and installed it in this one."

"Did it hurt? I mean, there was someone in this body, right?"

Torrent looked warily at Grandfather before answering.

"This was a cloned body, commissioned for this purpose. There may have been a consciousness here, but it wasn't a real person."

"Nobody was hurt, Christine," her grandfather said, "just a model like I said earlier."

"Oh, good."

Torrent continued.

"It looks like the animus module is integrating into your motor functions well, from what I've seen in the last few minutes. Consciousness integration has happened already. There are some things you will want to know about how this module works. I'll walk you through it. First, I want you to try to remember what it was like to be in that coma."

"In the coma? How could I remember that?"

"Are you trying?"

"Yes, but nothing's coming up."

"Okay, good. That's correct. This time, I want you to think about the animus module, that metal pellet I showed you, and then think about the coma."

She did as asked, and instantly, she remembered laying motionless and breathing through a tube in her throat. The drip-dripping of solution into her arm echoed in her ears. The image grew more substantial, and as it did, the light began to fade around her. Her pulse quickened as Torrent and her grandfather disappeared, and she became stuck, unable to move her comatose body.

"Christine, open your eyes. You're not there." Torrent's voice pierced through the dripping and sounds of machines.

Christine gasped as her breaths seemed futile, void of air. She squeezed her eyes as tightly as possible and then opened them again. Torrent and Grandfather stared at her with concerned looks across their faces.

"Are you okay, Christine?" Torrent asked.

"I think so," she replied. "Will it always be like that?"

"Practice, and you'll get better. What I was trying to show you was that you have two memory systems now. You have your normal remembering, like what happened the first time I asked you to recall being in the coma. You also have more detailed memories that you'll never lose. Normal memories happen in the usual way. Also, the animus module records everything that you experience since installation."

"Everything?" she asked.

"Everything. You now have your very own eidetic memory."

Christine didn't know what that meant but guessed it from the context. Now, she would forever remember everything that happened in her life. It was a strange but useful gift, she thought.

"One more thing, Christine," Torrent said. "The animus module also connects to the Labyrinth."

She felt her eyes widen at that. Usually, people had to be in haptic suits or at least headsets to interact in the Labyrinth. She looked around to see Grandfather smiling at her with his gentle smile. Her eyes passed him and landed on Torrent.

"Really? How do I do that?"

"Well, it's not a full experience. You don't get an avatar or anything like that. You can search for things, though. The animus module has its very own a.p. and so it'll work anywhere."

"What's an a.p.?"

"Ansible protocol," Torrent said, "I guess you would have to be more of a techie to understand. Ansible protocol is how the Labyrinth connects with almost no latency worldwide. To access, you have to have an assigned and verified a.p. address. You have one."

"Okay, so - using it?"

"Just think of something you'd like to know more about."

Christine thought of the ansible protocol, and immediately she remembered what it was, in more detail than Torrent told her. The protocol, modeled after the internet protocol version 12, contained strict requirements on everything from underlying technology bandwidth required to a.p. address formatting. She could tell from this that the fact that she had her own, personal, a.p. address and direct Labyrinth connection was nearly an impossibility. Yet here she was. She told Torrent, who only stared at her dumbfounded.

"Wow. I forget how impressive that is."

"Torrent, I think we're ready for a break." Her grandfather stood at the same time and grabbed Christine by the arm to support her.

"Break? Oh, yeah, okay. We can continue later."

The next morning, Grandfather was in her room just after the sun rose.

"Get up, sleepyhead."

"Grandfather, what do you see?" She asked, rolling over in her bed.

He smiled.

"My granddaughter," he told her, "and I'm the proudest grandfather there could be."

"But I don't even look like you anymore."

"You never looked like me, but you did look like your grandmother. Almost entirely."

Christine pondered that. She used to share features with a woman she had never met and had died before she was born.

Grandfather took a seat on the edge of her bed.

"Still. Why did you do all of this?" She asked him once his attention had shifted to her.

"You are a Hamilton," he said, "so you have a destiny to achieve."

"I guess, thank you," she told him, feeling the warmth of his love. She wrapped her arms around him and buried her face into his musty sports-coat covered chest. She breathed in slowly to calm herself down from the anxiety of the moment. She was a Hamilton so she could do it. And she could do it on her own.

Recovered, she pushed away from him, keeping her balance on both feet with her arms extended. Christine picked up her left foot, which hung wobbly in the air before placing it only an inch before the other. Her arms screamed in pain as she continued to keep her body up with them, afraid to trust the leg she'd planted. Slowly, she shifted her weight again, allow the leg to take on more of her.

"Good girl," Grandfather told her from the side.

Just then, she got a mental flash of a volantrae careening toward the earth - the ground approaching with frightening rapidity. The door wouldn't open that high up, and even if it did, there would be nothing to do but fall. She gritted her teeth as the ground came up to meet her. Christine screamed as she neared the earth.

"Grandfather!"

"It's okay, Christine, you just tripped again," came his calm, reassuring voice.

Free of the mental image, Christine still couldn't control her shaking.

"You're shaking," he observed. "What's the matter?"

"The accident. Can you tell me what happened that day?"

In her mind, an argument had ensued, mostly her fault. She'd screamed even before the car left the road, a petulant child. She saw the volantrae swerve out of its Strata and down toward traffic below.

"I guess you would want to know," her grandfather said, sadly. Then he continued.

"A clip by a semi-truck was all it took to knock off the control sensor, and then the vehicle didn't know which end was up. You all were on your way to the Canopy downtown for a play. I remember because of my Margie…"

He stopped for a minute and sniffed once.

"Margaret, your mother told me that she had a surprise for your birthday."

She nodded. She hadn't known it was her birthday, but a show would explain the orange and white dress the woman wore and the suit her father had donned. In her memory, he smiled the entire time, even when he argued with her. As she searched even farther back, she found more memories of his face. He was perpetually grinning.

"Your mother was on the phone with me when it happened," he went on. "You and your father were talking about flying bears, of all the strange things."

That comment, as he made it, brought a thin smile to his lips.

"Then there was a crashing noise, and then the screams. They seemed to last forever. At some point, though, you all just stopped screaming - and the last thing I remember of your mother is when she said she loved me. I think that was just before impact."

"How did you find me?"

"We knew where you went down right away. The car's positioning system told us. When we finally got to you, though, you were so badly hurt. We didn't think you were alive at first."

She felt her throat going dry and her new eyes welling with tears. Struggling to keep them back, she let out a sniffle, and then the tears just came. She cried for her father, and her mother, and then finally for herself.

# 10

## Prodigal Son

### *Thursday, June 21, 2201*

Guilt kept Harper inside, and she guessed Bodhi fared no better having not seen him since the evening before. Harper's son had retreated into the Labyrinth, aided by the new haptic gear that Aiden had bought - Aiden, who took the opportunity to visit some state-side friends. Harper was alone with her thoughts. She obsessed about her son's life while at the same obsessing about Kiera's opinion of her. She'd felt the bonds breaking between them as soon as Kiera learned about the procedure. There was nobody around to judge her except for the mirrors in the hallways, which she avoided by hiding in her room.

Harper's stomach rebelled against her self-imposed isolation. The replicator, so pliable in Aiden's hands, was a monstrous beast in hers. Instead of taking her chances with it, she used her communicator to call the front desk. Harper waited past three buzzes before she finally gave up. Hunger riled her, and Bodhi would need to eat soon in any case. Harper inhaled, filling her chest with air as she stood to her feet, and then let herself out of her room, clearing the living area. As she stepped out into the hallway, a booming voice caught her attention.

"Harper?"

Memories from her past forced her turn around. She looked, mouth agape, and there, blocking most of the hallway, stood Ordell Bentley. She ran towards him and threw her arms around him, squeezing him in her embrace. He only stood like a marble statue, before he put one big arm around her and lifted her from the ground.

"Ordell, you're here?"

When he placed her back down, she rocked until she found her balance again and gazed up into his broad grin.

"It's been too long, Harper. Far too long."

Harper couldn't keep the smile from her face as she stared up at the big man. She'd underestimated how much she had missed him until that single moment.

"It's good to see you."

Harper motioned to him to follow her as she turned to return into the penthouse, and he followed, ducking through the doorway as he entered.

"Maybe since you're here, you can convince the replicator to feed us?"

"Still not good with those things, huh?"

Ordell let out a thick chuckle as he crossed the living room and made his way to the machine. She followed him partway as he made the journey, stopping at the kitchen table.

"What would you like?" He asked.

"I'd settle for coffee and a pastry or something?"

Ordell punched in some numbers, and a few seconds later pulled out two coffees and a danish, which he delivered to her, plate and all. She accepted and took a seat at the table, examining him closely. His smile seemed real, but didn't quite make it to his eyes. He seemed fidgety as he took his seat and couldn't quite get comfortable in it. This wasn't just an old friend visiting.

"What really brings you, Ordell?"

"You. I heard something troubling, and I wanted to find out if it's true."

Her face dropped, and she nodded her head in confirmation to what she knew his question to be. Then she firmed up her resolve and met his eyes.

"Yes, it's true."

Ordell's shoulders dropped as he reached for his coffee. He brought it to his lips, and stared at her as he sipped. As he pulled the cup down to the table, he spoke. "It's murder."

Harper shook her head, tears filling her eyes, blurring her view of the pastry she no longer had the desire to eat.

"Don't say that, Ordell. Not you. Don't you understand that my son is dying?"

"And you think that justifies taking someone else's life?"

"Not someone, Ordell."

She clasped her hands over her mouth, preventing the next words from coming out, shocked at what she'd just said. Ordell arched an eyebrow at her and his voice went quiet.

"Just a model? A clone? You're rationalizing this now?"

"I didn't mean that. It's my son. What would you do?"

His eyes went glassy, and he exhaled through his nose.

"I don't know, Harper. But I don't have that opportunity, do I?"

"I think you would. And I don't think you would care whose life you bargain with."

Harper examined him closely, eyes narrowing.

"How did you find out? Did Torrent tell you?"

"No. Kiera is one of ours. She told us."

She lifted her head and looked down her nose at him.

"What are you going to do - kill me? Are you embracing violence now, Ordell?"

"It has its purposes, but this isn't that kind of situation. I'm here as your friend, Harper - remember how we're friends?"

Harper's face relaxed, and she met his eyes. There she could see her old friend, and the meaning of his furrowed eyebrows changed from agitation to concern.

"My son will die this year if I don't do something, and we've tried everything else. I wish there was another way, but there isn't."

She searched his face for acknowledgment and acceptance, but she found none. His concern seemed real, but he would never accept her arguments, however many times she repeated them. She smiled at him, but he didn't return it.

"Anyway, it was nice to see you again, Ordell."

She motioned to the door with her head, and taking the cue, he stood and made his way toward it. As he turned away from her, Harper knew then that their friendship, forged in the flames of her parents' deaths, might be over. She crossed a line that he never thought she would. For that matter, Harper crossed a line that she never thought she would. A lump formed in her throat as she covered the remaining distance to the elevator, focusing on the mission of food for her and her son. The rest could - would have to - wait. She left the penthouse, leaving the pastry untouched on the table.

*It's the right thing to do.*

The elevator advanced toward the lobby at such a slow speed that Harper felt herself aging. She imagined the lines developing in real-time on her face and her bones shrinking away. By the time the door opened to the lobby, she felt weak and frail, shuffling forth one tiny step before the other. Static imposed on the sounds around her, and the hall dimmed as her eyesight waned. A pillar to her right supported her weight when she found she couldn't walk anymore. Harper leaned against it and stared with glassy eyes across the lobby in time to see the crowd part at the entrance and Ordell step through the opening. She wanted to call out to him, but what could she say?

Three deep breaths of air smelling of pastries and buttercream swooshed in and out of her lungs and then out her nose. She straightened her back and blinked, focusing her vision. Almost there. She'd gotten Bodhi this far, and soon the question of whether to have the procedure would be over, and her son would live.

*It's the right thing to do.*

No matter how many times she repeated that line in her head, it didn't convince her.

Harper walked toward the entrance to the lobby on autopilot before she realized she was following Ordell accidentally as he departed. She stopped herself before she passed through and directed herself back towards the origin of the smells of pastries in the air. A small bakery was pressed up against the first-floor gift shop. Her mouth watered at the aroma of fresh-baked pieces of bread, a luxury she hadn't treated herself to in years. Very few places baked anymore since replicators killed most of the food industries. Dry, crispy pseudo-bread was all they could produce at her command when Harper didn't burn it. She saw several loaves of bread baking in an oven through the glass window, but when the doors slid open at her approach, the scene disappeared.

"Of course," she said to herself. Tiny projectors in the glass augmented the image, and other machinery produced the synthetic smells. Still, now that she was inside and already hungry, she made her way to the counter to order. A robot popped its head up from behind the counter.

"May I have your order?"

"Three sticky buns."

The robot said nothing else but whirled to head into the back to retrieve her replicated snacks. The smell of bread grew overpowering, and she felt herself getting light-headed. She shook her head slowly and regulated her breathing, but the feeling intensified.

"Ordell," Harper muttered as she stumbled toward one of the small bistro tables that littered the floor of the shop. Her mind swam, and the air pressed down on her forcing her toward the ground. She fell first to her knees and then to her hands. Harper went through the motions of breathing, but no air moved. She clutched at her neck with her left hand and supported herself with her right. Her eyes watered and stung as smoke materialized around her.

"Harper," a female voice called out from the mist. The call seemed to unlock the oxygen, and she finally caught a breath.

"What?" She rasped at whoever it was that called out to her. In the mist before her, Kiera stepped forward. "What did you do to me?"

Kiera pushed up her eyes into arches as she looked down on Harper's struggles on the floor. She took a step forward and stood by her head. Kiera licked her lips, turning them into a reflective glossy pink.

"You're doing this to yourself."

"Leave me alone. You're not going to convince me to kill my son!"

Kiera's face went stiff, and she tilted her head. "Your sticky buns are ready."

"Wh-?"

Kiera evaporated as the smoke dissipated. Harper breathed in steady gulps of air, and her eyes darted around, seeking Kiera, but she was nowhere to be found.

"Your buns are ready."

The robot pushed a box mechanically across the counter.

Harper stumbled but caught herself and grabbed them before swiveling toward the door. Tucking the buns beneath her arm, Harper collected herself and strode out into the busy lobby. She crossed the threshold to the elevator and took the dull ride back up to her room.

Aiden paced back and forth across the floor in the center of the room as Harper entered. Bodhi sat on the couch, his eyes puffy and red, half-dressed in his haptic suit. Aiden's face tilted downward, and she could see his eyes darting back and forth as he took each step.

"What happened?"

He shook his head briskly and didn't reply. Bodhi caught her eye.

"Aunt Kiera," he said.

"What about her?" Harper enunciated each syllable as she rapidly fired her response.

"She died yesterday," Aiden glowered at her. "They found her body in Winnipeg near the red-light district. We were going on a rescue after we got back, but I guess she wanted to do it alone. This whole thing is - was - hard for her to deal with."

Harper staggered to the couch and collapsed into it beside Bodhi. She fought back the tears.

"Yesterday? Ordell didn't tell me that she was dead." The words were more to herself than anyone else, but she'd made the mistake of uttering them aloud. The mention of Ordell's name caused both Aiden and Bodhi to pivot their heads and look at her, eyes wide. She now owed them some sort of explanation.

"He came by earlier. Kiera was part of the Order?"

"Yes," Aiden said. "She joined after I found her in Vancouver."

"You knew?"

"I assumed based on the rescues she kept asking me to help with. Since when was Ordell involved in the Siblings?"

"Lancaster used to be a friend of his. He's been close with them for a while."

Harper looked to Bodhi, trying to gauge how he was dealing with the information. His face was frozen, and the tears that streamed down it fell unaltered onto his chest and shoulders. Bodhi wasn't like her, though, and that was something of which she would always be proud. She'd always felt fragile, carrying anxiety around like a rabid tiger on her shoulders, waiting for an opportunity to jump into her life and destroy her world. Bodhi processed emotions better, and she felt that he would do better than she in this life. His stoic and unidirectional manner gave him a clear path where she'd always trickled through life like water.

"Are you okay, Bodhi?"

"Aunt Kiera," he said, "dead? Really? I talked to her before we left. She can't be dead."

Harper reached out and grabbed his hand.

"I'm sorry."

Bodhi turned to her and stared at her. Harper tried to read the emotions in his face, but the sadness seemed to overwhelm everything. He pulled his hand from hers, and she gulped as he turned away. He would never forgive her now.

"Bodhi…"

"I think I need some time," he said. Bodhi stood and walked toward his room in his haptic suit, waddling as the servos interfered with his gait.

"Don't forget it's almost time for the pump."

"I know."

Then he was gone, and she found herself alone with Aiden.

"Harper, do you have Ordell's ansible? If he didn't know, then we should tell him. I think he'd like to be involved in the funeral arrangements."

"I have one for him, but I haven't used it in a long time. I'll send it to you."

"Did you want to let him know?"

Harper shook her head no. Confronting Ordell again, armed with the fact of Kiera's death - she couldn't do it.

"He tried to talk me out of the operation, Aiden. Why is everyone trying to talk me out of saving my son?"

"Imagine if you were a clone. Someone grabs you off the street, and takes you into some room then puts something in your head. Then, everything that was you disappears, and someone else now wears your body around like a suit."

That didn't help.

"You hate me too?"

He looked away from her as he answered.

"I don't hate you, Harper. I couldn't do that. And I flew us here, and I'm paying for the hotel rooms. I'm as guilty as you are. I want to save Bodhi too."

"Why do you do all of this?"

"What do you mean?"

"I mean since the desert. You gave me a place to stay, and you took care of my son and me. You brought Kiera to safety. What's in it for you?"

"I have the means and the time, Harper. And at the risk of overstepping, Bodhi's like a son to me."

"Kiera? How did that happen?"

Aiden looked as though he didn't want to answer, but the time had come for them to be honest.

"It's a little embarrassing. I used to frequent the brothels in the states on the other side. Until I met you, I wasn't very attuned with models and the situation. I mean, I knew about it intellectually, but it didn't mean anything to me."

"So you didn't think about why those women were there?"

"Never crossed my mind. Kiera was always my favorite,

and I asked for her by name. When - when I met you, I started thinking about her as more. I made the mistake of asking her if she liked her work."

"What did she say?"

"She told me to fuck off with questions like that."

Harper smiled at the thought. That sounded exactly like Kiera.

"She told me that she did what she had to do, just like I did."

"But you still kept sleeping with her?"

"We developed a thing. But I guess Kiera got bored with me. Cut me off years ago and tried to leave. I asked her to stay with us. She thought it was a mistake, but she stayed."

"She's a good person."

"Harper, you need to come to terms with this treatment. Be in or be out. This extended guilt trip that you're on - it's affecting all of us."

"Thanks for the unsolicited advice."

"I mean it, and I'm sorry to have to say it. Bodhi's internalizing your projections. You hate yourself right now, and it's so obvious. He's doing something that you asked him to do, and that very act is tearing you apart. Whatever you have to do to get past it, please try."

Aiden was right, and she hated him a little for it. Her response was short.

"I know."

# 11

## Twenty-five Miles

*Monday, October 17, 2185*

Harper had been there for it all, the tumultuous history and the discovery that there was something she loved more than herself, or her self-righteousness. There was Bodhi - that miracle child who taught her what it meant to truly love. Her mind, as usual operating under its own license, visited those moments when she'd first learned of her son's disease.

Every time she saw him, part of her wondered what she could have done differently. What decision could she have made? And no matter how many times the question came up, it always ended with her baking in the hot sun of the desert on the American side of the border from Winnipeg, a struggle that still made her tremble to recall. The sun had beat across Harper's back as she trudged through the sand, alone on the former highway.

Dunes crested behind her like mountains against the sky. If it wasn't for the lack of trees, she could have imagined herself on a sunny afternoon walk out in west Texas. The illusion shattered at a hundred and twenty-five degrees Fahrenheit, though. She unstopped her water bottle, thankful that the supply held up so far. When she lifted the canister to her lips, she discovered that she had emptied it already. Giving it a couple of sorrowful shakes, she tossed the dead weight to the side of the road and fished out her backup supply from her bag. Warmed from the heat of the sun, the fluid didn't satisfy her thirst.

*Twenty-five miles. That's only eight hours.*

And she was already three hours into it. Tired and hot as she was, Harper knew she could make it by taking one small step after another.

Without warning, her stomach lurched, and she keeled forward. The water she'd just drank spewed from between her lips, and what didn't evaporate sprayed across the ground, along with left-over chunks of donut. Harper crashed down to her hands and knees in the burning sand, retching so violently that she fell over onto her side. The nausea passed over several minutes, costing her another half-an-hour delay and she couldn't fathom how much in fluids.

When she rose to her feet, Harper forced herself to drink again to replace what she'd lost. Trembling, she brought the container to her lips and drew in a short sip. That one went down okay, so she took a little more. When it seemed safe to do so, she pulled a deep draught from the bottle before she replaced the lid and rose to her feet. Harper had just gotten it back into her bag when she came crashing down to her knees again. The pain made her cry out as she pitched forward, face down in the dehydrating mud her vomit had produced.

Tears streamed down her face.

*Eight hours.*

Harper was only eight hours away from the border. She could even see a city in the distance across the flat surface of the desert. Eight hours was all she needed, but life wouldn't even give her that much. She struggled back up to her knees. Without being able to keep water down, she didn't know what eight more hours in the desert would do. Setting her sights on the city and clenching her teeth, she took one step, and then another. Then her stomach cramped again, and she fell.

Harper screamed at the top of her lungs as she slammed her fists into the dirt. Mud splattered under the force of her punches. Over and over again, she beat at the earth until she dropped from exhaustion.

In the distance, Harper heard the echo of a replicator fan. She lifted her head from the sand and tilted it, straining her hearing. The whine echoed again, reverberating in the distance. She struggled to get her knees under her, but she only bowed over again. All she could do was try to focus on the brown speck atop the far horizon line, kicking up a cloud of dust that now hid the distant city. Harper's heavy eyelids pulled together.

When she opened her eyes again, she bounced up and down, with each bounce sending a flash of pain through her abdomen. The city seemed closer now, and the dunes had been replaced with flat, crusted earth and the occasional pointed plant. A burlap bag provided some support to her head, and straps crossed her midsection, keeping her from flying up too far into the air each time the vehicle lifted. Someone screamed over the noise of the road.

"Found her in the desert. Yeah. I spotted her down there, on foot, if you can believe it."

There was a pause as part of the conversation passed on the other side of what she guessed was a communicator. Nausea swelled in her belly, so she closed her eyes and focused her energy on not being sick.

"I know you can't come to the states and get her. I'll get her to the border - you make sure the bus is ready for me. You'll see us - we had to bring a jeep."

A moment passed.

"I agree. Volantrae would have been better, but that would have taken to long to get through the checkpoint."

"Argnnnn." Harper groaned as the vehicle careened over a nasty bump.

"Slow down, David, she's waking up."

On command, the vehicle slowed, and the bumps lessened in severity. Harper opened her eyes again to see her face reflected into a pair of sunglasses. Behind, a large man with long, black hair pulled into a bun over his head smiled and talked to her.

"Found you in the dirt, Harper. It is Harper, right?" Her eyes shot open as she realized he knew her name. She struggled against her bonds.

"No, don't do that. We had to strap you in. It's a rough drive."

"How do you know my name?" The words came gurgled and foreign to her ears, and they trailed off at the end when she felt the nausea teasing at the back of her throat.

"Wasn't easy," he told her, then his grin widened. "We had to look through your stuff. Found a lot of money and a few data-coins. Your name was on one of them. Don't worry; we put it all back."

Harper had no energy with which to fight or worry. She closed her eyes and tried to drift off to an uncomfortable sleep, but the man wouldn't let her.

"I'm Aiden."

Harper managed a weak smile looking up at him.

"My hero."

Then she passed out.

\* \* \*

The next time she awoke, she gagged on something wedged into her throat. Harper's eyes shot wide, and she glanced around the room. A plastic apparatus blocked most of her view, but she saw Aiden asleep in a chair in the far corner of the space, tucked beneath a white coat. Her arms struggled against bonds somewhere beyond her field of vision. Harper tried to call out, but her muscles contracted around the tube allowing only a small groan to escape. A loud beeping noise sounded, alerting Aiden who jumped up to his feet as a stream of doctors entered the room.

"Calm down," one of them said. "We'll get the tube out."

She tried her best to listen, while one of the doctors slowly withdrew the tube from her mouth as another worked at her restraints. Saliva dripped down her chin when the plastic came free and the smell of rotting eggs assaulted her nose.

"Ms. Rawls, you're going to be fine."

The man spoke with a distinctly French accent. Somewhere in the background, she heard a nurse with a similar affect. This combination brought a smile to her chapped lips.

"Canada?"

"Yes, Canada. Specifically, Winnipeg. How do you feel, Ms. Rawls?"

"Fine."

"I'm glad you're awake. We had some questions for you that we were having a hard time answering. Just how long have you been pregnant?"

"About three months."

The doctor flashed a smile at her.

"It's a boy," the doctor continued. "We placed the age somewhere around three months, so that seems right. But his blood cell count production isn't where we'd like it to be. It's within a safe range, but towards the lower end. We need to keep an eye on it."

Aiden towered over the doctor, looking down at his chart

wide-eyed.

"We'll give you another couple of days to recover, then you and the father can go out. We'll give you some tools to continue monitoring. These things sometimes work themselves out."

"He's not the father."

Aiden looked up at this, face washed out and eyes bleary as though he hadn't quite woken up yet.

"I'm not," he volunteered. "I found her wandering in the desert."

"Do you mind stepping out for a moment while we discuss medical history?"

Flashes came to her about her first time in a hospital bed after her parents' deaths and the hours she spent re-living her nightmare alone.

"Wait," Harper interrupted, then focused on Aiden. "Can you stay?"

Harper implored with her eyes. The man sidestepped the doctors and walked toward the side of the bed, scooting a chair beneath him. The doctor tapped at the screen in his hands, looking for something or entering data - Harper couldn't be certain. She looked to Aiden.

"Thank you for saving my life," she told him.

"It was nothing others wouldn't have done."

"Nobody else did."

Her words seemed to make him uncomfortable, and he changed the subject.

"You don't look pregnant. I wouldn't have guessed."

"It's only been three months. It gets obvious soon, don't worry."

She held her breath as those words came out. Her joy at escaping to Canada, she realized, should have been Ordell's joy. She'd followed his escape plan down to the letter and now was in a foreign land, with no job and less of a support system than she'd had had in the states.

Smart.

"What were you doing in the desert?" Aiden asked.

"Would you believe I was looking for a new life?"

"I guess you found one."

Aiden laughed aloud, which made her chuckle in return, though doing so made her feel nauseated, so she cut the laugh short by locking her teeth together. The doctor waved a wand across her forehead and up her right side, then frowned at the thin pinamu screen he held. He jabbed at the pinamu with one finger with such ferocity she thought it might break, but the flat screen held off his attack. The doctor stared at her in a way that made her uncomfortable.

"Okay, let's get started. Do you know what day it is?"

"Not a clue."

"October 17, 2185."

"Do you have a history of mental illness?"

She shook her head no, but she could tell from the doctor's arching eyebrow that he didn't believe her.

"Maybe I should go," Aiden interjected. "I'll just wait in the hall while you get through the medical interview."

"Thank you," the doctor nodded toward the doorway. As soon as Aiden left, he turned to Harper.

"We can't get your medical history from the United States. There's no international agreement that allows that. You are the only way we can get this information. Please be honest with your answers. Do you have a history of mental illness?"

Abashed, she looked up at him.

"I can't go back."

"None of this information will go into your consideration for citizenship if that's what you're concerned about. Completely confidential."

She nodded and rubbed the back of her neck.

"I was diagnosed with an anxiety disorder. I used to have

an implant."

He nodded.

"We saw that in the scan. Would you like someone to talk to you about it? We can bring in a psychologist."

"No, I'm fine."

"Are there any other conditions you would like to tell me about?"

*My father murdered my mother right in front of my eyes, and the Human Pride Movement stalked me and tried to kill my best friend.*

"None. You've already discovered the pregnancy."

"Allergies to medications?"

She shook her head again.

"That's all for now, Harper. If you think of anything else that would make our job of caring for you easier, so we don't have to guess - please don't withhold it."

Message received. Don't piss off the doctor.

"One more thing," he continued. "Would you like us to issue you a new mood stabilizer?"

"No. I mean, no, thank you. I'm fine."

The doctor smiled a non-genuine smile and then turned and walked out the door. True to his word, Aiden re-entered the room and took his seat next to her bed. She settled back into her pillow and pulled the sheet up. She looked at Aiden, who, even sitting, was above her eye level. She smiled up at him.

"Thank you for staying."

"It's nothing. I want to make sure you're okay."

"I am. And now I'm really tired for some reason."

"For some reason?"

"Yeah, okay - crossing deserts takes it out of you."

Harper yawned widely and closed her eyes.

Harper awoke in the middle of the night with sweat pouring down her face. She pulled her blanket over her as chills shot through her body, but it did nothing to warm her as her body began to shake violently. Seconds later, the door to her room burst open as an influx of doctors and nurses crashed through.

"Hit the levitation," the doctor shouted, and a nurse bumped into the bed, then grappled around. Harper felt the bed detach and float a few inches upwards as the entire thing moved, a nurse on each side. Violent shivers rippled through her body as she began to vomit again. One of the nurses pushed her head to the side, so the vomit cleared her mouth and missed the bed.

"Where are we going?"

"Emergency triage," the doctor reported, as Harper tilted her head backward to make out the nurse better. "We need to take a look at that baby. Something's not right there, and it's throwing her system off."

"ET," the nurse parroted as she shoved the bed through the doorway. Down the hall they went, gliding smoothly while Harper wretched violently. She heard the schlinking sound of a drug administered under her skin through an insertion gun and fell into unconsciousness.

# 12

## Discovering Anemia

### *Tuesday, October 18, 2185*

"You're still with us."

The doctor didn't seem confident. He looked steadily at a bank of monitors before him. One of them displayed the rough outline of a female body, which Harper guessed was hers. The flashes of multicolored lights mesmerized her. A dim glow began in the chest of her two-dimensional clone then pulsed out to her extremities before going dark again. On another monitor, several time-series graphs displayed atop each other, one of them spiking with her heartbeat.

"So far," she replied feebly. "What happened?"

"The child happened. It's sucking red blood cells from your body. Your body is producing red blood cells at twice the normal rate. The child doesn't seem to be producing any of its own, and it's pulling yours. Maybe pregnancy anemia, but we've never seen it this bad."

Being killed by her unborn child seemed par for the course

with Harper's life story. She said nothing, completely unsurprised.

"Did you expect this?" The doctor asked her the question. Her chin quivered as she tried to explain. He turned to face her, and she realized then that he was the same doctor from earlier.

"This is just my life," she told him.

He turned back to the monitors and spoke over his shoulder.

"We can offset the drain, and he may be able to produce his own blood cells when he's a bit more mature. But we can't let you leave the hospital in this condition. Right now, we're infusing you with blood. We need to ramp production in your own body, which is possible, but it would require an implant. Do we have your permission to install a red-blood-cell production amplifier?"

She nodded quickly. Her son needed it, and she was willing to do whatever he needed.

"Thank you. We'll get you in probably tomorrow morning. Try to sleep - it won't be easy, I know."

He motioned to the mass of wires around her and the body harness strapping her down. Then he placed his pinamu down and seemed to be preparing to leave.

"Doctor?"

He notched up an eyebrow at her.

"Thank you."

The doctor nodded curtly before ducking out of the cocoon of screens. Her eyes caught another of the monitors from her reclined position. This one portrayed an image of a lumpy head attached to a pink globule with four tiny arms.

"Bodhi," she whispered to the screen, "just like your grandfather."

\* \* \*

## *Wednesday, October 19, 2185*

Once again, Harper found herself in a state of delirium. This time, having been expected, it was much more pleasant. The doctor floated before her like a specter and said intelligent things like 'more blood' and 'suture.' She lay on her right side, while on her left, she felt a tug and a push and another tug, but no pain. Her raised side pulsed with her heart. Then she fell asleep.

## *Friday, October 21, 2185*

"Ms. Rawls," came a voice, "are you awake yet?"

Harper licked her dry lips before she could open her eyes. Her body pulsed and throbbed as though bruises covered every inch. Supported by her right side, her right hip had fallen asleep. Opposite that, ribs exuded a warm heat that Harper felt was pain that she was still too groggy to feel yet. She braced herself as her body continued to awaken.

"Mostly," she told the person, "give me a minute."

With all of the strength she could muster, Harper forced her eyes open and saw a different doctor this time. He had green eyes and a stray lock of hair that swooped down across deep wrinkles in his forehead.

"Aren't you supposed to be operating on me?"

"The operation is over, Ms. Rawls."

The pain hit her, and she scrunched her face and bit her lower lip as her eyes welled. It was as though someone plunged five carving knives into her left abdomen all at once. The doctor's eyebrows raised, and he tapped some things into his pinamu. She felt the pain slowly reducing back to a dull ache and swallowed.

"Sorry," he told her, coming back to her side. "We misjudged your tolerance."

Unable to talk, she only moaned as the pain subsided.

"The operation was a success. There were some difficulties, but your stable now."

Her teeth grit together as she locked her jaw and stared intently at the doctor for any signs that he might give away - anything he wasn't saying. She saw by the way his eyes refused to settle that something else loomed.

"What is it, doctor?"

"I don't know how to say this," he told her.

"Bodhi?"

"He's fine. Everything worked as I said. It's just…"

"I can handle it."

Her insides wound into knots as she steeled herself for the inevitable disappointment to come.

"The child. His production rates are dropping. We'd hoped he would show some improvement, but it doesn't seem to be. He seems to be pulling even more from you and producing less red blood cells of his own."

The doctor took a deep breath and pushed the stray lock of hair up and away from his eyes.

"There's very little likelihood that he will get better, Ms. Rawls. He's going to need support for the rest of his life. And the rest of his life may not be very long. You need to understand the severity of his condition so that you can decide."

"Decide what?"

"Whether to continue with the pregnancy."

Harper turned away from the doctor the best she could, although propped up on her right side, this meant looking down at his feet. He wore sports shoes. She realized that she'd been expecting more professional shoes, but with someone who spent the day bouncing from room to room, it made sense. They were cleaner than she'd expected, cleaned of any blood spots. The bottom of gray scrubs leaned gently over the laces. These, too, were immaculate and not the sign of a person who'd just come out of an operation.

"What's today?"

"Friday. Ms. Rawls, did you hear me?"

She nodded mutely.

"It's better that you make the decision sooner, Ms. Rawls."

"I want to see him."

"Mr. Periam?"

Harper shook her head no, catching sight of machines as her field of vision swung up and down the doctor's body.

"No. Bodhi. I want to meet him. I need to meet him and to tell him how much I love him."

"Do you want to think about it? Perhaps Mr. Periam should join you."

"It's not his baby, doctor. It's mine, and there's nothing to discuss."

Anger welled up inside of her at his vacuous suggestion.

"I just thought a friend might help."

"You're not listening. I'm keeping this child."

The doctor stood and nodded curtly.

"You must understand though. To keep this baby, we're going to have to induce and place him in a holding tank and infuse red blood cells. He'll be connected to machines and may never come off of them."

"I do understand, Doctor. I need him."

He left the room as Harper, crushed with the weight of her decision, stared after him.

## *Saturday, October 22, 2185*

Harper's body seized up as the pain spread through her lower back. Sweat beaded up on her forehead and trickled into her eyes. She clutched the side of the bed hard enough to turn her knuckles white. Counting the seconds helped. She observed each one as she blew out and tried to resist the urge to push. It wasn't time yet, the doctor told her, and pushing early could hurt her little Bodhi. She focused on the seconds - 17...18...19.

"Three and a half minutes," the doctor told her, "almost time. Nurse, administer the pain treatment."

Harper felt a pain release in her lower abdomen, reduced to a tightening sensation.

"You're doing great, Ms. Rawls," the doctor told her. The nurse murmured something in his ear and then turned to Harper and smiled.

"Just great, Harper," he followed up.

Seven people gathered around her bed - two doctors, four nurses, and one more person whose presence she didn't understand. A woman stood near the door, just outside of which she knew Aiden waited. She was prim and wore a sleek red overcoat, contrasting with the drab grays, greens, and pastel blues of the scrubs everyone else wore. The woman was also the only individual in the room sans mask. Harper focused on her face, which at that moment, seemed to watch everything all at once. Then the woman's gaze shifted, and she locked eyes with Harper. Purple eyes seemed to drill into her.

"Push, Harper. Now's the time."

Harper closed her eyelids, and the woman's intense stare penetrated into her mind. A sharp pain told her the woman would have to wait. Harper pushed. Hard.

"Okay, stop. Take a break, and breathe."

She opened her eyes, and the woman had vanished. The doctor met her gaze and turned to see where she looked. He gave his attention back to her, and the other doctor stared at a set of monitors nearby.

"Are you ready? Push again."

Moments later, a nurse lay a tiny pink boy across her chest. He lay there so silently that she thought he might not have made it after all. Tears formed in her eyes and streamed out down her cheeks. Then the little body twitched.

"Harper," the nurse got her attention. "We have to take him, but I told the doctor to give you a few minutes. He's going to need to go into a chamber for a while. And we need to go over care."

Harper's eyes focused on the little pink head until it finally twitched. She wanted to hold onto him forever. Her world grew smaller until it only consisted of her and Bodhi. The hospital staff faded away into the background.

"Harper?"

Her mother, Aayushi's voice penetrated through her mind.

"Mom?"

"Harper, he's beautiful. He looks just like you. Look at that nose. And you can already tell he's going to have gorgeous brown skin."

"His father's half-black."

"What a strange thing to say."

"I mean, he's not brown."

Her mother wasn't paying attention, she could sense it, and her words confirmed it.

"Look at those feet. They're perfect. And those little hands."

Harper could imagine her mother standing beside her, touching each of the fingers and toes. Bodhi stopped rooting and turned to where she sensed her mother's presence.

"Mom, he's sick."

"I know, dear. So were you - don't you remember? I loved you just the same."

"Not like this. My problem is anxiety. Bodhi might die."

"Maybe. Or maybe not. But look at how beautiful he is."

Her mother's voice trailed off then, and something tugged

at Bodhi. Harper grabbed him tightly, only to hear a voice chastise her.

"Let go, Harper. It's time for him to go. His blood counts are dropping."

Only then did she notice the tiny wire dangling from the bottom of his left foot as someone lifted him away.

"Rest, new mom," the doctor told her. "You'll have a lot of work to do soon. This little one is going to keep you busy."

## *Monday, April 24, 2185*

Six months later, Harper returned to the hospital, where the doctors insisted that she stay for the full course of postpartum training. Her assigned postpartum room was tiny compared to the prepartum one. No monitors covered the walls, no endless flood of nurses and doctors either. Harper remained alone and isolated, with a holovid which showed her various facts about conditions Bodhi might have. But Harper knew that none of the videos captured Bodhi's situation. The nurses drilled it into her that nobody had ever seen Bodhi's situation before. Multiple red blood cell diseases hit her son at once.

Harper watched a video in dismay about possible treatments. At Bodhi's size, he couldn't get an implant to increase the blood production the way she could, and his body might not respond either. Her now-disabled implant was roughly the size of a half-liter beaker, though oblong like a squished heart. It would take up half of his body if they installed it. His treatment had to be different, especially with so many failures in the process.

One part of the treatment was a small enclosure about the size of a tomography scanning chamber. When it flashed onto the holovid, the voice caster announced that the device was an external erythropoietin pump. Red blood cells were complicated things to make. Kidneys encourage the body to create them by releasing erythropoietin, which promotes red blood cell production. The external erythropoietin pump used light wavelengths to trigger the kidneys to release the chemical.

A nurse entered the room as the video came to a close.

"Are you okay, Harper?"

Harper then realized that she had been crying the entire time she'd watched the end of the video. Multiple times a day, her baby would have to go into that tiny chamber.

"Not really," she admitted. "Does he have to have all of these treatments? It's just so much for him to go through."

The nurse nodded.

"Every one. The erythropoietin pump will help keep production up. The iron tablets will give him the tools to produce those cells. The dialysis machine will get rid of the dead blood cells to make room for the new ones."

"But that's his entire day. When will he be a boy?"

"There will be time, Harper. Just at his size and development level, we have to stay on top of it. Dialysis will be less frequent as he gets older. As his digestive system develops, you won't need the tablets as much. Even the pump will be easier as he gets older because he'll be able to do it himself with a wand instead of the chamber."

"All of this, and the feeding?"

"You can do it, Harper."

"Besides, you're not alone," came a booming voice from the doorway. Harper's heart leaped as she looked up to see Aiden blocking the entire door frame. She smiled at him and wiped away her tears.

"Aiden."

The nurse stood and flashed them both a smile before leaving, as Aiden skillfully maneuvered over to a window seat on the right side of her bed. He carried two cups with him, one of which was probably yaupon hot brew, his favorite drink. For her, regular coffee with a splash of creamer. He handed her a cup and then sat on the window seat.

"It's a lot, huh?"

"So much. Did I make the right decision? Will he get any joy in his life?"

"With you around, I'm sure he will."

"What if I make a mistake?"

"Just take it one day at a time. We'll get through it."

She switched her coffee from her right to left hand and reached out for him. He grabbed her hand in his, and she marveled at the size difference as her hand disappeared. He squeezed gently.

"It'll be okay, Harper."

"I couldn't do it without you. Thank you for everything."

"Not done yet."

He reached out to her and dropped a pink heart-shaped communicator into her hand.

"My number's in there."

"Heart-shaped?"

Aiden shrugged his shoulders and grinned. "It's what they had in the gift shop."

# 13

## Meeting Torrent

### *Sunday, June 21, 2201*

Something touched Bodhi's foot and he started involuntarily. He pulled himself free of his new helmet to see his mother sitting beside him.

"Hey, kiddo. Your father wants to see you."

He nodded in silence and forced himself to his feet. He tossed the helmet down to join the rest of his unused haptic gear on the bed. Without words, he followed his mother out of the penthouse and into the elevator. She pressed the button for the fourth floor, and they both waited until it came to a stop.

His mother's gait slowed near a door marked 'Alexander Toussaint.' She came to a stop before it. She reached her hand up to knock, but even this, she seemed unable to do. She stood staring as she mulled something over. Then she turned quickly toward him as her black hair lifted on the manufactured breeze of her motion.

"Bodhi," she told him, making eye contact the way she did when she had something profound to say. "Your father and I have known each other for a very long time."

"Okay..." he muttered, and continued looking at the sign, and then the door. Carvings embellished the glass's surface, with rough edges smoothed to make the door resemble ancient friezes, with Greek and Roman figures fighting. The figures in this frieze were all geese, flying at various heights, some hidden behind trees. Bodhi wondered at the significance of this. There was no title on it. Regular doctors, he knew from experience, had titles, like Pediatrics or Orthodontics. This door only had the three words on it, which comprised the man's name. He strained unsuccessfully to penetrate the frosted glass with his eyes.

His mother pushed the door open, and instead of a waiting area as Bodhi had expected, there was a man seated behind a cluttered desk. Frizzy graying black hair framed the man's face. Kind-looking oval eyes focused intently on something on the desk's surface, with laugh lines fully pronounced at the corners. Optical lenses rode the end of his nose and prepared to slip. Bodhi got a glimpse of what looked like a scientific printout, which the man's eyes scanned impossibly fast from line to line. When the door clicked shut noisily behind them, his father looked up. Torrent stood hastily and walked around the edge of the desk. Then he stopped as though he didn't know what to do next with himself. Finally, after an eternity of silent staring, he extended a hand toward Bodhi's mother. Instead of taking the hand, she knocked it aside and swooped in quickly for a hug. She wrapped her arms around his neck and pressed her cheek to his. Bodhi wished to look away, embarrassed by the spectacle. Before he could, they were already apart, separated nearly as quickly as they had come together.

Behind a handful of freckles on the tops of either cheek, he saw a blush receding from the man's face as he pulled away. Though apart now, they continued to hold hands as the pair spoke in hushed tones.

"How have you been, Harps? I've missed you."

"Fine, Torrent. Mostly. Thank you for arranging this."

He smiled and nodded.

"This treatment is experimental, you know. There are no guarantees, but I think it's the best shot. How was the trip?"

"Not bad. Aiden's jet got us here in a couple of hours. It's kind of nice not to have to wait in lines."

"Aiden?"

"Yes. My significant other."

"Oh, the stock trader."

Torrent pulled his hands from hers and backed away, but only about six inches. He turned and pushed a hand toward Bodhi, which Bodhi accepted and shook as expected, but didn't smile. Torrent then refocused his attention back on Harper.

"I wanted to see you," Torrent said, smiling sheepishly at her. Dark azure eyes seemed connected to her hazel ones by invisible wires as they stood apart. Then Torrent shifted his attention back to Bodhi again.

"It's not a treatment, not really. It's a transfer of consciousness."

"I know."

"Yes. The way that it works is that the animus module interfaces with your brain."

He turned his head and pulled forward his caramel-colored left ear, revealing a thin scar behind it.

"I have one. My prototype - first version. Your mother refuses though."

He turned to Bodhi's mother flashing a quick smile and then back to Bodhi.

"Twenty years, and no problems yet," he said, as though

they had had conversations about it for at least that long. "We implant this, then after it's there, it maps out your consciousness and starts to replace bits of functionality. Eventually, your entire consciousness runs from it."

"Then what?" The idea, as crude and painful as it was to consider, Bodhi still found fascinating.

"Then we move you. Instead of this body that you're in, you get a new one."

A new body. If his actions had matched what he felt inside, he would have been running around the room, jumping on tables, and giving away hugs. A new body was something he'd wanted every day for his entire existence.

"What does it do? In there?" he asked as he tapped his head with the index finger of his right hand.

"Nanites create networks that mirror your current neural pathways. Then they link into your senses and take over. You won't even notice that part. After a few days, your brain will essentially be redundant, as all of what you think of as 'you' will be on the animus module. Are you following?"

"I think so."

"Good. After that, we pick a model and then transplant your animus module into that new body. Once there, the module will begin to integrate and take over the body, making it yours. Clones, I mean, specific for that purpose. A partnership with…."

Torrent looked toward Bodhi's mother before continuing.

"…sorry, Harper. A partnership with Emergent Biotechnology provides us with the clones we need fairly inexpensively. They see this as an investment."

Bodhi and his mother had both known about Emergent Biotechnology's involvement. Still, he wouldn't have been able to tell from looking at her. Her face lost its dark tint and turned pallid, but she revealed her anxiety in no other way, except perhaps by the question she asked next.

"Have you seen Ordell, Torrent? He asked me about you."

"Funny you should ask. He's been by, and he's not happy about it. But sometimes we have to do things we don't like to move science forward. Emergent bought the patent for our cloning process, and part of the payment was access to clones for research purposes."

Bodhi's mother seemed embarrassed, as though she had only just remembered that Bodhi was in the room. She directed her next statement to him.

"You have some time. We aren't going to proceed unless you agree."

He could tell that it hurt her to say those words. If it were up to her, he would be under the knife already. Bodhi was inclined to say yes as well, and keep his promise. He also feared that he would die in the middle of the operation, or something else nefarious would happen. After all, the device would be tinkering with his brain. He only nodded.

"I heard about your timeline," Torrent interrupted. "Has it changed?"

"A year is what the doctor said."

The words came out of his mouth like knives and stabbed their way back in through his ears. One year. He could remember a year ago, and it seemed so close that it nearly took his breath away to think that all of the time he had left could fit into the memory he had of the last twelve months of his life. Absently he wiped one eye, which had started to burn a little, and realized that a tear had formed in the corner of it and smeared across his finger.

"Then we should move quickly. Take two days, no longer, to think this through. At that point, we will need to know the answer. It does take time to do the implanting part, and we'll need a while for the recovery."

Torrent's business-as-usual tone took set Bodhi more at ease than he had been with the knowledge of his imminent death. He thought about simply saying yes, but he wasn't ready. He was still convinced that things would go wrong, as they always did. He faked polite smiles and shook Torrent's outstretched hand when offered.

"I have to go," Torrent told him. "Other patients. Well, one. But remember, two days. Don't take any longer than that, please. The sooner we get started, the better off we'll be."

Something about the man's blue eyes pierced into his mind. Or possibly, he thought, it might have been the way that he talked or moved. Maybe it was the way his mother had treated Torrent that had done it, but suspicion was developing in Bodhi's mind. He struggled with asking the question as they walked across the hall and back toward the elevator.

"Mom?"

She seemed still flustered by the experience and struggling to hide her discomfort.

"Bodhi, what's the matter?"

"Torrent. Why did you…"

Once again, her face washed out of color, so he knew that she had understood what it was that he was trying to ask. She didn't answer at once, though, only entered the elevator and pushed the button to get them back to the penthouse. Then she turned toward him.

"Why break up?"

Bodhi nodded.

She smiled, and then that smile widened into an open-mouthed grin as she laughed.

"It was long ago."

But she didn't add any details, and he didn't press her farther on the subject as she didn't want to talk about it. Bodhi still had more questions to ask, but his strength began to fail him. He quickly checked his communicator for the time. It was just a little after one o'clock in the afternoon, and there hadn't been an opportunity for food. Still, he had had a late breakfast, so it was barely two and a half hours since the last bit of food he'd eaten, and four hours since his remaining iron tablet. He silently wondered what his body did with all of the iron that it burned through. He guessed probably he simply pissed it away.

"Mom, I need to …."

He wasn't quick enough, and he knew it. The upward momentum of the elevator overwhelmed him, and quickly he crashed to the floor. His eyes stopped working when he hit, but his ears continued to funnel noises toward his brain. He heard his mother scream and felt the elevator lurch to a stop, and the door creaked open slowly. His breathing slowed, despite his subjugating desire for it not to. The sounds also began to disappear, replaced with a cold sensation throughout his body. What he knew to be the cold metal floor of the elevator felt warm to the touch.

The episode caused him to fade in and out of consciousness. He felt carried one moment and then heard the muttering of hushed voices all around him, none of which he could distinguish from the others. Then the sounds faded out again. His eyes cracked open in the silent void. He caught flashes of blue and green and orange, and occasional flare-ups of light as he continued in a somehow effortless, yet rapid, pace down some hallway. Then everything faded once again, and he found himself in the quiet darkness.

"He's waking up," someone nearby whispered. He heard shuffling far away as he began to open his eyes. A flood of lights silhouetted the fuzzy outline of a woman. As his eyes adjusted, he realized that this woman wasn't his mother, and was around his age. Her eyes captivated him as deep pools of topaz so that all he could do was stare. He tried to think of something to say but felt so exhausted that even the effort to produce thoughts was strenuous. Instead, he took in the rest of her. She wore her blond pony-tail in a short braid that lay across her left shoulder. Her eyes were full of concern, he noticed, but why they should be, he didn't know. Since he'd never met her before, the idea that someone as beautiful as she was would be at all concerned with him. He smiled the best he could, which wasn't very good, and he felt it form into more of a grimace as he tried again. Her lips began to move, almost out of time with her voice.

"Are you okay? Oh, never mind. The nurse said you shouldn't talk. I know! Wink once if you're okay."

He tried to wink, but he could tell the eye didn't close because of the light that leaked in through his parted eyelids. Then, over the blonde girl's shoulder, he saw his mother suddenly appear. Across her face, he could see that whatever they'd discovered about his condition was even worse than they'd known before. He wanted to sleep.

"Bodhi, you're awake," she said, "good. We need to talk before you go back to sleep."

"Talk?" he managed to force through his teeth.

"Yes. You had an episode, and I asked Torrent to look at you again. He said..."

She couldn't continue. The tears she had been holding back with that angry expression that Bodhi knew wasn't anger began to flow down the sides of his cheeks. The girl beside him picked up the story where his mother had left off.

"...he said you're going to die in a month. Was it Bodhi? What a cool name!"

He tried to process her words. Would he die in a month? That's what he thought he'd heard, but it couldn't be right. A whole team of doctors had looked at him in Canada, and they'd said a year. Could things have sped up so much?

"Who are you?" he managed in a hoarse whisper that was only a marginal improvement over a cough.

"Christine Hamilton," she said and stuck out her hand

quickly. When he couldn't take it, she seemed slightly embarrassed and put it back down into her lap. He noticed then that she wore what looked like running shorts that matched her shirt.

"Bodhi Rawls," he told her, biting off the end with an actual cough.

"Nice to meet you. It's so boring here; you wouldn't believe it. When I saw your mother in the hallway, I had to help. I was coming from physical therapy, and I was a bit sore. But you needed help, so we got you to the doctor, okay."

Something about the woman seemed off. The way she spoke didn't quite seem to match how old she looked.

"Tell him what you told me, Christine," his mother said, "about the treatment."

"Oh, that, yeah. I got the treatment. See?"

She flashed her wrist at him, and he saw a model's bar code stamped across it. He recognized the striped tattoo - the same one his Aunt Kiera wore.

"You did?"

Finally, his voice seemed like his own again. Only a slight breathlessness marred his words this time.

"I didn't have a choice like you," she told him. "I was in a coma for… they say…something like twenty years, I think."

"Twenty years?"

"Yes. Torrent did the same thing to her that he's going to do to you. Christine, did you notice anything wrong after the treatment?"

"You mean with me? No, I don't think so. A new body takes a while to get used to. See?"

She lifted a leg slightly to show him her shorts.

"Physical therapy. You may not need as much as me because, you know, no coma. But I bet you'll need some."

The door cracked open, and an older man came in. The door then closed behind him, and he shuffled toward them.

"Christine, ah, here you are."

"Hi Grandfather," she said as she turned to smile at him. When she did, Bodhi could make out the small incision behind her ear.

"Grandfather, Bodhi is going to have the treatment too."

"He is?" The man replied, then turned toward Bodhi's mother.

"It's been far too long, Ms. Rawls. Where have you been?"

"Gallatin, it has. Thank you for agreeing to this."

"You always were my favorite Toussaint Labs employee, even if you did turn out to be a bit of a pain in the ass."

Bodhi's mother blushed a little at this before she retorted.

"Your lab recovered, and through licensing, you're making money hand over fist. I don't think you need to be too upset about that."

"It was quite the circus when you disappeared. We'll have to do lunch and catch up. But we have more important things to discuss."

Gallatin turned to Bodhi.

"Have you decided? I feel like we don't know yet. Are you going to take the treatment, or aren't you?"

He looked at his mother's expectant face and wished more than anything else that he still had two more days to think about it. There was so much more to consider. Bodhi could already feel the weakness creeping back into him as his strength dripped away. A decision had to be made, and if the choice was between being alive or being dead, there could be only one reasonable choice.

"Okay. We can do the treatment," Bodhi said with the last of his energy, then finally allowed his eyes to close again. A moment later, he was aware of being spirited away, and then nothing else.

# 14

## Loneliness

### *Monday, June 22, 2201*

Harper noticed the gradual change in the suite's interior lighting changed to eighty-percent brightness, an indication that beyond the walls of comfort, late-afternoon had fallen in the city. Aiden was gone on a business trip, planned months ago. She'd told him it was okay to go, begged him to go even when he'd threatened to cancel to see her through Bodhi's operation. Harper hated herself a little for sending Aiden away.

Her arm trembled as she raised her right fist to knock against Bodhi's bedroom door, so much that she paused a second to steady it. Once the shaking stop, she pounded three times quickly and let it drop to her side. Her heart raced in her chest. To her surprise, the door popped open just as her arm rested at her side, causing her to jerk backward a step.

"Bodhi, it's time."

The whisper croaked out of her, but she didn't try again on

the knowledge that the weight on her chest would turn all of her words into misshapen things.

"I know, I'm coming."

Did she imagine the hostility in his voice? The week before had been nearly impossible to endure. Her conviction never faltered, since the loss of her only child was something she refused to endure. Bodhi's reaction to her had been a slow drip of anger that she'd never seen in him before. Today was the last day, she told herself. Tomorrow he would be safe, and she would have kept him that way. She only had to make it one more day.

Harper resisted the urge to widen the crack in the door any more open than Bodhi had left it. Shuffling sounds of clothes moving around and other clutter moving about piqued her curiosity, even through the fog of dizziness she felt accumulate in her head. Not enough to knock her down, the feeling intensified only to the point of proclaiming its existence, and knowing that the cause lay beyond the doors opening did little to stifle it. She saw the opening grow and the silhouette of her child in the entry, and for only a second, she saw him again as a five year old, smiling up at her with wide, trusting eyes. That image disappeared as quickly as it formed in her mind, replaced by the complex studying stare of a boy on the verge of manhood who now weighed every word she said for truth.

As he pushed through and past her, she caught sight of his fingers, nearly as thin as those of the child she'd been thinking of. More emaciated than ever, she saw the signs of aging on him, even from the last week. She'd done the right thing in forcing him into this, hadn't she?

"You coming?" Bodhi's impatient voice cut into her. Harper looked up to see him staring back at her, and behind his eyes, she saw something besides anger. He hunched more than usual, warping the over six feet of his body into a small bundle that could almost be overlooked in a crowd. His sallowed skin clung to his face, and tiny beads of sweat sprawled over his forehead. The impatience was a facade, and some of the anger might have been too. She would love for that to be true. One thing was certain - behind those darting eyes was the scared little boy she brought into the world. Harper closed the gap between them quickly and threw her arms over him. This time, he returned the hug.

"I love you, Bodhi." She whispered the words into his ears.

"Me too, Mom. I'm sorry."

"You don't have to be. No matter what happens, you can always blame me for this. If it saves your life, I don't care."

That wasn't true. The week had taught her better, but they were words that he needed to hear, and at least she could do this much as a parent to her baby. He pulled away and looked into her eyes for the span of a second, revealing misty tears tucked behind his lower eyelids, and then looked away with a sniffle. He wouldn't cry, not in front of her. She'd never told him not to. One day, he'd just stopped doing it, and she'd missed those tears ever since.

"Shall we?" She asked the question as she turned toward the front of the suite. Bodhi nodded and followed her through the door and they made their way to the waiting area.

The room was barely larger than a kitchen, with couch-like seats and a replicator and desalination unit near the door. On the back counter sat a glass panel that separated whoever was in the waiting area from what may one day be a secretary, but now was just an empty space.

The door popped open beside the secretary's cubicle, and Harper's heart again began to race. There, in full scrubs as she'd never seen him before, stood Torrent, his thick goggles tucked behind a surgical mask.

"Are you ready?"

She nodded, but then realized he hadn't addressed her. His eyes focused entirely on Bodhi, who gulped and stepped forward. Harper's hand shot out to grab Bodhi's and she clutched him, squeezing his fingers tightly. The two of them waited for her to release her grip, soundless as death. Harper relinquished her son to Torrent then.

"Don't let him die," she pleaded with Torrent as Bodhi disappeared through the doorway. Torrent only stared at her with furrowed eyebrows, and promised nothing. He'd always been a scientist. The traits that now could save her son's life grated on her. How hard could a few consoling words be to eek out? But he wasn't hers anymore. And now Bodhi may not be either. Harper turned and made her way to one of the seats, then sunk down into it unsure if she would ever rise from the seat again.

## *Tuesday, June 23, 2201*

She must have fallen asleep, because the clicking shut of the waiting room door awoke her. As frayed as her nerves were, she may have even passed out, as the drumbeat in her skull told her may have been the case. Harper swiveled her head toward the door to see who entered, and in the doorway lurked a frightened looking young woman.

"Christine?"

"May I sit with you?"

Harper straightened up in her chair in response, offering up more space so that Christine could accept the invitation. The woman neared her tentatively, but then plopped herself down quietly, crossing her legs back under the edge of the chair.

"What time is it?"

"Seven o'clock in the morning."

Harper smiled.

"And you're here without coffee?"

Christine returned her smile.

"There's a replicator over there. Should I get us some?"

Pouring coffee on her anxiety would flare it up more, but she wouldn't likely pass out again with that going through her system, or she hoped. The idea of not being awake when Bodhi came out of his operation frightened her more than the idea of restless fear plaguing Harper's mind.

"That would be nice."

Christine prepared two coffees for them and then handed one to Harper and blew on the other, cupping it in her hands like cocoa.

"How long has he been in there?"

"All night since late yesterday. Do you know how much longer it would be?"

Harper rocked back and forth as she asked the question, unable to sit still. She also blew on her coffee and took a sip just to be doing something.

"I don't know. I was in a coma for mine. It could have been hours or weeks. Didn't Dr. Toussaint tell you anything?"

"He thought it would be a few hours only, but wanted to do it in the evening and let Bodhi sleep through the night. I haven't seen either of them since they left to the surgical room."

"I'm sure Bodhi will be fine, Ms. Rawls."

"Call me Harper, Christine. I'm not that old even if I look it."

"Oh, you don't, not at all."

Such a pretty lie brought a smile to Harper's lips. She watched Christine sip her coffee and make a bitter face.

"This is the worst stuff ever invented."

"Why are you drinking it?"

"Isn't that what we adults do?"

Adult body aside, Christine's mind was still fourteen, a thought that gave Harper a topic for a welcome distraction.

"What's it like, getting used to your new body?"

"It's weird. Getting around is okay now, but sometimes I forget how tall I am. When I'm trying to pull stuff down in my suite with my grandfather, I ask him to get stuff from the high cabinets still sometimes. Then he gives me this look that says 'get it yourself.'"

Christine laughed at her memory, and Harper joined in, feeling a little more at ease.

"What else? Tell me everything."

"People don't see me as me. I mean, nobody here but Grandfather would recognize me anyway. As human is what I'm talking about."

"Really?"

Christine held up her wrist and showed Harper the tattoo, causing her to swallow involuntarily.

"This is what they see, without fail. If I go down to the lobby to get a donut, I have to make sure the right person is working who will actually sell me one without asking questions. It's hard."

Harper's heart jumped as she realized she hadn't worked out how to get the tattoo removed from Bodhi's wrist when he emerged. Christine must have seen the look on her face, because she was quick to console.

"No, don't worry. Grandfather's going to have them removed for both of us. And he told me not to go down there. If you can't tell, I do what I want."

"I can tell." Harper smiled at the woman's self-assuredness, even through a twinge of jealousy that at the same age, Harper had been a fragile eggshell of a woman.

"That's not the worst part though. Bodhi won't have this problem, but the worst part for me is the twenty years. The skyways are so cluttered with volantrae and you can barely see the cars on the roads below. The replicators - those could only make soups and stews when I was young. Now they can make anything. And then there are the models. I mean, they're *everywhere* now. I remember like only the extremely wealthy could afford them. Everyone else had robots. Remember the clunky sentry machines and MiniMaids? I guess the latter are still around, but the doors are all guarded by models, models work in the lobby. I've never seen so many in one place."

"I helped make that possible," Harper said, partly as a confession. "I used to work with Torrent and we revolutionized the modeling industry." Her words hung aloof in the air as she clipped the end.

"You used to work with Dr. Toussaint?"

Harper nodded.

"While you were in your coma. I worked with your grandfather too. In fact, once your grandfather paid to send Torrent and I on the most wonderful date that I've ever been on. We soared above the city and looked at the stars together."

The thought spurred emotions Harper had long thought were dead. There was a time that Torrent loved her, really and deeply loved her. She felt a lump form in her throat.

"I guess that was a long time ago," she followed, dropping her voice to a whisper.

The door to the waiting room sprang open and a nurse in full scrubs bolted past them and past the secretary's station door, disappearing beyond. Another nurse followed shortly, pulling a stretcher with him. Harper jumped to her feet, as did Christine.

"What's going on?" She called after him.

When a third nurse came through, Harper grabbed the woman by the arm and wouldn't let go.

"What. Is. Happening?"

"Let go of my arm. The patient is slipping, and we have to catch him before we lose him. You are costing valuable time here."

Harper released her grip and wrapped her arms around herself. She pulled her arm down and put it back up to let it hang again at her side. Her body trembled as she felt her adrenaline spiking and her head start to swim.

"No," she told herself, fighting against her anxiety. After almost twenty years through her roller-coaster of a life, she wouldn't give in. Her knees weakened and the room began to spin. As she began to sway, unable to curb her panic attack any longer, she felt Christine's fingers interweave through hers.

"It'll be okay, Harper. Dr. Toussaint is the best doctor I've ever known. He'll keep Bodhi safe."

Harper turned and saw then that she wasn't the only one who felt the pain of Bodhi's absence. The only other person who could possibly understand what Bodhi was going through, isolated and alone just like Harper was, stood before her, tears in her eyes and speaking words of confidence that she didn't feel. Harper wrapped her arms around the woman and they stood together in a tight embrace. Then she whispered into Christine's hair.

"You don't have to lie to me, Christine. The odds are against us in this life, aren't they?"

They stood in silence, holding each other and waiting and hoping. The doorway by the secretary's nook opened and Harper gasped as she let go of Christine to look. Torrent stood, still in scrubs now turned red and purple with blood stains. His face was gaunt and haunted as he stood there. She felt anger rise up in her and present itself in a scream.

"You said he would be okay!"

His mouth went tight and he clenched his jaw muscle, but he didn't respond.

"You told me - "

"He's in a coma. We're not sure if it worked or not. The iron deficiency - he began to seize mid operation and we had to rush. We did the transplant, closed up his new body. He should be in there. I *think* it worked."

"A coma?" Christine asked the question.

"Not like yours, Christine. This one was because of the operation. The operation of the brain should have transferred to the module. I think the trauma is slowing the integration. The module seems operational."

Harper sucked in her breath. There were a lot of words in there that were guesses, like "should have" and "seems." Christine clutched tightly to Harper's hand still, and squeezed even tighter - a reminder that she wasn't alone. Harper let her breath out again.

"Okay, okay," she said. "I can do this. We can do this. Just patience, right. A few days."

Each day took an eternity though. Torrent had to go back in to monitor Bodhi, but Christine stood right by her the entire time, leaving to get them food and standing watch while Harper went to the facilities. They'd become a team over the the next few days, doing their best to distract each other with stories, allowing Harper, with limited success, to pretend that she wasn't about to explode from the anxiety. As each day passed, Torrent reported. No progress. No change. Still in a coma. Only when Friday arrived did Harper hear anything different.

"Harper," Torrent began when he emerged that morning, with multiple layers of sleepless wrinkles beneath his eyes. "There's been a change."

Harper looked first to Christine and then to Torrent, holding back the hope of what the change might be.

"He's out of the coma."

Harper squealed and jumped up, closing the distance to

Torrent before he could react. She threw her arms around him, and pulled him in tight, not letting go. He returned the embrace, squeezing her as tightly to him as she did. Then they awkwardly pulled apart.

"He's resting now, but you should be able to see him soon."

Harper looked toward Christine, who smiled back at her, a wide toothy grin.

"See?"

"You were right. Thank you."

Harper followed Torrent through the door, anxious to prove that Torrent's words were true. Christine didn't follow, and for a moment Harper wondered why, but the thought of seeing her son pushed her curiosity aside.

# 15

## Bodhi's New Body

### *Friday, June 26, 2201*

The first thing Bodhi noticed when he awoke was how chapped his lips had become. They were parched and he could tell by the sting as he ran his tongue across that they had split as well. He tried to close his mouth, but found that something like a plastic tube blocked his efforts. The tube had a metallic taste to it, as though it were made out of aluminum, but the texture made it seem as though it was plastic. His mind raced quickly as he considered what may have happened. He tried to move, but his body seemed not to care much about his desires. Even without the assistance of neck movement, he was able to see much of the room, which looked pretty much the same as the sanitized room he had fallen asleep in. The medical equipment seemed to have reproduced while he was under anesthesia.

In his periphery, he saw his mother in a chair near the bed, and Dr. Toussaint staring at the machines. Bodhi's chapped lips cracked with the movement as he spoke.

"W-what happened?" He spoke in a voice that wasn't his. It was deeper, and more nasal-sounding in his head. At first he thought it might have been that he could only whisper hoarsely, but then he remembered why he was there. "Did it work?"

Bodhi's mother threw her arms around his neck and squeezed.

"It worked!" she whispered into his ear.

"There were some complications," Torrent said from somewhere behind her.

"Complications?"

"The nanites use iron from the blood to build their networks. We gave you an iron drip to offset that, but it wasn't quite enough. You've been in a coma for a few days. I'm going to ask you a few questions now just to check your cognition."

His mother stood, releasing her grip on him, and pulled her hand to her mouth in one of her mannerisms that broadcast that she barely kept it together.

"What year is it?"

"2201."

"Correct. Who is the president?"

"Ramsey."

"Also correct. Finally, you know five people here. Can you name all five?"

"You, Mom, Aiden," he began, "Christine. Christine's grandfather too."

"You seem fine. The most recent memories are the more difficult to get right."

His mother's hand came down away from her mouth and she let out a sound that seemed like a gleeful yelp, and she accosted Bodhi again with hugs.

"Mom, I can't breathe."

"I know, I know."

But she didn't let go until ten more seconds had passed. Bodhi sucked in air afterwards, ignoring his trachea's soreness and the rasping, wheezing sound that it made.

"Is this my new body?" he asked. "I can't move anything."

"It will take time for the animus module to figure out how to move you," Torrent told him. "Usually only a day or so."

For Bodhi, it did take longer than a day. Upper body mobility returned in only a few hours, but the use of his legs took the most time. He couldn't get a really good look at himself until he wobbled his way into the attached bathroom to see himself in the mirror the next morning.

Gone was his head of curly black hair, and his oversized nose. His eyes were green now, and his nose was an appropriate Roman nose for his square-jawed face. His skinny body was replaced with a toned, muscular physique that he was sure would move effortlessly when he finally figured out how to use it. His new green eyes were intense, and it was difficult to break away from his gaze. He pulled open his hospital robe to see his chest, and his pecks were pronounced, his stomach flat and toned. He even had shoulder muscles, which he'd never had in his entire life.

Whoever had previously owned it had taken good care of it.

The thought made his head swim so much that he nearly fell to the floor in a fit of vertigo. The face that he looked at, symmetrical and strong, had undoubtedly belonged to a person who held the same traits. Within that body, that mind had a consciousness that had a will to survive very much like his. People spoke of models as though they were animals, incapable, or unclean. Some thought that the cloning process produced little more than child-like automatons, devoid of any real depth. Bodhi wasn't one of those people. At least, he hadn't considered himself one. He had never been able to see any difference between cloning and birthing a child. Still, he knew very little about the process, and had never felt the desire to learn more.

Only now he did want to know. On his wrist, like the wrists of every cloned body in existence, displayed a stamped bar-code that indicated who made him. He'd assumed that to be Aiden because models were prohibitively expensive for most. He wondered what other information the code held about the birth-date and target occupation. He couldn't read the bar code himself, and he wondered what the occupational description for hosting another person's consciousness looked like.

In the mirror, someone's green, staring eyes struggled to keep tears from falling. Bodhi thought it was strange that he couldn't see the lump forming in his throat.

As soon as he sat himself back down on the edge of the bed, something in his head vibrated. He tried to focus on the noise, to determine its origin, when suddenly it stopped, and in its place, he heard a girl's voice.

*"Bodhi? Are you there?"*

He looked around the room, seeking the source of the sound, but found nothing. Was it possible he was losing his mind?

*"It's me, Christine. If you're there, think something at me."*

He didn't know how to think at people, especially his imaginary representation of people in his brain, so instead, he spoke out loud.

"How are you doing that?"

As soon as the words came out, the heads of Torrent, Harper, and Aiden all turned toward him. Torrent seemed to be the only one who understood.

"We should go," he told Harper, while winking at Bodhi. "Let him rest some."

*"No. Think it. When you say it it's like you're yelling at me."*

Christine's voice bounced through his skull as his mother hugged him, then Aiden, and finally Torrent, who whispered in his ear. "There are some things you need to know, but I see you've got a teacher already." A few moments later, he found himself alone.

*"How are you doing that?"* he thought. Then he heard Christine laugh.

*"The animus module. Grandfather gave me your a.p. address. Are you out of the operation yet?"*

*"What's an a.p. address?"*

*"It's like your communicator number. Nobody told you about your module yet?"*

*"What? No, not yet in any detail."*

*"Oh, sorry. Do you want me to go?"*

He thought about that, and weighed the possibility that he wasn't certain that he wasn't losing his mind still. But, for him, a conversation Christine had so far been a welcome distraction from his thoughts, so he told her no, and that he'd love to chat more. She explained the workings of the animus module to him, and how he could call her through hers, just like a communicator with only a thought.

She gave him her a.p. address, so impossibly long that he would never remember. He told her as much, but she seemed to think otherwise.

*"You'll remember. You won't be able to forget. Trust me. Anytime you need me, just think of that number and, hmm... how do I describe it. I guess think about calling me. That seemed to work for calling you."*

*"Is that all these things can do?"*

*"Well, no. You can also link into the Labyrinth."*

*"Really?"*

*"It's not exciting. Grandfather says the interface will get better - they're working on it. You don't get the images and stuff, but you*

*can get information that way. It's very useful for things like the GED."*

*"I've already graduated high-school. Left early last year."*

*"Aren't you special? I was only just getting started. Grandfather arranged a GED test for me next month. He said that with all my free time, it should be simple."*

*"He hasn't been to school for a while."*

*"Right? These subjects are hard. And really, when am I going to in my life need to figure out the volume of a solid?"*

*"I can help you study if you like."*

*"Oh great! That'll give me an excuse to see that new body of yours. Is it weird getting used to?"*

He started to think the expression "you have no idea," but then, she was the only other person who actually would understand.

*"Yes, absolutely surreal. It's a nice body too, much better than my last one. God, to hear that coming out of my mouth – I'm not being cocky. It is a good one."*

*"Just think, Bodhi. When this one get's old, you can always go get another."*

He did think about that, and he wasn't sure that he liked the idea, but said nothing. What was forming in his mind was an evolution in the modeling industry. Instead of for laborious work and menial tasks, he saw models built as host bodies for immortals who threw out one body as soon as it began to develop wrinkles. Such people, he thought, could amass wealth and pass it to themselves over generations. These thoughts were somehow different than the deliberate thoughts he used to communicate with Christine, but he felt that some of it might have leaked through. Christine confirmed as much.

*"Immortals? I didn't think of it that way, but yes, you're right. In a way, we're the first immortals. Should we call ourselves gods?"*

He didn't respond at first, partially because if he was

legitimately going insane, then this thought process was a dangerous one to entertain.

*"I'm joking of course. Don't you have a sense of humor?"*

*"I used to."*

*"Well, get it back. You're going to live for a very long time. That body has gone through extensive physical preparation. Grandfather likes to talk about his projects. You're going to have to start thinking farther ahead than six months, and if you want to make friends, you'll need a sense of humor. Wait, I can find your body - I'm sure Grandfather has a picture."*

He heard her moving from room to room and shuffling things around.

*"Niiice. You may not need to worry about that sense of humor after all."*

The thought of her ogling his photograph embarrassed him, and he pulled his hospital robe tighter around his body.

*"Don't worry, it's only a head shot. Your modesty is protected. Hey, I have to go. Grandfather heard me and it sounds like he's coming to check on me. He's going to want to find me studying."*

"Okay Christine, see you later."

She was easy to talk to, always in a good mood, and, it seemed to him, always in need of attention, which was fine with him because he would never have tried to contact her on his own if their roles had been reversed.

The Labyrinth was something he had always loved to frequent. It was the perfect mix of his craved anonymity, and parade of people for people watching. Bodhi wondered at first how in-depth an experience he could realistically expect. Inhabiting the body of this person, whoever it had been, he owed enough to fill in some of his gaps in knowledge about models.

The interface into Labyrinth through his module turned

out to be very simple to use. All he had to do was think for about a second about the Labyrinth, and then some topic. He could then remember details about that topic, stuff that he couldn't possibly have known, surfacing like memories. The first few pieces of information that came up only echoed stereotypes about clones. Cloned men were considered simple-minded buffoons only good for physical labor. Women were oversexed beings, so eager to please that they didn't have personality traits other than subservience. His mother, through countless conversations, had shared these stereotypes before, and how wrong they were. It helped Bodhi to think that they were true, even for only a second. Then he stumbled across a news article called 'Clones Among Us.'

This paper, published some time before he was born, argued for a need for the Madison Rule to properly mark clones as clones. They were so much like regular people that they were nearly impossible to recover when they ran away from job sites. The bar codes solved that problem, and made leasing arrangements simpler with the tracking number stamped on their wrists.

The article set up a dilemma. How was it possible that simple-minded buffoons or seductive harlots could so easily hide in society? The article attacked the Madison Rule, saying that it was because of their similarity to "normal people," models had to be significantly more varied than the stereotypes suggested.

He hated that idea, but he knew it to be true. His body once belonged to a unique individual with ideas and dreams. Bodhi could have stopped looking at that point. He could have forced himself to believe the stereotypes and reinforced this perspective until he believed it. He didn't.

The deep thinking enticed him as he considered the possibilities. Swimming in ideas, Bodhi didn't notice the door swing open and Harper appear in the doorway.

"Bodhi. There's something I have to tell you." His mother stood there, smile from the previous day gone and replaced with a grimace. "Aiden and I have to go to Kiera's funeral tomorrow. We'd hoped that you would be able to come, but I talked to Torrent. He doesn't want you traveling yet."

He'd forgotten. A mind full of memory and he'd forgotten about his aunt's funeral. She was right, he couldn't go yet. The idea of flying with a fresh hole in his head seemed preposterous.

"Please tell her I miss her and I love her, Mom."

# 16

## Funeral for a Queen

### *Monday, October 10, 2185*

The jet ride back to Aiden's house took a few hours early in the morning, and Harper slept through most of it. The trip into the compound from the airport was just as forgettable. Nothing happened, and Aiden didn't even bother arguing with the driver. A somber mood lay over the trip because of its purpose - to bury a woman she'd known for most of her life with Bodhi. She couldn't help her mind slipping back to the time of their meeting.

Harper and Aiden had begun to communicate more, and though there hadn't been another kiss, he was nice to her and always had a smile and a kind word. Harper felt their relationship growing, and there were even days when she thought he might ask her to be with him officially, though with the demanding schedule of an infant, those days were few and far between. Still, she believed that they were growing closer. At least until the morning of October 10. Aiden had taken Bodhi in for treatment again, and Harper sought refuge in the kitchen. She was there only five minutes when a strikingly beautiful woman sauntered in wearing nothing but a long t-shirt.

"Hi, I'm Kiera," the woman introduced herself before taking a seat at the kitchen counter. "You must be his newest charity case."

All of the strength evaporated from Harper's body. The act of staying upright required her complete focus, and she missed a breath. Harper didn't respond, and only stared down at the countertop.

"Oh, shit. I'm sorry."

"N-no, it's okay."

"I am too."

The woman flashed her left wrist, revealing a sequence of fat and thin stripes.

"Kiera Caldwell," she said. "Yes, I'm a Caldwell."

Harper was still reeling from the comment. She hadn't considered herself to be a charity case. Was she? Did Aiden feel that way?

"I ... don't know what that means."

"A Caldwell? We're the backbone of the sex industry. The Emergent factory in Caldwell makes us and exports about half. We're global, baby." She smiled a wry smile that didn't reach her eyes.

"But not anymore, right?"

"You mean am I on the job? No. Just hiding out for a bit while people stop looking for me. And you are?"

"Harper."

She didn't include her last name on purpose. Models all over knew who Harper Rawls was, and she guessed this woman probably did too. Kiera's mouth dropped open and her eyes widened.

"No. Shit."

Harper was right. The last thing she wanted was to be friends with this woman. Kiera opened her mouth to follow up her exclamation, just as Aiden walked into the room. Harper turned her attention to him, to see him carrying little Bodhi. He carried the child over to Harper to hand him over, then he frowned at Kiera.

"You should put some clothes on."

Harper had stifled a laugh as she stood with her baby and left the room.

From that awkward introduction, it was hard to anticipate the bond that would eventually emerge between them, and even connecting all three. The common interest was always Bodhi, and at the end, Harper had taken Bodhi away from his Aunt Kiera. At least at her funeral, Harper would have an excuse for all the tears she knew she would cry that day.

## *Saturday, June 27, 2201*

Harper made her way into her room in silence after they landed.

That's when the fight with her closet began. Out of all of the people who had died during the last year of Harper's life, somehow, she didn't own a single black dress. It hadn't seemed important to pack anything like that when she fled across the desert. There also wasn't a lot of nursing mother clothing in black that she found appealing. Her bedroom consisted of teals and fuschias, not blacks and grays. By the time she gave up looking, everything she owned lay in a pile atop her bed, and an hour had passed.

Why?

She sat exhausted beside the heap. Part of it was that she didn't want to go. To go to the funeral meant possibly to see

Ordell again and other Siblings of the Natural Order who had once believed that she would win their freedom. She could handle stares of disapproval from the mass of them, but Ordell would seek her out. And when he did, he would ask about Bodhi and try to talk her out of the operation. Bodhi, who no longer looked like Bodhi, was recovering from his traumatic experience. What would she tell him? Someone rapped on the door twice.

"Come in, Aiden," she called out. "You don't have to knock. It's just you and me here now."

"I thought you could use this," Aiden said, and she looked toward the door to see him pass through, holding a dress out before him. It was long and black and in her size. She smiled at him. Of course, Aiden would remember - he always did. She took it from him.

"Can you be ready in ten minutes? I can get our driver here."

"Yes, it shouldn't take me too long."

Aiden turned and exited the room while she changed. The dress felt no better than any of the other items that she'd discarded onto the bed, but it had one redeeming quality. It came wrapped in Aiden's adoration, something she'd taken for granted for so long that she sometimes felt guilty about it. He had asked her to marry him only once, many years earlier. At the time, she wasn't ready, and now she saw what she had missed.

After she finished changing, she met Aiden in the kitchen.

"Driver will be here in five more minutes," he told her.

"This is where I met her," Harper told him.

"I know. After that, she told me all about it. She said we had to stop sleeping together that same day. Did you know that?"

Harper nodded.

"Her idea, not mine."

"Is that why you said no?"

Harper stared at him. Gray hairs had begun to show on his head, some far longer than she would have liked. Even in the perpetual man-bun, it was off-putting.

"No, it wasn't that. You scared me. What kind of man picks up strays off of the street and brings them to a compound in the middle of nowhere?"

"Hardly the middle of nowhere."

"Still, it is a little strange."

"Did you think I was dangerous?"

"You have so much money that you never have to suffer consequences. Bad decisions that would destroy other people roll off of you."

"I see."

She moved from her position in the doorway to a stool by the kitchen counter. His eyes followed.

"But if she hadn't been sleeping with me?"

"That wasn't it."

What sort of man took advantage of someone he was supposed to be helping?

"It was her idea. She insisted on paying me in trade."

Harper began to remember the rest of why she had never married him. As she opened her mouth to explain, the sky opened, and a volantrae came through the entryway in the dome. She began to talk as the vehicle landed.

"Okay, it was that a little. Of course Kiera offered - that's all she had. But you accepted, knowing of her desperate situation. What else could she have done?"

"Oh, come on. You know - knew Kiera."

He trailed off at the end, and she saw the pain in his eyes. They were tired-looking and filled with tears behind his thick glasses. She thought through what he said.

"I knew Kiera later," she told him. "At the time, I thought you were taking advantage. But I learned too late that she held onto her freedom with both hands. If she hadn't wanted to sleep with you, she wouldn't have. But I didn't get to know her right away. When you asked me…"

"You weren't ready. Are you ready now?"

Harper glared at him, through him.

"I don't mean will you marry me. I mean, would the answer be different? If sometime, I did decide to - do you trust my judgment more now?"

The volantrae came to a stop and the door popped open.

"I don't know," she told him. "I can't think about it with all of this happening."

He nodded and followed her in.

The gathering of people was smaller than she'd thought. If the Siblings of the Natural Order had representation there, it was only in the form of Ordell and a strange-looking woman who held his arm. Harper could tell by the fleeting glances up at him that the woman loved him, and by the glances in Harper's direction that the woman knew who Harper was. She kept the coffin between them while an ordained minister spoke. In the end, she grabbed Aiden's hand quickly and began to pull him away toward the volantrae. Ordell was faster than she'd remembered and had made it around the coffin and to her side before she could effect her escape.

"I'm glad you're here, Harper. Have you decided about Bodhi yet?" He cut straight to it, and she met his eyes with her directed gaze.

"It's already done, Ordell. Leave me alone."

He extended his arms and wrapped her in them, squeezing her in a gesture that was so familiar it felt like coming home. She let herself go finally and sobbed relentlessly into his chest.

"I'm sorry," he told her. "That must have been a horrible choice to make."

"You had no right to do that to me, Ordell."

He broke the hug and pushed away from her.

"I had every right. And it needed to be done. We should never have to make decisions like that. When can I meet him?"

She wiped her tears away.

"Why would you want to?"

"He should know about the life he took."

Harper cringed at that and backed away.

"Not today," he said, "but soon. He has to know what it means, and what that person's hopes and fears were."

"I won't let you."

"Harper, I was only asking to be polite to an old and dear friend."

"I won't. He doesn't deserve that."

"Come with me—you and Aiden. Let's talk about Kiera and Siblings and catch up. And let's talk about Rutger. Maybe I can change your mind."

"Rutger?"

"Yes. The man your son replaced."

Harper sucked in her breath and gulped. The man had a name. Harper, of all people, had already known what it meant. These extra cuts were unnecessary, but if that's what it took to gain Ordell's forgiveness, then maybe she would take the pain.

"Okay, Ordell."

Aiden tugged at her arm.

"You don't have to." He directed his words at her, but his gaze stayed fixated on Ordell. She imagined what he was wondering - how much of a threat was Ordell? The man was bigger than even Aiden by at least a fourth, and that wasn't an easy task. Aiden probably wasn't used to being in the company of people who could make him feel small. She ignored Aiden and addressed Ordell, nodding toward his date who stood near the entrance.

"Who is she?"

"That's Monica Caldwell," he said. "She went to the same Didactics as Kiera."

"She seems like more than a friend, Ordell."

He smiled at that comment and nodded.

"More, a lot more. We live together, although she's about as hopeless with the replicator as you were. You'll like her."

Harper smiled back.

"I'm happy for you."

"I still love your mother, Harper. That won't fade. This is a different kind of love."

"I didn't say anything. Mom has been dead a long time. She'd want you to be happy."

"Shall we?" He asked. He motioned toward the entrance to the cemetery, where a volantrae pulled up next to Monica.

Harper pulled on Aiden's arm and half-dragged him to the vehicle. Aiden dismissed his driver with a quick nod of the head, and they approached. The volantrae was almost the size of a bus, a perfect fit for the four of them. Inside, Ordell and Monica sat on one bench seat, and across sat Aiden and Harper.

"Faux Grey," Ordell said, and the fully-automated vehicle took to the sky.

The settlement money had never been more than a number on a document for Harper. The Faux Grey demonstrated in full how much money had actually been awarded in the settlement with Emergent Biotechnology twenty years earlier. Ordell escorted them into a private lounge that reminded Harper of her first real date with Torrent so many years ago, complete with detached building top floating up into the sky. This time, romance was less the reason than privacy.

"Now we can speak more freely," Ordell commented, and

loosened his tie with one hand. Monica seemed to relax as well.

"Harper," Monica said, "Ordell has told me so much about you." The woman stuck a perfectly manicured hand out in Harper's direction. To avoid appearing rude, Harper took the invitation and shook gently, eyeing the woman up and down. Harper examined her own hands, trimmed fingers and weathered knuckles from gardening. She knew that unlike Monica, she had creases around her eyes from squinting in the sunlight. Compared to her, Monica looked like a granite statue.

"How did you meet?"

The question caught Harper off guard. Her mind stayed locked on the fact that Ordell had tried to get Torrent's number from her, but she hadn't given it. Curiosity brewed behind her eyes. Looking directly at Ordell, she answered.

"I helped Ordell escape."

"No, I meant you and Aiden. How did that happen?"

Harper started into the story of the trip through the desert, in a flat and quick way to get through it without inviting questions. In her periphery, she saw Monica's eyes swell at all the usual parts. Afterwards, the four of them sat in silence, interrupted by the whir of the robotic waiter and the slow trickle of wine into the glass sounded like a volcano erupting. Harper kept her eyes on Ordell, and he on her, but neither opening conversation. Aiden sniffed absently in the background, which brought the emptiness of the soundscape front and center in Harper's mind. Nobody moved.

"To Kiera," Monica broke up the silence. Harper quickly grabbed her glass and responded in kind.

"To Kiera."

The others clinked their glasses together, and from that moment forward, the conversation steered clear of anything but her departed friend.

# 17

## GED Celebration

### *Wednesday, August 5, 2201*

Over a month after her new friend's mother returned from a funeral Christine passed her high-school equivalency examination. When she got the notice, she invited Bodhi to her celebration lunch. The next step on her road to success was Fouriedon University, or maybe Randen. She had forgotten which was her grandfather's alma mater, where she would be a legacy, but whichever it was, that was the one she would choose.

She focused back on attempting to find the restaurant on the upper floors. Christine had been to the cafe that overlooked the city once before. It was the perfect place for their celebration, but enough time had passed that she wasn't exactly sure even what floor it was on. She would be unfashionably late.

Out of embarrassment, she avoided calling Bodhi to ask for directions. Grandfather was out doing business things so that she couldn't bother him either. Considering her animus module told her that it was only a few minutes until twelve, she decided to ask at the hotel's front desk instead. The elevator opened before her and whisked her down to the main lobby.

The man behind the counter reminded her of how Bodhi used to look. He was tall and skinny and wore glasses, which served to draw attention to his rather severe acne. She cut to the front of the line to get his attention, ignoring the other customers' stares.

"Can you tell me how to get to the high cafe? The one on the upper floors?"

"Ma'am, there's a line."

"I know there's a line. Just tell me where it is. Seriously, if you just told me, I would be on my way already."

"Ma'am, it's restricted. You can't get to it if you're not on one of the top five floors."

She caught the man's eyes glancing toward her wrist where the bar-code stamp still showed in thick black lines. Something about the way he said "top five floors," as if it were an impossibility that she could be on any of them, grated her, so it was time to name drop.

"My name is Christine Hamilton. I'm in one of the rooms on the top five floors. I do have access, and my grandfather owns the building. I just forgot where the cafe is. Can you please tell me or find someone who is competent at their job?"

Flustered, the man stuttered its whereabouts, and she thanked him in a manner that she hoped told him that she was only doing it because of proper upbringing. It turned out to be easy to find. Once she left the elevator on the correct floor, signs pointed the way. Her heart fluttered as she saw Bodhi seated at a small table overlooking the city. He had taken some of her fashion advice and upgraded from t-shirts to sweaters, which were frankly more appropriate for the early fall anyway. She had been right to suggest it, and he was right to listen. As she'd anticipated, the sweater, coupled with his new sculpted body, signaled that he was a captain of industry and would be welcome in her circle.

She flashed a smile at him as she approached and found that she was just slightly edgy about being as close to the window as she was. There was a fear that she hadn't known she had. Her mouth went dry as she approached, but she kept the smile plastered on her face.

"Hey Christine, congratulations!" He told her as she took her seat. They traded an awkward high-five, but their hands didn't immediately separate. He held her hand until she finally blushed and pulled it away. Usually, it was other people who were embarrassed and backed down from her. She put her effort into beaming at him, perhaps a little too much this close, but she did it anyway.

Impulsively, she leaned toward Bodhi and put her arms around him. At first, he just sat there without making any motion at all, and it was like hugging a statue. But, to her relief, he wrapped his arms back around her shoulders. She pulled away after five seconds.

"What about you? Are you going to take any classes?"

He nodded.

"Now that I have, you know, an actual future, I have to do something with it. Aiden thinks I should go to college. That requires an entrance exam score, so now I'll be studying for that."

"Not me. Don't need to. My grandfather is a legacy. That means no entrance exam necessary."

"Hmmm... I wonder if I can get out of that too."

"Your mom?"

"University of Texas."

"Oh, that won't work. You need a private university. What about your dad?"

His face told her all she needed to know about his father. She wondered if they'd talked about family much before but couldn't remember him talking about his. She was pretty sure he knew everything there was to know about her own, including the accident. The only thing she'd kept from him was her step-father's abuse, but otherwise, she was an open book.

"Aiden's not my father," he told her. She had figured this much because of his insistence on calling him Aiden when he called his mother 'Mom' regularly.

"Do you know who your father is?"

He nodded in a way that made her wonder if he would tell her or attempt to change the subject. The conversation wasn't an easy one to have.

"Drinks?"

A woman who looked like an anorexic version of Christine lingered behind Bodhi while holding a pinamu tablet. She seemed ready to take an order, so Christine gave her one.

"Yes, a gin and tonic for me. And for him, a..." Christine paused and gave Bodhi an expectant glance. At first, he only looked at her blankly, so she decided for him.

"For my friend, a pale ale."

"I'm sorry, can I see some ID?" the waitress asked.

Christine pulled out the state identification card the her grandfather had given her and flashed it at the person, careful to keep her bar code hidden. As the waitress handed the card back, she looked at her picture on it. Pretty. Christine traced her face with her thumb.

"Turner?" Bodhi whispered at her and she looked at him and tried to read his face, but his eyes darted down to the license. When she examined it, she noticed that her name was no longer Christine Hamilton, but had changed to Christine Turner on her new license.

"What the hell?"

The waitress returned with drinks for both of them, ending the discussion about her name. The woman hadn't even bothered carding Bodhi, and Christine guessed his five-o'clock shadow sold his age as higher than the requisite eighteen. As soon as the drinks were provided, she turned to Bodhi.

"I don't know. I'll have to ask Grandfather. But we were talking about your dad?"

Bodhi took a long sip of the beer and made a strange face, which made her giggle like a little girl. She covered her mouth, but that made him laugh and seemed to break the tension.

"You know Alexander Toussaint?"

"Torrent?"

"Yes, him."

She felt her eyes widen with amazement.

"Torrent is your dad!"

"Whatever happened between my parents, it was pretty serious, I guess. Opening all of that back up would be hard."

"Well, I've got great news for you. I overheard Grandfather and Torrent talking once. Grandfather said that Torrent was a loser because he went to Randen instead of Fouriedon. They were only joking around, but Randen has a legacy program, and it's an amazing school."

And Randen was only a drive away from Fouriedon, but she left that part out, along with the fact that her grandfather had plans for her. Christine was the sole heir to Gallatin Industries. This global venture capital fund had ownership in hundreds of different start-ups, some of which became established companies. She'd almost made herself known when she heard that bit because she had to stifle a shriek of delight. The future he wanted for her was exactly the future she wanted for herself. She had imagined her face on the cover of Time magazine, and it seemed very likely that she could get there. He'd been duly impressed that she'd managed to pass the GED on her first try, even with the score of 600, only twenty above failing, but passing all the same.

"I didn't know that."

"I know you didn't. I know more about your father than you do, and that's kind of sad," she said, as she sipped on her gin and tonic and made her face. The gin had a lingering aftertaste that she hadn't expected. Alcohol was new to her.

"That's some face," he said, grinning at her.

"Yeah, I guess that's what I get for buying a grown-up drink."

"How did you do that?"

She fished out her state identification again and examined it closely. Stamped across the front was her correct birth month, but the year was 2181. Christine flashed it at him.

"I'm over eighteen on this."

"So let me think this through. You're fourteen in your head, eighteen on paper and in your body, but your total time on this earth is forty years?"

"Only for another two weeks. Then I'm fifteen in a nineteen-year-old body."

"Happy birthday?"

"Thank you. To be honest, I'm a little afraid of it."

"Of your birthday?"

"Yes. It's going to be my first in the new body. It seems strange to celebrate a birthday that this body never had, you know?"

He nodded his head in agreement, and his face went serious.

"Yes, I do know. You know what else? It seems strange that whoever this was," he motioned to his body, "won't be celebrating any more birthdays. I sometimes wonder if they ever did. Do models celebrate birthdays?"

She could tell that he was about to ruminate again on the

idea that he stole the body from some living thing. Christine could never understand what his problem was with that. Models had no futures, not really, and especially not these. These models that they inhabited would not have existed except for her father's decision to commission them and have them made, and for a lot of money. Her own body, she knew, had been several hundred thousand dollars. She steeled herself to listen politely, though, because no amount of talking him down had ever worked before. Bodhi had to work through on his own. To her surprise, his eyes brightened.

"I've been researching artificial intelligence, Christine. Did you know that there's a significant application programming interface for the Labyrinth?"

"O...kay. What does this have to do with models or entry exams?"

"Nothing, directly. But what if instead of doing what we did and take over these bodies, people could move into something like a virtual world?"

"Would that be living? I mean, this is the real world, right?"

"Well, yes. I haven't worked it all through yet. But I think that if someone managed to do something like that, we wouldn't have to worry about killing people."

"Killing people?"

"Come on, Christine. You may as well admit what we are. We're murderers. It may have been legal, but there's nobody else in this body but me. That means whoever was here is dead."

"They're not people, Bodhi," she said before she could stop herself. His face fell at her words, and she immediately struggled to back-track.

"I don't mean it like that."

"How do you mean it?"

"I mean that they wouldn't exist except for us having them

made. There's no reason to feel bad about using what you own."

"That's not better."

"Fuck you, Bodhi. You know what I mean."

"No, I don't. Do you mean you don't feel anything about the fact that you took this body from someone?"

"Not some*one*. Some*thing*. Models don't feel like we do. They're barely able to think properly."

Bodhi went silent. His green eyes focused on hers as though he were trying to see into her soul. For some reason, she desperately hoped that he found something redeemable in there. How could she explain that if she looked at it any other way, it would crush her? Models couldn't be human, because he was right. That *would* make her a murderer, and Christine couldn't live with that.

"Well, you didn't have a choice, did you?" he asked, clearly not intending for the question ever to be answered. Then he continued. "Let me ask. If you had the option of a fully virtual world to exist in, instead of taking a body, which would you do?"

Instead of an answer, she stood and turned and left him there to celebrate her success alone. She felt her cheeks burning and the threat of tears, but it was only a threat. She was the master at not crying. When she passed by the waitress, the woman tried to make small talk, but Christine ignored her.

"Christine, come back! I'm sorry!" he called after her. It was too late. She had no intention of going back. She stormed through the cafe door and down the hallway to the elevator. Once there, she had a change of heart and held the door-open button open for almost thirty seconds before she gave up on the idea that he might pursue. Angry then at herself for needing his approval, she rapidly and repeatedly pushed the door-close button until the metal doors met in the middle.

Then she stood and focused on regaining her composure.

She almost had it. She had slowed her breathing and focused on it, and by the time the door opened, she was a new person. Just as she left the elevator, though, she felt the familiar buzzing of the animus module. She let it buzz once, twice, and then three times. When it got to fourth, she thought that she would have to answer it, or he might never stop. Walking down the hall toward her room, she engaged in conversation.

*"Christine, don't disconnect."*

*"What do you want, Bodhi?"*

*"I'm sorry. This was supposed to be a celebration for you, and I'm happy for you. I didn't mean to get bogged down about the models."*

*"You get that it's hard for me too, right? I have this body I didn't ask for. At least you had the chance to say no. And your bullshit question wasn't fair. What would you do in that situation? You don't know. You can't know. Nobody can know in situations that big unless you're actually in them."*

*"It wasn't fair. Where are you?"*

*"Going to my room. I don't feel like celebrating anymore."*

*"Yeah, I figured. Turn around."*

She turned, and there he stood, smiling and leaning against the wall casually in a pose that she guessed he'd been working on while they were talking via the animus module. She tried to stay angry, but the feeling melted away as soon as she saw him.

"I didn't mean to upset you, Christine," he said to her, his green eyes locked again into her blue ones.

"Well, you did," she said, but she didn't storm off, which surprised her.

"I've been feeling guilty about this," he admitted. "I knew what I was doing, and I did it anyway."

"It's called surviving, Bodhi. You and I get a second chance.

Nobody else in the entire world knows what that's like or what they would do given the same situation. We know. We've been put into an unfair position and are trying to make the best of it."

"I know that," he replied, "but it doesn't change that someone else died for me to live."

"I understand." She stepped toward him and wrapped her arms around his neck, placing an ear against his chest. "It'll be okay, Bodhi." He seemed vulnerable and in need of reassurance, so she gave it.

"Maybe," he muttered into her hair. "It doesn't bother you?"

She let go of the hug and backed away slightly, and thought for a moment.

"Only when I'm with you," she laughed awkwardly, resisting the temptation to turn away. He followed her in laughter.

"I suppose it's time to talk about better things?"

"Yes, let's please."

"Like…your grandfather increasing his stake in Emergent Biotechnology?"

"You saw that? Something about it being easier to steer the company when everyone's afraid of you."

"What an interesting man," he replied.

She considered his words.

"Yes, I think that's right. Interesting, for sure. Try living with him."

# 18

## Meeting Torrent

### Saturday, August 8, 2201

Ordell had failed in his first goal - Bodhi had killed Rutger, who hadn't deserved to die. The boy was a special commission Caldwell, which had the least amount of genetic tampering. Rochester told him the boy had had a good life, was fed well and worked out often. He never wanted for anything, and probably didn't even know that the procedure he went in for would be the last time he would exist. That was the best situation he could have hoped for, but the fact that they'd gone through all those pains mean that they were already preparing the corporate framework under which Immortality would surface. In a way, Rutger's lack of suffering condemned them.

The possibility of immortality for polli had been validated not once but twice now. As a result, three on the council wanted to kill both Bodhi and Christine, and their resolve had hardened. They wanted to send the message that if polli participate in the program, they would not avoid death. Participation should be a death sentence. Caldwell and the other two still listened to him - Caldwell for obvious reasons, and the others probably because of the deference Lancaster gave him.

Other duties drew his attention away from the problem. His responsibilities as Captain and high-council representative required his presence and consumed most of his time. The idea of leaving Caldwell to try to save a former friend, one who saw his arrival as a burden to suffer, didn't fill him with encouragement. Still, he found himself once again leaving the SeaTac airport with a bag draped over his shoulder that would last him about a week. His plan had changed, though. This time, his focus would be on Alexander Toussaint. Ordell hoped that there might be a thread of conscience running through him.

He wasted no time in getting to work. After depositing his bag unopened on the plush hotel bed, he made his way to the lobby, seeking a way up. The last time he'd gotten lucky, and someone from the cleaning crew ignored him up to the penthouse. This time, he became fortunate in a different way. As soon as the elevator opened on the lobby floor, a man with frizzy brown and gray hair and freckles entered beside him. This man, by his attire in a dark navy-blue suit with a shimmering silver tie, he remembered as Torrent - still one of the flashiest dressers he'd ever met. Deep in thought, Torrent hit the key for the penthouse before he glanced in Ordell's direction, and from his reaction, he didn't see him. On the double-take, Ordell knew that his presence had registered.

"Torrent," was all he said, as the man's eyes shot to the rapidly closing elevator doors.

"Ordell."

"It's been a very long time, hasn't it?"

Torrent nodded, his exploding hair following his head

through the motion.

"How have you been?"

"I've done well. Food, a roof, an uprising. You?"

"I heard rumors, but I wasn't sure it was true. Do you know what we're doing here?"

"Some."

Torrent turned his body toward Ordell and met his eyes.

"The National Science Foundation disapproved of my application for consciousness research. The pill strategy we'd decided to implement is still stalled at the FDA. Gallatin would only continue funding my research if I saved his daughter. It's that simple."

"His daughter is fine now. But here you are, still involved."

"Harper's son was dying. You do remember Harper, don't you? The woman who saved your life?"

Torrent's eyebrows had shot together into a tense glare. Ordell looked at him placidly, willing his emotions to stay contained. It amazed him how willing Torrent was to trade one polli life for thousands, even millions, of models.

"Torrent, think about that. You didn't just save one life. You validated a business model, one that will set the proposition of everlasting life against the rights of models. How do you expect us to garner public support if polli have to give up on immortality to support us?"

"I - I hadn't thought about it that way."

He was sure Torrent hadn't. Everything Harper had ever told him about the man indicated that he was interested in exactly one thing: discovery. That single-focus made him a wunderkind scientist and, now, pushed him relentlessly to pursue his consciousness research. Ordell changed tactics.

"We need to stop it, Torrent. If you want to do consciousness research, we can pitch it to the modeling community and ask for volunteers. That wouldn't be hard. I can't tell you the exact numbers, but SNO is huge now. If I can get you the assistance you need, can you drop this project?"

He could tell from the look in Torrent's eyes that it wouldn't happen. The research wasn't the entire purpose anymore. He'd witnessed immortality and he was now an aging man, just as Ordell was. Torrent awoke with the same aches and pains that Ordell did. As in response to his observations, Torrent stepped back six inches and collided with the elevator wall.

"I can't."

"Because?"

"I just can't."

Somewhere, a model was waiting to be replaced by Torrent's consciousness. How much could Torrent learn about the universe over multiple lifetimes, multiple murders? What could Ordell offer to compete with that prospect?

"Let me rephrase that. Stop. The Order knows who you are and what you're doing. The only thing keeping you safe is my influence. I've convinced them that they can reason with you. Stop the program."

"I don't mean that I won't. I can't. I've signed a contract for four more years."

A contract. Ordell blew out his anger through clenched teeth. The door opened, and Torrent stepped quickly into the penthouse hallway, motioning Ordell to follow.

"But maybe I can help. We need to get somewhere private. You're kind of conspicuous. Come to my room, and I'll fill you in on some of what your intelligence missed."

Ordell admitted to himself that perhaps he'd misjudged. Whether it was the not-so-veiled threat or the possibility that a mind like Torrent's could be as myopic as to miss the implications of his work, Ordell didn't know. But Torrent seemed much more pliable, and information from him had to be better than anything Rochester collected so far, so he followed.

## *Sunday, August 9, 2201*

Torrent offered little in the way of new revelations, and he refused to commit to any additional assistance. The man disappointed Ordell with how little intelligence he would be willing to offer. The entire conversation was an exercise in frustration.

When he found himself at the lobby bar on Sunday afternoon, he looked up from his auburn lager to see Bodhi standing across the hallway in Rutger's body. Ordell dropped a cash-coin that left a much too expensive tip for the bartender, who pocketed it without checking.

Ordell crossed the distance between them at a rapid gait. Just as he was about to overcome the last few feet, a short blonde girl appeared from behind a pillar and enshrouded Bodhi in a quick hug. The girl then muttered a few words that Ordell couldn't make out while he tried to hide his massive frame behind a potted plant. Bodhi smiled at her, and she pivoted away to do something. From the impatient way Bodhi looked after her, it seemed as though she was doing something temporary and would be back soon. Ordell's eyes sought out where the girl disappeared, and when he glanced back at Bodhi, he realized just how futile his effort to hide behind a fern had been. Bodhi stared right at him, eyebrows furrowed as if trying to place him. Ordell smiled and stepped around the fern, which to his surprise, didn't seem to intimidate Bodhi at all. Instead, Bodhi progressed towards him, hand outstretched.

"I know you," Bodhi told him, without breaking eye contact. "You visited my mother a few weeks ago."

Ordell took his hand and shook it quickly before suspending his arm back to his side.

"You saw me?"

Bodhi nodded. "You're a lot bigger than I thought."

"I get that a lot."

"Are you back to see my mother?"

"Right now - I guess I'm here to see you."

Ordell couldn't think of what to say. The boy had already transferred bodies, so it wasn't as though he could somehow bring back Rutger. He simply stared for a moment.

"Why?"

"I've been trying to convince everyone around you not to let you have the procedure. It didn't work. I should have just talked to you about it."

Bodhi shifted his weight, and his eyes fell to the ground. He lifted his hand to his forehead, but his hand didn't quite make it to his temples. It was as if he had missed-aimed for his head. Ordell continued.

"That was a person, you know? Someone with dreams, and hopes, and fears. I doubt they even told him what the operation was for. He just went in, got strapped to some machine, and then no longer existed."

A splash of sadness washed over Bodhi's face as tears began to form. Guilt set in as Ordell realized that the person he was facing wasn't the person he was lecturing in his mind. His conversation was meant for Harper. She of all people should know better.

"I'm sorry, Bodhi, it was a hard choice, wasn't it?"

"I didn't have a choice. I said I didn't want to do it. I told Mom no but she kept asking."

Ordell stuck out his hand to stop him.

"What happens next is the question. You are the second successful transfer. Do you realize what this does for their ability to get investors and to publicize? They only need a few more to push the procedure through. By this time next year, or maybe in a few years, I'm not sure - but soon. Very soon, thousands of models a day will churn through their process. A thousand invisible deaths."

Bodhi grabbed his elbow, but to his credit, didn't break eye contact still.

"I told you, it wasn't my idea. I was willing to die."

"But you didn't, did you?"

"No. And now it's too late."

"You can still help, Bodhi. You can prevent others from going down the same road."

"I'm fifteen, Ordell. I just need to survive."

"That's the problem, isn't it? There was a time when your mother thought…"

"My mother."

Bodhi's lips curled when he said the words, and Ordell finally understood. Harper had done something that she'd probably preached against for her entire life. She had become very nearly an activist by the time she left League City, Texas, to cross the desert. Then she pivoted and told Bodhi to save his own life. The tie between them had become frayed - and perhaps, he thought, feeling a slight tinge of guilt - maybe this was something he could use to save lives.

"She protected me, at her own risk. I thought she understood what was at stake, but really, I think she didn't. I think that your mother protected me because she knew me, and she protected you because she loves you. I don't think she ever really had a modeling position."

"For fifteen years, she did. Every day she talked about the cruelty and abuse. And then - then she does this to me? She wants me to live so badly that she gave up her beliefs. I didn't ask her to do that."

"It's not for me to say anything else about your mother, Bodhi."

Ordell caught a glimpse of a blonde head coming out through the elevator opening and knew he had to act quickly.

His influence would pale compared to whoever the girl was, and he had a suspicion that it was Gallatin's granddaughter.

"Listen, Bodhi. Just do what you can. You don't know what kind of danger you all are in now. I need you to promise that you'll do what you can. We need this program to fail. Can you be a part of that?"

A light went on behind Bodhi's eyes.

"I hadn't thought of that," he said. "I suppose I could give you information. Aren't you SNO? What do you need?"

Ordell smiled.

"Nothing yet," he said and flipped a data-coin to Bodhi, who caught it in his hand. "My contact information. Send me yours, and we'll be in touch."

"Who's your friend?" The girl had arrived just as Ordell was about to spin away.

"Nobody," Ordell said and pivoted quickly, disappearing into the crowded lobby.

## *Monday, August 10, 2201*

Ordell began to feel that this trip had also failed. As he packed his bag, starting with shoes and working his way to shirts, he reflected on what he would report back to the order. The one thing they all agreed on was that there was time, and the need for discretion was paramount. The knee-jerk response of some had faded into more practical arguments than "just kill them." How many times would the other high council members be willing to let him try? And, equally as important - how many times was he willing to do so? He felt the anger lurking just beneath the surface of his skin. The lengthy arguments he'd had with Harper, the fact that she'd gone through with it anyway, was a stab in the back. She'd twisted the knife in, and he felt it every time he thought about her.

But she had saved his life before. He had to remember that. She wasn't just some polli - she was Harper. Three knocks rapped echoed from the front of his room. Not expecting company, Ordell quickly crossed to the entryway in time to see an image formed on the door panel of Harper, pacing back and forth just beyond. He pulled the door open to greet her.

"Har-"

"Don't you ever come to my son again. You had no right to do that to him."

He backed up as she pressed the offense, with her finger dangerously close to his eyes.

"Harper, this is bigger than you know."

"I know exactly how big it is. Listen, and listen well. He isn't a part of this. I forced him into the decision, and it's not his fault. Whatever you - or your order - may think. He's innocent."

The door slid shut behind her as Ordell stumbled down onto the couch cushion, not paying attention to where he'd backed away. Then, as abruptly as she'd begun, she stopped and just stared into his eyes. Tears gathered in her lower lids and began to stream down her cheeks.

"This wasn't easy, Ordell," she finally said. "I can't eat. I can't sleep. It wasn't easy. He's my son. You can't know what that feels like, to watch your son fade away into nothing. Then to have the opportunity to yank him out of the jaws of death. You can't possibly know."

She was right - he couldn't. Forced sterilization ensured that he would never know what that was about. But he was still a person.

"That's a boy that you killed. Come here."

He reached into his bag and pulled out a data-coin, then tossed it onto the coffee table. Immediately an image of Bodhi popped up.

"I visited Torrent too. He gave me this. Look at that smile, that hope in his eyes. That was the boy who lived in that body before Bodhi. He had an entire life ahead of him, but he couldn't possibly know that he would never see it. Or maybe he did. I don't know. Imagine stuck in a hall with twenty other people, and one by one, each is called forward, never to be heard from again. That's what it must have been like for this boy."

She slid down on the couch beside him, her hands cradling her face as tears fell freely.

"You have no right," she muttered to him. "No right to include Bodhi in this."

"He's in this. And so are you."

"Just leave him alone."

She dropped her hands and glared at him, and he recognized the look. Ages ago, when he had sworn that he would take care of her, and she told him she could take care of herself. That was the look she flashed now, and his heart dropped in his chest. Had they drifted so far?

"I'm trying to keep you safe. The order knows about both of you, and some of them want to kill you. I want to leave you alone, but I can't. This trip - was the last try, as far as I know."

"Too fucking late."

"Maybe. But let's be honest, you wouldn't have listened anyway. I'm sad about your decision here, but maybe this is an opportunity. We just want the program to end. Can you help us?"

"Will you leave Bodhi out of it?"

Ordell hadn't planned to talk to Bodhi again anyway. He didn't see the boy as useful since he was so young, but there was no reason to let her know. He gulped down the shame he felt for leading Harper on.

"I think so. If we had someone on the inside who could

keep us up to speed on what's going on - that would be very convincing. Can we count on you?"

She turned away from him and walked toward the door. Then she paused and turned back, staring at him, or staring through him - he couldn't tell.

"All you had to do was ask, Ordell. I hate this shit too. I hate what I did, and I hate that other people will do it. I hope you're wrong about not being able to have children. I hope you can feel what it's like. You would understand then, and maybe there's a chance somehow that you would be able to forgive me."

With that, she crossed through the door and left him speechless. He scooped the data-coin back from the table and watched the boy's face slowly disappear. Even with the same body, he could see right away how different they were from each other, Bodhi and this boy. The boy had a shine about him like life oozed free from his pores. Bodhi had inherited the sadness. His mother, his grandmother, and now him. Sad souls who passed through this life, tragically alone.

# 19

## A Better Vision

### Thursday, August 13, 2201

Bodhi let his mind wander through the various ways he could work with the Labyrinth programming interface. Afternoon light poured in through the window and turned the skin on his arm a warm honeyed tone. The slight temperature variation was enough to snap him out of his daydream design session. The list of ways was short, made that way because he had no programming knowledge at all. So he vainly attempted to form something tangible from the ephemeral mist of his lack of understanding.

Bodhi would learn, though. With his animus module, he found it easy to track and research different circuit-board patterns and wiring diagrams, so he was becoming quite adept at hard technology. Through patience and many hours of trial and error, he was slowly mastering electronics. He intended to move on to programming next. He could feel the possibility bubbling in the air, which is what made the thing that he'd decided to do so hard. Bodhi sighed, raised his fist, and banged on the door in front of himthen waited anxiously for the door to open. He only had the strength of will to knock once, and when there was no answer after several seconds, he spun and walked back down the hallway. On the way, he saw Torrent, and with no courage left, only nodded as the man flashed a quick smile.

Asking Torrent for a legacy reference made sense when Christine told him to do it. In-person, he didn't know how Torrent would react. Sporadic calls had always been terse, brief things between them. Torrent didn't owe Bodhi anything, and they didn't really have much of a relationship, so Bodhi chickened out, and he thought, quite wisely so. Instead, he made his way back to the penthouse, where Christine would want a full report.

But a full report on what?

As he tramped down the hallway he didn't see the walls, or the doors. Nor did he feel the carpeting that gave way beneath his feet. The expiration date had come off of his life, and as soon as it did, another destiny overwrote his own ambitions. This one was driven by the goals of the only other female than his mother or Aunt Kiera who he had ever met in person. She'd decided which schools they would attend, why they would go - for reasons lost to him as she was poised to inherit a fortune. He wondered as he traversed the space whether he had given up his new future too quickly. What if he was meant to do more? The question plagued him as he continued back toward his family's penthouse suite. Then, rife with guilt of failing a burden that he felt was unfairly his, Bodhi stopped and called Christine.

*"You didn't even ask him?"*
  *"I couldn't do it."*
*"All you have to do is ask him and let him know that this is the*

*only thing you'll ever ask for. It's not hard. Do you want me to do it?"*

Nothing was ever hard for her. Bodhi envied how she navigated through life, making decisions that would work out in her best interest without fear of failure or repercussions. He couldn't figure out how to make that work. Guilt pulled on his decisions like tar.

*"No, I'll do it. You're right. It's not hard."*

He swallowed and turned back into the hallway. Bodhi felt only angst as he approached the man. The only reason he crossed the hallway and toward Torrent's door now was to avoid having to explain to Christine that he was once again too scared to do it.

It was a dumb idea. Torrent knew that Bodhi was his son, and they had a relationship of sorts. He shouldn't be as nervous to ask such a simple question as using Torrent for legacy status. Deep in thought, Bodhi navigated his way around the corner and nearly collided head-first with Aiden.

"Bodhi," he said, "how are you?"

"H-hi Aiden," he stammered, thinking simultaneously of his mission and the fact that if Aiden was on his way back to the penthouse, his mother might be with him. Bodhi scanned the area, but his mother wasn't anywhere nearby.

"Are you okay?" Aiden asked. The way that Aiden looked at him seemed different. Bodhi cocked his head a little more than usual and narrowed his eyes into slits, almost as though he were sizing up an opponent.

"I'm fine," he remarked, as casually as he could. Then he slowed his pace to a fast walk and swung around Aiden to continue his quest. As Bodhi's pace slowed, he noticed that Aiden didn't move behind him. He felt the brown eyes piercing into him, as though he had done something wrong, and all that was left was to catch him at it. Even though he'd come to Torrent's door, Bodhi picked up his pace again until he rounded into the next hallway. Once there, he waited until he heard the door to their penthouse clang shut before he found the strength to go back to Torrent's room.

As he approached the door, he felt his animus module buzzing.

"Christine?"

*"I can help, Bodhi. Keep me on, and I can walk you through it. It's easier for me, and you won't have to obsess so much."*

The feeling of her thoughts materializing in his mind calmed him. He agreed and knocked twice before he heard shuffling from inside, indicating that someone was coming to open the door for him.

The door cracked open a wedge, and Torrent's face peered with just-emerging crows feet around his eyes. Without the graying hair and glasses, he wouldn't have seemed nearly as old.

"Do you have a minute?"

"Yes, come in."

Torrent pushed the door further, and Bodhi did too as he stepped through. At first, Bodhi couldn't tell what kind of room he had entered. He'd expected a living room or foyer. If there was a couch, it was impossible to know through all of the clutter. Torrent motioned to a pile of clothes and then quickly moved it to reveal a hidden couch cushion.

"This won't take long."

*"Think about what it looks like - I want to see."*

Dutifully, Bodhi closed his eyes and scanned the room in his mind.

*"Wow, that's exactly what I thought it would look like."*

"Really?" he asked.

*"I thought it would be messy. Torrent seems like a packer to me."*

"What did you want?" Torrent asked, more directly than Bodhi had expected.

"Well," he began. "I've been thinking about this for a while."

Torrent smiled and stared as though he relived happy memories from their shared pasts.

*"Tell him. Just blurt it out. It'll be okay, I swear."*

Bodhi paused momentarily.

*"Seriously, just ask him already."*

"I'm not asking for anything. Well, nothing that would put you out, I mean."

*"He can't be interested in all of that. Pop the question and get out. He'll say yes. What happened between him and your mom anyway?"*

*"No idea."* Of course he knew, but now wasn't the time to get into it.

"I just wanted to ask if you can help me get grandfathered into Randen." As the words came out, Bodhi felt a sense of relief as well as defeat.

*"Yaaaay! You said it."*

Torrent swiveled around and sloshed golden liquid around in his glass as Bodhi got a glimpse of a mini-bar behind him.

"Sure, I can help."

*"Say thank you, and leave."*

"Thanks, Torrent."

He stood there in silence, half-expecting Torrent to say more while Torrent took a sip from the glass. That moment never came. The man's eyes stared ahead through Bodhi for a few seconds. Then Torrent shook his mane and seemed to see Bodhi again.

"I'm sorry. It's been a long day."

Taking the cue, Bodhi helped himself out of the room.

*"I told you he wouldn't mind."*

*"You were right, I guess."*

*"Are you okay?"*

*"I think so. I'll talk to you later."*

They disconnected. Bodhi had gotten what Christine wanted - a much lower entrance barrier into Randen. That was perfect and exactly what he had planned to do.

Christine was often right about people and people's reactions. Her ability to switch her personality to adapt to the situation scared and impressed him at the same time. Part of him wondered if she steered him toward Torrent and Randen just to see what the reaction would be. He dismissed the idea as quickly as it occurred.

Bodhi returned to the penthouse to find his mother and Aiden on the couch. As he passed through the door, the first thing he noticed was that the two of them jumped a the same time. It wasn't as if they left their seats. They both simply shook quickly, once, and then settled back down. He immediately thought back to Aiden's reactions in the hallway.

"Bodhi, welcome home," his mother told him when she recovered, acting as though the lurch never happened.

"Thanks, Mom," Bodhi replied, as he also casually nodded to Aiden.

"Where've you been?" Aiden asked. Bodhi took his tone to be antagonistic, but nothing about his features brought about that conclusion. It must have been Bodhi's guilt.

"Nowhere," he said, shrugging his shoulders.

"Were you visiting Torrent?"

This question came from his mother, and Bodhi wondered how she knew. Then he remembered the look that Aiden had given him earlier.

"I was with Torrent," he said, nodding in confirmation. His mother's face dropped. She looked down, and then to the side, and anywhere to avoid meeting his eyes. Aiden scowled.

"Why?"

Bodhi considered what it must look like to the man who

had raised him as a son when he snuck off to find his biological father. The evasive way Bodhi reacted to him in the hallway must have been more hurtful than strange. He considered that Aiden might think that he had found a different, replacement father. Until that moment, he hadn't considered the possibility, but now, he thought he understood. Then Aiden asked another question that made him wonder.

"What did he tell you about the module?" Aiden asked briskly.

Bodhi turned to him and asked, "What about the module?"

His mother only sat with hands over her mouth and said nothing.

He could tell that his mother had been thinking the same thing that he had, about seeking his father. But Aiden was on some other mission.

"What about the module, Bodhi? What did he tell you about it?"

"Nothing. He didn't tell me anything about the module. We weren't talking about that," Bodhi responded.

His mother chimed in with a wavering voice.

"What were you talking about?" She asked softly.

He knelt in front of her and took her hands in his.

"Mom," he said. "I only asked him to help get me into Randen."

Then she stood, and he backed up enough to prevent himself from tripping and give her some space. She squeezed him into a hug while Aiden, being Aiden, wrapped his long arms around everyone, and made Bodhi squirm. Bodhi then backed away from the group. He looked at Aiden.

"I didn't know you wanted to go to Randen. Are you ready?"

"I don't know, Mom. I've got to do something. I can't waste this body, you know?"

She bit her lip and nodded.

"Aiden, what about the module?" Bodhi asked the question, remembering the conversation Aiden had tried to start. Aiden sighed in response.

"I thought he'd told you already," he muttered, but he didn't answer the question directly. Then he paused and turned towards Bodhi's mother as they both exchanged a glance. Then Aiden looked at Bodhi again.

"It's the life expectancy," he said. "The module's integration in the new body is untested. Torrent thinks it might only last around twenty years or so, for reasons I really didn't understand. They're working on a new model that will last longer."

Bodhi looked at his mother, who nodded in confirmation.

"But Bodhi," she told him, "this is twenty years that you didn't have. It's twenty years that I get to have you with me."

He put on a smile as he tried to choke down the thought that what this meant was that he would be in the same position looking for another body in twenty more years. He would look for another body, another host, to hold the Bodhi parasite. Bodhi's mother didn't need to be a part of any of that.

"But he's had his for way longer than that."

"His doesn't do everything that yours does. His is the prototype - no ansible interaction or even Labyrinth. It does only one thing. Yours - and Christine's - those are the new market versions," Aiden responded.

Bodhi surveyed the room, soaking in the downcast expressions. Everyone stared with unblinking eyes, awaiting his further reaction, while he had none to give them. The time had passed for his decision. In the last week, he had morphed from a victim of circumstance to a murderer. He hated himself for his fear of dying. He made his way to the door in silence, and flashed his mother and Aiden a smile. For the second time that day, made his way to the office of Dr. Alexander Toussaint.

"What do you want? Sorry - I mean, what can I do for you?" Torrent asked, over thick glasses.

"Only twenty years?"

"You heard."

Torrent didn't seem surprised or stressed. He stated a fact.

"Twenty years until I murder again," Bodhi murmured, not entirely sure what he expected the man to do about it.

"It was the best I could do," Torrent told him. "There's a lot we don't understand about the technology still. I told him it was too early to market, but Gallatin made a good point."

"What point is that?"

"Whether it's twenty years or a full lifetime, a new model will be needed eventually anyway."

Bodhi blinked at that. He would become a serial killer, and there would be others. He was certain that there would be millions of others some day. He could see the farms now, factories churning out bodies after bodies - fodder for other people's immortality. And people who couldn't afford an entire body? Those individuals would bargain for parts. He closed his eyes and shook his head, then opened them to see the man's eyes focused on him.

"Why would you do that?" He asked.

"I'm not doing it," Torrent told him, "Gallatin is. Beckett-Madeline enterprises, and Emergent Biotechnology. I'm only a consultant."

The way he said the word seemed to absolve him of all guilt. Bodhi wondered if Torrent thought that was true; that he was guilt-free just because he wasn't a direct hire.

"That's dumb. They can't do it without you."

"I saved your life," Torrent reminded him. "To close the program means to close the medical recovery part of the program. How many people are in comas right now who could come out? Would you deny those people lives?"

Bodhi then imagined all of the outside comatose individuals, millions of them throughout the world. Why shouldn't their lives be extended? Then he shivered at how easy the rationalization was. They traded an uncertain death for a certain one.

"I'm sorry," he apologized, suddenly aware that he'd charged into the man's room and began accusing him of things.

"It's okay. You are definitely your mother's child. You have that straight moral compass. Not everyone does." He looked askance, which Bodhi interpreted as a confession of sorts that Torrent didn't have the same.

Torrent shifted to the left from the couch where he sat and patted the seat beside him. Bodhi didn't move.

"It sounds to me like you don't want to be a murderer," Torrent told him.

"I already am."

"No, you're not. I did the murdering."

Bodhi considered this perspective but shook his head to the contrary.

"You're guilty too," he suggested, "but I hold some of the blame. How do you get past this?"

"I don't. I'm not you, Bodhi. To me, this is just good science."

"What can I do to stop feeling this way?"

He asked Torrent he didn't know for advice. When the realization dawned that the gulf between them was insurmountable, he backed towards the door.

"Sorry for wasting your time."

"Bodhi, if I were you," Torrent replied, "I think that twenty years would be enough time to come up with an alternative. Don't you?"

Bodhi backed farther up before nearly tripping over a table. He caught his balance just in time to lean into the door, which pushed open with ease. Out in the hallway and toward the suite, Bodhi ambled on, gathering his thoughts.

# 20

## Fouriedon Acceptance

### *Friday, August 14, 2201*

In true Fouriedon fashion, Christine's acceptance letter arrived by postal delivery carrier. The university had paid someone an exorbitant amount of money to have the letter hand-delivered from their campus just outside of Missoula, Montana, to H Hotel in Seattle, Washington. Even her grandfather's business partners sent every correspondence via Labyrinth, or ansible if the message was timely and extremely important. She held the letter in front of her, examining it closely for close about how she should manage her future.

"Congratulations," the bartender said, reading the letter upside down from where she stood on the other side of the polished wood.

"Thanks," she replied, starting once again from the top. The words "Dear Christine" made her heart leap as much as it had the first time. She skimmed ahead to the body.

"...are pleased to inform you that you have been accepted to Fouriedon..."

She looked up from the document to the bartender.

"First try, you know," she said automatically, as though she had something to prove. The bartender gave her a quick disinterested nod before hurrying away to help someone else.

The person Christine wanted to tell was only an ansible call away. He could be talking to her in a heartbeat, telling her how great she was and how they would be only an hour's flight from each other by volantrae. No doubt her grandfather would provide her with the most expensive one he could find.

Christine looked at the paper once again then rubbed her tired eyes. After "Christine," the name printed there wasn't 'Hamilton,' the name of her father and her grandfather. It was 'Turner." Christine Turner. She examined the tiny blonde hairs on the back of her borrowed wrists.

Turner.

She'd forgotten about the name change. She took another sip as her vision clouded from the sadness and she wrinkled her nose as the aroma of alcohol lingered.

How could she explain to Bodhi the sadness that had come with that letter? Her entrance to the school that she'd been trying to get into was accomplished. The life journey she had chosen for herself lay before her. Her first initial step into it wouldn't be in her body, and it wouldn't be her name either. What of her was she bringing on this journey?

The name wasn't an accident or a misprint. Christine Hamilton lingered on the edge of death in a coma in a hospital across town. Christine's former body, with legs too short and stubby arms, lay attached to a breathing machine. Nothing was happening in that mind, and only devices kept the lungs expanding and contracting. The name protected the new and improved Christine Turner from scrutiny.

*Name or not, I'm a Hamilton.*

Christine choked back the rest of her drink and stood, crinkled papers now secure in her left hand. Then she wiped her tears away with one hand and put on a smile that she hoped was genuine enough to fool the bartender. She made her way out of the bar in steady, confident steps. There was one more thing to do to take ownership of the body, and that was where she headed. She lifted her left hand and shoved up her massive set of bangle bracelets when she was alone at the elevator, revealing the bar-code tattoo she'd concealed beneath. It was time for tattoo removal. Somehow that made her sad too. The last vestiges of the real Christine Turner, or whoever used to occupy her body, erased.

As she approached the rehabilitation room a her grandfather had directed her, Christine felt her pulse quicken and her stomach churn. However benign the laser sweep should have been, the idea of having a layer of skin essentially burned away made her queasy. Taking a deep breath, she pushed her way inside. The assistance bars in the middle of the room were gone. In their place sat a table and a man holding what seemed like a proton rifle with the barrel flattened into a four-inch-wide millimeter-thick oval. He was short - about Christine's height - and he fiddled with the device as though he'd just discovered it, turning what seemed like an excessive amount of knobs on the left side of it.

To the left of the man, she smiled involuntarily to see Bodhi there near an empty chair. He waved her over, and she approached to take her seat - or she expected it to be as it was the only other chair aside from the one immediately in front of the burly man. She surveyed the room for her grandfather before leaning in to give Bodhi a quick peck on the lips.

"I missed you," she whispered.

"Me too."

He reached out and squeezed her hand. She felt more her pulse slow and her breathing came easier in his presence.

"Bodhi?"

Bodhi broke his gaze with her and looked up at the man in response to the sound of the man's rough voice. The man tilted his head toward the free chair, and Bodhi pulled his hand away and stood and walked to where the man stood.

"Hold out your wrist, please."

The man was fatter than she'd initially thought. When he said the word 'hold,' he huffed as though he were an elephant about to charge. She watched Bodhi's wrist extend, and the man clicked a button on the device he held. He waved the oval over the bar code, and in one pass, it lightened, and in another, it was gone altogether. Instant tattoo removal, and painless. The possibility for escaped models doing exactly what Bodhi and Christine did had increased the price of such an operation to several tens of thousands of dollars. The simple gun the man held alone must have costed over a hundred and fifty thousand.

"All done," he gasped. Christine could see sweat shining from his forehead despite the coolness of the room.

"You're next."

Bodhi took his seat next to Christine, squeezing her hand as he did so in the process.

"It didn't hurt," he told her. "That's the NeverWas Laser System. It burns off layers of skin so small that you won't feel a thing."

She appreciated the fact that he tried to make her feel better. The imposing-looking device scared her a little. She walked across and extended her wrist. The sound of the instrument was more evident this close. The click was only one of several tiny clicks as the device slid up over her tattoo and backed down. Bodhi was right, though - it didn't hurt. And in a few seconds, the tattoo was gone, with no sign that it had ever been there.

However she was feeling before, the feeling she now experienced was that of relief. The body was now wholly hers. Whoever, whatever, the body had been through before was gone now. And, if she had to admit it, there was a power in re-inventing herself. If she were to be Christine Turner, she would be the best Christine Turner she could invent.

Christine and Bodhi left the room together and re-entered the expensive hallways of the hotel. Faux-Persian rugs smashed underneath each footstep as the smell of antiseptic lingered in the air. She felt a buzz of excitement course throughout her body as she chanced to slide her fingers between his. He didn't resist and they held hands in silence as they continued up the pathway until they eventually reached the elevator.

"I guess I should leave you here, "she said.

"We could go back upstairs."

She glanced up at him and saw the desire in his eyes. She felt more connected to him at that moment, as though they had undergone some horrific event together and forged bonds from the pain. In a way, she guessed they had. Christine laughed as soon as the elevator opened and pulled him inside, then hit the button to take them back up to the café.

The rest of the afternoon passed in a whirlwind of conversation, beginning with his first struggle with the disease. Christine tried to imagine what it must be like to go through an entire lifetime without being able to trust your body.

They sat across from each other, this time fingers interlocked and gazing longingly into each other's eyes. From the dark blue irises to the chiseled jawline, she found herself captured in his gaze.

When the night came to a close, it brought with it an

indescribable sadness. She couldn't take him back to her grandfather's suite.

"What are you thinking about? "He asked.

"Nothing."

"Certainly seems to be something going on in there. "

"I was just thinking about the first day I saw you."

"The day I collapsed?"

"No, before that when you first came to the hotel. I was in the lobby, and you walked through with your mom and your dad."

"Not my dad," he reminded her and squeezed her hand gently but didn't let go.

"You know what I mean. Aiden. What's the deal there anyway? Not-your-dad Aiden, your mother? It certainly *looks* like there's something there."

He went on to tell her the story of his past, and his parents' past. She shared the story of her own parents' deaths, and followed her impulse to ask more and more questions, searching for who he was in his answers. He seemed to be the kind, passive person she believed of him, someone who enjoyed his small family. For a while, his disease had made him cynical, but now he was working through that to try to become someone worthy of a second chance. Christine related to that drive to make something of her life now that she had it back.

At the end of the evening, they walked back to her room, hand in hand. Bodhi politely said his goodbyes, but when he turned to leave, she couldn't let him go. She pulled him closer toward her. He gave willingly, and then on impulse, she planted a gentle kiss on his lips and smiled.

"Thank you for a wonderful night," she said.

"I miss you already."

"Me too," came another voice from behind her. Bodhi's ears took on a reddish hue, and he put his arms to his side, and shoved them into his pockets. Christine turned quickly to find Grandfather standing in the doorway, and pulled pulled her hands back to wrap them around her waist.

"Ah, young love," her grandfather said as the couple separated. Christine stared at him, trying to discern his thoughts yet finding nothing betraying the smile on his face. She gave Bodhi another brief goodbye hug, then pushed past her grandfather into their suite, irritated by the interruption. A moment later, she heard him turn to follow as the door clicked closed.

"Wait, Christine," her grandfather said, his tone gentler now.

"No," she responded and kept going, only to be stopped as he grabbed her arm and turned her around.

"You don't think that's a mistake?"

"It's *my* life." As she looked on, a heavy sigh shook through him as he squinted his eyes, folding his skin into wrinkles at the corners. Grandfather did that when he thought through challenging problems. She took the opportunity to interject.

"You didn't have to embarrass him like that."

"Embarrass him? I don't think he was embarrassed."

"He was. And why did you come out anyway?" She felt the hostility in her chest balloon up and swell to fill her insides. Whether or not Bodhi had truly been embarrassed, she had been. Her grandfather closed his eyes and let out a breath. When he opened them again, his expression became more rigid.

"We should talk, if you want to see that boy. Remember that Bodhi Rawls is Harper Rawls' son, and Beckett-Madeline Enterprises is partnering with Emergent Biotechnology."

"And?"

"Harper led a very high-profile lawsuit against Emergent Biotechnology twenty years ago. If you get involved with

Bodhi, it will get messy. Your life will be so much… easier if you don't complicate matters."

"Oh? If Bodhi is such a problem, why did you bring him here?"

Her grandfather shook his head in denial.

"I didn't bring them, Christine. Torrent did. He told me Harper's son - his son - was dying and insisted that we help. I needed another experiment volunteer, and helping Torrent buys loyalty and trust. That doesn't mean you should start dating him."

She glared, and he seemed to soften.

"I've always liked Harper. It's just not a good idea to create problems on the cusp of our joint venture launch."

Her heart sank into her stomach, and she stumbled as she shifted her weight and caught herself. Her chin trembled and tightened.

"You are the future of Beckett-Madeline Enterprises. There's no one else, Christine. It's just you. We don't have the luxury to indulge in frivolities."

Frivolities. That's what Bodhi was to Grandfather, a curiosity or plaything that she would tire of and cast aside.

"I love him, Grandfather."

The exclamation erupted from her as an all-consuming force, but the violence that she felt fell uselessly before him. He didn't even blink at the words.

"I believe you probably think that," he told her sternly, but without anger.

"I know it."

"You are only fourteen, little one. There's a lot you have to experience in life still. This isn't loving."

She hadn't been fourteen for over a month and a half. Every time she looked in the mirror, an eighteen-year-old stranger stared back. Nothing she did was typical fourteen-year-old fare either. She'd taken a GED and gained entrance into Fouriedon University. They intended to admit an eighteen-year-old Christine Turner, niece of Gallatin Hamilton, into their prestigious university.

"It's love if I say it's love," she insisted. She stomped heavily through the suite to her room, ignoring his pleas behind her. Christine tried to slam the door behind her, but the hinge slowed the door to an unsatisfying soft thud. Then she threw herself onto her bed and felt her body shake.

Forcing her face into the pillow, Christine released a scream that nobody heard but her. She closed her eyes and focused on the love she felt, that warm feeling every time Bodhi was around. She clothed herself in it, and it lifted her heart back up to her chest and then spread to fill her entire room.

## *Saturday, August 15, 2201*

Christine's grumbling stomach awoke her in the same position in which she'd fallen asleep. Fully clothed, she lay over the top of her bed as sunlight licked the room. The taste of batteries in her mouth told her that she'd not eaten or brushed her teeth since having drinks with Bodhi the day before. A fluttering in her belly accompanied her memories of what she'd felt and brought a smile to her lips.

Christine left her bedroom into an empty suite. Her grandfather had already gone to Texas. A note lay on the counter, but she had no desire to read it after the evening before. She considered calling Bodhi. He wouldn't be awake yet.

Acceptance to Fouriedon had been the last item on her list of things to accomplish over the summer. Now, however, she faced the unusual problem of having to find some way to entertain herself without GED study or obsessing over the lack of a response.

A knock on her door captured her attention. She opened it slowly, peeking through the crack, and broke into a full smile as soon as she saw Bodhi standing there.

"I was just thinking about you," she said.

"You're awake. Good. I had to see you - I couldn't sleep."

"My grandfather didn't intimidate you away?"

"Wha- no. He seemed polite enough to me."

"Come in," she told him as she moved out of the way for him to pass and closed the door behind him. Bodhi knew nothing of the conversation she'd had with her grandfather after Bodhi left. She decided to tell him, and watched wondering if she'd made a mistake as Bodhi listened. At first, his smile wavered, and a few times, he opened his mouth but said nothing before closing it again. When she finished, he stared at her, confused.

"You love me?"

Her chest tightened. She had told Bodhi more of the conversation than she'd wanted. It was out now, so she had to decide what to do. Confess to it? She could play it off like a joke.

"Y-yes," she admitted, looking down and away from him, afraid to meet his eyes.

"I love you too."

He said the words like they were a fact. It was as though it were a truth that he pulled from the universe to hand to her. It was complete and honest and reminded her of all the reasons that she loved him. She threw her arms around his neck and kissed him firmly on the lips.

They breathed together, lips pressed upon lips, and sharing the same air.

"Grandfather's not here," she whispered into his ear, as she separated and grabbed his hand. Then she pulled him back toward her bedroom, and he followed, glancing back over his shoulder as they dodged the furniture.

\* \* \*

## *Sunday, August 16, 2201*

The next morning, Christine found herself awake before six o'clock, despite the late-night with Bodhi. Grandfather wouldn't be back yet. Full of energy, thoughts bounced around in her mind. She closed her eyes and recalled the memory of his scent as they rolled together in her bed. The sheets still held his aroma.

She stood and made her way across her bedroom. Christine pulled the pinamu from her desk, and it sprang to life as it recognized her biometric signature. On the screen were all of the notes of things she'd tried the day before. The last line was about the chamber Christine had discovered. Closing her eyes, she imagined herself separate from everything, drawing a line in her mind between herself and any physical experience.

When she opened them again, she was no longer in her bedroom but was in a grainy virtual room with walls covered in knobs and switches. Markings decorated sections of the paneled wall. One panel held a symbol that seemed to be for communication, adorned with concentric circles indicating a signal of some sort. Another one displayed a long green bar - some sort of status that flickered, then shrank and grew as she watched it. She reached out to this bar, touched it, and it projected words in the space before her.

"Animus Module Status: Active - Christine Hamilton"

Animus Module Configuration?

She closed the display with a thought and touched the signal button. A panel popped up before her with multiple boxes. One held Bodhi's face, pixelated almost to the point that she didn't recognize him. Three others hovered nearby. Christine reached out with her fingertips to touch Bodhi's face, and then the room flickered before her and disappeared into black. When the room came back, the pop-up panel had disappeared and she stared at what looked like the same two symbols before her - signal and status. Otherwise, nothing seemed to have happened.

Christine then touched the panel with the signal symbol on it again, and a similar series of boxes opened before her, only this time she saw her own face staring back at her, distorted. She then willed the containers closed and moved back to the green bar. This time, when she touched it, the message had changed.

"Animus Module Status: Active - Bodhi Rawls"

Could it be?

She moved back to the other panel, this time opening the menu with the image of herself. More buttons appeared, displaying symbols she didn't recognize. One looked like a link that was gray and black. She touched it with her fingertips, and it changed colors to bright green.

Connect?

Christine touched the image of her face, and the room flickered to black again before coming back. She understood the system now - it was like navigating in the Labyrinth, but less well-designed. The menu navigation system seemed clunky, like an operating system. When the room came back into view, she clicked on the signal menu again. This time, it showed Bodhi's pixelated face. Beneath it, the link was highlighted green. Early or not, she had to try it out. If she were right, she'd just turned on auto-connect between them. No more annoying buzzing. First, she needed to be back in reality. Christine squeezed her eyes shut, and when she opened them this time, she was on her bed. Then she tried it out. Instead of calling using his ansible number, she thought of Bodhi and willed her message to him.

*"Are you awake?"*

Laying in bed, staring at the ceiling, Christine sent her

message out into the ansible network. She imagined it pinging from node to node, seeking out Bodhi, finding him in his bedroom in the penthouse. Christine picked at her blanket as she waited, her heart beating more loudly with every silent moment.

*"How did you do that?"*

It worked. Christine smiled to herself. *"Do what?"*

*"Your voice just popped into my head. Is this my imagination, or is it you?"*

*"You auto-accepted my call. Isn't this cool? I've been playing around with the configuration."*

*"How did you do it?"*

*"I thought you'd want to know. There's a virtual room…"*

She walked him through the steps as she went back into the configuration menu and followed along.

*"Wow. What does this one do?"*

*"The one with the weird face on it? That's me - it just looks funny."*

*"No. By the link, there's one with a face on."*

*"The one with three squiggles?"*

*"Yeah. That's a face, right?"*

*"If you say so."*

*"I'm touching it."*

*"Don't you think we should…"*

Christine couldn't finish the thought. The feelings she felt inside magnified to a stifling extent as she struggled to catch her breath. Fear lurked beneath love, and an intense longing for something. Slowly her mind adjusted to the new levels as she realized that she was the intensity's target.

*"Wow! Is that how you feel?"* Christine asked Bodhi.

*"You felt that too?"*

*"I think so. What are you afraid of?"*

*"Maybe that wasn't such a good idea."*

The flood dissipated to a trickle and then stopped

altogether. She grabbed the feeling in her mind and clung to it as it evaporated, leaving her drained.

*"Bodhi, can we turn it back on?"*

He didn't answer right away. Christine knew how he was, though. He weighed the consequences, and she thought she could feel the scales shifting under the weight of his analysis. Christine could turn it back on herself. She could simply touch the button. The wall of emotion collided with her and filled her again with the experience she craved. They were connected, the two of them and no-one else in the universe.

# 21

## Departure

### *Sunday, August 23, 2201*

Time passed too quickly. In a only nine days, until Bodhi found himself alone as Christine packed in her suite. His eyes watered as his mind fixated on her departure.

"I'm going to miss you too. Can you meet me downstairs?"

Anxiety and excitement dripped around the edges of their connection. Christine was leaving for Fouriedon that morning, and he wanted to make sure he could say goodbye.

"I will. On my way down now."

He had only a few minutes until she finished packing. If he hurried, Bodhi could get down to the gift shop before she made it to the lobby. He sprinted through the door.

"Bodhi?"

His mother's voice rang out behind him.

"I'll be right back, Mom."

He didn't bother to turn his head. The elevators were two suites away, and he didn't have time to be delayed. He caught one just as it closed and jumped through the closing doors, surprising a housekeeper as he almost knocked the man over.

"Sorry."

The man only grunted at him.

When the elevator finally stopped, he slipped through the opening doors and sprinted to the gift shop in the lobby. There, he paused. He didn't know what to get. The stuffed animals seemed inappropriate, and the fake flowers seemed banal. The real flowers in the window were prohibitively expensive. Except… there was a little white flower in a vase.

"Excuse me, miss?"

He flagged the shopkeeper, who looked human from the back but revealed android features when it turned toward him.

"This flower?"

"Eidelweiss. Seventy-six dollars."

"Charge to the penthouse, please."

"Very good."

The android scanned him to confirm his identity before retrieving the flower from the glass. He grabbed it and turned just in time to see Christine emerge from the same elevator chute he had. He bolted out the door of the gift shop and then slowed to a calm stride. The stride didn't last as he stumbled the last few feet to her. He shoved the flower at her impulsively. This seemed to amuse her somehow, as she reached out and grabbed it with a whimsical smile across her lips.

"Thank you."

"You're welcome."

He reached for her free hand, and she grasped his in return. The pair walked toward the front door to the hotel. He couldn't find words to tell her about everything he felt. His body was on fire with longing for her not to go. They could stay as they were, living in this hotel, forever. Her grandfather and Aiden both had enough money that neither of them would ever have to work. They could spend their days and nights together, living one unified life.

The feeling became too strong to contain. Then it became more potent in a way he didn't know was possible. He struggled to breathe in it. He forced himself to meet her eyes, and he saw it there too. The way she looked at him then, as if nothing outside of the two of them mattered. He felt her love also, mixed together with his, growing exponentially. They settled onto a bench in front of the hotel, and he wrapped his arm across her shoulders.

"Where's Grandfather?"

He posed the question with masked casualness as though he could care less. The moment was to linger forever, and Grandfather would interrupt it. When he arrived, they would be torn apart.

"I asked him to stay upstairs," she assured him.

"I'm going to miss you," he told her. This close, he felt the heat from her skin, and her aroma saturated the air. The fear and stress and desire for her weaved into the physical sensations, clouding his mind and making it impossible for him to think.

"Maybe we should disconnect for a while?" Tears threatened to stream from his eyes, and he saw the same in hers. She nodded at him and wiped her eyes. Then the sensation of oneness disappeared, and he could no longer feel her heart.

"Christine, time to go." Her Grandfather's voice called out from behind her as a volantrae appeared, descending down toward them. She gave Bodhi a kiss before swinging her legs over his, now leaving him physically alone as well. He watched as the luggage was loaded in, and she climbed into the back.

# 22

## Fouriedon

### *Sunday, August 23, 2201*

The jet landed with a skid on a private runway on the Fouriedon campus. When the door opened and the staircase extended down to the ground, Christine stood behind it, waiting to take in the scene. Massive deciduous trees covered the campus, spaced enough to allow swathes of green grass to wander among them. She already knew that some of the campus buildings were hundreds of years old. Christine thought she could distinguish which by the amount of ivy covering the buildings.

Grandfather coughed behind her, and she started forward down the steps and toward the runway. She smiled back over her shoulder then continued downward to meet the gentleman who had come to greet them.

"Pleased to meet you," the man said, shaking her hand aggressively.

"You as well," she replied with a grin. The air was

deceptively cool in the brightness. She reached out her hand, and the man escorted her down to the tarmac. Once he'd positioned her just to the left of the stairs, purse in hand, he turned to give her grandfather similar treatment. In a few more minutes, he stood beside her.

"Quite the show, eh," he asked.

Three separate volantrae with gold trimmings around the vertical boosters descended from different directions to land in a row just in front of them.

"They like to show off," her grandfather said.

Suddenly she felt small in the face of the destiny they'd both decided for her. Fouriedon would be the first place she would go without her family. She supposed Christine Turner had no family anyway. Then it struck her that if Christine Turner had no family, she couldn't be in on legacy.

"Grandfather?"

"Yes, Christine, what is it?"

"How did I get accepted here as a legacy if they know me as Turner here?"

"When you pay for a building, they tend not to look too closely at things like entrance requirements."

He stepped toward the middle volantrae as the door opened for them to enter. At first, Christine followed until he waved her toward one of the others.

"You need to go check into the dormitory," he told her, motioning to the third volantrae in the row. "Your luggage will be there by the time you finish checking in."

She looked up at him, eyebrows raised. She hadn't expected him to abandon her so soon. His stern eyes locked onto her determined ones.

"You have to learn how to run an empire, Christine, just like we talked about, remember? There are twenty years to make up for."

Her impulse was to grab him then, and hold him and

refuse to let go. The word her mother had used was driven, as though he were an expensive volantrae that had no control over the situation. In the same breath, the woman had often compared her to him. Depending on the woman's mood, the comment oscillated between insult and encouragement. Just then, Christine began to understand better the impact the man had had on his mother's life and why she had never been interested in taking over Beckett-Madeline Enterprises. He softened a little and reached forward to pull her into him for a gentle hug before pushing her back out to arm's length. She searched his eyes for the tears she felt gathering in her own, but found none.

"It's okay, princess, they'll take good care of you. I just have to talk to the University President about a few things."

The door opened before her, and she stared at the empty interior. She moved toward it, unsure whether she would be able to enter. At that moment, she felt like the fourteen-year-old she actually was.

"Go ahead, Christine. You'll be fine."

That little nudge was enough to get her in. Instinctively she probed out with her mind looking for Bodhi's connection but then paused as she remembered that they'd severed it intentionally. He would have to get over it, she thought. As she slid into the volantrae, she attempted to connect.

*"Miss me already?"*

The familiar feeling of Bodhi's presence soothed her as she fastened herself in.

*"Grandfather is abandoning me to go check-in."*

*"Abandoning you?"*

*"He's not coming with me. There's a volantrae here to take me to the dormitory for check-in. He's off to talk to the president or something."*

*"Ramsey?"*

*"Not that president. The university president."*

*"That makes more sense, I guess. How are you?"*

She did a quick mental inventory. Aside from being nervous, she felt excited that her life was finally able to begin. Her excitement only grew as they approached the dormitory, where older kids entered and left in groups. The volantrae came to a stop in front of the entrance, and the door opened for her to exit. She could see hovering signs that read 'registration.'

*"I miss you, Bodhi. I've got to go figure out the check-in process now. Can we talk later?"*

*"You never even have to ask. We can always talk later."*

She disconnected as she stepped from the vehicle back into the sunlight.

"You're Christine Turner?"

A man's voice caught her attention. At first, she didn't understand that the question was directed at her and not some other Christine. She told herself that she would have to do better. She swung around toward the voice to see a man who seemed the right age to be a student charging toward her. He slowed before reaching her.

"Christine Turner?"

"Uh - yes."

"I'm Jacob Barnett, the resident advisor for dormitory three. Ann asked me to come to check on you. She's a little busy."

"Ann?"

"Sorry. Ann Taggart, the resident advisor for your dormitory. She has a class at this time so can't meet you herself. She asked me to help you get settled in."

"Barnett? Like the Emergent Biotechnology Barnett's?"

His mouth split open into a huge toothy grin.

"That's me - guilty. My parents own the company. But I understand I'm well met. You're related to Mr. Hamilton?"

She marveled at the smallness of the world and how business relationships followed into 'normal' life. Her father's company, Beckett-Madeline Enterprises, at one time had owned stock in Emergent Biotechnology - not a majority, but enough to influence the direction and to get three loyal members on the board of directors. By his influence, the board of directors poached Barnett from Innovation Strata, the company's only significant competition at the time. Afterward, her grandfather had funded the move to retake the company private, installing the Barnett dynasty. Here, helping her to her dorm room, was the heir apparent to one of the largest bioengineering firms in the world. She smiled at him and corrected her posture as subtly as she could.

"I'm his niece."

"I think your uncle knows my dad. Come with me, we can chat while we walk. It'll be great to get to know you."

She considered how likely it was that her grandfather had just happened to schedule his arrival when her RA was missing. How much of a hand had he in the determining of her destiny?

"Do you go by Christine?"

She flashed a smile at him and turned her head toward him slightly to answer.

"Christine usually works. You?"

"I don't go by Christine, no. But you can call me Jake."

His attempt at humor failed, but that he tried made her giggle.

"Okay... so the quick run-down here. Stay away from those guys."

He motioned across the yard toward something that looked like a small hut. In front, a group of six seemed to be loitering and talking. Nothing about them seemed unusual to her.

"Is something wrong with them?"

"No, just not likely to be major players. You and I know how this works, right? Some people have influence, some don't."

Those words caused desire and ambition to rise up in her. This was a game she knew, and Jake seemed a lot like her.

"Of course," she said and meant it.

"Those over there," he motioned to a group of girls, "they are from the Orphan Program. No family, no connections. They're pretty nice, though."

He smiled and waved as one of the girls looked toward him, and then the other faces joined. All three of them were tall and gorgeous, and all of them waved back. Christine felt a jealous pang at the interaction, and she corrected it in her mind. There was no reason for her to feel that way about this man she'd just met.

"Ah, here we are." Jake stopped before a building that looked identical to the building where she'd been dropped.

"Dorm 4?"

"Yeah. As I said, I'm in dormitory three, or Edgar Rollins Hall. This is dormitory four, Octavia B. Jackson Hall. And I think you're on the second floor."

He turned abruptly through a doorway she hadn't noticed and up some stairs. She followed quickly and tripped as she passed through, stumbling head-first toward the stairs only to stop just before the collision. Strong hands pulled her back up to her feet.

"Sorry, I should have warned you. That step is tricky if you're not used to it."

Christine felt flush from the near-fall but refused to betray her embarrassment. She righted herself, and the pair continued up to her room.

Jake left Christine alone in her room, number 206. Unlike others, she didn't have to share. Her entire room was hers alone. And her luggage had somehow beaten her to it, as attested by the stack of bags leaning precariously against the far wall. Sunlight came in filtered through a curtain that turned the pinks of her luggage into browns.

Besides her luggage, the room held a bed, a dresser that looked barely large enough to contain her three bags of clothes, and a tiny refrigerator. Otherwise, the room was someone else's idea of elegant. Billowy sea-foam curtains accented dark red hardwood. A tan chair rail followed along the walls, pale green on top and dark-forest green on the bottom. A writing desk adorned one corner, ancient and faded, but sturdy-looking. To the right eyes, it might have seemed lovely, but all she could think about was how quickly she could at least change out the curtains.

Christine began her marathon job of unpacking. Everything went to its proper place, and by the time she was done, she was prepared to drop over from exertion. Or it could have been hunger. Three raps on her door caught her attention, and she opened it, surprised to see Jake back again.

"Lunch?"

The protest began in her throat, but her stomach grumbled and betrayed her.

"I guess so."

"Great! Come on, I'll show you the cafeteria. One of the perks for Fouriedon is the great food, so you really need to take advantage."

The day passed in a flurry of activity after that. Jake took her to the registrar's office to verify her schedule and then gave her an impromptu tour of the entire campus. She'd already missed the official orientation, so Jake's personal tour was welcome, although he walked quickly as though he had somewhere else to be that she kept him from. It didn't help that she stopped periodically to discover something new that hadn't even existed before her coma.

"MiniMaid ten?" She stopped to watch the robot suck dust from a corner of the ceiling, hovering silently overhead.

"Yes. You didn't have one of those?"

She caught herself before revealing that when she'd gone into her coma, the version of MiniMaid out was only two and had those had wheels and clumsy extendable tubes. They certainly couldn't fly.

"Just haven't seen one for a while. What version are they up to now?"

He shrugged.

"Not sure. Maybe twelve? Right through here."

Jake wasn't rude exactly. He was friendly and never complained, and they even laughed a few times. She guessed that he tried really hard, but his accompanying her was out of obligation more than interest. The act almost broke when she stopped again to gawk at a trio of boys who walking by. One of them had silver skin, one had a thick red stripe across his entire face, and the last one had what seemed to be a metallic device protruding from where his left ear had been. She'd never seen anything like it before.

"Are you coming?" Jake asked her with a thinly veiled hint of exasperation in his words.

"What. Are. They?"

He glanced where she looked.

"You've never seen body mods? It's all cosmetic. The latest 'shock me' body modification. Probably to surprise their parents."

"Is it permanent?"

He looked at her through the corner of his eyes with a look that Christine knew meant she needed to stop gawking at what he considered normal.

"No, not for them. I'm sure their parents are as rich as ours. Well, mine - maybe not yours. By senior year, they'll be back to normal. Are you ready?"

She followed him through a sliding doorway into what appeared to be a long hallway. So intent on watching the boys outside, she hadn't noticed the size or shape of the building, but the hall seemed to go for at least the length of a city block.

"For first year, a lot of your classes will be in here," he told her. "Orientation, and a few of the basics. Do you have your calendar?"

"I- I don't know."

"They would have sent it to you by now. You should check your messages."

Christine pulled her pinamu out of her bag, and saw three missed alerts, two of which were about classes. Opening the last message, a list of courses appeared. Jake took the pinamu as soon as he saw and scoured the list.

"Yeah. These two will be down here," he said, pointing to her introductory English and Statistics courses. "Those others though - wow. That's a jog. At least you get lunch in between, but still. The cafeteria is on the opposite side of campus. You'll have to walk pretty quickly to get there."

"That bad?"

"Same thing happened to me. I had to sprint to make it and even then was late half the time."

He became obsessed about the timing of her courses and the distance between them. Whatever important event she kept him from had either already been missed, or it was possible that she'd misinterpreted his actions. He was slow and deliberate as they timed the walk and found that she could make it just in time if she left precisely when the lunch bell chimed.

When they returned from the tour, she found Grandfather seated on the edge of her bed in her dorm room.

"Mr. Hamilton, pleased to meet you," Jake said, moving past her to shake his hand.

"The pleasure is mine, Jacob. I've heard wonderful things

about you. How is that Second Chance Tutelage going?"

"It's going well. The dean is going to let me advertise in the main buildings. We have over fifty seniors employed now."

"Good, good," Grandfather said.

It hadn't occurred to her that starting a business would be something students might do.

"What's Second Chance Tutelage?" Christine asked.

"We provide tutoring for students who may have a difficult time in some courses," Jake said.

"It's more than just that," said Grandfather, "Jacob has worked out an arrangement with the university to get a discount over the premium rate if the school provides referrals. He gets more business, students get more help, and the school get's the publicity of pro-actively helping students achieve."

"So you have been keeping up with me, sir?"

"Absolutely. Your father speaks highly of you."

Jake seemed to take the cue and flashed a quick smile at Christine before turning and leaving the two of them alone.

"Well? What do you think?"

"About the school," she asked, "or about Jake?"

"Whichever you want to talk about," Grandfather replied, with a twinkle in his eye that let her know that she was right about the coincidence.

"He certainly seems nice enough. But…"

"Yes?"

She sighed. At some point, she would have to be her own person. Grandfather did love her, however controlling he came across. He probably wouldn't stay mad for long.

"I'm dating Bodhi, remember."

"He seems *nice*."

His tone was different than it had been days before in their suite, though the way he said 'nice' still exuded disapproval.

Christine had expected much worse from him, especially after such an obvious match-making effort.

"He's more than nice," she retorted. "He's wonderful."

"He's also in Seattle."

There it was. Her real situation was that now, the boy she loved lived halfway across the United States. From her grandfather's perspective, Bodhi was out of the picture - probably for good. She would see what her grandfather's reaction changed to when Bodhi got into Randen, only an hour away.

"I'm not asking you to marry Jacob. I wanted you to meet him so that you could have an ally here and not be so alone. He's a good person to stay in touch with, and I think he will be a good person to know."

Christine blushed slightly at the realization that she had originated the idea of dating Jake. She was suddenly glad that she had broken the connection with Bodhi earlier.

# 23

## Building Tomorrow

### *Monday, August 24, 2201*

Almost an entire day passed without any communication from Christine. In his room, Bodhi lay across his bed wondering what might be occupying her time. As evening descended, he decided to call her and find out.

*"Christine?"*

He heard a click and felt her presence.

*"Bodhi?"*

*"Hey, how are you doing?"*

*"I can't talk long. Things are going great! Grandfather and I are about to go out to dinner, then I think he's going back to Seattle."*

*"Okay. Just checking on you - we said we'd talk every day, remember?"*

A feeling of annoyance washed over him and caught him off guard. He wasn't annoyed, or at least, didn't think so. He realized then that he received the emotion from her.

*"I'm sorry. I didn't mean to interrupt."*

*"No, I miss you. I'm sorry. I have to go, okay?"*
*"Call me later?"*
The feeling was still there, making him insecure.
*"Sure, yeah. Okay. I'll call you later."*

She disconnected first. Bodhi couldn't help the rejection that he felt with her departure. She would, of course, be busy. This wasn't the first busy day they'd spent apart. The difference was, he couldn't go to her. There were thousands of miles between them, and the ansible communication made it feel as though she were still downstairs in her grandfather's suite. But that wasn't true. Tomorrow he would want to see her in person, perhaps at the cafe. She wouldn't be there.

Relax though. He'd gotten into Randen. It'll be only a matter of time. He needed to be patient. And he desperately needed a hobby.

## *Tuesday, August 25, 2201*

The next day apart didn't improve Bodhi's demeanor. Missing Christine brought him spells of melancholy. Another concern also plagued him. Every time he looked in the mirror, he saw a face he didn't recognize. He could only think of more and more bodies being stolen from their rightful owners, as must be the logical consequence of his and Christine's procedures' success. He could already see the market forming, and he was a part of it. So he did the only thing he knew to use his new-found gifts to find an alternative. The animus module sucked up information as he tested its bounds, exploring everything from circuit design to network communication. The more he learned, the more he wanted to know, and unlike his old body, his new one could keep up the pace.

In Labyrinth, he kept his avatar unchanged. He liked being himself, if only in the virtual world. Poorly defined structures that resembled buildings drifted by - information hubs and portals into different games. Floating through the digital pseudo-reality was the only time he did feel like the Bodhi he used to be.

He sought information. Somewhere in the Labyrinth was an alternative to cloning, but he'd yet to find it. Robots, for all of their practicality, still fell short in tasks that required creativity and imagination. Models had become less expensive than robots to produce en masse for jobs like construction, and sex work was always going to need models. Even the most perfect androids fell short in comparison to humans, where sexual intimacy was concerned. Bodhi felt his the pressure rise in his overwhelmed mind as he sought a solution. Perhaps he didn't need to solve all of cloning to prevent what he witnessed in his mind.

With another two weeks to wait before his own school term began, he filled the available time with research. His time with Christine during the window shrank to nearly nothing as she found herself also overwhelmed, but with schoolwork. The GED was nowhere near enough preparation, and she needed perfect marks for her chosen course through life. Time in Labyrinth kept him from missing her as much.

Billboards dotted the virtual landscape. Some were for household products, and others were for high-end volantrae. Some are marketed for practicality, and some for luxury. Some were x-rated, and he felt embarrassed floating past them until he remembered that nobody was there to judge him. The thousands of avatars that floated by were not people he knew or needed to know.

One advertisement caught his attention. It wasn't x-rated content, but the word "immortality" flashing across the top caught his attention. As he approached, the artificial gravity it created increased and sucked him toward the intangible flashing billboard. Curious, he let himself be pulled into the immersive experience ad.

He was an enfeebled older man. He lifted his wilted arms before him, struggling under strain. A man's voice spoke, bold and direct.

"A full life well lived shouldn't bring a death sentence."

The next second, he stared at a young, vibrant arm. He flexed his toned muscles and his arms lifted easily. He sprang to his feet and jumped a jump which turned into flight. He felt himself soaring through the air.

"Achieve serial immortality. Brought to you by Emergent Biotechnology."

Then he was back out of the experience. The ad had been vague, probably intentionally so that other modeling companies couldn't compete. Bodhi got the message. What happened to him was going mass market.

What happened to him.

What he had chosen - to live the rest of someone else's life - had been his decision only. He could have said no. Then his life's choices got a lot simpler as he would be dead by now. Part of him longed for simplicity over the guilt that followed him around and struck at him every time he looked into the mirror at someone else's face.

Soon anyone with enough money could do it.

An idea flickered in his mind. He swirled back around and re-entered the immersive ad.

He was an enfeebled older man.

He was an enfeebled older man.

*He was.*

# 24

## Immortality 2.0

### *Sunday, August 30, 2201*

By his own volition, Ordell was the duty officer for the week. His reason for volunteering involved spending time with Caldwell, whose office sat just around the corner from the duty office, and he liked to keep her company when he could. Typically, their schedules were so hectic that duty weeks were the only times they could really talk. Emergent Biotechnology performed Reclamations overseas now, and the industry had followed. The Siblings of the Natural Order had shut down the reclamation industry in the United States and thus deprived themselves of suitable targets.

"Coffee?" Caldwell showed up in his doorway as though he'd summoned her. He smiled, and she brought in a cup of black yaupon brew, which she'd taken to calling coffee, even though it wasn't. But it wasn't tea either, really, and had a consistency somewhere in between. He accepted his cup and pulled it up to his nose to let the aroma wake him up a bit.

The evening shift wore on, and it was destined to be a quiet night.

Then his communicator buzzed, which caused him to jump, spilling coffee down the front of his shirt.

"Ouch," Caldwell commented, watching him and stifling a laugh. The communicator buzzed again, and she rescued it before it vibrated itself off of the table. She clicked the button on the side, and a projection of a blond-haired eighteen-year-old boy smashed against the wall across from her.

"Who's this?" She asked as Ordell cleaned himself. He looked up at the image.

"Bodhi?"

"Ordell, it's really you. Oh, shit."

"Yes, it's me."

"I don't mean to bother you - sorry. I - I should go."

"No, no. You're fine, Bodhi."

"Who is that?" He asked, pointing to his left. Ordell guessed that he probably meant Caldwell but just wasn't used to the communicator's projection mode.

"Monica Caldwell," she introduced herself.

"Like Aunt Kiera?"

"Like Kiera," she said. "A little different." Caldwell offered no more of an explanation, and after an uncomfortable, expectant moment, Ordell decided to move the conversation along.

"You can trust Caldwell. What do you want?"

"An idea. No, a thought? A - it might not be anything. But I was thinking about what you said - all the models being killed to extend people's lives. What if people could live forever without serial immortality?"

"I have no idea what you're talking about."

"The animus module does the hard part - offloading consciousness and providing an interface between that and the body. I've been studying - you know this thing gives me an eidetic memory, right? Anyway, my point is - what if we could put people in virtual reality?"

"Like a video game?"

"Yes, like that."

"I would think part of the appeal of immortality is being able to be with loved ones - in the real world. Or pursue dreams, or gain knowledge," Caldwell responded.

"What if you could still do all of that? What if people could visit you, and you could feel them touch you? All of that happens in the brain anyway. Imagine all of the immortality and none of the moral dilemma."

The ideas reminded Ordell of a young Lancaster - someone who picked a direction and went in it, regardless of the obstacles. He wasn't as knowledgeable about the higher electronics, like how the Labyrinth worked, and only vaguely understood the animus module. If there was a way to combine the two, it wasn't apparent to him. But the longer he looked at Bodhi's expression, the determination set behind his eyes, and the focus - part of him wanted to believe. Caldwell interrupted his thoughts.

"And you know how to do all of this, do you?"

"No. But…"

Bodhi trailed off then, and his fierce eyes faded as he changed focus. Ordell understood what he was going to say.

"I have a debt to pay, Monica, and it's a pretty big one. I've been thinking a lot about it. This technology is out there in the world. Christine, me - we exist. There's no stopping it now, and when I think about it, I'm not sure there ever was. For something as pivotal as Immortality, I'm sure the how-to is shared across servers all over the world. What I can do is commit myself to provide an alternative. What do you think?"

Ordell chewed his lip and examined the boy. Then he looked to Caldwell, who kept her bearing. He could still tell with the relaxed way she met his gaze that she thought his plan was progressing if nothing else.

"I think it's a start, Bodhi. And it's something I'm willing to help with. I can't do much with the technology, but I do have money, and I can help fund this little project as an investor. If it works, then it could be the carrot to enticing people away."

"That's what I wanted to ask. And I need you to know something else."

"What?"

"I'm sorry." He turned to Caldwell next and told her the same thing.

"I'm sorry because I lied to you. I'm afraid of dying as much as anyone, and I jumped at the chance. My mom was only an excuse - a way to rationalize. It was my decision - and I hope I can make it up to you both someday."

He ended the call there, and Ordell looked to Caldwell to gauge how she really felt, now that they were alone.

"I don't know if he can do it," she admitted. "But he made some good points. As soon as Immortality was advertised, others started looking at the possibility, I'm sure. The genie was out of the bottle as soon as the idea materialized."

"I kind of feel like, maybe - maybe there's a chance. Let me ask. If you didn't think he could do it, why be supportive at all?"

"It's win-win for us. He won't be advertising Immortality if he's actively working on a competing project. Also, since it's illegal for basically any of us except for you to actually have money, we need a laundering project. New investments are always good for that. Finally, suppose Bodhi's strategy does succeed. When we start blowing up Emergent Biotechnology office spaces, people might be more inclined to go with the safer option."

"There's a long way from here to there anyway," Ordell sighed. "Do we delay our strikes until we see if this can become something?"

She nodded.

"I think if we present it like that they might agree to this new plan."

Ordell's heart lifted. He hadn't realized how much stress he carried with him. However much he hated Harper's actions, cutting her away from his heart was impossible. And the people who loved her were caretakers of someone who was an integral part of who he was, no matter how distant they may be. He had worried daily about the council, and each time they met, he struggled to convince them to stay a gentler course than killing his friends. Maybe this would settle them for good.

"What next?"

"Well, we're here, on duty, with nothing really happening. Want to run this by Rochester?"

Once again, Ordell found himself in Caldwell's office talking to Rochester. This time, she was an image pasted against a far wall instead of her real self, not actually being on duty with them at the compound.

"I'm sorry, what?"

Caldwell had just explained the idea, and Rochester seemed to be struggling. Ordell had pitched her for the intelligence job, so he knew her technological savvy was unmatched. She couldn't have misunderstood the situation unless maybe Caldwell's explanation left something out.

"I said he wants to compete…"

"I know what you said. Hold on, I'm thinking."

Ordell looked at Caldwell and smirked. She flashed him a grin in return. It wasn't often that Rochester had to take the time to think about things. This meant there was a possibility.

"I want to be part of this project," Rochester told them flatly. "I think it can work. But it's going to require some serious intelligence. We need to know more about the module and the interface, and we can't do it by yanking the module out of Bodhi's head and rendering him useless. And ...I have some ideas."

Her eyes sparkled when she said that, and Ordell knew she was hooked. If she believed that it was possible, then their chances in front of the rest of the council members went up exponentially.

"We'll need to find a new intelligence chief if you take on this tasking," Caldwell said. "I'm not sure how the council will feel about that."

"Let me figure it out, Captain. I'll put together something to sell the idea. Once they understand how truly possible it is, I'm sure they'll see this as better use of my time."

Ordell still couldn't see whatever vision it was that Rochester had latched on to. It wouldn't be the first time she had proven to have better acuteness at understanding the consequences of things than he. That was why she had the job she did.

"I'll back you, Rochester."

"Me too. And if the two of us do, then half of the council will come with us. If we talk to Lancaster and get him to make one of his rare appearances, then we might have the votes."

"Or he could just make the call," Rochester said. "He is the General, after all."

"You know he doesn't work that way. We'll keep that in our pocket, though."

"I've never seen him do that," Ordell said.

"The last time he did was to bring you on board," Caldwell told him. "Feel special?"

"I'll reach out to Lancaster. Can you schedule the meeting?" Caldwell asked him. He nodded.

\* \* \*

## *Monday, August 31, 2201*

Five faces peered back at them through separate panels on the wall. Ordell and Caldwell made up representation for the mid-southern and south-eastern regions. Ordell knew the Captain of the North-Eastern area personally, as they worked together to manage the entire eastern waterfront's SNO membership. The mid-western, middle, and western regions were wild cards in any vote.

"I'm glad you're all here," he told them, staring at the faces who seemed, except one, to be irritated by the interruption of their regular duties.

"Why are you calling us? Aren't you on duty - is something happening?"

Ordell's stomach clenched at the question. He had failed to realize, in his excitement, that even on a Monday, a duty call would send a message that an emergency was before them. Captain Desmond Medora, representing the mid-west, was particularly sensitive to interruptions, and it was he who spoke.

"No, this isn't that kind of call."

"Then get on with it," Desmond responded.

"It's about the Immortality program," Caldwell offered.

"Oh, that again. Why haven't we eliminated that problem yet? Weren't you going to talk to them, or kill them, or something?"

The problem was so much larger than that. The idea that acting against people who were arguably victims themselves in order to undermine a global corporation's marketing strategy was asinine. But having made the argument repeatedly, Ordell avoided stepping into it again. The council lacked imagination, something that even the core of he, Caldwell and Rochester struggled against daily. Their preferred solution was usually some form of direct action, usually violence, directed at some individual. Alternatively a change in propaganda was also acceptable. It didn't help that their options against Beckett-Madeline were limited by the fortification of most of their facilities after SNO's brief attempted uprising.

"Talk to them only," Ordell said. "And I have. What we bring to the council are the results of that conversation."

"Well?"

Caldwell glared at Desmond, who glared back. Ordell interrupted the stare-off by opening with a description of his trips, including the recent phone call they'd had the day before. When he ended, he gave the rest of his time to Rochester, who reinforced the idea with facts and numbers that had less meaning to him than - he hoped - to the rest of the council.

"This is what you brought me here for?"

"Captain Desmond, this is an opportunity. Do you have any idea what we're trying to head off?"

"You're running away from something you imagine might happen. I'm not going to be a part of it."

Desmond exited the call, often his modus operandi as a way to flex his power. Sometimes, he got others to leave with him, but this time, Ordell and Caldwell were fortunate to still have a quorum.

"I call a vote," Caldwell chimed, before anyone else could talk, or more importantly to Ordell, before anyone else could leave and render a vote impossible.

It occurred to Ordell that the vote was a silly thing to do. His money didn't belong to the order. If it wasn't for the fact that Desmond quite publicly supported blowing up the H hotel and everyone in it, he wouldn't have bothered. He didn't really know the other three Captains, but he guessed that for Desmond to be so public, he must have support from at least one of them.

"Three for, and three against," sighed Caldwell, examining

the vote count in the bottom right of the screen.

"We know which way Desmond would go," said Captain Willson, the western region head.

"He forfeited his vote by leaving," Caldwell corrected. "There's only one way to decide this now. It has to go in front of Lancaster."

All of the heads began to speak at once, and Ordell could make out a few of the words. "Take it to your buddy" was one phrase he caught in its totality, though he couldn't tell from who.

"Who said that?"

"I did," Willson responded. "We all know how the three of you are. Why did you even bring us here if you were going to override our decision?"

"Desmond did that when he left," Caldwell replied. "You don't know which way Lancaster will go with this."

"The same way he always goes with his rescuer and golden-boy."

"You're out of order," yelled Rochester; Willson's face went dark red.

"Who are you to tell me I'm out of order?" He screamed at her.

In a flash, he was gone.

"Thank you all for your time," Caldwell said to everyone else, and then they dropped off the call one-by-one. When they were all gone, Ordell turned to Caldwell.

"That went well."

She laughed and looked to Rochester, who also erupted in a quick laugh and then stopped.

"I guess we talk to Lancaster then?"

"We already did. Now we just do it."

# 25

## Jake

### *Monday, September 7, 2201*

Finally, she could breathe. The first two weeks of classes, she had barely gotten to speak to Bodhi at all. Christine hadn't foreseen the level of studying she would have to do just to get to where all the other students already were. Her grandfather had been right - he'd brought her in, but if she really wanted to succeed, she would need to do it. And she had, so far. Christine had excelled in every class, which meant that she could take time off to call Bodhi for a change.

*"Bodhi?"*

He connected almost instantly.

*"Christine? Hi, how are you."*

*"Surprised?"*

*"A little. I was just working on something - that's all."*

*"How are your classes? Are you catching up?"*

*"Mostly A's. The math still gets to me, though. It's not easy."*

*"Well, I knew you could do it."*

*"I'm so sorry it's taking time away from us. I can't wait until you get here. When does Randen start?"*

He didn't immediately respond.

*"When are you coming, Bodhi?"*

She needed him. With the introductory classes that universities generally require, they could study together at least. And she could spend nights at his house, sometimes lounging around and doing nothing at all. She would have him to hold onto. The room where she'd felt at first privileged to be alone now seemed like solitary confinement.

*"Christine."*

*"What, Bodhi?"*

She knew that she projected anger across the connection, but she didn't bother filtering.

*"I'm starting a company, Christine. A lot has happened in the last two weeks."*

*He was being evasive. What did that have to do with anything?*

*"Great for you. When are your classes starting?"*

*"I'm not going to Randen, Christine. I'm not coming to Montana."*

*"You're not coming?"*

*"No."*

She disconnected from him. The disconnect wasn't malicious. She only realized at that moment that she'd been building her future without him anyway. When she thought about inheriting Beckett-Madeline Enterprises, she never saw herself with him. The work that it would take and the future that lay before her required more sacrifice than she'd been willing to admit.

His not coming was the least important thing in her life at that particular moment.

That night, Christine lay awake. The other students' sounds had long since died down, and the multitude of cicadas that frequented the trees around the dormitories had come to life. A peace lay over everything around her, but she found none. She waffled on whether to call Bodhi back or not. In only an instant, she could reconnect with him, and she was sure he would answer. But to do so would be to show weakness. He should be calling her back and apologizing. For a few precious minutes, she allowed herself the fantasy of him hopping on the next flight to come to surprise her and beg forgiveness. He would show up unannounced outside of her dorm room. She would usher him inside against the rules of the dormitory, and he would stay with her. Somehow, they could hide him from the advisor and other students. That world she could enjoy.

The a.p. call had given her too much information for her to believe that. Beneath his announcement, she'd felt Bodhi's resolve. He wouldn't be coming. And she had a legacy to fulfill that locked her into place.

Christine stood quietly from her bed and began to pace. Strength was a family trait, and he was just some outsider. Christine would eventually own entire companies and through them nations when she inherited her grandfather's company. Then there would be no end to the men pursuing her.

But none for love. If he loved her, he would have called her back.

Unable to sleep, Christine made her way to the common dormitory area to get a drink of water from the mini-kitchen there. Occasionally she heard the sounds of snoring emanating from rooms as she passed. In one room, there echoed the suggestive sounds of grunting, unusual for a Sunday night. Though, she guessed, she still had a lot to learn.

As she entered the kitchen, she stepped into something wet and cold. Disgusted, she pulled her foot up out of a puddle. A wayward piece of ice must have landed there. Turning to her left, she passed by the skinny refrigerator and the replicator nestled up against it. Briefly, the idea of ice-cream passed through her mind, but she thought better of it. She wasn't sure that she would be able to stop if she started.

Instead, she grabbed a glass from the overhead cabinet and filled it to a quarter of an inch. She took a seat at the tiny table that took up the kitchen space and sipped it. She needed to get ahold of herself. Long-distance relationships sometimes did work. Rarely, but it happened. If Bodhi wouldn't come to her, perhaps she could go to him.

She heard a throat clearing around the corner and immediately prepared to go into hiding. There was no way she would greet anyone in her pajamas.

"...and that's all that has to happen, really. We'll set them up in tents."

"That could work."

She recognized Jacob Barnett's voice coming around the corner, followed by Ann Taggart's response. Curious, she lingered in the doorway to watch and see if she was right in who they were. Sure enough, Jacob rounded the corner first and immediately made eye contact.

"Christine, you're up?"

"Just getting some water."

She waved her glass at him, and a splash of water escaped to create another puddle on the floor.

"I'm crashing, Jake," Ann said. "Thanks for your help tonight."

"No problem," he said. "We can pick up tomorrow."

Ann quickly left the room, as Jake helped himself to a glass of water as well. Then he turned to Christine.

"Trouble sleeping?"

She nodded at him, and he continued.

"When I first got here, I had trouble sleeping too. Of

course, for me, it was that my suitemate snored. But if I recall, you don't have that problem. Want to talk about it?"

"It's my boyfriend," she began and then told him about Bodhi and their relationship, leaving out the stuff about the cloned bodies and the ansible connection.

"That's unfortunate."

"I know. He should come out here and be with me."

He reached out and grabbed her hand.

"No, not that. I didn't know you have a boyfriend."

She pulled her hand back quickly. Heat flooded from her cheeks and made her eyes water. At that moment, she missed Bodhi more than she had since she'd arrived.

"Sorry, I made you uncomfortable."

An already horrible night had just gotten much more strange. He looked at her as though his entire world hung on the balance of the next words she had to say. Looks like that hadn't happened to her since her pre-coma days. She had forgotten how it had felt to have that kind of control. She met his eyes and forced an unwavering stare.

"I'm not uncomfortable."

Again he reached for her hand.

"I should have said that long-term relationships are hard. You can't blame yourself if it's not working out."

"But so soon? I thought just a few months, you know?"

"You can't blame yourself."

Christine didn't blame herself.

# 26

## Breaking Up

### *Tuesday, September 8, 2201*

Bodhi called her the next morning. The first few times, he remained cautious about interrupting her classes and spaced his calls out. By the afternoon, his patience had evaporated, and he'd called her five times in a row, to little avail. She could be like that sometimes, though, and he admitted that she had every right to be pissed. The plans that they put together had fallen through, even though she'd done her part. She had pushed him along and helped him hold up his side of the agreement too. With that thought, he tried one more time. To his surprise, this time she connected even if the connection carried with it a feeling of aloofness.

*"I wanted to talk to you about it. You've just been so busy lately."*

*"I know, Bodhi. Maybe it's time to admit that this won't work."*

*"We can still work, Christine. I just need a little time to get established, then I can come to Missoula."*

*"Glad I come in first."*

*"It's not like that. Everything I need to get moving is here, on the west coast. I can't leave now."*

*"It doesn't matter. Obviously, we're young, and we want different things out of life."*

*"I don't want to break up, Christine. I just want to…"*

*"You just want me to wait for you to finally decide that being with me is worth the effort."*

*"No! I just - there has to be an alternative to the body snatching."*

*"Is that what this is about? They're just models, Bodhi. They wouldn't exist if not for the market we created for them. They're lucky to have been created at all."*

Revulsion flashed up inside of him before he could intervene. It spread out over the ansible connection faster than he could think to stop it.

*"So, that's the truth. I repulse you?"*

*"It's just what you said. No, you don't repulse me."*

*"You can't lie over this thing, Bodhi. The truth is there."*

*"But it's not the whole truth! It's just how I felt at that moment."*

*"You can't change it, Bodhi. It doesn't matter anyway. You don't feel the way I do. Your guilt eats at you and drives you to do -whatever it is you're doing."*

*"Virtual worlds, Christine. Virtual bodies, certified, actual-entire virtual worlds."*

He felt awe in the fluctuation of the ansible response. Christine liked the idea; she thought it was amazing. But for some reason, he knew that she hadn't changed her mind.

*"That's a good idea, actually."*

*"I know. And I've been researching how to do it. I almost have it figured out."*

*"Bodhi, just think for a minute. You over there. Me over here. Do you see a future?"*

A startup company meant at least a year or more of sixteen-hour days, traveling, and meetings. Even with Aiden's support and resources, there was too much to do. He flipped the idea around in his head and analyzed every angle he could think of. In the end, there were only two ways he could see it working. One was a long shot. She could give up the future she'd planned on since she was a child and glue her dreams to his. And the other, he knew, would never happen - he could give up his obsession and go to school after all.

"Do - you want to come to join us?"

"What do you think?"

He sighed. There wasn't a chance that would work. He sensed through the ansible connection that the initial hostility of the call had dissipated. He felt no animosity either.

"Bodhi, I'll always love you - we're just not meant to be. Not right now."

"I know. I love you."

"I love you too. And Bodhi?"

"Yeah?"

"Stop calling me so much. It's really distracting during my classes."

"Sorry about that."

"I'll see you when I come back for the holidays, I'm sure. We live in the same building, after all."

The connection was over, and so was their relationship.

The disconnection felt final. Bodhi lay in his bed staring at the ceiling.

It's over.

His eyes welled with tears as he lay unmoving. Even breathing seemed to take more effort than he felt willing to commit. Bodhi hadn't anticipated that she would react so harshly. She gave up without trying. Thoughts accosted him of the times they spent together. He felt connected to her in a way he'd never felt about anyone else before.

Bodhi writhed in his bed, clutching his stomach and chest as the feeling of loneliness exploded through his body. The universe overwhelmed him, and his mission now seemed pointless and dissatisfying. The ideas that before had lurked in his mind, seeking their escape, now cowered in her absence. Some things were too important, though, so he began his work.

Concentrating on the technology brought him solace as he sought refuge in the design process. He visualized the many tendrils of the animus module's nanite web. The number of tendrils varied based on the individual brain neural network, so a universal docking station wouldn't work. He had to be more creative than that. The tumult of his break-up subsided while he worked, so he clutched to it and let his brain follow. Bodhi pulled himself upright on the bed and focused on his animus memories. He found the one with the design plans for the module and reviewed it.

When installed through ingestion, the pill exploded, and nanites flooded the bloodstream. Of the thousands which emerged, only around ten percent cleared the blood-brain barrier to eventually find their way to the hippocampus. They performed two essential functions: connect together to form switching networks, and build more nanites. These switching networks eventually expanded to build memory banks and replace neural processes. By the time the module finished installing, it would cover approximately thirty percent of the brain.

As Bodhi's had been, the modules installed through surgery to speed up the transition came with a pre-formed nanite cluster that acted as a central hub for nanite activity. This localized the module around the ingestion site, and it expanded out from that point into the surrounding brain.

To provide a viable alternative for immortality to cloning, Bodhi needed a way to pull the entire module from the body, a tricky prospect. Further, he needed a way to install the module into a virtual reality program. This was the interface he attempted to design.

He closed his eyes to better visualize a representation of the module expanding into the brain. Bodhi felt his pulse quicken as an idea formed. His vision of the interface device had been the haptic suit he used or the ports the haptic suit connected with. However, what if he used a nanite mesh instead? The animus module sought out and simulated energy flows. As long as there was enough resistance to provide conductive pathways through a type of gel, then the animus module's design would build in to emulate those energy pathways.

With guidance and pre-forming of avatars separately, the module could grow into the avatar control similarly to growing into the human brain.

Excitement replaced the sadness as he turned the idea over in his mind. He would have to talk to Torrent about that, but it felt right. His animus module had already allowed him nearly Torrent's level of expertise. Still, Torrent always seemed to see things he missed. Intuition was not something he got for free with the upgrade.

# 27

## Never Alone Long

*Friday, September 25, 2201*

Christine broke up with Bodhi on principal. The fact was, her long-term plan hadn't included him - not in a real way that accounted for him being more than an accessory. She sometimes had let herself fantasize about the possibilities but had always known that the relationship was doomed. It was better to stop sooner than later.

Why did it hurt so much?

She struggled to get out of bed for her classes. The animus module was the only reason she continued maintaining her grades, as her eidetic memory recorded everything she read. She longed to get past the malaise, but it held fast for two long weeks. The only thing that wrenched her out of it was Jacob Barnett. When he asked her out for a date after class one day, she accepted without the expectation that anything should come of it. She used Jake to distract her from her pain.

Even though he lived in the next dorm over, Jake arrived in

a bright silver volantrae that landed illegally in front of her building. She hadn't even known he owned one but should have guessed. The heir apparent to Emergent Biotechnology would naturally have significant resources. However, she didn't have a volantrae, and she was the heir apparent to Becket-Madeline Enterprises. Her grandfather had told her that she didn't need one to remain focused on her studies. She agreed at the time, but she appreciated the convenience of on-demand transportation.

Christine greeted Jake at her door in a light-green dress with yellow adornments. His high collar and tails were a disappointment that she kept that to herself. Besides, even if he was on a date, she wasn't.

"Christine, you look great!"

"Wow, you too, Jake. Nice volantrae."

"It's a hand-me-down. Dad got a new one, which is still pretty new, so he gave it to me. Shall we?"

He extended his arm, which she immediately took. They boarded from the back doors and sat together on the wide bench seat in the back. The vehicle rose quickly into the air, with little perceivable inertia. Jake began the conversation.

"I know that you just broke up with Bodhi. I want you to know that if you want to we can just, you know, hang out together. Don't feel pressured or anything."

She immediately felt guilty about already deciding the date's outcome. She would like to actually date Jake someday, and she might not get a chance.

"It's okay," she assured him, "it wasn't going to work out anyway. You don't have to tiptoe around me."

She flashed a smile she didn't feel, and he grinned back.

"Okay, then. We're going to have a wonderful time. Downtown Missoula has a performance coming through of Maudling Aggression. It's that show about the Siblings of the Natural Order."

She did remember the group—the largest terrorist group in the United States consisting solely of models. Making rounds in the theaters was the story of the tragic romance of the organization's leader, Phineas Lancaster. Many of their performances suffered from protests because of the glorification of violence, but the show was about love.

"I thought that was sold out?"

"It is now. I bought tickets just after you got to campus."

"So your original date canceled?"

He looked somewhat ashamed at this, and for a moment, she thought she would have to demand to be returned. Christine refused to be a second choice.

"Not exactly. You're going to think that I'm weird."

"Why?"

"I wanted to ask you out as soon as I met you, Christine."

Christine hadn't considered the possibility. Jake was friendly and someone she had confided in often. The idea that he was pining away seemed a little ridiculous.

"What if Bodhi and I hadn't broken up?"

"Then I would have had an amazing time in the front row of one of my favorite musicals of all time. And I would have been happy for you."

The energy that they shared prevented Christine from maintaining her defenses. She enjoyed the musical, even so far as to get teary-eyed when Lancaster was discovered by the site-boss with his daughter, Tess. The consequential beating was widely considered what launched Lancaster on his trajectory toward becoming one of the most feared leaders Siblings of the Natural Order ever had.

After the show, she and Jake walked from the playhouse to a wine bar. The owner came out to greet them personally and whisked them away to the VIP section overseeing the musical acts which followed, one after another, below. She found herself reaching for Jake's hand as they took their seats. It seemed natural to do so, and he smiled at her and squeezed hers in return.

The evening passed perfectly. Even when Jake dropped her off, he landed his volantrae in precisely the same position and walked her to her dorm room. Jake didn't try to go in and only gave her a kiss on her cheek.

"Thank you for a wonderful evening," she'd told him and meant it.

"I enjoyed tonight. Do you want to go out again soon? I feel like we should and see if we get sick of each other."

She laughed at that and stepped toward him.

"Yes, I would like that."

She leaned up and gave him a quick kiss on the cheek as well before disappearing into her room. On the other side of her door, she clutched her hands to her chest and smiled widely. Jake was perfect. Like her, he was on the same professional trajectory. They would be a power-couple - the symbolic combination of Beckett-Madeline Enterprises and Emergent Biotechnology, soon to be made real. Their children would be born into royalty.

# 28

## Obsession Blooms

### *Saturday, September 26, 2201*

The idea forming in his mind captured Bodhi's imagination. As long as he built, he didn't feel the rejection and loneliness that lurked in his heart. He'd plotted a course and only needed a little money to get some tools that he needed. He rubbed his eyes and stared at the wall, exploring mental possibilities. That's when Aiden unexpectedly walked through his door without knocking. He shifted his gaze to the man's figure in the doorway.

"What's on your mind?"

Aiden used his most fatherly voice, higher than his usual, and leaning into the inquisitive upswing at the end.

"What if you could gain immortality guilt-free?"

This caught Aiden off-guard.

"Guilt-free?"

"Yeah. In the Labyrinth, I saw that Beckett-Madeline Enterprises have teamed with Emergent Biotechnology to offer the animus module to people. They're calling it Immortality. The catch is that you have to kill a model as I did."

"You feel guilty about that."

Something about the way Aiden said it - as though it was an observation and not a question - irritated him.

"Only as guilty as I *should* feel, having killed someone. But that's not what I want to talk about. Imagine if there was another option?"

"Like what?"

"Like virtual reality, Aiden. What if you lived forever in a perfect world?"

"Heaven?"

"No. Like earth, but before Equilibrium, and before Akson. And a world in which you only die if you want to see what it feels like."

"I'm not sure I understand."

"Sure you do. I'm this."

Bodhi reached his index finger up and tapped the scar behind his left ear.

"It's talking to my body, telling it what to do. But this module has severed my need for it. If I die tomorrow - this could go into another body, and I could pick up where I left off. It's simple - the idea anyway. Why use a body at all?"

With that, Bodhi explained the latest incarnation of his new idea. A nanite mesh gel could guide the animus module to integrate with virtual reality.

"This is possible?"

"I think so. I ran it by ..."

"By who?"

"Don't tell mom."

"Bodhi, who have you been talking to?"

"I ran it by Rochester. She seems to think that it can work."

"And who is Rochester?"

"It's imperative that you keep this a secret. I'll tell mom, don't worry."

Aiden squinted at him, which looked so ridiculous behind his tiny rounded glasses that Bodhi realized he hadn't seen that look of distrust from the man before.

"Tell me."

"Ordell Bentley - the model mom saved. He came by a month or so ago. We talked a bit about another possible approach to immortality. He's going to give me some money to keep looking and some help. Rochester is the help - she's a technical genius and is trying out some of these ideas."

The look disappeared from Aiden's face. It was replaced by the far-off look of concentration he sometimes got when he considered whether or not to buy a particular company. Bodhi took that change as a good sign.

"It's a good start. What if your virtual world was a sovereign nation?"

"Can that be done?"

"I don't know. But a lot of people want to interact in the world still. If it was an entity - a nation or even a state - that could allow trade negotiations. A virtual world would have social problems just like this one. Why re-invent the wheel? That's a huge undertaking. Are you sure you want to take that project on? That's a lifetime project, and you're not even sixteen yet."

"This body is eighteen years old. His name was Rutger Briggs. I'm not even sure he knew that he was dying. If I'm old enough to carry his death on my shoulders, I'm old enough to work to redeem myself."

Bodhi didn't look at Aiden after that - he didn't have to. He could feel the pitying sadness dripping from Aiden's gaze already. That wasn't the point. He continued to stare at the wall, imagining the life that Joseph might have had when Aiden interrupted.

"Okay. So you'll need a business plan and probably need to do some market research."

"Market research for immortality?"

"Well, yes. You're not the only option. I understand what you're trying to do, but you can't let your idealism get in the way of the business. That's how I tanked my first company."

Bodhi's turned his head back toward Aiden, eyes wide. He'd known that Aiden had money, but they'd never talked about where that money came from.

Aiden continued, "My first company was in water desalinization technology during Equilibrium. The process, slower than the ones that ultimately took the market, was completely carbon-neutral. I assumed there would be enough interest in not making the Equilibrium problem worse so that folks would buy, even at four times the price."

"What happened?"

"Well, the business failed, of course. I lost several million dollars of other people's money. I couldn't get more than one round of investment, and that evaporated quickly. I would do a proof-of-concept first and estimate the cost. If you can segment the market, then you have a chance. Start at the high-end, and make it fancy. Make it seem sexier than physical bodies, and you have a chance."

Bodhi took in Aiden's tie-dye shirt and bun and unassuming glasses.

"I forget you're a businessman sometimes."

"By design. People are much more forthcoming if they think you don't know what you're talking about."

Aiden winked, then sighed and shifted his weight. He pulled the loose strands on the left side of his face and tucked them behind his ear.

"I made my first hundred-million by the time I was twenty. Now, all I do is venture capital. I invest in companies all over the world. I don't like to talk about it. Once people find out, everyone has an idea they need money for. I'd like to help you out with this - if you want. You don't seem to need money, but some business knowledge might be useful. A working prototype is the best move you can make right now. Create that virtual world. Get an animus module integrated into it, and show that it works."

"I'm not sure how to do all that. I need a live animus module to do the integration."

"You need to talk some more with Torrent then. Start knocking down some of these barriers. Only I wouldn't mention Ordell or Rochester to him."

"Yeah, I didn't think that would be a good idea either. Thanks Aiden."

"It's no trouble. And Bodhi," Aiden said as he turned to leave, "talk to your mother."

He would, but first he had to do what he'd been putting off since the idea's inception: talk to Torrent.

The only trouble Bodhi had after revealing the idea to Torrent was getting him to shut up about it.

"You can absolutely do that," he spat out. "Very innovative - nice work. To test mine, I exposed two ports on the module that I used to do virtual simulations with it outside of the body. The one that you had installed still has those ports - since the generation two model requires a pill to ingest, and we didn't have that kind of time. I imagine you could use those as a template to grow a port interface, and then probably you might be able to see for yourself if it works."

"You mean like a docking station for to my implant?"

"Yes, something like that. I ran all kinds of external diagnostics before I did the implant."

"How do I 'dock' - to what?"

"Well, you'd have to expose the ports, of course. They're under the skin."

"Expose the ports. Do you mean cut me open?"

With that, Torrent lifted his right arm and pulled up his sleeve to reveal an ugly scar.

"We all make sacrifices for science. But I think we can do yours with a lot less scarring. Just need to put in a transdermal patch."

"Okay, great. That's all."

"It wouldn't be hard," said Torrent, "but anything happening to your animus module is risky. Talk to your mother. If you get her permission, I can help."

Talk to your mother - again.

His mother was napping on the couch when Bodhi entered the suite. That seemed to be her favorite place now. Without the garden that she usually cared for, there wasn't much for her to do. Bodhi adjusted well to the new body, which meant that his hyper-diligent mother lacked enough work to keep her thoroughly engaged. When he woke her, she seemed disoriented.

"Mom, are you awake?" He asked her, knowing she was asleep.

"Wha - yes. Bodhi, hi." She smacked her lips and slowly pulled herself upright.

"Good. Do you remember the business I wanted to start?"

She nodded slowly, still groggy.

"I think I figured out the last part of the problem. I talked it over with Torrent, and he agrees that it might work."

Her eyes shot open at the sound of Torrent's name. He cut in before she could say anything - that wasn't the question he wanted an answer to.

"But it would take one small modification on my animus module to test."

Bodhi thought he saw her shake briefly and then stop. She stared at him as though she saw through his head. But she didn't say no.

"Are you sure that's wise?"

"Mom, they're pre-selling immortality now. I saw an ad in the Labyrinth. How many people will die because of that?'

"After all of this - is it worth putting yourself at risk again?"

"Yes. People will die."

"Does Aiden know?"

Bodhi nodded.

"Then I guess that's that."

She gave him a weak smile and reached out to hug him. Her arms were viselike as they pulled him in. Bodhi realized that she hadn't asked what the change was. Likely it didn't matter - it was all danger to her. He tried to pull away, but she wouldn't let him. Three more seconds passed before his mother finally released him.

"One more thing, Mom."

She looked up at him, and he saw tears in her eyes. "What else?"

He took a deep breath.

"I've been talking to Ordell."

Her tired eyes shimmered for a second, then looked down and away. She deflated like a balloon that had just been pierced.

"I thought that might be behind this."

"It's not behind this. This is my idea - he's just helping."

"It's okay, Bodhi. It's not as though I have a right to judge. Get help where you need it - just be careful? SNO - they hurt people sometimes - whatever Ordell tells you."

"I know. I am careful."

"I love you."

"Me too, Mom."

He meant it. The anger he felt towards his mother would probably never go away. But there was more to her than being his mother - depth he hadn't noticed before. Her body quaked when he held her as he felt her tears fall gather on his shoulder. She reacted to that moment as a moment of loss while he vibrated with excitement that his creation was one step closer toward becoming a reality.

Without the animus module, and inhibited by disease, Bodhi's life before consisted of gaming on the Labyrinth for short stints, and sleeping most of the rest of the time. His new body, and the animus module memory storage, gave him energy he'd never known possible. The idea that other people lived life without the constant threat of collapse and with the mental energy to focus was a thought he still hadn't completely grasped.

He'd thought the first thing that he would do was spend more time gaming if he was ever well enough to spend longer than half an hour a stretch. Now, that seemed like a waste of the strength that he'd been given, and in a sense, a waste of the life he'd taken. Instead he would make a difference in the world, and he thought the animus module was the place to begin. The device had already successfully carried his entire consciousness from one body to another - so the hard part was, in a sense, done. He would build a virtual world - one with which the animus module could integrate. A world like that would be better than reality. Death would have no meaning, there would be no sacrifice of life. Guilt-free immortality was better than becoming a serial killer.

From Torrent, Bodhi learned that the human brain held over one-hundred billion neurons, each one reinforcing messages between some neighbors while dismissing messages from others. They were like tiny galaxies within the head of every one of the fifty trillion people that existed on the planet. These factories processed every thought or sensation that came into the body.

After learning and growing and forging connections, the brain's function reduced to five inter-dependent networks. Each network controlled sub-functions that together built an entire personality. Memories informed, feedback loops developed, and interconnected neurons segregated into areas of functionality that behaved independently of each other. These are the components that the animus module emulated, the building blocks of a person. Rather than attempt to model behavior on the neuronal level, which would have required a hundred-billion nanite clusters, each larger than an actual neuron requiring the space of a small house, the animus module and nanites worked to identify and model regions of behavior, reducing the work to the chip itself, which also recorded every sensational experience in more detail than the brain was capable, and tendrils that stretched from that into the brain region that looked, if removed, something like a jellyfish covered in slime mold.

Designed to work in the mind, transplants between bodies were straightforward. Upon extraction, a special tool was used to "wind" the tentacles together and compress the entire network into something the size of a fingertip. This same tool could be used to insert the chip into another brain and accelerate expansion back into the new brain.

The most significant question that he needed to answer was how to interface with a virtual world when there was no brain into which the chip could extend, as Torrent explained. The ports could work for short-term testing out of certain parameters, but eventually, there would have to be a way to connect an animus module in all its extended, messy, glory to whatever virtual world that Bodhi could create. This was only one complication.

The other, Torrent continued, was that each animus module synchronized events from different sensory inputs and automatically adjusted timings so that experiences happened together. This gave the impression that sights and sounds came together, even if they weren't actually perceived at the same time. In the world, events propagated and audio and visual data followed the natural laws of physics. In a virtual world, these laws had to be programmed in. This meant a lot of processing, even beyond what drove the Labyrinth, if he wanted to be able to compete at a scale that would make a difference.

This is where having a direct connection to the Labyrinth coupled with a new eidetic memory paid off. After the chat with Torrent, Bodhi began searching for what the Labyrinth was comprised of. He learned that the entire system was hosted in three different locations equidistant around the globe from each other. Banks of twelve 128-cubit quantum computers, each with operational performance of -135 Ha. Though impressive, the devices were state-of-the-art when Labyrinth was founded decades before. Newer hardware topped this performance easily.

The Labyrinth separated its virtual interface into different enclaves with access controlled by the annoying user interface that Bodhi hated. The reason for this, Bodhi also learned. Processing between QPU outside of a bank introduced latency that threw off the immersive experience. The experience was "glitchiness," and while that was fine for Labyrinth, a system that was used largely to find information quickly or use as a launch-point for games, actually spending twenty-four hours non-stop living in that type system was impossible. Bodhi tried for seventeen hours and found the experience unbearable.

The solution was known, only didn't really exist. Connecting the banks together in real-time meant speeds that technology couldn't handle. Even ansible protocol would lag under the type of information flow necessary to create a believable virtual world.

Bodhi dedicated a day and a half to solving that problem. He took meals in his room, and pared back useless interactions as he scoured the Labyrinth for a solution to a problem he only barely understood when he stumbled onto a small company out of Waterloo in Ontario, Canada.

Positrons. The long-neglected anti-matter relatives of electrons, were being used in Waterloo by Graystone Machinations to create a network topology of switches. For this system, the network itself managed switching, as opposed to requiring specific switching hubs - the model used for generations. The system used both positrons and electrons as communication energy flows in two networks that mingled together. Different points in the network caused the flows to interact giving off tiny bursts of energy. The graphic simulation showed it as interwoven wires with bursts of light flaring up and disappearing.

The speeds were faster than any known network on the planet. But with only an experimental prototype, and no practical at-scale application yet due to cost, the company struggled financially. The stability of their network approach was in question, and even the major tech players didn't want the risk that could come from the energy potential of such a network of opposites. In a year, several business analysts predicted the company would be out of business. "Maybe positrons will be used in technology someday, but today is not that day," stated the president of Prescient when he weighed in.

Unlike Bodhi, they had choices. The speeds that they needed weren't the same as the ones Bodhi was after. For his idea to work, he needed a problem solved. And Graystone Machinations may have had just the solution.

# 29

## Salesmanship

### *Saturday, October 30, 2201*

"The problem is that nobody can tell what your plan is. Do you have a plan?"

The words cut as Caldwell threw them at Ordell. Two months prior, they had been a united front, and even then his plan had been more of an idea. Supporting Bodhi solved two problems. The first was that it kept his friend's child out of harms way for the time being. As long as he worked to undermine the Immortality program, they would never use him as a poster child, and even Siblings of the Natural Order wouldn't consider him a reasonable target for violence. The complication, and the reason Caldwell's voice escalated when she talked about Bodhi, was that the boy stayed in such constant contact with someone who all were convinced would be a real problem for SNO should she continue on her trajectory. Ordell likewise saw the threat.

"You want me to do what, exactly?"

As he shifted to stand, he placed one hand beneath Caldwell's head and lifted it from his lap as fiery red tendrils fell through his fingers. Then Ordell slid sideways from beneath her, laying her head gently on the cushion which had just supported him. His eye caught the two dark smudges on the carpet as he did so. It would have taken so little to replace the carpet in the room, or even put in the more durable single-mold flooring most modern homes used. His construction skills could easily have handled the job in an afternoon, yet nearly sixteen years after he'd lost his first love, he had never brought himself to do so.

"Authorize the strike."

"She's in Fouriedon. How many lives will be lost if we attack? How much public opinion will we lose if they find out we did it?"

"This is the time to do it. Send in Rochester's girl. She doesn't have any tattoos. She could get in and out, and nobody would notice."

"For what the girl *might* do?"

"No. For what Emergent Biotechnology will do with that girl. She's their *piece de resistance*. Without her, the entire program fails."

"It's still killing, Caldwell."

He propped his head between his hands as he sat, now with his back to her. He felt her fingers slide over his shoulders and her head press into his back.

"I know it's hard, Ordell. That's why we're Captains. We make these decisions."

"I know," he muttered. "And after the raids on the reclamation facilities, this should be nothing. You didn't see how he looked at her, Caldwell. He looked at her the same way I look at you."

He felt her lips press against the back of his neck.

"That's why I love you Ordell. You're so empathetic."

Ordell shrugged off her kiss and slid out of her arms before turning to face her. If Caldwell was already turning on his idea, then how could he expect to convince any of the other five?

"Caldwell, I need you to back me on this."

He met her eyes, which had morphed back to purple from green, aligning with her more combative mood. Her nostrils flared and she pressed toward him, filling in the gap that he'd left. Her tense neck muscles strained and her shoulders tightened as he looked on. He could see the struggle playing out in real time in her mind.

"Ordell, I backed you already. You said we should support Bodhi, and presented him as a wunderkind who would give us a non-violent way to wage this war. I agreed with you, and I put my name down beside yours. So did Rochester. Even Lancaster signed on, remember? Our names are right there with yours. If this fails, then we all may get demoted, or worse, excommunicated."

"It's only been three months, though. How much could you expect him to accomplish in three months?"

"That's not the problem. The problem is that there doesn't seem to be a plan. Willson asks when we can expect to see results, and it doesn't seem like Bodhi's any closer to a solution than day 1. If there was an actual plan, that would be something we could take to them."

"But we do have a plan."

"What is it?" She tried to wrap her arms around him again, but he again shrugged her off.

"Ordell, don't take it out on me. We're on the same team. Would you rather I told you everything was fine only to find ourselves homeless on the streets?"

"Would that be so bad? I've got money, and we could go to Canada. We'd be really free then."

"And Christine would die, right? If that's the case, why not just authorize the action and not have to flee? We - I - have a lot of work to do in the states. I can't go to Canada and leave this for someone else to clean up. Can you?"

"I guess not." He rubbed his hand across his face and finally turned back to face her again. "Let me talk to him this afternoon. I'll work with him to put a timeline to it, and we'll have something for the group tomorrow."

"Today, Ordell. Willson is making inroads and we can't wait."

"Fine. Today."

"I love you, Ordell."

"Me too." He let out his breath and twisted his neck until it popped. Then her fingers dug in as he straightened his head back up and Ordell closed his eyes, focusing on the muscles that the fingers pressed into as she kneaded his neck and shoulders. He wished for a plan. The conversations he'd had with Bodhi revolved around the animus module, but he couldn't fully understand the science. Partially, that was because like the animus module, the science for what Bodhi thought would have to happen still had to be invented. Ordell didn't know how to put a timeline to that.

A short while later, after Caldwell left for the office, Ordell decided to give Bodhi a call and relay the position they were in. Bodhi answered, and after Ordell informed him, he met silence for five seconds.

"A schedule?"

"That's what they want."

"When we don't even have a prototype?"

"I know, it's not easy. But we have to give them something, or else, well…"

"They kill Christine. But this isn't a month's long thing we're trying to do. Even with Torrent helping unfettered, it's going to be a couple of years before we can even get a prototype working."

"So two years?"

"For a prototype. *If* it works on the first try, which it won't."

"Four years?"

"Closer. At least that gives us a shot."

"And how long until the Immortality program starts?"

"I don't know. What did Rochester say about it?"

"Last time we spoke, she said they hadn't had another success since the two of you. So a couple of years at least, but it's going to be close. Four years?"

"I don't know, Ordell. I really don't."

"I'm going to tell them four years then. That's at least something and gives us some breathing room."

"Okay. When are you coming back out here?"

Ordell pondered the question as he watched the image of the boy pace against the mantle in the living room where Ordell sat.

"I can come out if you need me. What's the matter?"

The image paused.

"N-nevermind. I'll be fine."

This was the other part of the problem with Bodhi heading a project. The most significant stressor in Bodhi's life was the body in which he lived, and which he could never escape. Bodhi began again.

"I signed a DNR the other day. If I die, there won't be another for me. I - I thought you'd want to know that."

Ordell could hear the guilt underpinning those words. Before he could respond, his communicator chimed in his ear. He wasn't expecting any calls.

"Bodhi, I have to go."

He disconnected and connected the next call, projecting an image of an agitated Caldwell pacing.

"Oh, good. You're there. Ordell, they're moving to kill her."

She stared at him from behind a wayward strand of hair that she didn't bother to move.

"Did you hear me?"

"Wh-"

"It was Willson. He built a coalition, looks like he got the East on board."

His mind raced through his options while part of him posed the ever present question of whether he'd done enough already. Christine wasn't the ally that Bodhi had become, leaving his relationship behind to pursue a strategy to help Ordell's cause. Then it occurred to him what Bodhi might have been upset about earlier. The boy was only fifteen, no matter what his body said. That step must have been monumentally difficult for him. Bodhi thought back to Aayushi. It never got easier. If they killed Christine, and remedied the problem that they feared she would become, it would go the rest of the way toward crushing Bodhi. How long until he was next?

"Ordell?"

"I'm thinking. Do we have any friends in Seattle right now?"

"Rochester's on the way to Maine. Her intelligence network is there, but she'd never ask them to go against orders."

"Any idea when or where this is going to happen?"

"They were very vague about it. I don't think they trust us. Willson is carrying it out."

"Christine's at university now, right? Missoula - is that correct?"

"I think so. At least we don't have any branches there. What are you thinking?"

"Not sure. If they kill that girl, we lose Bodhi. He'll ask me if they did it. He already knows the stakes."

Her image leaned back as though she rested her shoulders against an invisible wall. He forgot sometimes how beautiful she was.

"Are you going to go?"

"I think I have to. Is there any other way to handle the situation? She's not going to believe some strange model calling her from nowhere. I just need to go, and keep an eye out. Maybe I can talk to whomever Willson sends and explain the stakes. I know you don't believe in this approach anymore, Monica. Thanks for telling me."

"I love you Ordell. You know I'll back you. Guessing you won't be there when I get home?"

He smiled and shrugged. "Probably not. I'm going to finally get an education."

Caldwell laughed and smiled back at him as she took a few steps forward and then her grin faded as her now olive-green eyes pierced into his. That was her color for sadness.

"I mean it, Ordell. Be safe and don't get in the line of fire. Just have the conversation, model to model, and come back to me."

## *Sunday, October 31, 2201*

Ordell exited the tiny plane into the cool, crisp autumn air of Minnesota. He felt a warm blast from behind him as the airplane gave up the last of the exported League City climate. A regional airport, there wasn't much more than a tarmac before him. No terminals or anything else, and a single angry-looking taxi driver graced the stand, waiting, it seemed, for anyone other than a large model with a half-decimated bar code across his wrist. Given that Ordell was fifty-percent of the cargo of the small plane, and the rest was made up of brown boxes carefully netted together, the irritated man had little choice but to take him on as a client.

As Ordell approached, the man jumped out of the vehicle to retrieve what looked like a plastic wrap from the back of the car and spread it across the back seat, muttering something he couldn't quite make out and that Ordell was quite certain he didn't want to hear. Instead, he focused on the mission, understanding then that he was the least conspicuous choice for the job. Still, he hadn't much of a choice in the matter if he wanted to save the girl. Nobody else, not even Caldwell, wanted her saved. The granddaughter of the untouchable Gallatin Hamilton made a compelling target for kidnapping on any day. As a blow to the man who now owned controlling stakes in the two dominant cloning organizations in the United States, her death would send an unforgettable message.

Perhaps. Bodhi had told him she was enrolled as a distant cousin, a message that he'd relayed back to the rest of SNO leadership when he thought the idea of a strike was behind him. The general public wouldn't get the message, perhaps. Her death would be a tragic accident. Ordell even doubted that Gallatin would get the message to change course away from the Immortality program. He was the type of man who hit back harder. On all levels, the idea of her being a target made no long term sense. All it would do is ease the nerves of a few unimaginative people.

Ordell picked his bag up from where the worker, who wasn't a model, had dropped it on the pavement without so much as a greeting. He turned his attention to the taxi, which to his surprise, now waited with the door open for him. He slid in, ignoring the rumple of plastic beneath him. This wasn't the first time he'd been too unclean to share the seat that others took for granted.

"Where to?"

"Missoula, sir."

The man seemed to perk up at the formal address that Ordell had delivered with the intent of conveying the message that "this was a good one." As long as he didn't stray too far from the subservient model here on his master's business, then this man, now standing on the other side of the door he'd just passed through, would take him wherever he wanted to go.

"The university?"

"My owner wants me to deliver this bag to one of the professors there. He would have come himself, but he's giving lectures and its too far out of the way."

The man closed the door and crossed around the car, entering into the driver's seat. Once he settled in, he looked at Ordell in the rear view mirror.

"What's in the bag?"

"Don't know sir. He only asked me to deliver it. I suppose it's too important to send on its own."

"Sounds like a big responsibility." The man pulled the vehicle over the pavement as Ordell marveled at the feeling of the tires beneath him. It had been ages since he'd been in an actual car.

"Yes, sir. If I do it right, he'll give me a steak tonight."

"Sounds like a good man."

The entire time the man spoke, his eyes kept darting up into the rear view mirror. At first, Ordell thought it was his size that caught the man's attention. Then he realized that the man's eyes kept drifting downward to the bag that Ordell had brought with him - a bag full of clean clothes and his pinamu tablet. The man had bought into his story a little too well. Ordell clutched the bag more tightly to drive it home that he was protecting it, and the man's attention turned back to the road.

"There are good people out here. We don't get many of your kind."

"I'll be gone as soon as I can, sir."

"See to it. There are people out here who aren't as open minded as I am."

The rest of the trip passed in silence while Ordell pondered just how open-minded the man thought he was, given his reaction and ease of navigating the role that Ordell had invited him into. Doubtless in his own mind the man's actions of layering thick plastic over the passenger seat was the pinnacle of acceptance. The car wound up and down the hills, and Ordell began to understand why they were in a car instead of a volantrae.

There were no towers. The volantrae navigated by use of global positioning for location, and periodic markers for indications of where the proper lanes were. These were established by the use of towers that marked the skyways. Without the towers, volantrae had to follow the paved roads just like other cars, which meant that their utility was a lot less out here. It wouldn't have made a lot of sense to drive a volantrae out here without any of the benefits.

He began to see towers finally as they passed a sign that Fouriedon University neared, which made Ordell breathe an involuntary sigh of relief. The feeling passed as soon as it had arrived when he realized he didn't have a second stage to his plan. The man dropped him at the university gate and he looked out over the campus lawn at rows of metallic structures that all looked the same to him. In one of those was Christine Hamilton, going by Christine Turner, and possibly her would-be assassin.

# 30

## Stalker

*Sunday, October 31, 2201*

Christine was well aware of the envious stares of other girls who probably, like her, only attended church because Jake was there. She'd made friends, or at least, acquaintances among some of her jealous rivals that went as deep as her skin, and the superficiality had become grating. Christine was good at it. Her entire childhood consisted of silent competitions and subtle behavior cues and controlling the conversation when she wasn't even in the room. That was fourteen-year-old Christine though. Just as she'd taken over a more mature body, her emotions had grown to fill it. The constant threats and veiled attacks had quickly morphed from inducing entertain and exciting nostalgia to producing anxiety and exhaustion. Were it not for Jake's religious conviction, Christine would have foregone the battleground of church altogether.

The one redeeming quality for her was the excuse it gave her to buy and wear expensive dresses. With her grandfather's money, and her mother's taste, this was one area at which she'd always excelled. Nobody in the pews attracted more attention than she did. If the preacher had been actually present instead of a hologram giving sermons at multiple churches at once, Christine was positive that her gold-flecked green gown with ivory kerchief and matching gloves and lace veil would have even distracted him. The veil was admittedly overkill, but she saw it and had to have it.

"Beautiful sermon today, don't you think?" One of Jake's want-to-be groupies touched Christine by the elbow for greeting. She plastered on a smile and turned to face her opponent.

"Poignant what he said about envy, wasn't it?"

The other woman's innocent grin wavered for a moment, just long enough that Christine saw confirmation in the flickering emotion and turned away before she could reply. Oblivious Jake extended an elbow, which Christine took, and the two stepped toward the exit of the building, making the necessary greetings and waves and nods.

"I hope you weren't too bored," he said as they crossed the threshold out into the cool autumn air.

"Bored? No, I wouldn't say that."

"What would you say?"

She turned to face him, careful to smile and meet his eyes. Just a few inches taller than her, she tilted her neck as she did, and he rested his hands on her waist, meeting her gaze.

"Devastatingly bored. Is this every week for you?"

"Draining, isn't it? I know. But I made a promise to my parents before I came that I would keep up attendance. Thank you for coming."

He leaned in for a kiss and out of the side of her eye,

Christine noticed the girl that she'd slighted staring at them. She closed her eyes and pushed her lips upwards to his, hopefully driving the point home that Jake wasn't on the market anymore. His lips were soft like kissing a velvet pillow, and dry. He didn't even part them a little. Christine couldn't help her mind reaching back and comparing the kiss to the passionate wet kisses passed between her and Bodhi so many months before. She pulled way quickly before Jake could pick up on her body language, and turned, to see the vulture of a girl still circling, with a wide grin on her face. She saw.

"Can we leave?"

"Back to my dorm room?"

She looked him in the eyes and nodded slightly. It would be one of those lazy days in bed, and after an emotionally exhausting morning, that was fine with her. She scanned the perimeter to see if any other harpies hovered nearby. Not that she had to worry. Jake was the type of man to do exactly what he committed to doing, and right now, he was committed to Christine. That made her smile as she pulled in to place her head against his shoulder.

That was when she saw a man standing next to a tree in the distance. Something in her memory matched the man with someone she had seen long before, but she couldn't place the memory. Jake must have felt her body tense up, because he directed his gaze toward where she looked.

"Do you know that man?"

"No, what about him?"

"They're filthy, aren't they? Look at how big he is. Does he really think nobody sees him there? He has no business on a college campus."

"I think I've seen him before."

"Really? How can you tell? They all look alike to me."

"No, I mean it. Maybe...I can't remember. The scar on his

face, that's something you don't forget."

"Has he been following you? That's even worse. I heard they do that sometimes."

She pushed back away from him.

"What are you talking about?"

"Models. No souls - that's what I heard. They can't help it. They're just not like us."

The hate in his eyes projected daggers toward the man, who seemed to detect them and turned to walk back to wherever he'd been before deciding to watch the church exit.

"No souls?"

"Ask the preacher what he thinks about it. He'll tell you. They're only here for one suffering. Sons and daughters of Ham, they're made to toil the earth."

"You actually believe that stuff?"

He turned his gaze back to her, and his face softened more quickly than she had thought possible. He turned from a hostile, angry person back into Jake in less than a second, putting on that cool smile that he always wore.

"Oh, no, that's just what I heard. That's all. Did you see the size of him? He made that tree look like a twig."

With that, he laid his arm over her shoulder and steered the two of them back toward his dormitory while she tried to make sense out of what had just happened. They'd tripped over something in him, and she wanted to know what. But how to start that conversation while avoiding the hostility was something she knew she would have to work out. As they crossed the quad, she thought she caught a glimpse of the man hiding behind the library, but couldn't be certain because of the shadows.

Christine left Jake to entertain himself in his room. The comments earlier had disturbed her enough that the idyllic morning she'd hoped for had become irrecoverable. Instead, she resigned herself to studying in her room alone, even though she'd gotten to the point that studying wasn't technically necessary for her anymore. But she felt guilty not putting in at least some work. The sun warmed up the day so that by the early afternoon, the quad filled with students and she found that she had the dormitory building mostly to herself. She flipped through a book on business strategy as her mind wandered.

As it always did, her brain settled on Bodhi, and not the post-operation Bodhi. She though of the boy in the elevator, who collapsed and whose mother she had become friends with. That thought reminded her that she needed to call Harper sometime soon. She had neglected that relationship for far too long. But it was Bodhi who captured her attention. Even after the operation, whenever they connected through the module, it was always the skinny black-haired boy she saw. The fact that he had broken his word and left a scared girl to navigate this new world alone brought her close to tears every time. She longed to reach out and connect with him again, but she knew she would only try to convince him to come, and he would only say no again.

Angry at herself, Christine rose to her feet and decided on what her distraction had to be. The schoolwork wasn't enough, and Jake had become irritating though she was certain that feeling would pass soon - it hadn't yet. The only alternative was tea. A warm cup of chamomile was exactly what she could use. She slid her feet into thick slippers and left her room, taking the brief hallway to the shared kitchen. As she turned the corner, she froze in her tracks.

"It's you."

"Yes, Ordell Bentley." The man was larger than the refrigerator, though the way he moved was fluid and smooth. There was something unnatural about it.

"Where do I know you from?" She asked the question and

searched her organic memories at the same time. Her animus memories are what answered the question though. The scene popped into her head of being in the H Hotel lobby, talking with Bodhi, and being interrupted by this tower of a man. At that time, he hadn't seemed so large, but that may have been because the lobby ceiling was so high that everyone who entered shrank.

"You remember. I can see it in your face."

"I do." She stepped around him, faking the bravery that she didn't feel, and punched her code into the replicator. It began whirring in the background as she turned to face him.

"Why are you here, Ordell?" She made careful eye contact when she did so, letting him know that she wasn't intimidated. This was a lie.

"Watching you," he said. The words sent a shiver up through her spine and into her shoulder blades. She stepped back from him before she was aware that she was doing it.

"No, I don't mean it like that. I mean, I'm keeping an eye on you."

"Try again," she told him.

"It will take a minute to explain," he said, and motioned to her to sit at the table.

"No, we can't talk here. Someone will walk in."

Her tea beeped its completion, so she retrieved it from the replicator.

"Come with me."

After checking the hallway for occupants, she shimmied quickly across and up the stairs to her room, Ordell in tow behind her. She felt insane allowing this man into her personal space, but she felt that there was something important in what he had to say. She seated herself on her bed while he paced.

"Your grandfather is a problem for us."

The way he said the words cut through her. Worse than the

words was his gaze with sunken eyes and lacking any attempt at kindness. Something about him wasn't quite right. He continued, and the conversation didn't improve.

"I've been trying to save your life," the man said as he slumped down. He took up almost half of her bed and it sunk beneath his weight. Christine didn't understand - her life wasn't in jeopardy.

"Listen carefully, Christine. You and your grandfather are targets of an assassination plot. The Siblings of the Natural Order consider you both to be threats."

Nobody was supposed to know that she was Christine Hamilton, but the very people who they'd designed the subterfuge to circumvent already had the information. She would have to tell her grandfather that someone inside of his organization couldn't be trusted. She thought back to the conversation with Bodhi, which the large man had previously interrupted. Was it possible that on top of failing to keep his word and leaving her stranded, he was also the reason that this man sat in her dorm room?

"Bodhi did this."

He didn't answer, and only stared at her.

"Okay then. You're here. What, are you going to kill me now?"

He seemed shocked at the idea and pulled his body backwards almost falling over.

"No, not me. This isn't a threat. I'm here to warn you."

"You warned me then. What good is that other than to scare me?"

He ran his hands through his hair and looked lost. He hadn't thought it through - that was written all over his face, and the idea that he'd come to her without fully thinking it through told her that whatever the threat was, it was also imminent.

"I don't know," he admitted to her. "Caldwell and I didn't

talk through that part."

"Caldwell? Like Bodhi's aunt?"

He shook his head.

"No. Like my girlfriend. She warned me and I came here."

"Are they sisters?"

As soon as she asked the question, she knew better. Ordell was a model. Caldwell was probably a model. And though Bodhi hadn't told her so explicitly, Aunt Kiera must have been a model too. So many models around him, she began to understand his reaction to the treatment and the cold way he'd treated his mother after awakening. Ordell didn't acknowledge her question. Instead, he only walked to the window and peeked through the curtain.

"I don't know when, and I don't know how. You're right, this is the most useless rescue attempt ever. But if I didn't try, Bodhi would never speak to me again. And neither would Harper."

"Welcome to the club."

He let go of the curtain and turned to face her.

"What are you talking about?"

"Bodhi doesn't speak to me anymore either. Rather I don't speak to him."

"You two seemed to get along well. What happened?"

"He happened."

She didn't say more about it, and instead changed the subject back.

"If you're here to warn me, thank you. I'm sorry I was rude." It wouldn't do any good to lash out at the man, and it wasn't fair to do so. Well thought out plan or not, the fact was that at least she would be aware of who and why when they eventually tried to attack her.

"Why not leave? Your grandfather could afford that. I mean, I can buy you a ticket if he won't."

Why not leave? A very good question. Bodhi wouldn't be

joining her and after Jake's display - well she wasn't as sure of them as she planned.

"I'll ask," she told him. "Maybe with a death threat over my head, my grandfather will bring me home."

"It can't be home, if you mean Seattle. In fact, the best you can do I believe is to leave the country. There are a lot more of us than people realize."

She froze.

"Us?"

"Didn't I say I have been trying to save your life? I've been trying to convince the other leaders not to do it, that it would at best be a stopgap to kill you."

"A stopgap is how you think of me. Another living, breathing human being?"

"Let's not lie, Christine. You have to realize that we know this isn't your original body. You've already killed once."

"I was in a coma. It was hardly a choice."

He moved closer to the door, and she stepped aside to let him.

"I know."

He reached for the doorknob.

"Wait, Ordell. Don't go. Please."

His hand hovered over the knob.

"He won't believe me. You have to tell my grandfather what you told me."

His broad shoulders slumped and he slowly turned. "I will, okay."

The conversation with her grandfather lasted maybe three minutes total. As soon as she told him where she was and that there was a strange man in her room, her grandfather laughed at her. But when Ordell spoke up, his deep voice confirming everything as he stepped into view, her grandfather became very serious, very quickly.

"I'll send a volantrae immediately," her grandfather told

her, and when he said immediately, he meant it. After they hung up, Ordell was about to leave when a knock echoed through the room. She stood as still as she could, and she could see by Ordell's trembling frame that he debated what to do. He reached out his shaky hand to pull the door open slowly, peaking through the ever growing crack of light.

"Who are you?" The sound of Jake's voice bounced off the walls as he shoved his way past Ordell and into the room. The big man stepped through and was gone. He must have known that Jake wasn't a threat because she doubted Jake could have pushed past him without him allowing it.

"That was Ordell."

"What?"

"Sit. Let me explain."

For the second time in fifteen minutes, she told the story. The next time the door sounded, it was the volantrae ride for the airport.

"I'm leaving, Jake."

"Now? I know you said…"

"Yes. Now. Are you coming or staying?"

"Coming." He didn't hesitate or dawdle, didn't have other plans to give back to the modeling community or a bag of guilt chaining him to Missoula. Jake only had eyes for her, or if he did have any other ambitions, they were so well hidden that she doubted seriously that he could even find them.

# 31

## Desperation

*Monday, October 31, 2201*

Sometimes when Ordell was alone at night and drifted off into an uneasy slumber, he dreamed of Aayushi. Her raven-colored hair and sad smile and the smell of Lavender. At times it was little more than those sensations as he walked through a field or meadow. Other times, he held her in his arms as he once had while they watched a Zephyr match on the holovision, something he hadn't done since her death. But when he awoke, she was always gone and usually he was accompanied by a flood of guilt when he discovered Caldwell beside him.

Aayushi had left a hole that Caldwell hadn't filled. Instead, she'd caused him to grow as a person, so that there was room enough for him to love her too. The evening after Christine left, his dream involved Aayushi and Caldwell together, and they both told him the same thing.

Run.

And he had run. For hours through the night he ran through cities, through the desert, and over hills in Texas hill country. Exhausted, he still ran on, legs pounding beneath him and breath escaping faster than he could catch it. No matter how much he strained, his legs never moved quickly enough, and their combined voices ushered him forward.

Until the low electric whine of a proton rifle roused him from his slumber.

When he opened groggy eyes, Ordell thought he was back in his pitiful first home in Tribeca, a by-the-week motel that he'd shared with prostitutes and car thieves. Not volantrae thieves, but car thieves, because in Tribeca, there hadn't been any volantrae to speak of. No one who lived there could afford them. But when his eyes fluttered open, what he saw wasn't his set of velvet curtains that Aayushi had told him for months to discard, rather the end of a proton rifle, held by what looked like a Boston, thin and wiry and capable of fitting in as just another polli, and engineered to be smarter than most.

"Good morning sunshine," the woman said, without pulling her weapon away from him.

"*You're* the assassin?"

"Messenger. I'm the messenger sent to do the will of the Order."

An acolyte. Of course it would be someone who worships at the altar of the religious sides of the Order. She probably had the entire Gemini Book memorized.

"Those who work against us in speech are no better than those who work against us in action."

Yep. An acolyte. Probably one of Desmond's lackeys.

"What was your plan?" He asked the question, curious and marginally confident that even an acolyte wouldn't kill another Order member without approval. That would come after a trial - of sorts.

"Gas leak."

"I figured it would have to be something like that. You do know these buildings are powered by fission reactors though, right?"

The woman shrugged. She might have been beautiful had it not been for the weapon still aimed steadily at his face.

"Overload then."

"And wipe out the entire campus?"

"It doesn't matter, does it? Where's the target?"

"Not certain. Far, far away from here though - you can count on that."

"Give me one reason I shouldn't execute you right now."

He looked at her eyes, and saw the wild fury beneath them. Ordell guessed then that she was a rescue, and probably had made it as far as one of the reclamation vats, possibly even filling with decomposition chemicals, before the Order freed her. That's where most of the acolytes came from, but with this one, he could tell that she'd been broken by the experience. That kind of trauma left marks, and it was all over her face. Ordell's confidence that he would survive to trial took a sharp dive.

"Gemini 3-6. But our actions must be tempered in reason, or like the polli, we lose our right to inherit the earth."

He'd had his religious days, and now, they might just save him. She lowered the tip of her rifle as confusion washed over her face. She struggled internally with a decision, but she didn't want him to know it. Ordell wondered if she knew that her struggle was broadcasted by her tense jawline and unblinking stare. He knew better than to mention it. Her face relaxed, which indicated to him that she'd made her decision. When she lifted the weapon back up, he considered that he may have ended up on the losing side. Then she reached into her pocket and pulled out what looked like metallic zip-ties and launched them at his face. He lifted his hands to catch them and prevent them from hitting his eyes.

"Put those on."

Ordell suppressed a grin. He would make it to trial after all, but what happened next he had absolutely no idea. Moments later, he walked from the motel room at gunpoint, cognizant of the fact that in the neighborhood he was in, such an exit happened almost weekly, and there would be no help from the locals.

The volantrae ride only took about three hours to make it from Fouriedon University to Desmond's SNO branch headquarters in Forsyth, just on the edge of the desert that spread through most North Dakota, South Dakota, Nebraska and Kansas. Equilibrium had killed whole cities in that corridor. Ordell had heard a rumor once that Desmond killed traitors by marching them out into that desert. Desmond had a bit of a religious streak too, and could react harshly sometimes, but Ordell had always considered that to be a useful rumor.

Desmond would be upset, but the by-laws of the Order require a full trial attended by at least five of the seven leaders. Ordell guessed that Caldwell probably wouldn't be invited. Rochester wasn't technically one of the seven, and the other five were the entire group who wanted to assassinate Christine in the first place. They wouldn't take too kindly to his perceived betrayal, however misguided their decision was. He thought about trying to convince them that it was a knee-jerk response when a long-term strategy was needed, but he knew already that they had probably all rationalized that decision away.

He couldn't blame them.

Once the reclamation units shifted overseas, their primary recruitment tool evaporated. The fortification of the modeling facilities meant that heavy firepower was necessary to get through, or they had to have a person on the inside - which was harder and harder as screening intensified. SNO had a pretty far reach, but the types of weapons they needed were heavily monitored by the government, the targets out of reach or always in such public surroundings that attacks risked losing what little public opinion they had. They had become sidelined and the leaders, including he and Caldwell, were looking for a way to continue being effective.

They now gravitated toward soft targets, like dependents, family. But that could only win the battle, and would cost them the war of public opinion. He tried to warn them, but Ordell wasn't charismatic. He was a Cassandra, howling his message that nobody except Caldwell and Rochester heard. Even Lancaster approved of soft-targeting, though in this case he'd landed on Ordell's side.

That might save him.

Ordell's history with Lancaster stretched back farther than some of the leadership had been alive. They'd gone through Convocation and Didactics, training for models on how to do their jobs and integrate into society, together many, many years before.

But he wasn't sure. Lancaster had also been a rescue, and tended to be more spiritual and prone to interpretation of signs and the conviction that came along with it, which made him a great figurehead, but difficult to predict.

On approach, the first thing that Ordell noticed was that the headquarters branch there had one entire glass wall facing the desert. Solar panels lined the grasslands that separated the building from the unrelenting heat of the sandy dunes. He'd forgotten that Desmond's branch was self-sufficient, and had no footprint. Even the roof was designed to deflect satellite surveillance. This was the fall-back location in case things went horribly wrong at all the other branches. More of it was underground than above, extending several strata downward and using the insulation of the earth to help maintain climate.

It was a useless marvel. When Ordell looked at it, he saw the weapons they didn't have and the diminishing recruitment streams. Desmond had commissioned it during the uprising, when they though that the uprising would garner the focus of the entire nation and that models in the SNO would be hunted. That hadn't happened. What had happened included an overwhelming corporate security response making further attacks impossible, and wall-to-wall negative coverage. The Order still hadn't figured out how that was managed, but the needle of public opinion moved hard in the wrong direction.

The hallways stretched up to the sky, jutting above him as the acolyte marched him toward their destination. Ordell's head pounded from the sunlight that he guessed the others had grown used to. When they reached their destination, it turned out to be a small room with only a couple of chairs in it and a wall of screens. Faces of the other leaders already adorned the monitors. The chatter hushed as soon as he breached the doorway, but he was encouraged to see Caldwell's face in the one in the bottom left-hand corner. A quick glance garnered him a smile and a testament to the gravity of the situation.

"Order, please," Desmond called out. Since Ordell was now in his jurisdiction, he would preside. It couldn't get much worse than that. "Calling the meeting of the Council to Order."

All chattering boxes went silent at once. Ordell's captor, the would-be assassin, left the room, leaving him to Desmond's guard, alone for just a second and Ordell considered the possibility of fleeing, but the eyes of all the leaders rested on him, and maybe now they would listen. In a sense they would have to, as part of the trial had to include his motivation. The window of opportunity closed when two Briggs models entered the room to stand behind Desmond and stare menacingly. Ordell wondered if that was part of their jobs - the stare. Would one practice such a stare?

"May the Siblings Rise," Desmond said. In unison, the attendees repeated the phrase, including Ordell."We are here to discuss a tragic matter where one of our own interfered with an active operation. This fact is not in dispute, so I ask you to remove your doubts, and not to consider the innocence or guilt in this matter. The only question we have to answer here today is whether and what sort of consequences could prevent such an occurrence again."

"Desmond, that's not the question," Caldwell interrupted. "The question is whether and what sort of consequences his motives deserve. Was he attempting to undermine the Order? Was he attempting to further the cause of the Order?"

She glared unblinking straight out from her box. She must have been glaring at Desmond, but unfazed, he didn't shift his gaze to address her directly.

"During the trial, the defendant will have time to present his case, it's true. And these concerns will, of course, be weighed when considering the consequences. Any further… interruptions?"

Ordell could see the hate collecting in Caldwell's flushed face. At least he had one ally, but Rochester, ally or not, wasn't on the council, so he *only* had one ally.

"Good. Ordell, you may present your case."

Ordell began to stand up, but the movement of the Briggs guards behind him indicated to him that this part of the ceremony would have to be performed from his seat.

"Good Siblings of the Council," he began, careful to make eye contact with each of the remaining six in turn - even Desmond, whose eyes never wavered. Ordell had never considered himself a man for long speeches and wielding influence. "Siblings," he tried to begin again. Finally his tongue loosened.

"Friends. None of you can possibly doubt my loyalty to the Order. I fought alongside you in the Reclamation Uprisings, Desmond. David and Katy, I was on the raids that intercepted you on the way to reclamation - remember that? Phineas knows me."

It was that moment that Ordell noticed Lancaster's absence. A trial such as the one he was in could carry with it the weight of treason, the only crime in the Order which could result in execution, and Phineas Lancaster was nowhere to be seen.

"Of course you have a reason. Personal relationships with the polli Harper Rawls, her son, and by extension, the Hamilton girl," Desmond sneered at him. Ordell could tell from their vids that David felt the same way.

"Maybe two months ago, when we had this conversation, that was part of my concern. But think about the other arguments I made in the following months. It's enough to brand us terrorists to go after high targets in these corporations. If we start killing relatives, friends, family members - where does it stop?"

"Need I remind the council that the person in question is proof positive of the viability of the Immortality Program at Beckett-Madeline enterprises? This program will cost the lives of models at a scale we could only have nightmares about. She's not just a friend or family member."

Ordell scowled at Desmond. So much for impartiality in sentencing. Desmond was trying to get him killed - something he would not soon forget.

"No, she's not," Caldwell interrupted. "But how do you think that would play out in the press? She's parading around as a niece, not even a close relative. Suddenly, nobody is safe."

"Nobody should be safe," came a voice from the doorway behind him. That's when Ordell noticed that the eyes on the screens before him no longer focused on him, but looked to the back of the room. Ordell turned in his chair to see his old friend, leaning heavily across two supporting crutches. Ordell's jaw dropped as he processed the words.

"We're not a terrorist group, Phineas," he said, addressing him by his name instead of by his title. The break in protocol didn't phase him.

"Aren't we? The press says that we are. Ramsey says that we are. The intelligence community says that we are. All of this for saving the lives our brothers and sisters who lined up in concentration camps awaiting their turn to die."

"Hearts, Phineas. Minds. Remember? The direction *you* gave."

The man's thick eyebrows turned down toward the ground before him and Ordell saw his body slacken before the man turned his gaze to the wall, staring into space.

"And what has my direction gained us?"

"Humans. There are polli who support us in court battles and show up to protest our mistreatment."

"In the tens. Perhaps the hundreds."

"What about the Bellingham festival?"

"Hundreds. With over a billion people in the United States, percentage-wise, the needle isn't moving. It hasn't moved in years, Ordell."

"But to become the terrorists that they say we are?"

"It's the only option left to us, old friend. That, or irrelevance and eventual self-destruction. If people see what you did, and that emboldens them - then the rift in the Order is no longer just among the leadership, is it?"

"We can't *be* terrorists, General Lancaster," came Caldwell's voice, drawing Ordell's attention back to the bank of monitors. He scanned each and didn't like what he saw.

Only Captain Wasatch nodded his head in response to Caldwell's statement.

"Old friend, the decision was made before this meeting began," Phineas continued. "Desmond was told to convene this conversation if you interfered, and he did as I asked."

Ordell's back went stiff and his shoulders tightened. His oldest friend in the order planned against him.

"Phineas, how can you not see what this means? Do you think you can take on the government? Peaceful protest is the only way, strategic bombings that free our people. These are the things we can do. What you're suggesting is…"

"It's the only way left to us. Now, the time is here to vote. I wish this ended differently."

"It can," Caldwell shouted form her monitor.

"It can't!" Phineas's gravelly voice rose to a roar, the tone that he used for speeches and to rally the troops. This wasn't a conversation, Ordell realized. As the saying went, the volantrae fell and all that was left was to decide where to crash it.

"What say you for recommendation, General?" Desmond fell into the formal trial speech. The general didn't have a voice in the trial, but he could make recommendations.

"Old friend, I'm sorry," he told Ordell as his eyes locked in like a gray storm settling over the east coast. "Life, in prison."

Ordell's heart fell, even though he'd known the risk. The idea of getting captured hadn't seemed an actual possibility. Even then, these were his friends, and not just officers.

"What say the council?"

Caldwell's vid disappeared, probably as a refusal to vote in what had obviously been a corrupt trial from the start. The others fell in line to the person, including Wasatch. Ordell couldn't blame him for that. The vote was lost before the trial began, he realized. If Phineas had said death, it would have been death. He supposed he should have counted himself fortunate that wasn't the case.

Still, as the two Briggs escorted him from the room, and down the lengthy hallways of the unfamiliar complex to a temporary holding cell, the betrayal seeped into his heart. Phineas Lancaster, the man who'd been with him through Convocation and Didactics, and who disappeared before emerging again as the leader of the Siblings of the Natural Order, tossed him aside. Without Lancaster's insistence, Ordell wouldn't have even joined the SNO in the first place.

Ordell's jaw clenched as the bolt slid into place behind him. An entire wall of the cell was made up only of glass, permitting the desert sun to raise the temperature to sweltering heats. Desmond was an ideologue, and believed in suffering. Even this late in the evening, as the sun set behind him out of sight, while pink and blue clouds stretched across the sky, he already felt the sweat collecting on his forehead.

He sat on the lone bench and stared past the grasslands into the dunes. It was impossible not to think of Harper and Bodhi, and the order's new direction.

How long would it be before they made the kill list?

# 32

## Disappeared

### *Tuesday, November 15, 2201*

Bodhi's calls went unanswered. For two weeks, he'd wondered what he'd done to offend Ordell enough to disappear from his life. His first instinct was to reach out to Caldwell, but worse than Ordell, instead of receiving on a prompt to record his message, Bodhi head a pre-recorded indication that he had been blocked. Only Rochester answered, and that was only after he'd worked up the courage to dial her directly on a number he had "in case of emergencies".

"How did you get this number?" Her response lacked the warmth it once had when they conferenced prior.

"Nobody's returning my calls, Rochester."

"Lose this comm number. Don't call me again." He felt in her voice that she was about to disconnect.

"Wait, don't go, please. I'm worried. I haven't heard from Ordell in a couple of weeks now, not even for the status reports. No response. It's like he disappeared."

He switched his communicator over to projection mode, but only saw the SNO logo on the wall. She kept hers off.

"Listen to me closely. Do not call this number again. Don't call his communicator. Don't call anyone in the Order. Things have happened."

"What things?"

The pause filled the room as he sensed her trying to decide how much to tell him. He pushed himself away from his workbench and stood with nervous energy. The air crackled with uncertainty.

"Ordell has been charged with treason against the Order. He won't be coming back. This program has been discontinued."

Bodhi went silent. His chest felt tight and his stomach twisted.

"I didn't mean to-" he began, but Rochester interrupted.

"It wasn't you. It was your girlfriend." Of course it would have been Christine.

"She's not my girlfriend."

"It doesn't matter."

"What happened?"

"I can't tell you that. It's classified. You need to find the rest of your funding elsewhere. For now, the Order seems to have forgotten about you. Stay quiet, out of the news, and out of sight."

Bodhi felt the hair lift on the back of his neck as the words bounced through his head. He paced back and forth across the room.

"Rochester, will Ordell be alright?"

She sighed audibly into her communicator.

"I don't know, Bodhi, but there's nothing you can do about it. We're working on securing his release, but if I'm honest, it's not looking good and if we keep pushing…"

"You'll be accused of treason too." He knew how that would work - video game knowledge was a dangerous thing.

"I have to go, Bodhi. Don't call me back. We need to make sure you stay forgotten. Caldwell and I have taken precautions to protect you and your family, but it won't work if you draw attention to yourself. Stay hidden."

Rochester disconnected then, without another word, and Bodhi stared at the wall where the logo of the Order once hung. Her words seemed far away and jumbled as he tried to make sense of them.

Ordell captured, Bodhi's family under threat, and Christine was involved.

He wouldn't call her. She wouldn't answer anyway.

Bodhi wiped his hands one more time, and examined the gel interface prototype in pieces across his wide workbench. It was so far from complete that it hurt to look at. Translucent blue fluid leaked out and joined the other stains on the bench that had begun as a pristine white and now dulled to gray. Whatever Rochester told him, Ordell was in trouble because he tried to protect him. It was through Bodhi that Ordell met Christine at all.

It wasn't enough. The five stacked disks in the corner represented all that he had of the world he imagined. Servers networked together at ansible speeds. Most of the money that he'd gotten from Ordell had been funneled straight into the hardware. It was simple enough to load a virtual reality environment onto them, something basic. Getting his animus module to work correctly with it - that was the job of the collection of discarded parts before him. The gel interface had been Torrent's idea, but the design was completely Bodhi's, and it wasn't even to the point that he could test it.

The process took too long. The Immortality program, with millions if not billions of dollars in backing, had to be moving more quickly. The odds that he would beat an international corporation to a market for immortality seemed ludicrous at best. It seemed like monthly another eccentric trillionaire signed another contract with Becket-Madeline. Funds were rolling in, and the SNO focused on his family, and Christine, and locking Ordell away?

His mind swirled with the ridiculousness of it all. His heart wouldn't slow down, but he had work to do, so he ignored it. Bodhi reached for his electron welder on the lab bench. The welder sprang to life and he immersed himself back into his work with the satisfying clicking noise and blue-green heat rising from the device. As the wand neared the back of the gel interface, his hand trembled and the device slipped away, burning a hole in his desk. His heart pounded and would no longer be ignored. Bodhi reached for the device to turn it off, but only managed to push it away from himself. His breath quickened and no oxygen came through.

Christine. She lurked in his mind, whether he wanted it or not. The lights around him swirled into a blur while he tried to push her memory away. Ordell.

But there was one more wasn't there? One more body that had no name, that he stole without a right. And right now, that body betrayed him. He tried to stand and to shout for help. The laboratory was several floors below the penthouse and nobody would hear him. He fell to the floor under the weight of his guilt. As he lay there struggling to breathe, he heard a voice, or was it a memory?

*"Bodhi? Are you okay?"*

The last thing he heard before he lost consciousness was Christine's voice.

When he awoke, the first thought that sprang into his mind was that once again he'd forgotten to do his treatment. His groggy mind still believed that the anemia hovered over his life, casting a shadow over everything he did. Fifteen seconds later, he remembered that he no longer had the disease. Then why had he collapsed? And where was he?

"Thank goodness you're awake." He forced his lethargic eyes open and turned toward the sound of his mother's voice.

"Mom?"

"We found you on the floor. You've been working too hard, Bodhi. You can't fix everything at once."

"What happened?"

"Panic attack," Aiden's voice chimed in.

"Just like me," Harper said, her voice tinny and distant.

"No. I don't have panic attacks."

The room they gathered in was small enough that even with the two of them and him as the only occupants, it was already crowded.

"You do now. That's another gift I gave you."

Bodhi refused to respond to the baiting, knowing that she had already latched onto the single panic attack he could ever remember as more evidence of how she failed him. Instead, he examined the tiny room that the three of them barely fit into.

"Where are we?"

"Christine called me," his mother began, then stopped. He watched her hazel eyes quiver her lips flatten into a line. "Christine called and told me you weren't answering her calls. Then she told me that Ordell saved her life. When I asked her what that meant, she told me that the Siblings were trying to *kill* her. Did you know that?"

He nodded his head, too quickly as the throbbing told him.

"Then we packed everything up and left H Hotel," Aiden continued. "We're in Tacoma, a southern neighborhood, near the interstate."

Bodhi tried to sit up but the room began to shift into unnatural angles.

"Relax Bodhi," Aiden said. "We got your servers and hired some people to pack up your lab. It'll be here tomorrow and we can set it up in the attic."

"Ordell's been locked up," Bodhi told them. They needed to know sooner or later, and now seemed like a good time. "SNO locked him up for helping Christine escape."

His mother pulled her hand to cover her mouth as she gasped at the new information. Bodhi closed his eyes and lay back before continuing, speaking to nobody. "Yeah, Rochester told me. There's no more project. No money and no technology. We barely got off the ground and now there's no stopping the program."

"I can get the money if you need it, Bodhi. It'll just take a few days, that's all."

"What are you both talking about? What about Ordell?"

"There's nothing we can do for him. We don't know where he is, and for all we know, we could be next on the list. This is what we need to do - stay here and stay off the radar." Aiden let the words out with a volume that echoed afterward and filled the room. Then there was only silence.

"This will help Ordell," Bodhi added. "If we can get this program going, it will prove that he knew what he was doing, and maybe they'll let him out."

His mother only smiled and Aiden didn't even do that much. In his heart, Bodhi understood that Ordell's outlook was bleak, being a captive held by a terrorist organization. If there was a way he could help, he would. But this project was the only thing he had that could even have an impact. Now, he had to figure out how to fund it fully. It may not have been the right time, but he only knew two people who had the money to buy what he knew he needed.

"Aiden, I need money. Without Ordell and the Siblings

backing me, I can't buy the positronic cache backbone I need to connect the quantum cores. Latency is going to be a big problem at scale."

"One step ahead of you. I sold my shares in Prescient already. Frees up about a billion give or take. Will that be enough to get your positronic cache backbone?"

"Maybe."

"It's a big spend, Bodhi. How much of this cache are you going to need?"

The pieces fit. One after another he added to the schematics in his mind. Bodhi was almost ready for the next step. To do that, it was time to talk about Graystone Machinations. Time was the killer - and quantum cores could only do so much. The positronic cache was new and the only company that made it had formally filed for bankruptcy.

"All of it. We need to buy the company."

# 33

## Heat

### *Monday, November 30, 2201*

Ordell's curled beard hung down an inch below his chin. He peered out of a red, dehydrated face, awaiting the fullest blast of the sun to steady his shivering body for the forty-five minutes to an hour before the heat became unbearable. The sunlight already peaked over the horizon, sending rays directly into his cell and forcing his day to begin. He slid off of the bench that doubled for a bed, and twisted his massive body to pop his aching back.

Then he thought of Caldwell.

He'd been like this before, trapped and isolated from everyone he loved. Then, he'd maintained himself by meditation and he'd had a secret ally. Ages ago he recalled the experience, washing his clothes and exercising daily, keeping his mind fed by the news and planning his eventual escape. Back then, he hadn't realized how necessary access to information, even bad news daily, was to helping him cope.

This time was different. Every morning before he opened his eyes, he saw Phineas Lancaster's smile. Every day he remembered the first reunion with bitter anger.

Caldwell was there. In fact, it was the first day he'd met her sixteen years before. He'd been denied while trying to buy his volantrae at the dealership where she worked. As something of a consolation prize, she'd offered to take him to a place they'd often wanted to meet.

"The Stern Lectern," she told him, as though he should know what that meant.

"What is that?"

"It's the only model-friendly bar anywhere near League City. Where do you go to drink?"

"I used to go to Jarro," he replied, naming the source of his greatest triumph and most dismal undoing. Her face screwed up in disapproval as she glanced over her shoulder at him.

"No wonder you got into so much trouble."

He smiled at that. For a model, the best way to manage life was to become and stay invisible. He had definitely broken the cardinal rule by becoming key in a national lawsuit to overthrow the Madison Rule.

Just then the crowd before Caldwell began to thin, and models parted on either side. He only just noticed that the cacophony around him diminished to nearly nothing. Caldwell then ducked to her right, and before him, seated at the back of a round table and surrounded with other models, sat Phineas Lancaster, grinning from ear to ear.

"Ordell Bentley," his gravelly voice echoed over the table and boomed against the silence.

"Lancaster."

Ordell glanced at Caldwell, who took what seemed to be her natural seat to Lancaster's left. She grinned mischievously at him. Ordell diverted his attention back to

Lancaster. The man hadn't aged. His face was still flat an unperturbed, with the exception of a smile that still looked out of place. His hair had grown coarser, and was now a dark black nest topping his head. His face had the weathered look of a figurehead, without the grace.

"How are you, old friend?" Ordell asked, barely able to get all the words out as his eyes clouded over with tears. Lancaster shoved someone to his right, who gave up his seat and produced a hole that the entire side of the table stood for Ordell to fill.

"We have some things to talk about, don't we?"

Meeting Caldwell turned out to be more than a coincidence. Phineas Lancaster had set that into motion the same way he'd set into motion the wheels that locked him into his exposed prison. A knock on the door broke his concentration.

"Friend," came the voice, through the closed door, as though Ordell's anger had somehow summoned him into existence. Ordell squinted at the door as it slid away from the wall and watched the large man hobble in.

"Lancaster," he muttered through clenched teeth, not bothering to feign civility.

"Is that any way to greet an old friend?"

"You use that word a lot. What do you want?"

"Just your time, Ordell."

Lancaster shuffled through the doorway and slid with jerky hesitation down onto the bench beside Ordell.

'Why are you here, Lancaster?"

"I wanted to talk to you."

"About?"

Ordell turned his gaze to the floor and shifted his weight, putting Lancaster behind him as best he could without leaving his bench.

"Society, Ordell. You don't understand."

"I understand that you're turning the SNO into a terrorist organization, full stop. There's no more ambiguity once you start picking off innocents. How do we recover from that?"

He could hear the man's head shaking behind him.

"You really don't understand."

"There's nothing to understand. I'm not going to rationalize this away."

"I'm not asking you to." Ordell cringed as Lancaster moved his crutch to his right hand and placed an arm over his shoulder.

"This isn't working," Lancaster continued. "Do you know how many years I've been at this? Trying to sway the public, trying to change minds and reach hearts? Nothing has a lasting effect."

"And you think terrorism will?"

"No. And yes. I spent the last several months wondering why. Why can't we move the needle? Why won't people listen? You know what I realized? Polli don't *have* to. It's not their children and loved ones being dissolved in tanks of acid. It's not their sons and daughters being tortured on sadistic whims. It's not them dropping into mining caves and never coming back out again."

"I repeat. You will change their minds with terrorism?"

"No. I won't. *You* will."

Ordell shifted shrugged the arm from his shoulders, and Lancaster let it fall. Ordell then turned to face his old friend, and saw as his muscular frame sagged under the weight of his responsibility.

"What are you talking about?"

"You will be the next Gandhi, the next Martin Luther King. You will be the voice of reason, and people won't listen to you at first. Polli will think you're just another angry model."

Lancaster's eyes narrowed and somehow the light shifted

to draw shadows beneath them, stretching his face into a distorted scowl.

"But they will listen when they realize that *I* am the alternative."

"You've lost it."

"Maybe, but you have a choice, don't you? Take Caldwell, take Rochester, and *be* the peaceful alternative. Play the role I've set before you for the good of our people."

"Or?"

"I love you, but you will spend the rest of your life in here watching the desert sun rise and wishing you'd taken my offer. Either way, I know that our friendship is over."

His voice trailed off at the end, and Ordell stifled a dry laugh. Their friendship had been over since the betrayal. He'd lost count of the mornings he'd spent cursing the day he met Lancaster in Didactics.

"Sometimes," Lancaster continued, "sacrifice is required. Now, make your choice. Be my nemesis, and forge the middle ground, the accommodating position, for polli to look to as an alternative. Be my enemy."

Ordell met Lancaster's eyes and what he saw there were the eyes of his friend, misted over with tears unlikely to ever fall.

"There's a better way, Phineas. We don't have to do it this way. They will listen."

Ordell was wrong. One tear escaped, and ran down the man's rough cheek.

"I wish that was true. If only that was true. You've always been more idealistic than me."

"Not always, Phineas. Remember?"

"I remember. Do you remember what they did? Do you remember what love costed me?"

Lancaster rose to his feet, pulling up onto one crutch and then the other.

"The door will be open after I leave. Desmond doesn't know, so you'll have to be careful leaving. I will get him to the conference room. Look for Caldwell when you make it to the door."

"She's here?"

"Of course. How far did you think even the great Ordell Bentley could make it into the desert on foot? Caldwell and Rochester are both here, and they are waiting. Make your decision."

With that, he turned away from Ordell and shuffled his way back out the cell door into the hallway, letting it creak to a close as he left, but not locking it. Ordell waited long enough to be sure the guard and Lancaster both were gone, and then shoved the door open and pushed through into the empty hallway.

Plodding down the length of the hallway revealed to Ordell that his legs had grown accustomed to his sixty-four square foot cell. A spike of pain shot up through his left knee forcing him down until he crashed down on top of it, exacerbating the forming pain. He flexed it in response and worked his way to his feet before walking the remainder of the way toward the exit. His entire escape depended on Lancaster's ability and true desire. If Lancaster kept Desmond and his lackeys occupied until Ordell could clear the facility, leaving could be as simple as walking at his staggered pace down the remainder of the hallway and past the front desk, down an elevator and then out into the stairs. Otherwise, he wouldn't make it to the end off the hall before guards circled back around again and put an end to his escape attempt.

Five steps to go.

Four.

Three.

Two.

One.

On the other side of a door was the guard's desk. The test was what happened next. Ordell pushed the door open a crack, and it stuck. He put his shoulder against the door and shoved it hard. Something large slid across the floor as the door opened and through the crack he could see a boot sticking out past the opening. When he gave it one more shove, the door swung open and he saw two plasma rifles aimed at his chest.

"Ordell?" Caldwell lowered her weapon and motioned to him to come forward. "You look like shit."

"He wasn't lying," Ordell replied.

"No. Not this time. But we have to go before anyone shows up."

"Volantrae?"

"We're 'stealing' his. He was foolish enough to leave the keys in it." Rochester smiled at him. "It's good to see you out of that cage."

The trio passed through the doors of the facility just in time to hear shouts behind them. Ordell pushed as hard as he could, struggling to keep up. By the time he made it to the vehicle, Caldwell and Rochester were already seated in the back. Caldwell extended a hand and yanked him forward just as a proton blast ripped a hole in the panel where his leg had been.

"Better move, Rochester."

"Got it."

Ordell was only partway in when the volantrae rose up into the air. His feet dangled out of the door as he scrambled to pull them inside and out of the line of fire. Another shot missed and went over the top of them, charging the air as it passed. Ordell rolled the rest of his body through the opening with Caldwell's help, and lay panting staring at the ceiling. A tangled mass of red hair blocked his view as Caldwell fell on him, kissing his mouth and face with an intensity so great he pushed at her to tell her to stop, while returning every kiss that met his lips. When they finally parted, she smirked at him.

"You need a shave."

"I know," he told her, unable to hide the smile of being free and with his true love again.

# 34

## Graduation

### *Thursday, May 17, 2204*

Two and a half years later, Christine joined Jake in graduate seating on the stage of Exeter University in Southern England. Jake had already been across the stage to receive his diploma. Christine held her head up high as she listened for her name. When the announcer made it through the "h" names, her heart jumped at the idea that she'd been skipped. But she was Turner, now - although there had been rumors that she might be a Barnett soon. Some of them she'd started herself - why leave things to chance.

Three repetitions of Pomp and Circumstance later, and the announcer finally landed in the T's. Christine, smiling broadly, approached with a quick gait to the steps when her name was called. Up and across the stage, she went to collect her diploma. Looking out over the crowd, Christine laid her eyes on Grandfather, who had yet to take on a new body even after all this time. She urged him to take the treatment every time she saw him, mostly as he complained of increasing little pains here and there. Christine smiled again and waved at him briefly before turning to leave the stage.

Instead of going back to her seat, however, she sat nearby in a chair designated for her alone. In three years, she had not only graduated but had skyrocketed to achieve summa cum laude among her new proper-sounding peers. Partly, that was to do with the fact that she wanted to graduate alongside Jake, who had started off a year ahead. She still had her sights on becoming a captain of industry, which meant that knocking aside competitors would be her life going forward. Of course, she always maintained a veneer of geniality, no matter what.

One more Pomp and Circumstance later, and the stage emptied. Christine shifted her weight before standing up and rubbed her hands together quickly. She walked back up to the stage, stepped over to the microphone, and gave her brief address. Words flowed from her mouth about a future, rising stars, and owning tomorrow to make a positive change in the world. As she was about to deliver her closing address, something buzzed near her head. She turned toward the sound as it buzzed again, pausing briefly. Nobody else seemed to notice it. She looked at Jake, and he smiled but seemed confused at her stopping.

Then she remembered.

Bodhi. He was still the only one in the world who used her a.p. since her grandfather even used the more traditional communicator. She ignored the buzz and continued with her speech. The buzzing stopped halfway through.

As she walked off of the stage, the buzzing began again. She grabbed the railing as Jake, seeing her distress, ran to meet her.

"Are you okay?"

"Yeah, I'm fine. It's nothing."

She'd never told Jake about the link she had with Bodhi. There hadn't ever been a reason to, and now didn't seem like the time either.

"Just a little stress," she told him. "I'll be fine."

"Okay, Chris. Do you want to ride with me to the apartment? We can get the volantrae later - the lot is fine for twenty-four hours."

"That would be nice."

What she could use was a nice bath. She leaned on Jake's arm, wondering what in the world Bodhi could be calling her about after three years of silence. Unsolicited, Jake helped her into the house as though she were fragile and likely to break. She wasn't, but she was too invested in wondering about Bodhi to pay attention to the condescending way Jake treated her. Jake was like that - it was a habit she found irritating but had gotten somewhat used to. He'd learned to hide his flagrant disregard for models, especially since his parents had been visiting more frequently and dropping hints about him taking over the company when he graduated. He would be the youngest president ever.

Home in their apartment, Christine locked herself into the bathroom and filled the tub. She was about to lower herself into the water when the buzzing returned. She ignored it for two cycles until curiosity got the best of her, and she answered.

"Hello?"

"Christine? Don't hang up - it's me."

"I know it's you. Why are you calling me?"

"It's a long story. Please don't hang up. I've been alone in here for hours."

"In where?"

She felt the fear beneath his voice. He was trapped somewhere and alone - it was all there. Christine nearly fell over. She'd forgotten how intense those emotions transferred.

"I'm in Mijloc. It's my prototype project. Remember the company I started?"

The mention of it pushed flashes of anger through her mind. She had never realized how truly angry she was about the way he had forgotten his promise to her so easily. Christine didn't bother trying to hide her disgust.

*"How could I forget?"*

*"I'm sorry. Just - how could I let all of those people die?"* She didn't want to re-hash the past. It was over.

*"You got it to work?"*

*"Kind of. There's nothing here yet. It took us this entire time to get an empty space functioning. It works, but I can't get out. What time is it?"*

*"In Pacific time? I guess about six in the afternoon, probably."*

*"Damn. Four hours and counting. I hope they can figure something out soon. I don't want to be stuck in here forever."*

*"Why did you call me?"*

*"I was going crazy in the blackness. There's nothing there. Not a single thing at all."*

A knock interrupted the conversation.

"Are you okay in there, Chris?" Jake asked.

*"I have to go. Good luck with your project."*

*"No, wait, please."*

*"I have a life, Bodhi. I'm not just here for whenever you get into a bind. If you like, I can pass the message on to your mother."*

*"She knows. And I'm sure she'll give me a lecture when I get out."*

*"You deserve it. You're an only child, and you risk yourself like this?"*

*"Okay, look, I'm sorry I bothered you. I'll go back to staring at the pitch black now."*

*"No, Bodhi, I'm sorry. I shouldn't be angry with you. Hold on a second."*

She shouted out loud enough for Jake to hear. "I'm taking a

long bath. What time is dinner?"

"We have about an hour," he replied.

"I should be out in about half that."

"Okay, babe. Let me know if you need anything."

*"You really like him, huh?"* Bodhi's thoughts interrupted her own.

*"He's nice. And he's here."*

*"Ouch - I kind of deserved that too, though, I guess. I really am sorry, you know."*

*"I know."*

*"What about you? I wasn't trying to break up. I was just trying to get this stuff worked out, you know?"*

*"It would have happened sooner or later, Bodhi. I really don't want to talk about this. Is there something else we can discuss? How about your project - want to fill me in?"*

*"Okay. So it's kind of gross. I have to interface with this because I've got two electrodes permanently installed in my neck now. I lay down in a vat of gel, and it just connects. Then it's like I don't even have a body anymore. I just exist in this black space. I can move around in it, but the scenery doesn't change."*

*"Doesn't sound like much of an option compared to cloning."*

*"We're almost there. The world design is something we can hire out. The hard part is this bit, which we're doing. I just can't get out."*

*"What about legal issues?"*

*"Way ahead on that one. And we have funding too. And getting out - that's not even a requirement to prove anything. For most purposes, this prototype worked."*

*"That's amazing! Congratulations, Bodhi!"*

She meant it. At least she hadn't been abandoned for an idea destined for failure. She'd rather be the ex-girlfriend of a successful man than of a disappointment.

A click sounded across the connection.

*"Christine, sounds like they can pull me out. Thanks for talking*

*to me. It really is hard to only partially exist for a time. Really messes with my mind. You helped."*

"Sure, Bodhi."

She disconnected after that and stripped down to let herself into the now tepid water.

"Water, eighty-five degrees," she blurted out. Lights flashed into the tub, and the water warmed instantly. Heating this way wouldn't retain the temperature for very long, but she only had fifteen minutes of her luxurious bath remaining anyway.

Thirty minutes later, Jake took Christine to Cedric's River Shore. The little restaurant straddled the river, complete with imported beach and volleyball. Christine's nerves were still on edge from her conversation with Bodhi earlier.

She couldn't tell if it was a manifestation of her own anxiousness, but Jake seemed a little on edge. He stumbled as they approached a table by the sand and whispered something to the bartender as they ordered drinks. She assumed he'd corrected a drink order or gotten more fries.

Just before live music began, a massive spotlight blasted on their table. Jake, face set as stone, knelt before her in the dirt. Her heart fluttered as she saw what he did. She knew there was only one reason, and before he'd even fully opened the box to show what she already knew would be a massive diamond ring, she said yes. Being Jake, he ignored the first yes.

"You make me the happiest I have ever been. I don't want to ever imagine a life without you. Will you be my wife?"

"Yes. Yes, absolutely, yes."

A look of relaxation swept over his face as cheering erupted from the crowd. The establishment then brought rounds after rounds of cocktails to their table. The moment was storybook and would have remained that way had her mind not wandered back to Bodhi.

# 35

## Contracts

### *Friday, May 18, 2204*

"You could make a call through there?" His mother asked, referring to his experience after telling her about talking with Christine when they pulled him out.

"Yes, it worked - no problem at all."

"We should probably fix that," Aiden said, "at least until we get certified."

"I agree. But that's not what's important. Right now, it worked."

"Fine, Bodhi, celebrate. We can get the lawyers to draw up the contracts to get the ball rolling on filing with the World Government."

"What do you think the likelihood is that they'll give us sovereign nation status on the first try?"

"Nonexistent."

Bodhi sighed. He knew that was the answer. His mother was the only person left on this top-secret project who had the time to familiarize themselves with becoming a sovereign nation.

"What would you suggest then?" He asked her the question with a good-hearted snarky twang.

"We could buy an island," Aiden offered, unsurprisingly. His opinion came in two flavors - buy it, or scale it back. Bodhi was glad Aiden seemed to see the same necessity for sovereignty that Bodhi did.

"Why? It's virtual space we're talking about, not tangible land. Wouldn't that only make it more complicated?"

"Well, if we bought an island far enough outside of international waters, we could claim sovereignty. Nobody would care. There happens to be one for sale right now."

Aiden shuffled up to the kitchen table in the dinette and waved his hand across.

"Show Salamander Island."

The tabletop activated, and Bodhi grabbed his notebook off of it. An image emerged of an island shaped like an hourglass. On one side sat a clear beach, and on the other a jungle. No man-made structures appeared.

"I've had my eye on this one for a while," Aiden continued. "It's small and just outside of international waters. Still in trade waters, so there are trade laws we'd have to accommodate. That might work out in our favor, though."

Bodhi's mother frowned at that.

"Couldn't we just do it here? We don't need to be a nation; we just need to let people reach their loved ones and buy and sell stuff. That's it. You both seem too excited about this national sovereignty thing."

"Fifteen thousand people are queued up for the Immortality program, according to Gallatin. Imagine how many more are likely to sign up for the low-cost and humanity-friendly option?" Aiden asked.

Bodhi could imagine. He didn't quite understand the low-cost part of Aiden's suggestion, but Aiden seemed to believe that was true, and he'd worked out the numbers somewhere.

A knock rattled the door in its hinges. Bodhi answered, surprised to see Torrent standing beyond. Torrent looked first to his mother, then at Aiden, and then stepped through the doorway.

"It worked," he said and dropped a data-coin onto the table. Bodhi's heart jumped. He had experienced nothing but black while in his prototype virtual world, Mijloc, so he couldn't verify anything from his position. Aiden turned to Torrent.

"Better than expected, even. Four hours worth of data really drives the point home. You were in Mijloc"

Bodhi smiled a sheepish half-grin.

Aiden grinned at him. "Accident, eh? I think we knew what we were doing."

"All interfaces with your physical body ceased. The movement you felt only manifested in the virtual world. The gel worked, the connections worked. Just a minor oversight that we didn't plan a way back."

Bodhi laughed at that. It was easy to laugh now that he was no longer in the void.

"What next?" he was the first to ask.

"Well, it's up to you, Bodhi, Mr. CEO," Aiden told him. "Now that we have the technology, we can try to patent it, or we can keep it a trade secret. Nobody needs to know how we do this stuff."

"What's the difference?"

"Trade secrets stay secrets forever - if you can keep them. Patents are non-compete, but you only get a few years."

"What would you do?"

"Wait to decide."

Bodhi didn't even have the opportunity to make a decision.

Two days later, an encrypted datagram arrived in his inbox on his pinamu. He selected the message from his communicator. It immediately projected to the wall a picture of a Caduceus flanked by fire - the unmistakable logo of Emergent Biotechnology.

To Mr. Bodhi Rawls:

We regret that we must ask you to cease all development in your Mijloc Animus Module integration. Patent No. 100495238, "Animus Module General Integrations," covers all Animus Module extensions in such a manner. Emergent Biotechnology is developing similar capability as an exercise against our patent.

We have attached a copy of the patent in question for your consideration. Emergent Biotechnology believes that your work falls under the aforementioned patent. We would prefer to avoid legal action, but should we discover that you have not ceased, please understand that we will use the law's full extent to enforce our claims.

President and CEO,
   Emergent Biotechnology Incorporated,
   Jacob Barnett

Bodhi's hand shook as he picked the communicator up and placed it into his pocket. He hadn't known that Jacob would land immediately in the CEO position directly out of college, but he could have guessed. He'd probably already taken on the responsibility. Christine must have passed on the information to him. Bodhi immediately dialed her.
   *"Christine, why did you do it?"*
   *"What?"*

"Why tell Jake about Mijloc? I told you that in confidence between friends."

"Bodhi, we're getting married. I'm not going to keep secrets from him."

"We looked at that bullshit patent. It's about the Labyrinth connectivity. There's nothing in there that related to us."

"Look, Bodhi, I don't care. I'm not involved - Jake is doing what he thinks is best for the company."

"You were involved enough to tell him."

"You and I aren't a thing, Bodhi. There's nothing here between us. Jake is my fiancé."

"That's not true, and you know it."

"Stop calling me, Bodhi. This isn't good for either of us."

"Tell your boyfriend that I'm not scared."

"Bye, Bodhi."

He felt tiredness along with her goodbye.

"You should be afraid," Aiden told him without affect, startling him. At the moment, he'd forgotten they were in the room. "This is years of court battles. Even if they don't win, it will still eat years and may delay us long enough to kill our prospects."

"Really? They can do this?"

"Yes. And if you want Mijloc to see the light of day, you will need to prepare."

"But the prototype is almost done."

"Hire someone. You need to focus on this, Bodhi. This case is serious."

He didn't think she would tell Jacob. Even now, when he thought about Christine, it was the girl who had just changed bodies and tried equally hard to impress her grandfather and piss him off. That wasn't her anymore. Three years later, she graduated early from the university, and she would be out in the world soon. With Gallatin Hamilton's backing, she would be in the headlines in no time. She would achieve her dream. Wealth, power, and influence - everything she foresaw would come to fruition. And now those dreams came at the expense of his.

"We can fight this," his mother said. "We will fight this."

"Aiden may have a lot of money, Harper - but he's not Beckett-Madeline. And I'm not Emergent Biotechnology. We don't have the resources to fight this."

Her eyes teared up, and she bit her lower lip. Bodhi recognized that look. She had no intention of backing down.

"Harper, we have to fight, but we don't have to win. This doesn't have to be a replay of the past," Aiden told her, touching her shoulder.

Torrent folded his arms before him as he turned away, shoulders hunched so that Bodhi no longer saw his face.

"I can't be a part of this anymore."

"Why not?" Bodhi asked.

Torrent first answered with a head-nod in the direction of the pinamu.

"Non-compete. Now that this letter's been sent I'm sure there's one just like it on the way to me. If I stay involved, it will come up in court."

He continued.

"You don't need me anyway. The prototype worked. Now it's just a matter of building up."

Torrent edged his way to the door, paused, and turned back. His hands shook slightly, and his glasses seemed to flare up. He stared directly at Harper.

"Gallatin is nice and he seems to like you, but he's business first."

# 36

## White Wedding

### *Saturday, June 15, 2205*

They were in the H Hotel. Three years out of the country and her grandfather thought it was time now that she had graduated to call the bluff of those who had threatened her. The threats and lack of follow through had all faded into history. Still, she wouldn't have picked the H Hotel if it hadn't been for her grandfather. The place where it all started, and she was certain he also wanted to use the wedding to let slip some hints about the Immortality program. More and more seemed to be leaking about the program lately, and knowing her grandfather, the leaks were not accidental. But she had more important things to worry about than his businesses. She pulled the shoulders up a centimeter on her dress.

The white gown fit her torso perfectly. Elbow-length gloves accented the simple white top. The silk synthetic fiber sleeves tickled her arms, a sacrifice she endured for their beauty. The skirt extended down to the floor under the weight of heavy plaits, only to evolve into a train as the color transitioned from white to midnight-blue. As she huddled in the back of the church, awaiting the Bridal March, she knew with full confidence that she was the most beautiful woman in the entire building.

The march began, and Grandfather opened the door and extended his arm toward her. She took it and, as gracefully as she could without trampling her train, she began the slow walk toward the hall.

"Nervous?" Grandfather asked under his breath.

"A little," she confided. "What if he doesn't show?"

"He's out there. We talked earlier."

"What if he doesn't say yes?"

Grandfather paused just outside of the nave. He looked at her.

"My beautiful granddaughter. You have been through more in this life than anyone in that room, yet here you are. You, my dear, are a Hamilton to the core. If he says no, he's an idiot."

Her heart felt lighter after that and lighter still as he continued.

"And if he's an idiot, that brings into question a lot of our business arrangements with Emergent."

She laughed.

"Grandfather, you're bad. Stop it."

He would never use his business dealings for revenge - she knew that. Still, it made her feel better to hear him say otherwise.

"Ready?" Grandfather asked. Christine nodded, and he pulled her veil down. "Here we go."

The door opened on cue, and the pair proceeded into the hall. Christine delighted at the packed pews and the extra gallery to the side where reporters gathered. As soon as she cleared the doorway, they flew into action, turning cameras and chatting busily amongst themselves. Christine caught her eyes bouncing from face to face in the crowd as she and Grandfather slowly cleared the sitting area. She knew what face she was seeking, and she also knew Bodhi wouldn't be there. Christine imagined him standing to object to the wedding and played the results in her head.

Last chance, Bodhi. Now or never.

She arrived at the altar, and the priest motioned for the parishioners to take their seats. From that point forward, everything seemed to speed up. Grandfather gave her away, and Jake, handsome as ever, received her. The priest asked some questions, then asked if anyone objected. Her heart fluttered just for a moment, and the priest ended the silence by having them recite their vows.

Grandfather held the reception in the H Hotel in the Grand Ballroom. Swept away by the moment, Christine barely registered the gathering crowd as they passed through the hotel lobby until she caught sight of Bodhi Rawls. He stood near the back of the hall, watching the procession as they passed. She made contact and smiled at him, and she meant that smile. Being back at the H brought forward so many of those old feelings that she felt that they'd never really separated.

That was wrong, though. Christine's husband had sued Bodhi to stop his idea from gathering force and possibly displacing Emergent Biotechnology's market dominance in the new Immortality segment. Whatever Bodhi's smile represented to her, he couldn't have meant it.

There was one way to be sure.

As she slowed her gait crossing, she looked toward him again. The smile still adorned his face, and he seemed genuine. Almost without thinking about it, she called him without slowing further.

*"Bodhi, you're here!"*

*"Of course. I wouldn't miss your marriage, even if I wasn't invited."*

*"It's not like it was exactly a secret."*

She felt over the connection that he was genuine. Perhaps, like her grandfather, he could completely separate business from personal affairs.

*"You're not angry?"*

*"Why would I be angry? You don't run Emergent Biotechnology - your husband does. Besides, he's underestimated us anyway. I'm not worried."*

She stumbled for a step on her gown but corrected herself with Jake's assistance. Christine flashed Jake a smile. He leaned in to kiss her, but she had already shifted her gaze back to Bodhi.

*"I'm sorry about all of this. You're my oldest friend, and we shouldn't be on opposite sides of a corporate battle."*

*"No, don't worry. I'm just happy you're getting the life you want."*

*"Regardless, tell me you'll come to the reception? It's upstairs in the Grand Ballroom. Will you?"*

At first, he said nothing. His smile wavered before he responded.

*"I guess I can if it's important to you."*

*"We just haven't seen each other in so long."*

*"Okay, I'll be there."*

Jake nudged her to get her attention on a member of the press corps who wanted a picture. She obliged, and when she turned back, Bodhi was gone.

Bodhi never showed at her reception. She looked for him and even tried to call him after a time, but he refused to answer. Christine should have known that he wouldn't show. She knew that after cutting him out of her life, she had risked permanent damage between them, but it seemed like the only way to manage the situation. It was hardly appropriate for him to be calling her whenever he wanted to.

"Are you okay, Chris?" Jake asked her, not for the first time. She eased his concern.

"I'm exhausted," she told him, smiling. "How are you doing it?"

"Fumes," he assured her, "fumes for sure. We can leave whenever you want."

"But we haven't cut the cake yet. We probably should at least eat some."

"Yeah, you're right. Fumes - see?"

She laughed, and he laughed. Jake was funny, and smart, and witty, where Bodhi oozed brood and judgment. She'd definitely picked the better deal - yet she found herself surveying the crowd again.

"May I have this dance?" Jake asked, extending his hand.

"Of course, husband," she replied, taking his hand. The two stepped out onto the dance floor.

Christine asked to visit the Rainbow Mountains of China for her honeymoon, striped with pinks, reds, and teals. Save the extended stay in London, Christine had only ever seen Mt. Rainier. Leaving the state exposed her only to the flatlands of the midwest and the hills around Missoula. She felt that even the seas of red and yellow flowers would fall short of the vivid mountains she had seen in the Labyrinth. Jake took her there in a private jet but insisted they only stay for a day because of business.

Christine, once again, found herself in lessons paid for by her grandfather.

"If you want to lead an empire, you have to learn how," he'd told her.

She didn't know if that was what she wanted anymore. At

least, she didn't realize that Beckett-Madeline Enterprises was something she wanted. The firm exuded power, and owning it would set her for life. No matter how well she did, though, she would always consider it her grandfather's success. She wanted her own success. With the animus module, her grandfather could easily keep his success for himself.

She shook her head to clear it. When Jake traveled, Christine found that she became self-reflective. At that very moment, he was somewhere in New York, and she was tired of being bossed around all the time. That had to have been what it was.

Lessons closed early that day, and Christine had a few hours before she would feel up to starting her next batch of studies. She let herself out of her cramped hotel room, once again in the H Hotel, and caught the elevator to the top. It was in the cafe that she found what she wasn't looking for.

Head tilted down, deep in thought and working on something, sat Bodhi Rawls. She caught herself staring when his head lifted, and he caught her eyes.

"I didn't expect you to be here," he told her.

"My grandfather owns the hotel."

"I know, but Jake's in New York - I figured you were with him."

"Surprise," she said and gave a little curtsey. "Need company?"

"I guess."

He picked up three data-coins from the table and placed them into his pocket. Doubtless, they were his most recent changes to …what was that thing he said… Mijloc? What kind of name was Mijloc? It was unmarketable, and nobody would want to be plugged into some machine when they could have bodies. She slid onto a chair across from him.

"What are you working on?"

Bodhi's eye twinkled at her.

"I can't tell you," he said. "Last time, it didn't work out so well."

"Bodhi, I told you - it's not my fault. I didn't tell him to send the letter, and it's not like he's done anything to you since then."

"Still..." he replied and stopped.

"Fine. Then I guess we'll just have to talk about the weather. Or maybe, why you didn't come to my reception?"

He tilted his head up further and cocked it to the right.

"You really don't know?"

She shook her head side-to-side vehemently in response.

"How could I go? It took all the strength I had to stand there and wave. When I saw you, I - it doesn't matter."

She could have sworn he blushed as he lowered his head. Christine changed the subject to spare him more embarrassment.

"Why are you here, anyway?"

"Angel Investor conference downstairs. I have to pitch my spiel and see if we can get more funding. Thanks to your husband's stunt, we lost two early investors. Aiden's money is already earmarked, so we need more."

Unfazed, Christine kept eye contact until he continued.

"I'm presenting tomorrow."

"Do you want some help? Remember, I have a degree in business and finance. I'll be glad to help you prime it if you want."

"No thanks. You'll just take it all back to Jake."

"It's my grandfather's hotel. If I want to attend your presentation, I can. Anything in the conference rooms I can get. You might as well just take the help I'm offering."

He glowered.

"I didn't mean it as a threat. I just mean, use me. I feel bad about the investors. I can help you get that funding. Who knows, maybe Emergent will invest."

This caught his attention as he raised one eyebrow.

"Okay. I guess there's not much in the investors' pitch that you don't already know anyway. Will your husband mind?"

"Not when I give him all of the inside info," she joked and immediately regretted it. Bodhi's face flushed, but then he smiled.

"Yeah, like I'm going to give you any insider information."

That seemed to break the tension between them, and suddenly, they were Bodhi and Christine again, just two lost souls who had nobody in the world but each other. The practice turned into drinks, and the drinks turned into nightcaps.

Nightcaps turned into morning.

Christine woke alone and smiled to herself. She hummed as she got up to clean the room. They'd spent the entire night talking in her suite until there o'clock in the morning. Only with reluctance did they finally part, and she fell asleep on the couch shortly after that. The day seemed bright, and they'd already made plans to meet for brunch. But brunch wasn't for another hour, so she thought she might pass her time watching the news on the holovid. Before she could turn on the display, a buzz distracted her. She smiled, knowing that the familiar tone was Bodhi calling.

When she answered, something was wrong. The emotions connected to the call were fear and sadness.

"Christine."

"What, Bodhi?"

She felt her heart quicken with every passing second.

"It's Jake. Turn on H4. Or any holovid channel. It's all over the news."

"Apartment, H-4."

Since she was in the kitchen, the counter projected an announcer's head just above its surface.

"...last night in New York, two-hundred dead at the Bentley factory. Twice that many models were destroyed in the blast - easily a loss of nearly two-hundred billion dollars. Emergent's fledgling CEO Jacob Barnett was caught in the explosion and is in serious condition at Clayton Hospital. Doctors have been quiet as to whether or not he will make it."

"Christine, I don't know what to say."

A lump constructed from the guilt for her evening with Bodhi formed in her throat. Someone knocked on her door and broke her concentration.

"I'll be... I... "

She couldn't form the words. She hung up without further explanation, and the pounding on her door grew louder and more insistent.

"Mrs. Barnett," came a loud voice.

"Coming," she replied, quieting her voice from wavering.

She opened the door, and two men stood there with dark suits and serious faces. One grabbed her arm, and the other bolted past her to search the premises.

"Mrs. Barnett, come with us. We'll keep you safe."

"I will do nothing of the sort."

"You will," came a voice from behind the men, "immediately, Peach."

She looked up as tears fell from her eyes. There stood her grandfather, equally stern-faced. She wiped her tears with one hand and nodded her head.

"What do we have to do?" She asked.

Two days later, Jake still wasn't home. Bodhi called several times, and once again, she found herself without any desire to talk to him, so she ignored his calls. Her grandfather, as always, was all business.

"It has to be done," he told her. "The lawsuit must go forward."

"I don't own the company, Grandfather. You'll have to wait until Jake gets out."

"It's a private company, Christine. If Jake can't manage it, then the responsibility falls to you."

"Not my responsibility."

"It is. I've spoken to the board, and you are the interim CEO. Frankly, you're the best we've got."

"Jake will be out soon. Just wait."

"Business doesn't wait."

"It has to wait," she said, as tears once again flooded from her. The tears seemed to break Grandfather's focus for as long as anything ever did. He stepped forward and put his arms around her.

"I know, darling, but you have to do the work. Especially now that the Bentley factory is gone. We can't keep everything in models. We need to diversify, and Paivana Thoughtforms is in the way of that.

"I know it's bullshit. You know it's bullshit. There's nothing in our company that envisioned a move to virtual reality. That's all Bodhi, and you know it too."

"It doesn't matter where the idea came from. What matters is who can act on it and who can't. We can, but we can't do it well if there's a player already in the way. He's the enemy, Christine. Not in life, but in business. You must stop him."

"Grandfather, I can't. I love him."

She clasped her hands over her mouth as soon as the words escaped. Then she knew it was true. Part of her cried for Jake, but her heart bled for the future she couldn't have.

"Never speak of either of these things again," her grandfather said, glaring at her. "There is no future in Bodhi. The future is Emergent Biotechnology. And your husband."

Christine wiped her tears away for the last time.

"Okay. Okay, I'll do it."

She stood.

"Please leave."

"Christine, I'm sorry. I had to get your head-on."

"Leave."

She glared at him as he turned and passed over the threshold. Then she closed and locked the door behind him. Christine took a deep breath.

"House, schedule a flight to New York."

# 37

## Defensive Position

### Monday, June 17, 2205

"Brigid, it's good to see you," Harper said as she embraced a tall red-headed woman who'd entered their home.

"Good to see you too, Harper," Brigid replied.

"I'm sorry I disappeared. I had complications."

"I'll say," Brigid chimed, eyeing Bodhi up and down in a way that made him squirm a bit. She seemed to be staring at his insides.

"He doesn't look anything like you, Harper," Brigid said.

"That's not his original body."

"Immortality?"

"Bodhi's one of the first."

Brigid took a deep breath a whistled the air out between her lips.

"I'm not a patent lawyer," she told Harper, "but I want to be involved. We've brought in a patent firm to help with the details."

"Do you think they have a case?" Bodhi asked, tired and ready to get to the point.

"No, I don't. But I do think they have a lot of money. And I think they're in bed with Beckett-Madeline Enterprises. There's no end to their resources. So if they've decided you need to be shut down, they'll throw their resources at you until you crack."

The statement silenced the room. Bodhi's mother drew her hand to her mouth; Aiden looked casually away in a carefully calculated nonchalance. Bodhi was the only one whose eyes popped out at the way her response sounded more like a defeat than an actual plan.

"What do we do then?" He asked.

"Take them to court."

"Why, if we're just going to lose?"

That's when Aiden's attention pivoted back to the conversation.

"Because," he said, "we're not playing to win or lose. How far are we from an actual working bare-bones world?"

Bodhi had watched the calendar meticulously over the last several months, each month creeping by slowly. Since the proof-of-concept, everything seemed to come to nearly a complete halt. Each step forward since had been painstakingly tested and incrementally built. Since being trapped, his mother had insisted everything be tested twice as much before he could make the next attempt.

"Three months," he responded to Aiden, guessing based on how far they'd been the last time he was in. Thanks to Aiden's money, they had a team working on it. But Aiden's money couldn't do both the development and the legal work. There was a limit to it.

"Okay. That means we need to find clientele within that time period. If we have people actually in it, then the lawsuit, however meaningful it might be, could never shut us down.

To do so would be effectively killing the people."

"Exactly," Brigid said. "As your attorney, I think your best shot is to string this thing along and double-down on finding some clientele."

Bodhi and his mother traveled to Walsh, Moody, and Kostic twice a week as Brigid's team took them through the 200-page patent claim section by section. While he wanted nothing more than to contribute to his project. As the CEO, Bodhi found himself unable to break free of the continuous stream of discovery coming from Emergent Biotechnology, most of which was unrelated to anything they did.

One day, he stepped into Brigid's office and into an unwelcome surprise. His mother had gone separately earlier in the morning. Bodhi had selfishly taken some time to review the progress.

"Bodhi's here," prompted one of the associates. The announcement turned all of the heads in the room. Brigid and his mother sat side by side, poring over her desk screen. Brigid looked more or less like she always did, but his mother's shoulders tensed up, and she pressed her lips together.

"What?" Bodhi asked, directed at nobody in particular. "Is something wrong with the case?"

Brigid shook her head no and immediately ducked down, focusing again on the tabletop.

"Come here," his mother motioned. "Remember that explosion?"

Bodhi slid around the table and looked over her shoulder. There in front was a document he hadn't seen before. It looked like another version of the cease and desist.

"What am I looking at, Mom?"

"The signature."

There, at the bottom, Bodhi saw it. Scrawled across the

bottom was a signature that she would never fail to recognize. Beneath the signature, printed finely, was the confirming print: "Christine Barnett, Acting CEO."

"This doesn't make sense," he muttered as he stepped back and shook his head.

"It's a private company, Bodhi," his mother explained. "She is qualified to lead. And she'll do well with the right team."

"But we were just talking after her reception. I thought we were getting back to speaking terms. What happened?"

"She's acting CEO," Brigid chimed in. "Try not to take this too personally. I'm sure she's just keeping going whatever Jake had started. On paper, this whole thing makes financial sense."

"Maybe even more now," he admitted, "without the Bentley plant."

"Exactly," Brigid continued, not looking up.

Even the words he spoke failed to quell the feeling in his chest. He reached out for a nearby seat and staggered to it, arriving in time to collapse. He slid back into the chair.

"Mom," he muttered, his voice cracking, "it was bad enough when it was Jake."

She stood and walked to him, wrapping him up in her arms.

"I know," she said. Bodhi felt her warmth and pulled her tightly to him. Tears threatened to fall from his eyes.

"Bodhi, don't stress, it's just business."

"No, it's not."

On the first day of trial, Bodhi barely recognized Christine sitting on the prosecution bench. She pulled her hair up into a bun and wore slacks and a long coat with a black undershirt. She looked very much like she'd come in from a funeral, which wasn't too far off since Jake was still in critical condition.

Bodhi didn't participate in the trial at all. He was never asked to take the stand or was even asked to substantiate a question from where he sat. The lawyers droned on and on about different patent claims and how their terms should be construed.

Bodhi stared at Christine, resisting the urge to call her. Her eyes were puffy and red, and she occasionally nodded along with her attorney's statements. He wondered why she was even there. Emergent Biotechnology had a legal department. There was no reason for her to be in the courtroom at all. Maybe she didn't know that - new to the job. Paivana Thoughtforms, on the other hand, had only one legal representative - Bodhi himself. Bodhi failed to focus on the trial at all. His mind wandered back to when the two of them had studied together for her GED.

For a moment, he lost himself in her. She tucked some of her hair just behind her right ear, and he remembered when he did that for her. She had invited him to her room to help study for the GED.

"I told you," he laughed as she lay beside him, "seventy-five percent of the animals are kangaroos. The other twenty-five percent are koalas. Kangaroos eat four-hundred grams of the dry matter daily. Koalas eat 300 grams of leaves a day. If you have a hundred animals, how many grams of food total will you need?"

"It's a stupid question," she said. "Why would you ever care how many grams of food total?"

"Maybe you need to ship it and see if the truck can handle it?"

"Yeah right. Know of a lot of kangaroo-koala farms?"

"Not in the states. But maybe in Australia."

She shook her head no as she grinned widely. This caused a strand of her hair to drop in front of her face. Instinctively, he reached for it to put it back in place.

"Sorry," he said when he saw her blush.

"No, thank you," she said, continuing the smile.

"So, more about koalas?"

Christine pulled closer to him, so close that he could breathe in her lilac perfume. He pulled his face toward hers slowly. Bodhi watched her tongue flick across her lips. As their lips connected, he felt his heart pounding through his entire body. Then she pulled away.

"I'm sorry, that was probably too much."

"I liked it. Don't be sorry."

He was sorry now, staring across the courtroom, unable to divert his gaze, as the future of his company and all of model kind unraveled before him.

Emergent's attorney raised his voice, committed to convincing the judge of their position, no matter how unfounded. Bodhi snapped back to the present to see that Christine had locked eyes with him. He saw a tear in the corner of her eye. He mouthed the word "why," only to have her turn away.

He never saw her in the courtroom again.

# 38

## Less than Jake

### *Monday, August 26, 2205*

They returned Jake to her broken.

At least that's what she thought when he walked through their door, escorted by two burly models. They placed him on the couch and then left, and he said nothing. He didn't greet her, nor did he look at her. Instead, he turned over into the cushions, buried his face, and lay still.

For two days, he lay like that. No amount of enticing brought him to the table for dinner or even elicited a response. His only activity was to shuffle back and forth from the bathroom the first day and the second; he didn't even do that much. She supposed that without drinking or eating, the bathroom was less urgent for him. By the third day, she grew sick of his inaction.

"Get up," she told him. "You have a company to run."

He ignored her.

"Get out of bed, now."

Still, no response - until she pulled so hard on his arm that he fell from the couch down to the floor.

"It's my fault," he said. "I thought I could change it."

The only words that he'd spoken in three days made absolutely no sense. His voice rasped as he breathed. Aside from a few bandages, he seemed fine. But the rasp sounded nasty - smoke inhalation probably did that to him.

"It's not your fault. It was a terrorist organization. Jordan Helm took credit for it already."

Jake locked his gaze with her and seemed to be aware that she was there. He smiled sardonically.

"How convenient," he muttered.

"Convenient?"

"It wasn't Jordan Helm. It was me."

"I - I don't understand."

"This."

He waved his hand in an exaggerated gesture, then pulled himself up to sitting so that he used the couch for back support.

"This is built on blood money. What we do, what we do... it's grotesque."

"What are you talking about?"

"Pumping these creatures out into the world. Every day, it sickens me. "

What would Jake think if he knew about her and her body? Her grandfather had been right to keep that a secret. Unless. She stared back into those brown eyes and saw something she hadn't noticed before. She reached out for his hand, but he recoiled.

"What? It's just me, Jake."

He shifted his weight and reached into a pocket to pull out a data coin.

"It's not just you," he told her.

Jake plopped the coin onto the coffee table before her. In

horror, she watched as headlines from news reports flashed over the screen. Christine hadn't even been paying attention to any news outside of Jake. There was a story to which she should have paid attention: "Gallatin Hamilton pulls the plug on his granddaughter." Grandfather hadn't even told her.

"I know who you are," he muttered, then his face turned to a scowl, "and I know what you did."

"I didn't do anything, Jake. I woke up in a body. It had nothing to do with my choice."

"No? Well, you sure kept it. And were you planning on telling me? Why did I have to find out this way?"

"What way?"

He nodded toward the table. The data-coin hadn't finished spewing data. When the documents finished unloading, a logo appeared that looked like an h attached to a backward p.

"Human Pride Movement."

He nodded his head with embedded, sunken eyes.

"Did they make you do something?"

"You don't understand yet, do you?"

She didn't. There was nothing about Jake's words that made a modicum of sense to her.

"I did it on purpose. I was supposed to die in the blast. This is inconsequential. You're one of those things."

Christine closed her eyes and shook her head. That couldn't be true. The man who she had fallen in love with was sure of his place in the world and wanted nothing more than to steer his family's empire to greater success.

"No, Jake, that's not you. You love the business and your family."

"Don't tell me what I want. I've been waiting for years, and I finally got to the point where I could make a real difference. How many fewer models can Emergent make without Bentley?"

She switched into damage-control mode.

"Okay, it's not a problem. We'll just put you back to work and let Jordan Helm take the credit. He wants it anyway."

"I'm not going back."

She reached out for him again, and he lurched to the side.

"You were in the middle of a huge explosion. You're probably still not thinking straight."

"I've never thought any differently."

"Jake." She reached for his arm again with the same reaction. She felt desperation well into her chest. "Your parents, my grandfather. Emergent. What was all of this to you?"

"It needs to be stopped, Chris. I can't be part of it anymore."

"Who - who's going to run the company?"

"I heard you were doing a bang-up job, Ms. Hamilton."

The stab made her cringe. Jake really did know, and now he drove the knife in further. It wasn't fair. Whether her name was Turner or Hamilton, she was only Christine, his Chris. How long had he known, she wondered. Was their entire relationship a lie?

"I don't love you," he said. "I don't even know who you are."

That was the last hit she could take. She strained under the stress of running a company that wasn't even hers, bringing Jake back from New York, and betraying a childhood friend to keep his company moving. None of it was what she wanted. She left him on the couch and retreated to the safety of the bathroom. A bit of cool water over her face brought down her temperature. When she looked up again, she realized that she'd expected to see her fourteen-year-old self. Christine wondered what that girl might look like at seventeen. Nobody would expect her to bear the weight of the world at that age, even if she had graduated summa-cum-laude from a prestigious university. The biological age of the body was a trap.

The door to the house slid open and then shut again, and she knew he was gone.

She skipped the next day at court. Christine didn't have to be there. When it had been Jake's cause, she'd believed in it enough to fight for it. She no longer knew what the fight was for. Why had he gone along with this battle when it diametrically opposed his view on pretty much everything? Trying to stifle a fledgling industry that could make the Immortality Project obsolete seemed contrary to what Jake had professed to believe in.

That day, she meticulously thought through her life. The prior evening was a vicious blow, but she could overcome, she knew. She was, as he had pointed out, a Hamilton after all. First, she needed to beat Jake to the press. If he exposed her, then it would be a scandal. Suppose she held herself up as a vivid example of immortality achieved. In that case, it could be a marketing boost to the program. Jake would be easy to discredit, especially if he moped around guilt-ridden about the explosion, claiming responsibility when a well-known terrorist group already had. She could spin that he'd been brain damaged by the blast and she had to take control of Emergent Biotechnology.

The more Christine considered the idea, the more she liked it. And with Jake out of the way, there was one thing that she could take solace in: Bodhi. He'd loved her since they were children together. Could he still love her, even after all of this? She didn't know. Christine was sure she loved herself a lot less. Coming out on top was more of an instinct than a testament to self-worth. She was a Hamilton. They always come out on top.

Using her Animus module, she tracked down Channel 4's number and dialed.

"Gordon Berry," a man answered. "Channel 4 news."

"This is Christine Barnett, of Emergent Biotechnology. I have some news to share."

# 39

## Awarded Contract

### Tuesday, August 27, 2205

The trial ran short that day because of late discovery. That had been Brigid's latest stalling tactic. She and her team had gone through every item in discovery provided by opposing counsel. They found a series of patent documents were missing. They were ridiculous documents, which in no way impacted the case, but discovery was discovery. She claimed that they did, and how could she know if she hadn't been able to look at them? The judge agreed and adjourned ninety minutes early.

This gave Bodhi the window to finally do what he'd planned to do for weeks. He made his way to their Tacoma facility as he smiled to think that he now had a facility. The house had proven too cramped. Once he'd hired the team, having strangers in and out impacted his mother too much. She'd given an ultimatum, and grumbling, Aiden had ponied up enough cash for a facility down-town. Bodhi had to take a bus to get there because he'd spent every dime he ever made on Paivana Thoughtforms, including money he could have used for a volantrae or car.

During the bus ride, he noticed a couple of strange looks from riders. He checked himself in the window, but nothing seemed any more out of place than usual. He'd developed a few worry lines, for which he was far too young, but that came with the territory of entrepreneurship, or so Aiden told him. As a fix, he'd joined Aiden for meditations on Sundays to reduce stress. Still, nothing about his appearance seemed too untoward. He stared back at one man in the back who quickly glanced away.

The bus dropped him a block away. Bodhi walked the route often, and this time was no different. He made his way along the cement sidewalk to see a crowd slowly building, getting denser as he approached. He eventually had to push through to make progress along the street, at one point stepping into the road to get around the mob. Someone in the group noticed him, and a path opened up before him. Since it was leading in the direction he wanted to go, he decided to change it. In Tacoma, sometimes people were just nice.

When he saw the camera drones, he started to get anxious. All he could think about was the massive explosion in New York, and the idea occurred to him that his mother and Aiden might be in danger. He sprinted the length of the sidewalk and pushed through the last group of people to find his entrance blocked by more news crew.

"Mr. Rawls, how does it feel to be the youngest entrepreneur with a multi-billion dollar contract?"

"Wha-what?"

The door popped open, and Aiden walked through. Instead of tie-dye and jeans, he wore a pressed suit and an expensive-looking tie. He greeted Bodhi with a big smile. As he got closer, he whispered, "Just smile and wave."

Bodhi turned to the crowd, smiled once, waved a shaking hand, and turned to go inside, with Aiden behind him.

"What happened?" He demanded.

"We don't have to worry about the lawsuit anymore," Aiden said. "The world government gave us the first exclusive virtual world contract ever."

"Mijloc? We can do it."

His mother interrupted that time.

"No, not Mijloc," she said. "They want a prison. It's too expensive to house inmates, especially those without the possibility of parole. Instead, they want to use the animus module to move them into a virtual prison."

"Prison? That's not what we wanted."

"No, it's not. But it defeats the patent. There's no more case because interest and ability make us the only company around who can do it in their timeline. Two years to launch." His mother smiled from ear to ear.

"What about Immortality? That's what we're after."

"Think about it. It's perfect. We work out the kinks on hardened criminals and then petition for the sovereign nation status for Mijloc. It's a step in the right direction, Bodhi," Aiden insisted.

A prison? Bodhi pondered the idea. The savings to the world government and then to other government systems would be massive. The money they would make had to be as well.

"How many billion?" He asked, finally coming around. This was a prime opportunity, and if it got Christine off of his back, the better.

"Fifty billion for the first year, and several hundred million a year in maintenance," his mother replied.

"Does that put us on foot with Emergent?"

"Closer. We just created an industry, kid. This is going to be a wild ride."

\* \* \*

The buzzing of his animus module interrupted the conversation. Bodhi motioned to his mother and Aiden and then to his ear, the universal sign for the incoming call through communicator implants. His mother's face twisted up into concern. He walked out into the hallway from the group and down toward the VR chamber, seeking privacy. He answered the call.

*"Bodhi? It's Christine."*

The emotions flooding the line were dark and desperate. Bodhi knew that he projected concern back, no matter how angry he was at her actions. Still, he chose to take the safe road and keep the distance between them.

*"What, Christine?"*

*"Congratulations. I saw the news. How did you ever swing that without us knowing about it?"*

It was easy, he considered. All Aiden had to do was not tell him, and Christine would never have been the wiser. He mentally kicked himself for the fool he had been. Aiden had been right to keep the secret.

*"I didn't know about either. I'm sure you would have gotten it out of me otherwise."*

*"I'm sorry, Bodhi."*

*"That's what you said last time."*

*"Things have changed. Without the patent, we can't compete with you in this area. Paivana and Emergent aren't enemies anymore. You and I, we aren't either."*

How could she just turn it off and back on like that? He never could figure it out. But there, in the emotional aftershock, was the truth. She couldn't hide the concern and longing from him, or maybe she didn't try to. Then again, from what he'd been through, maybe she only played it up so that he would be sure to get it over the connection. She'd always been better at managing her feelings than he had.

*"It's not a trick, Bodhi. I didn't want to sue. I had to sign off on what was already underway. It wasn't my company then."*

*"And it is now?"*

*She paused for a few seconds, and he thought she might say no.*

*"Not yet. But by this time tomorrow, I think it will be."*

*"What does that mean for us? You're still pushing the Immortality program, right?"*

*"Wrong."*

*"What?"*

*"You heard me. The writing's on the wall. When even the inheritor of a modeling empire can't justify the program, it's only a matter of time. We're on the wrong side of history."*

*"In so many ways. But what's really going on?"*

*"We want in Bodhi. I want in. Emergent needs to move away from modeling, and we need to diversify. I always thought Mijloc was a joke, but here you are - making news."*

*"So you think it can happen now? And you want a piece?"*

*"Professionally, yes."*

He could almost hear her sighing.

*"But that's not all, Bodhi. Watch the news tomorrow. I have an announcement that's almost as big as yours. Just a couple of things I have to tie up first."*

*"That's it? I don't know why I even bothered to answer."*

He felt the hurt he inflicted, with conflicting emotions: satisfaction that the punch had landed and dismay that he hurt her.

*"I miss you, Bodhi. You don't have to believe me. I feel like you're part of me, and I'm part of you. It's been like that forever."*

Bodhi gulped.

*"Don't answer,"* she said. *"Just know it's the truth."*

With that, she hung up. Bodhi sat dumbfounded for a moment, puzzled at what to believe. After their rocky past together, he knew he was better off believing nothing. Still, somewhere deep inside, he felt a tiny glimmer of hope.

# 40

## Christine Rising

*Wednesday, August 28, 2205*

The mansion was as large as she'd remembered it from the first time Jake had taken her home to meet his parents. The self-driving volantrae descended just in front of the drive to deposit her by the steps. As she left the vehicle, she reminded herself that she belonged to this crowd. Christine and Jake owned a significant home of their own (that she'd been to exactly once). She didn't know if she could remember how to get to it, but was certain someone could get her there if she asked.

Christine approached the door, balking when it swung open as she advanced. She nodded curtly at the man and woman standing there, the real force behind Emergent Biotechnology. They both returned the gesture with a similar detached air, then turned to make their way back inside, leaving the door open which she took as an invitation to follow. She followed them through to a formal receiving room, where brandy and little circular cakes were lingered on tall, silver serving trays. A butler stood in the back of the room, stoic, and holding a cloth over one bent arm.

"Christine Turner Barnett," the woman said with a smile. "You've turned out to be quite a good person to have in the family. Your work as interim CEO has been spectacular. Of course, we knew you would be. That's why we've been keeping an eye on you all these years."

Christine didn't ask about that. Between Jake and her grandfather, she'd grown accustomed to people being overly-interested in her life.

"Mr. and Mrs. Barnett," she said. "We need to talk."

"Of course we do," the woman said while the man stood strangely silent.

"Did you know that your son is an idealist bent on destroying your company?" She blurted the words out, intending to catch them off guard so she could see their reaction. Nothing passed over either of their faces.

"We suspected," Mrs. Barnett replied. "We weren't absolutely certain. He seemed to change when he met you. We hoped…" She trailed off.

"Then you know that the blast was his fault?"

"The official position is terrorist attack," Mr. Barnett chimed in.

Christine took a deep breath, hiding as much of it as she could from them, before continuing.

"I want permanent CEO. I can't work as his temporary replacement. He's gone, and he's going to attack the company in the press. I have to be able to respond properly."

"Are you saying that you're more loyal to Emergent Biotechnology than to my son?" The woman asked the question without judgment, and Christine weighed her possible responses.

"He lied to me. He lied to you. I'm not even sure he loved

me. So yes, I'd say that's about right."

The two looked at each other, and then the woman's eyes changed, now fierce with rage. At first, Christine thought Mrs. Barnett's anger directed at her.

"He's disappointed us for the last time. Jacob is not part of this family."

"What's my answer?" Christine asked. With the position formally hers, she could scale back the Immortality program and jack up the price. With contracts already in place, it was the best she could do without dismantling it altogether to the cost of billions of dollars. As the entire board of directors, CEO was up to the two people standing before her.

"Granted," Mrs. Barnett told her. "Tell me what you mean about Jake attacking us in the press?"

"I should have said attacking me. I'm Christine Hamilton, not Turner."

"The poor girl in the coma who died a week ago?"

"I'm round one of the Immortality Program. I am the proof of concept. His intention is to use that against me."

The man cocked his head to the right slightly as his arms twitched. Christine was confident that at least he hadn't known that. But the woman was harder to read.

"So you say," she nodded. "And being permanent CEO will help?"

No, it wouldn't, and the excuse was weak. She'd known that when she presented it. The fact is, they had nobody else anyway who ready to fill her role anyway, so she'd hoped that would be enough. The excuse was just that.

"It doesn't help, not really. I've scheduled a press release for later today to deal with that. What I need the CEO position for is to negotiate with Paivana Thoughtforms. Their new contract puts them out of reach of us *in court*. But we may still be able to get a piece of the pie."

Neither of them seemed encouraged by the idea. They

stood in silence, which she took as an invitation to continue.

"The tide is changing. It's only a matter of time before the Madison Rule is overturned. If we want to remain in business, we need to diversify."

"Into?"

"That prison contract is eighty-five billion dollars. That's money we're not getting."

"And you think, after all this, that Paivana Thoughtforms is just going to let us play in their sandbox?" The man asked.

"I know the CEO well. He's a good person and not the kind to hold grudges."

She left off the part that he wasn't the type to hold grudges against her.

"And you think he's just so kindhearted?"

"No. But we have technology he needs—the cloning bays, for example, and the animus modules. By re-purposing the bays, we can scale his operations far more quickly than he can from scratch. We have what he needs, and now that he has the contract, he's on a deadline, even if he doesn't understand that yet."

"He's been very vocally opposing us. And you think he'll jump into bed?"

*He will for me.*

"Yes."

"Okay, let's do it this way then. Take over full CEO and get that partnership. Do that, and we'll keep you. Fail, we'll find someone else."

She wanted to ask who else. Jake was an only child, and there had always been a Barnett in the CEO spot. Christine supposed they could find some extended family member somewhere.

"Why do you think the modeling industry is on the way out?" Asked the man, interrupting her thoughts.

"Ramsey. He spouts his nonsense, and in the process, he's

stripping away the illusion that models are second-class citizens. Every time he rails against them, he alienates people. Aside from that, the last Madison Rule challenge only failed because..."

"Because Paivana Thoughtforms CEO's mother dropped the lawsuit against us."

Christine resisted bringing her hands to her face. With confidence she didn't feel, she reasserted her position.

"However it happened, the industry is waning. The future is in virtual, and we need to be there."

Later that day, Christine stood behind a podium in a conference room in the H Hotel. Her grandfather stood in the back of the room, smiling broadly at his daughter's ascent. He'd been the easiest to convince that the conference was a good idea. He seemed to relish the idea that another Hamilton would join him in the spotlight.

The room buzzed with energy. Members of the press crowded together at the front, an archaic tradition that seemed entirely pointless with the hordes of camera-drones hovering over the podium. Christine raised her hand; the buzzing changed to a low roar, and she spoke into the microphone.

"Excuse me," she stared and waited for the noise to die further. Then she glanced up again to take in the crowd. Neither of the reclusive Barnetts was there. But in the back of the room, she saw a face she recognized. It reminded her of seeing him at her reception, except this time he didn't smile. Bodhi stood stoically against the wall, surrounded by several reporters who had recognized him and clustered about.

"Excuse me," she said one more time, and the crowd went silent.

"I want to talk about the Immortality Program joint venture between Beckett-Madeline Enterprises and Emergent

Biotechnology. And," she paused for effect, "I want to congratulate Paivana Thoughtforms on their most recent contract."

She smiled, and the crowd went up in a murmur. A second later, she lowered her hand again, and there was silence.

"Most of you know me as Christine Turner, great-niece of Gallatin Hamilton. That's an illusion I would like to shatter."

She took a deep breath.

"My name is Christine Hamilton. I was the first successful proof-of-concept for the Immortality program."

Hands shot up in the air as the press corps vied for her attention. She silenced them with a look.

"In light of recent events, we will be temporarily suspending the program. We plan to determine how to produce sub-models - devoid of personality or any semblance of humanity and eliminating the moral question altogether. This will yield a rise in program entry cost, but all existing contracts will be honored. Nobody should have to feel the guilt that I do carry for taking life from another human being."

Her eyes met Bodhi's across the room, and for the first time since she began talking, his lips parted in a tentative smile.

"I hope that this little effort on our part will be enough to convince you that Emergent Biotechnology takes our commitment to all of humanity seriously. We will be worthy of your respect. That recent bombing as a wake-up call. All of us here at Emergent are committed to creating a better society for everyone. No questions, please."

She turned and left the stage. On the way, she called out to Bodhi.

*"Did you like that?"* She already had the answer from the tenor of the connection.

*"I did."*

*"Meet me for dinner, and I'll tell you the rest."*

His response didn't come as quickly as she'd hoped. Christine was mentally preparing for him to hang up on her when he went the other direction.

*"I can do that. Where?"*

*"Why not the diner upstairs."*

Another pause. Perhaps choosing the place that they'd so often frequented together when they were young lovers was a bit too forward.

*"Eight?"*

Her heart jumped, and she tried to clamp it down before the feel of it flowed through their connection, but was too late. She could tell from Bodhi's emotional response that he'd felt it.

*"Eight is perfect."*

The press corps accosted her every step, and she ended up giving a follow-up interview to a gaggle of reporters on her way out of the lobby. Fortunately, she didn't have to leave the hotel, but only hop a quick elevator ride to make dinner with Bodhi.

She wondered what kind of mood he would be in, or even if he would show up. Christine never forgot being stood up at her reception, though she understood why. Their relationship had only gotten worse since then, so she could easily imagine another no-show. She accepted the risk, though. If someone had to bleed for the chaos she'd been part of creating, it might as well be her.

But the pantsuit had to go. In Christine's hotel room, she tried out several different outfits in quick succession. The straight green t-shirt dress with flats seemed too casual for the rooftop restaurant. However, it would ensure that nobody recognized her on the way up. She didn't anticipate this being too much of a problem, given the quality of people in the upper-levels of the hotel, but she called Grandfather via her communicator anyway.

"Grandfather, can you close the rooftop tonight? Just me and Bodhi?"

"Business? Or pleasure?" He asked her the question, but she knew there was only one right answer.

"Business negotiations."

"Okay, done. Nobody will interrupt you."

"Grandfather, what if I had said pleasure instead?"

"Sweetie, I would always do anything for you. I was just curious because of your history. If this is just a date, that's fine too."

"You've always pushed me away from him."

"When I thought he was a daydreaming loser, you mean? Of course I did. He's clearly not what I thought, though, is he?"

Nobody could call Bodhi a daydreaming loser anymore. He had bested Emergent Biotechnology, after all.

"I guess not," she answered, then thought for a second. "It's definitely business. Only personal if I'm lucky."

"Have *fun*, Christine."

Something about how he stressed "fun" implied that she hadn't been very much fun in a long time. As she thought back, she guessed that was probably true. Even the fun she had had, dinners and shows with Jake, had been rendered moot in her mind's eye by his betrayal.

That moment, she realized how angry she was at Jacob. She relished the idea of crushing him with all of the force of the company he once controlled. Even sweeter was that she would build the future that he wanted but lacked the imagination to create. He'd not been worthy of her.

She smiled at the thought. All this time, she had concerned herself with finding someone worthy of her long-term plan, and she had settled. Jake had been the safe bet that Bodhi never was. But unlike Jake, Bodhi was as constant as the moon.

Christine sat down to dinner at just before eight and ordered a Chardonnay, promptly delivered in a skinny wine flute. Bodhi arrived half an hour late. She caught the bartender in the corner of her eye staring at them - two icons thrown together in an empty restaurant.

"Bodhi, you made it," she spoke, both nervous and excited. He didn't smile, and she hadn't expected him to.

"Christine," he said and nodded quickly before taking his seat. The waiter nearly tripped while rushing to their table.

"Whiskey, neat, two fingers," he said to the waiter, who bounded off again.

"Wow, whiskey now?" She asked the question as a joke, but his scowl told her that she might have been part of the reason he drank whiskey.

"There's a lot you don't know about me," he retorted, taking his seat just as the waiter arrived with his drink.

"Bodhi, cut the shit. This can be fun. We don't have to be hostile enemies. It doesn't need to be business *all* the time."

"With you, it does," he remarked. Christine had no comeback from that. She had her own betrayals to worry about.

"Fair. Then let's get to it."

"Let's."

*Fuck this.*

She called him and watched him jump as the ansible call connected.

*"Why are you calling me?"*

*"Why are you being such a dick to me, Bodhi?"*

*"Why do you think?"*

Three questions in a row. The evening was so far going spectacularly. Christine took a sip of her wine.

*"I'm not trying to get you. Now, everyone knows who I am. It*

*will only be a matter of time before they connect the two of us if it hasn't already happened."*

"So?"

*"So let's be honest, okay? I'll tell you nothing but the truth. Any question you have to ask, I promise to answer."*

"Why did you break up with me?"

She shivered at the question. Bodhi caught her off guard by asking out loud. The fury preceded her response.

*"You broke your promise. You were supposed to come to Randen, and we were supposed to be together. I did my part, and you didn't."*

"I thought we would just re-connect on the other side. Paivana Thoughtforms is a good thing - for everyone."

*"You were just a guilt-ridden boy with a romantic streak, remember? You gave up on me - so I gave up on you. It was that simple."*

"And Jacob?"

*"A rebound. A really, really long rebound, but still - we had nothing like what you and I have. He's just another human, Bodhi. You and I, we're immortal."*

Bodhi disconnected and stared at her as though she'd said something crazy. Then his look softened.

"Christine, I love you. I have since the first time we met."

She doubted this was true and suspected that she remembered the first time they met better than he did. Still, she didn't interrupt as he continued.

"I don't know if I can trust you. Are you here for you, or are you here for Emergent Biotechnology? Beckett-Madeline? Which Christine are you today?"

"All of the above?"

"I can't do that."

She looked around. The waitstaff openly stared at them. This was the life she'd always wanted - to be a power couple and the object of envy. It felt so empty.

"I - I - "

"Which?"

Christine paused. Would love be enough to sustain her, despite her ambitions? Then again, she thought, she had her vision for the future. Her idea involved the slow dismantling of Emergent Biotechnology from a modeling company to a diversified umbrella corporation - her own version of Beckett-Madeline. But what if, she wondered, what if Paivana Thoughtforms was the umbrella company?

As the thought went through her, she caught a glimpse of how it could be. With Bodhi and Paivana Thoughtforms, she could build him into a force to be reckoned with. The Barnett's would never forgive her, of course, if she jumped ship. But how much would it matter?

Modeling was a dying industry. The Barnetts just hadn't realized it yet.

"You, Bodhi," she whispered, so softly that she barely heard her own words.

"What?"

"You, Bodhi. I'm just me, and I want to be with you," she stated loudly, enunciating every syllable as fodder for the waitstaff's gossip. As she said the words, she understood that they were conduits to the Labyrinth. Before she made it back home, the story of yet another betrayal would be circulating. Her concentration broke as she felt his hand close around hers. She looked up to see his gentle eyes.

"I've missed you," he said. And Christine knew it was true.

# 41

## Several Mistakes

*Friday, August 29, 2205*

Bodhi and Christine walked hand-in-hand together down the skywalk on Strata twenty. Blue skies stretched into the distance as he looked down on the city, volantrae rumbling through the skyways beneath. The thin air filled his lungs and mixed with the lilac perfume that he always remembered Christine wearing. The sun shone down casting their shadows as one at its odd angle and the white cap of Mount Rainier stuck up through the clouds. He felt at peace for the first time since he'd helped her study for her high-school test that now seemed like a lifetime ago.

"When did you really decide to be with me?" He asked the question, not knowing that he wanted an answer for it until it sprang from his mouth fully formed. She moved in slow-motion, head swiveling toward him and then she stared directly into his eyes, unblinking, breathing gently. She parted her lips, and a whisper issued forth from between them.

"I don't know that I have yet."

Bodhi went stiff as he examined her seeking out the truth in her eyes. A tangle of anxiety caught and he freed his hand from hers, bringing it up to rub his temple.

"I'm joking, Bodhi," she laughed, her hair blowing as a gentle breeze passed through it. He didn't laugh. Their journey had been fraught with too much deception for him to find her lie amusing. His heart fell as his mind unraveled the implications of that fact on any future that they could build together.

The distance between them shrank again as Christine advanced, putting her lips against his. As she did, he felt a tug in his mind. He resisted the invitation to connect. The vulnerability of it, letting her into his entire emotional landscape, was too much for him when he couldn't tell if he could trust her. Deep beneath the layers of scars formed from the multiple betrayals she'd heaped on him, there was a part of him that wanted to trust her, and the only way that happened was if he could feel her the way he used to. She couldn't hide from the ansible connection any more than she could.

Bodhi connected to Christine, swimming in her as she now did in him. Bodhi probed with his mind as their lips touched lightly. Feeling for deceit, he found longing instead, to be with him, and then as quickly disappointment. Christine pulled away and met his eyes with her own.

*"You still don't trust me."*

*"Can you blame me?"*

The connection closed abruptly and he felt more alone beside her than he had ever felt in his life before. It was Bodhi's turn to extend the invitation, to let her feel what he did. She accepted his connection and a new sensation emerged. Bodhi couldn't tell if it was from him, or from her.

That feeling that channeled through them both was the question of what their combined futures held, and the fear of losing each other magnified it for every second their minds touched.

Bodhi's mother erupted out from the hotel onto the narrow walkway as he watched. She waved something and seemed to be yelling. Bodhi turned toward her to see what she wanted, but he couldn't make out what she said. Her lips moved open and closed, and just as he started to grasp it, he felt the skyway tremble beneath him.

A second later, the skyway evaporated and he felt himself falling farther and farther down. Fear shot through him and he realized that it was Christine's fear he now felt as he plummeted, twisting through the air. He caught one glimpse of her, a tiny dot on the platform, just before he collided with the earth.

## *Saturday, August 30, 2205*

Blackness surrounded Bodhi - a blackness that continued forever. Images returned of falling, but he couldn't remember actually hitting the ground.

"Bodhi?"

"Christine?"

*"You're alive! I thought we lost you, Bodhi. That fall was over twenty strata."*

*"Why is it so dark? Did I lose my eyesight?"*

Christine didn't respond. He realized then that the words he had spoken hadn't moved past his lips. Rather, he couldn't feel his lips, or is face, or head. Systematically Bodhi checked his neck by trying to tighten his muscles, but again felt nothing.

It's an ansible connection.

Devastation flowed through him as he tried to move his

fingers and toes, but the feeling wasn't his. When he finally exhausted all of his body parts, discovering none, he turned his attention back to her.

"Where am I?"

"It was the only way, Bodhi. The fall - you hit the ground, you died."

"Mom?"

"She survived."

He felt trepidation and duty. Something else brought Christine to him, something important, but she avoided it. She had to know he could tell over the ansible connection.

"Siblings of the Natural Order claimed responsibility. They tried to blow up Grandfather's hotel."

He remembered his mother running toward them, screaming in desperation.

"Mom knew?"

"Ordell told her. He took nearly a third of the Siblings of the Natural Order and they denounced the violence of the SNO on national news."

The word punched fear, hostility, and gratitude through the connection as her mixed feelings about Ordell seeped across. An annoying tug told him that there was more still.

"They were trying to kill me, Bodhi. They wanted me dead and the Immortality Program stopped for good. They tried to kill me and killed you instead."

He felt the pain and the guilt flowing through her. It wasn't her fault. He wanted to say the words, but they wouldn't come out. She paused as though expecting them, and an awkward second later, Christine changed the conversation.

"I have a very important question for you. Your mother wanted us to put you in another body right away. I said you wouldn't want that. It was a fight, Bodhi, but we got you into Mijloc so we could ask..."

"If I want another body?"

Again, the question that plagued him for a lifetime. He knew what a body would mean. It would mean holding Christine, working through the trust chasm between them with a possibility for reconciliation, aided by physical touch. It would mean kissing his mother's cheek and giving Aiden a warm hug for being there throughout his life. He wondered then what it must have been like for the man, not quite a father, and not quite a friend.

Now was the test. He soaked in the darkness with the knowledge that if his answer was no, this would be his life.

*"The answer is yes? I can feel you - you're going to say yes."*

*"I do. I want it so badly I can taste it. I want to hold you again."*

*"Oh."*

Disappointment washed over him. She had been right about what he wanted, but she knew he wouldn't change his mind. Christine had still come into the darkness to ask the question, and he felt himself growing toward her, radiating outward and expanding into the empty universe.

*"I'll be okay here, Christine."*

*"Bodhi…"*

She trailed off, but he knew by the undulating patterns in her signal that she already missed him. No doubt she did love him, in some way that only she understood. Did he trust her enough to make her his conduit to the world, and his partner? Even now, in the eternal darkness, with nothing but the two of them there, Bodhi couldn't tell, and that was finally an answer.

*"One more thing, Christine. After this, after you tell my Mom, please don't contact me again."*

Shock. Anger. These two emotions spiked over the rest, followed by shame and embarrassment.

*"I thought we could do it right this time."*

*"You're like nothing I've ever felt before, Christine. As much as I try, I can't seem to shut you out. It's like I'm trapped floating*

*around you."*

*"You think I will burn you?"*

*"Do you?"*

She said nothing, as there was nothing to say. Of course she would burn him. It was as inevitable as the moon, and whether she loved him or not had little to do with it.

*"How will you communicate outside of here?"*

*"After last time we began work on an interface. It should be nearly complete, and I can be patient. It will suck, but I will have to be. I have a lot to plan anyway."*

In the silence he felt resignation.

*"Do you mind if I stay with you a few more minutes?"*

*"Stay, of course. Can you see what I see? It's beautiful here. I can see the trees, Christine, and the mountains just beyond. They're waiting to be born."*

He let his imagination fill with the future that he created in his mind. They rested in silence together experiencing each other in their naked truths, finally honest with the limitations of the love they shared. For Christine, there was an heirship at Becket-Madeline enterprises, and regardless of the Barnetts' decisions, Emergent would be hers too. For Bodhi, a world waited to come to life from the darkness. The future was as limitless as the void that surrounded him.

## THE END

## *Dear Reader*

Dear Reader,

Thank you for taking the time to read Bodhi Rising. Part of the reason I write is so that I can share some of these ideas with others, and present some possibilities of the future. It helps me to keep writing when I get feedback and know that readers like you are enjoying the experience of reading my works of fiction! Please let me know by leaving an Amazon review, which can also help others find my works too!

Please Leave a Review on Amazon!

Thank you so much for your time! Also, keep on reading! I've included the first chapter of the next and final installment in the trilogy. True to the name Reality Gradient, we get further and further from the "real world", taking the final leap in **Libera, Goddess of Worlds**.

Goodbye for now,
   Andrew

Bodhi Rising

# PART ONE

## LIBERA, GODDESS OF WORLDS (BOOK #3)

*The Creator*

*Wednesday, October 4, 2237 - Seattle, Washington - Earth*

Suspended in the air, hair splayed out and body tensed into a statue, Ada coaxed a land mass upward from the depths of the luminescent virtual ocean. Water cascaded downward as the glassy surface gave way to a mountaintop, sliding ever upwards and sending ripples outward to weak and slowly dissipate into nothingness. When enough earth cleared the mirrored surface for her to recognize the shape of Pangea, she stopped, gave herself two breaths and then formed reptiles and amphibians with her thoughts and spread them across the shorelines and into the shallower parts of the Panthalassic. With a flick of her wrist, she dropped four humanoid families down onto the coast along the Tethys sea. Separating from the nascent jungle by a rocky ridge, they would be safe from the more hostile creatures. They would still need to overcome insects as large as dogs; she didn't want to spoil them. Even with the bugs swarming and picking off the weakest, she still expected the groups to survive on their own for generations. That would give her more time to build.

The act of creation calmed her, which was as near to happiness as she ever got. When she started, there was only a gas nebulous. Her mind summoned errant rocks together with managed gravity; she had controlled the planet's entire history. The variables that she influenced formed patterns in her mind that mingled together like strands of electricity in a plasma ball. In a frenzy of energy, she had birthed a world, and she knew it intimately, with all of its moving pieces. Aida understood the distribution functions that led her ferns to spread from their origin into new territories. She knew where every grove of trees began. Her world was comfortably predictable.

A laugh drew her attention to the shoreline. The people she made ran around bare, which was going to be a problem. The design of the game made humanoid nudity an invitation for sex. She watched, irritated, as the beachside frivolity quickly degenerated into a mass orgy. If she could entice them to invent clothes, then they shagging long enough to evolve an actual society.

Aida turned down the heat, and the climate-adapted. Declining temperatures worked through Pangea as a severe cold front, causing the cold-blooded Sauropsids to become lethargic. She had now deviated from history. Permian-Period animals became dinner for her humans and warm-blooded

Therapsids, smaller creatures more capable in the cooling climate. Years passed in minutes while she watched on, detached.

She'd guessed there would be a die-off, but she hadn't foreseen the storm. It materialized around her as she elevated herself higher to be free from it. Her lime green hair whipped about as the winds picked up force. Humanoids scattered from the sea beach to hide in nearby caves, and of course, she knew what they would do there, naked and free from predators or the impact of weather. Her plan wasn't working.

A typhoon large enough to cover half of the global landmass raged before her. If she weren't careful, the anomaly would kill her humans and everything else on her planet. She gritted her teeth as she watched, angry at herself for having missed this possibility. Of the seventy-three variables controlling weather patterns, twenty of them changed related to temperature. She did the equivalent of turn down all twenty at once with only a thought. A chip-less android would have known that such a drastic temperature swing could tank her entire climate balance. But it was too late now. In the immersion game Event Horizon, time only flowed one way. The storm couldn't be un-made, at least not quickly.

A flash caught her attention as a bright ball of light penetrated the atmosphere. An orb-shaped spacecraft came to a slow stop beside her, and the top slid open like a helmet shield lifting. Inside, sat a man, an annoying interruption - and he hadn't been invited. He probably wanted to be friends.

"Hey! I saw your storm from space – awesome!" he said.

Yep, friends.

She heard but didn't acknowledge him at first, hoping that he would leave her alone. She felt his stare as the hairs stood on the back of her neck. Ada made a mental note to turn down physiological responsiveness in her haptic suit as she considered what her response should be. He had been friendly, so the rules dictated that she should reciprocate, even if she hated small talk. She ran a hand through her hair.

"Thanks," she replied. "It's an accident."

She played for modesty. In her experience, people seemed to respond well to that. Besides, it *was* an accident.

"I'd keep it," he grinned with his brown eyes sparkling in the ambient light. "Early planets can get pretty boring. Your storm spices it up."

She thought about what he said, now watching him with her peripheral vision. The storm seemed stationary, like the one on Jupiter. Even though it took up half of the planet, and the air currents had stabilized. She could leave it there for a while and see what happens next. It might be interesting to watch the patterns unfold and chart out the hundred or so variable changes that they impacted. Her humans lived far enough from the typhoon to be safe for a time. She remembered then that it was essential to respond to people when they talked. That was a rule.

"Interesting idea, maybe I will."

Perfect, she thought. Not a commitment, but not a complete dismissal either. Her mother would be proud.

"Jordan," the man provided his name without her having asked for it. "Jordon Helm."

She cringed. She would have to introduce herself now. That was also a rule. Since it was his real name and not some fiction, she decided to provide hers instead of Libera, which he had to have seen by now by checking her stats.

"Aida," she said. "Lothian."

"Great to meet you, Aida."

Thankfully, that was the end of the conversation. Jordan closed the shield, and the ship elevated back up through the atmosphere and into space. She stayed in the air, watching the storm to see if it was going to move after all.

She decided to think about it for a while before making a decision. She turned the temperature back up just a nudge and then left her planet to evolve. It was late, and she had work in the morning.

Free of the virtual reality system, Aida pulled at the skin-tight haptic suit. As it came free, she scratched at the pink indentations it left behind in her flesh. Even a seventh-generation Thoughtforms Special couldn't quell that post-immersion itch. She unbuckled the fully-sensory lockout helmet that kept her free of distractions during gameplay. Then she peeled away her stretchy haptic gloves, comprised of the same silicone-like material as her suit, but using tiny servos instead of nanites for better manual responsiveness.

Once removed, the suit only weighed about as much as a portable replicator without its protein packs. Aida tossed it into the box-like cleaner, which sealed with a hiss and began processing, bringing a smile to her face. Her previous rig had consisted of cheap gloves and a light aluminum resistance body-frame. Aida had hacked it into something resembling a full-immersion suit, but it was far too bulky for the sanitizer, so she'd had to clean it by hand. Even with a chemical bath, contamination remained about 0.8 colony-forming units where she could reach. Bacteria on hidden surfaces lingered around 2.1 c.f.u. and growing all the time. With the pulse xenon ultraviolet light, her entire setup got sanitized to about 0.9 c.f.u., including the places she couldn't see.

She gathered together her discarded work clothes, black vinyl shorts, platform heels, and a purple valuer jacket with the white halter top, before cracking the door to step back out into her master bedroom Ada turned into the bathroom to redeposit her pile of clothes atop the mounds from the previous days. She would eventually have to brave the company of other house members long enough to wash her work clothes in the communal laundry. But, she sighed involuntarily in relief; today wasn't the day. That was good, as Jordan Helm had depleted her reservoir of casual conversation.

After a quick shower, Aida slipped into a fluffy faux-fur robe and pulled down a copy of the *Celestial Bodies Connecting* for some comfortable evening reading. She settled into her magnetically-suspended reading chair and pressed backward to recline. Aida twitched her fingers in the motion command to summon her lamp. Wrapped tightly in the robe, she engrossed in the tactile sensation of turning pages and the smell of slowly decaying trees.

Aida couldn't focus on the book. The storm and the man named Jordan Helm gnawed at her subconscious. Her autism was at least partially responsible for the way he'd rattled her, but she thought there was more to the strange interruption that she couldn't figure out. She put the book aside and focused on the problem.

In Event Horizon, people trekked the cosmos to find Libera, Goddess of Worlds, and extract secrets from her about achieving in-game godhood. Aida Lothian never met their expectations. Her rules weren't complete enough to get through actual human interactions most times. Jordan had asked no difficult questions. The nonchalant way he had treated her made her think that he didn't know who she was, which was, of course, impossible in Event Horizon. Planets shared her name across the virtual cosmos. He couldn't have been unaware.

Was it Jordan's name that bothered her? She searched her mind for references to the name Jordan Helm. She hadn't recognized it right away, but people made up names all the time, so it may not have been real. Her animus module, the brain implant that she'd received when she turned eighteen, would remember.

The module was a strange hybrid of physiology and technology, which was 'installed' by taking a nanite-filled capsule orally. The tablet's nanites made their way to her brain and then built a network taking over higher-order cognitive function. Taking the pill had been a problem for her. She remembered her mother desperately forcing her mouth open and returning the capsule over and over again every time Aida ejected it. She knew now why her mother had been so desperate. Once Aida had the module, she was immortal. It was a brain backup that could be, for the right price, re-installed in another body.

Accessing the module was as seamless as thinking. Very quickly, Aida found her answers about who Jordan was. Images spun up of explosions at cloning worksites and wanted postings throughout Labyrinth, the virtual web. Probably the man was a teenage boy with delusions who had picked up the name because it was edgy. She'd hoped that he would at least be interesting, and the name would be a handle that she could track into other virtual systems. With a name like Jordan Helm, it would be impossible to identify one person. Thousands of teenage boys probably shared that same name in every virtual platform there was.

She picked her book back up and delved into the world of the slowest burning alien invasion there ever was. She particularly loved the imagery of nature and the world that existed three-hundred years before. The romantic notion of countries wrestling for global control, spying on each other, fighting wars - all things which didn't happen anymore - appealed to her. The Globalists eventually won, so now there was a single government, the World Government, which regulated the relationships between nation-states. There hadn't been a war for nearly a hundred years since individual national armies dispersed. Unlike in her book, no alien invasion had been necessary.

As pleasant a mental journey as it was to recall globalism's historical origins, Aida realized that she had read the same paragraph three times but hadn't processed any new words. She gave up on the chair and moved to her bed instead, disrobing in the process. Aida pulled herself into her bed's floating mattress, which molded around to her body. She felt the temperature in her room warm immediately to a comfortable seventy-eight degrees Fahrenheit. She lay sans blanket, a decoration only useful on cold nights when the heating system failed to keep up. The lights dimmed for her, and calming violin music played thin notes in the background.

Sleep wouldn't come as the incident with the man gathered more and more significance in her brain until she gave in to curiosity again. The instant she arose from the prone position, her room lightened to three-hundred and seventy-five lumens, allowing her to see the plain white dresser against the far wall that housed all of the clean clothes she owned. She didn't need the light since she didn't intend to leave her bed. She searched the Labyrinth again using her animus module implant and sent out a single query.

"Jordan Helm, Event Horizon"

Her animus module returned information like memories surfacing, each of which contained more details about the link between the man and the game. He was known to play the game often and used it as a recruitment tool for his activism. She wondered if the person she saw had been the real Jordan Helm.

She sat bolt-upright in bed when she received another memory, an image of his avatar. The avatar looked similar, though he was supposed to be a level seventy in Event Horizon, which meant he didn't need a ship. He'd attained godhood so long ago that he had the power to apparate between worlds and didn't even need to fly between them as she did. However, he enjoyed flying around in his orb-shaped ship out of nostalgia. He used the helmet-like Orb because he liked to, and being level seventy, he had little else to do but free play.

The sound of a landing drone caught her attention. At first, she thought it had come from somewhere in her master bedroom, perhaps a joke from one of her flatmates. A few seconds later, she realized it was from her animus module, and what she'd been experiencing wasn't a drone at all but an incoming call. She sucked in her breath as she mentally connected the incoming call to Jordan Helm.

That was silly.

Even knowing she was Libera, Goddess of Worlds - he couldn't have gotten her animus a.p. address. But as she thought about that, she realized the obvious truth. She could have gotten the information. It wouldn't have taken more than a few minutes because the people she had known before she joined Paivana Thoughtforms had tendrils everywhere.

Answer the call, she told herself. It's a rule.

"Hey, Aida, how's it going?"

People always ask that. When she was younger, she responded to the question with an enumerated list of good and bad things that had recently happened to her. She now had a rule against that. Conversations meant reciprocity, though, so she responded.

"Jordan?"

"Yes, it's me. Sorry, is this a bad time?"

It was always the wrong time for her to talk to people, but her rules indicated that she should never tell someone that. Instead, she avoided answering the question altogether.

"Why are you calling me?"

"I'm a little bored. I signed off of Event Horizon about an hour ago and haven't been able to sleep. I've been thinking about you since we met."

He hadn't.

When Aida was twelve, a little boy had told her that she was pretty, and she'd thought that might be true. For two days, she had believed that it was real and asked her mother to help her with her hair every day, brushed forty times on each side. It wasn't until a pep-rally two weeks later when he claimed ignorance of her that Aida had realized she'd been lied to. Her mother swore she was pretty every day for two months afterward because she cried every single day. That became her first rule: don't believe people who say nice things. Jordan was an extremist, a man who believed in his cause so fervently that humans had become expendable. He was a criminal, which was interesting. But he was also a person, so any nice thing he had to say to her was probably a lie.

She wouldn't argue about it though. There never was any point.

"Why?"

"Why have you been searching for me on the virtual web?"

And there was that. Of course, Jordan knew about that. Aida would have known if she were him.

"Not the same."

"That's fair; it's not. But listen, I have a proposition for you, and I'd like you to hear me out, Goddess of Worlds. I've been looking for you for months. That job you did in Jamaica was impressive."

It was worse than she thought. Jordan *had* been thinking about her then; that part wasn't a lie after all. But what did he want?

"I don't do that anymore."

"I know you're clean. I know. I only have one question to ask, and if the answer is no, I won't bother you anymore."

"No."

"But I haven't even asked the question yet."

"Fine. Ask the question."

"I need your help to disappear."

She had hacked into global government organizations, banks, and military bases. It had been interesting - so she had done it. Network protocols and the interconnections called to her. Even reminiscing, she could still feel the tug to explore the plethora of patterns that formed and evaporated every day. There were endless possibilities, all layered on top of basic communication rules. All she did was learn the rules and how to use them. She could make him disappear, but would she?

If she were to help, it might mean rebuilding bridges and issuing apologies to people who'd felt wrong by her leaving. She might have to provide restitution, or possibly just get killed, depending on how much her apologies meant to certain people. Even if none of that happened, she was never entirely sure how free she had managed to get herself. For all she knew, every single one of her scant contacts had turned informant.

People were hard.

She wondered why he couldn't do that job himself. He'd tracked her down quickly enough. All of this, she thought through rapidly and felt the urge building to disconnect the call and block him, if she could figure out how. As she pondered all of the reasons why helping him would be a horrible idea and would likely end in catastrophe, she heard her voice as though someone else worked her mouth.

"I'm listening."

Made in the USA
Columbia, SC
15 June 2021